REBELS LIKE US

REBELS LIKE US

LIZ REINHARDT

seventeen FICTION
FROM **HARLEQUIN** TEEN

Recycling programs
for this product may
not exist in your area.

ISBN-13: 978-0-373-21220-0

Rebels Like Us

Printed in U.S.A.

To Steph who refused to answer the phone
until I swore this book was done, (despite my charms, pleas,
and disgusting levels of self-pity) because she knows
the purest form of love is also the toughest.

The world is full of awesome best friendships—Napoleon and Pedro,
Claudia and Stacey, Jessica and Hope, Frog and Toad—
but "Steph and Liz" is and always will be my fave.

I love you to the best doughnut shop in Brooklyn and back, bestie.

ONE

Sartre said hell is other people, but he obviously never experienced a winter heat wave in the Georgia Lowcountry. Six weeks ago, my best friend and I were drinking cocoa laced with swiped rum, huddled under covers on the couch, oohing over the fat, lacy snowflakes that drifted into frozen piles on the sidewalks. Today, I'm trying to resist fainting from the broiler-like temperatures. *In winter.*

No wonder there are twelve churches within a five-mile radius of my new house. If this is the kind of fiery heat Georgians deal with on a regular basis, the idea of hellfire must be a terrifyingly real threat.

The sun follows me like the creepy eyes in a fun-house portrait as my sneakers sink into the melting blacktop. I hesitate and stare at my distorted reflection in the glass of the school's double doors. I'm still attempting to decode the movers' unintelligible boxing system—yesterday when I opened a box marked Art I found my collection of Daler-Rowney watercolor paints tossed in with an eggbeater and a dozen of my mom's old yoga DVDs—so my antifrizz balm is still MIA. With it, my hair falls into lopsided curls. Without it, I have to deal with my current situation—a dark cloud of frizz with a life of its own. It probably didn't help my hair's general health that I guilted Mom into letting me get the underside stripped, bleached, and dyed bright pink before we left the city. I need a hair tie. Or to get out of the pummeling sunshine before it fries my hair beyond recognition. I seriously love my curls, but I do *not* love what this crazy humidity is doing to them. Before I left the house this morning I decided that, despite my life going off the rails, I looked smoking hot. Now I look like I just made a quick run to the store and back for one of my aunties on a scorching August afternoon in Santo Domingo, even though all I did was walk across the school parking lot in Georgia. In the *middle of winter.* The only deliverance from this heat is inside the squat monstrosity that is my new school, Ebenezer High, so I need to make a decision: go inside or die of heatstroke.

"*Coño*," I mutter, and it's like I can feel my father frowning an ocean away. *Why is it the only Spanish you ever speak is slang and curses, Aggie?*

I shake his words out of my head and take a long look at the place I'm going to call my academic home for the second half of this, my all-important senior year, and I have to wonder if the builders accidentally opened the schematics for a psych ward or a minimum-security prison and didn't realize their mistake until appalled administrators and teachers showed up postconstruction.

I fill my lungs with a final gulp of suffocatingly hot air, then push into the cool building, cross a lobby showcasing dozens of glittering gold sport trophies, and I'm in a generic front office where a woman with a big smile and bigger hair inputs my information into the computer at a snail's pace. I heard things are more relaxed south of the Mason-Dixon, but if they're *this* relaxed, I may never make it out of the front office.

When my official schedule is finally approved, I'm introduced to the guidance counselor, who leads me into a hallway that smells like yesterday's cafeteria fries, bleach, and fresh paint. I crane my neck to better take in my new school and wonder if the dingy gray-blue color they've chosen for the walls is also a leftover from some institutional torture chamber. I'm used to seeing art displayed on every wall and bright splashes of random colors painted in crevices too small for anything else. This sterility is strangely claustrophobic.

While I'm trying to breathe without the help of a paper bag, I wonder again why I'm even here. My brother, Jasper, told me point-blank that he thought I'd lost my mind the day I announced I was migrating South for the spring term, like some freak-of-nature bird. My father insisted we phone conference half a dozen times so that he could lecture me in Spanish on the merits of a New York City or Parisian education over an education from Georgia—which he insisted was an oxymoron. My abuela says my dad has been *manso*—very chill—since the day he was born, but talking about my future is the one thing that can make him *quillao*—super upset. Ollie, my sister from another mister, would have shared her tiny bedroom with me in a heartbeat if I'd asked, but I'd never stoop to asking. I'm well aware my passionate, motivated bestie needs every available inch of room so she can focus on her intense practice schedule and the whirlwind of spring recitals. And Mama Patria, my abuela, has room at her apartment but she lives two subway lines and a half hour bus ride away from Newington—that just wasn't a commute I could've tackled twice a day, every school day, especially during the longest, coldest winter to hammer New York City in fifty years.

As far as Paris goes, I'd never admit it to my father, but my French skills have slipped—*a lot*—since he and Jasper moved and there was no one to ignore me until I asked for the salt or the remote or the time *en français*. To say my language skills have rusted would be an understatement—my French is basically a series of crumbling linguistic holes.

On top of all that there was the lingering poison-gas fog from my breakup with Lincoln—my first love and one of my best friends turned mortal enemy—which would have suffocated me slowly if I'd stayed at the private school he and I both attended. Lincoln and I started dating when we were sophomores, the year his parents started an exchange program for Maori soccer players with Newington High, and there are reminders of our coupledom sprinkled around every corner in the school where he was basically treated like royalty. I reveled in the fact that I couldn't pass the main hall without seeing our entwined initials on the art tile we'd painted, or his gorgeous face—broad jaw, wide nose, sparkling eyes, dark skin, plush kissable lips—on the Newington VIP board in the main hall. Lincoln pulled me close and kissed me for the first time in the courtyard under Newington's legendary oak while gold and orange leaves swirled around us. I'd never once passed that tree without running my fingers over the bark and smiling—well, I never had *before*.

The last months of senior year are so useless and so meaningful all at once. Everyone solidifies college choices, skips any day they possibly can, and gets disgustingly nostalgic about the people they're going to leave behind on graduation day. The last thing I wanted was to spend months dodging the yearbook photo montages and avoiding fondly retold memories that would only reinforce what a total lie my entire relationship with Lincoln turned out to be in the end.

I have to look at my decision to flee less as losing out on the last months with my friends and more as moving on a little bit early. I've always had an independent streak, so I might as well run with it. It's best if I consider my time in Georgia a kind of study-abroad semester before the adventure of college begins.

My tour guide's bubblegum drawl interrupts the panic that threatens to tunnel me under despite my internal pep talk that this will all be okay.

"It's wonderful to have you at Ebenezer High. We realize it will take a few days for you to get settled, but we'll let you jump right in. The good thing is you've only missed one day of second semester, so you should be able to catch up easily. First day of a new semester is mostly just the syllabus breakdown anyway." She gestures to a wooden door, and I peek through the tiny window into what looks like a lab full of students dying from a combination of boredom and heatstroke. "This here will be your first class tomorrow, Agnes. Mr. Hemley, AP physics. At this hour you'd be in the middle of your second class, which is…"

Newington was once some founding senator's house and had windows so huge, it never even felt like I was indoors. The windows in this school remind me of the slits in medieval fortresses that archers shot arrows out of. What the hell is the modern purpose of windows that narrow? As I pass the classrooms, I see sad ribbons of sunlight, bitterly determined to brighten the gloom.

Give up, sunshine. It's a damn lost cause.

"…this one right here." We stop in front of another nondescript door whose tiny window reveals my fellow cell mates. "The peer guide I've assigned to help you through the day is in this class. She'll give you a more thorough tour, and if there are any questions she can't handle, feel free to stop by my office anytime. The door is always open." Her silver fillings wink at me from the back of her mouth when she smiles. I can't remember her name no matter how hard I shake my brain.

"Thanks, but I'm pretty sure I'll be able to navigate all right on my own." I turn the schedule she handed me so that the map printed on the bottom is oriented, and bend my lips up in what I hope approximates a smile.

"Whatever you'd like, Agnes." She shifts from one sensible pump to the other.

"Okay. Thanks again. I'm, uh, going to class now." I point to the doorway I don't particularly want to walk through.

What's more awkward? Walking into a classroom full of seniors as the new girl? Or standing in the ugly hallway of your new school losing a staring contest with a guidance counselor whose name you can't remember?

Lamest game of Would You Rather. Ever.

Coño, I have to choose, so I walk backward through the classroom door, keeping that demented smile wide until Mrs. What's-Her-Face disappears into the shadows of the hallway.

"Good morning. You must be Agnes." A woman with a no-nonsense voice gives me the evil teacher eye over tortoiseshell glasses that perch on the end of her broad nose. Even with her springy, salt-and-pepper curls factored into her height, she only grazes my chin. But the fact that I tower over her doesn't stop me from squirming under her laser gaze. She has the same huggable, curvy figure and beautiful, soft, dark brown skin as my grandmother, but I cannot picture her taking a tray of warm *coconetes* out of the oven. I *can* picture her silencing a class of hooligans with one fiery look. "I'm Mrs. Lovett."

"Good morning." I modify my smile from demented pretend to real. I hate unnecessary authority, but I absolutely love ball-busting, no-nonsense bitches. I get the latter vibe from Lovett already.

"Ms. Ronston wanted me to let you know your peer guide will be Khabria Scott. Khabria, please raise your hand." Mrs. Lovett's voice snaps, and a hand pops up in response. I approve of my tour guide's bold nails—matte black except for a shiny white ring finger nail, gold fleur-de-lis designs glittering on each one.

Because I'm nervous, I resort to a goofy, toothy smile, and feel extra dumb when Khabria folds her arms across her chest elegantly and gives me a tight-lipped, polite smile in return. She's got this whole regal Nefertiti/Beyoncé vibe that's intimidating and impressive all at once.

"You can take a seat second row, fourth desk back, Agnes." Mrs. Lovett makes a mark in her roll book, and I slide into my chair while too many eyes dart my way, sizing me up because I'm so shiny and new. It's uncomfortable but not mean.

"Hey. Hey, new girl?" A tall, good-looking guy with a bright yellow basketball jersey sitting just behind Khabria nearly falls out of his chair calling to me and waving his gorgeously muscled arms over his head. "Where you from?"

"Crown Heights." I watch his face screw up like I answered him in Finnish. "Brooklyn."

"Where?" He kicks the back of the Khabria's chair as he tries to settle into a desk that clearly wasn't designed for people over six foot six. Khabria whips her head so fast her black and strawberry braids are a blur.

She mutters, "Holy hell, you a *moron*, Lonzo."

"New York City, man. C'mon, you're makin' us all look ignorant." I can't see who said it, but that deep, slow voice that rolls like a warm wave in the ocean is the most Southern voice I've ever heard—and I'm shocked by the fizzy glow that warms through me at the sound of it. I like it. I like it a lot.

"Why'd you move here?" The tall guy kicks my chair with the sole of his shoe to get my attention. When I turn to look at him, he grins wide, the way I smiled at Khabria before. "Too violent in your hood?"

"What?" I snort as thoughts of the last co-op meeting flit through my head. Old Mr. Madsen almost got in a fistfight with the "young hipster" who dared to adorn the communal herb garden with his found-art whirligigs, which Mr. Madsen screamed were "pretentious trash." The meeting ended with Mr. Madsen knocking all the disposable coffee cups off the snack table and vowing to recycle the young hipster's "eyesores" if they came anywhere near his flat-leaf parsley. "I lived in a really nice neighborhood. Not a *hood*."

I mean, sure, there were the Crown Heights Riots, but that was way back in the '90s. Ancient history.

"So why then?" Despite the twitchiness of his limbs, his dark eyes are calm.

When he repeats his question, more eyes turn to me from around the classroom. Shiny-haired cheerleaders and flexing jocks, slackers trying to pretend they aren't dozing, nerds clutching their notebooks—two dozen faces fade in a kaleidoscope of dark and light as my vision tunnels.

Being the new girl sucks.

"Uh…"

"You hate snow?" He rubs a hand over his tight, dark curls and clicks his tongue when Khabria stomps her sneaker in frustration.

"No, you need to stop, boy. Who would hate snow?" She throws her arms out and rolls her eyes like it's the most ridiculous concept she's ever contemplated.

"You ever even seen snow?" He juts out his chin.

"No, but I *want* to. You trying to say you don't want to ride on a sled? Or throw a snowball?"

"I heard snowballs hurt your hand." He holds out his own hands, so big they could probably palm a basketball with zero problems. He flips them, studying his knuckles and then his palms like he's trying to get a gauge of the damage a snowball could do.

I'm shocked silent. No snow? *Ever?* It's a lot to wrap my frostbitten brain around. Despite the intense heat here, I feel like I still haven't thawed completely from the last cold snap back home.

"Alonzo Washington, please stop harassing Agnes and come discuss the status of your term paper proposal with me immediately."

The guy—Alonzo—leaps out of his seat and says, "Yes, ma'am," like he's a soldier in a very obedient army.

I'm about to go back to imagining a life devoid of snow when I hear a little alien-baby voice whisper, *"Agnes?* That cannot be her name. That name would be ugly if it were my grandmother's."

I swivel my head and face the kind of blandly vicious sneers that always seem to infect a select few in any group. My cousins in Santo Domingo would say they're *bocas de suape*—mop mouths. In translation, they're two losers who don't know when to keep their traps shut. They're so generically pathetic, if life was a movie, they wouldn't even have names in the credits. They're even wearing *cheerleading uniforms*. Could they be more cliché? Generic Mean Girl One is giggling like mad along with Generic Mean Girl Two. I turn full around in my seat and stare at them, ignoring my new teacher's obvious throat clearing.

"Is there a problem, ladies?" she demands.

"My name," I announce, still looking at the two overzealously spray-tanned, hair-tossing idiots in their cutesy matching uniforms. I love the way their cackles dry up and their perfectly made-up faces fall. "Apparently it's *hilarious*."

"Agnes." I turn to look at my teacher, whose pursed lips and cocked eyebrows tell me she is *clearly not amused*. "Whatever this nonsense is about, it stops now. I don't tolerate fools, and I don't put up with time wasting. In fact, it's really starting to piss me off that I wasted this much time already."

A few people gasp or snort when she says *piss*, as if our innocent, nearly adult ears have never heard a single naughty word before.

"I'm sorry for wasting your time," I say, sitting straight at my desk. I can take care of the Generic Mean Girl Twins later. Right now, I'm going to make it a priority not to "piss off" this woman. For all I know, this class might be the highlight of an otherwise miserable few months.

"Ma'am." She crosses her arms over her wide chest. The idiotic giggles start again. I'm drowning fast.

"Me?" I point at myself. Mrs. Lovett's nostrils flare very slightly.

"Me." She points a thumb at her chest. "When you speak to *me*, your instructor, you refer to me as *ma'am*. Clear?"

"So, not 'Mrs. Lovett'?" I swear to baby Jesus, I ask only to double-check, but I guess I've already walked too close to the edge of the smart-ass line, and now my classmates are hooting like I'm the Pied Piper of classroom anarchy.

"Do *not* test my patience today, Agnes," Mrs. Lovett snaps. She slaps a paper packet and a copy of *The Old Man and the Sea* on my desk.

I leaf through the tattered pages, hold it up, and attempt

one last smile that's basically just me grasping at straws. "No friend as loyal."

Mrs. Lovett's lips twitch, and I curl my fingers around the old misogynistic tale of oceanic triumph and New Testament allusions, waiting to see if her lips will twitch up or...

Up. Smile. Score!

But now that I bought her love back with a cheap quote trick, I have to be on my best behavior while we scribble notes about Hemingway's boozing and hunting and womanizing—and that means keeping my mouth firmly shut. Because, despite my best intentions, whenever I open my mouth, trouble finds me.

Also, I'm still not sure about the whole *ma'am* thing.

When we're finally dismissed, Alonzo drags Khabria over to me.

"Agnes, tell this know-it-all that it hurts your hand to make a snowball."

"Um, if you don't wear gloves, it stings," I admit reluctantly. I'm breaking a deep, unwritten girl code by siding with Alonzo, even on a matter this insignificant, but...

"See! I told you! Ooh, you so wrong!" Alonzo crows, shimmying his arms at his sides and strutting around Khabria in a weird, end zone type celebration dance. "My daddy *told me* when he was in Lamaze class with my mama they made everybody squeeze an ice cube to let them get a taste of labor pain."

"Um, it's uncomfortable, but I don't think it's anything like labor," I cut in, but Alonzo is flapping his elbows like a chicken while Khabria sucks her teeth and sputters. I fear for Alonzo's life if he keeps poking this very beautiful, probably lethal bear. "I mean, it's mostly fun, not painful..." I trail off, and Khabria shakes her head.

"Ignore that fool. He actually *enjoys* being a dumb ass."

It occurs to me that I could stick out my hand and introduce myself—no! Maybe that's too weird?—but before I determine if the chance to make a new friend outweighs the incredible social awkwardness, Alonzo's sauntered up to his group of cronies and Khabria is gliding away to join a clutch of girls wearing navy cheerleading uniforms that match hers—including both plastic airheads from earlier. Ugh, maybe I should be glad social awkwardness won out before I tried to befriend someone who hangs out with the twit twins.

I try to convince myself I dodged a social bullet, but it doesn't feel awesome to be left hugging my books and wishing I could teleport to my next class so that I won't have to suffer being the one and only student at Ebenezer High navigating the halls alone.

And then, suddenly, I'm not.

"Hey! Hey, Agnes!" Khabria's tiny cheerleading skirt swishes around her long legs as she jogs down the hall after me. "I'm your peer guide today." She tucks a loose red braid back into her updo and gives me a slightly bigger smile than when we first met.

It's probably just a coincidence that the clutch of cheerleader clones she left down the hall erupts into squawks of laughter at that exact second.

Probably.

Panic feels like quicksand sucking at my ankles and threatening to pull me under. I half choke out my next words.

"Uh, no worries. I have this handy map." I flutter the wrinkled paper between us like I'm waving a white flag. *I surrender to social isolation—leave me alone in my misery.* "I've been riding the subway alone since I was a little kid. I'm sure I can manage the halls of a high school."

Khabria nabs my schedule and cocks an eyebrow. "Really?

Because your next class is back that-a-way." She jerks a thumb over her shoulder as I grab the map back and try to get my bearings. I usually have a decent internal compass. I guess I'm just off-kilter today.

"Right. That way. Okay. I got turned around, I guess."

Senior year. I'm supposed to be directing freshman to the nonexistent fourth-floor pool, not getting lost going down the main hall.

"I know it's not the subway, but finding your way around here can be tricky. Let me give you a quick tour at least." Khabria's dark eyes warm with the kind of sympathy I'm used to giving, not receiving. I definitely prefer being in charge, not being led around. But I guess I don't have much choice now.

"Okay. So...I see my next class from here. After that I have to head across this courtyard...or, wait? Is that a stairwell...?"

"C'mon." Khabria marches me to my next classroom and bats her lashes at the cute young teacher manning the door. "Mr. Webster, this is Agnes. It's her first day, and I'm her peer guide. Is it okay if I take her on a quick tour once the halls empty?"

Mr. Webster crosses his arms over his wide chest and sighs. "Ten minutes, Ms. Scott. Agnes will already be playing catch-up."

"Fifteen? Please, sir?" she says, bartering with a flirty edge to her voice and biting her bottom lip for good measure.

Mr. Webster looks decidedly uncomfortable. He takes off his nerdy-cute glasses and cleans the lenses with the tail of his half-tucked dress shirt. "Fine. Go, quickly, so you can get Agnes back as soon as possible."

"Thank you, Mr. Webster," she singsongs. We leave him frowning at his polished shoes.

Khabria whirls me down the hall, giggling the whole way,

and I feel normal for a split second. When we're at the stair-well, she tugs me close, glances over her shoulder, and dishes some seriously crazy gossip. "Webster tries to play it cool, but everyone knows he's dating a girl who just graduated last year…and they started seeing each other *before* school was out." Her eyes go wide and her perfect eyebrows rise up until they almost disappear in her hair.

"Did they get caught?"

There was a rumor about one of the teacher's aides and a senior at Newington when I was in tenth grade. But the rumor barely had time to circulate before the aide was gone without a word. I can't imagine what it would have been like if we found out the rumor was true, then passed that aide in the halls every day…

"No, but we all know it's true. He was at a few high school parties over the summer, always looking like he wanted to disappear. Oh, here are the math labs, and your next classroom after you leave Webster's class is the middle one." She waves a hand at a cluster of rooms filled with students silently scribbling complicated geometry equations on whiteboards, then sneers. "I don't know why he'd risk showing his face where there could be students around. I mean, it's not like anyone told on him, but someone could've, and now he can't get respect no matter how tough he tries to act because how do you respect someone with that little sense? Last year, he was one of the strictest teachers we had. This year, I think he's just waiting on us to graduate, so one more class that went to school with his little girlfriend will be gone and out of his hair."

Khabria's words cut like a razor through tissue paper, and I realize she's almost gleeful. I kind of get it. Right or wrong, there's a certain thrill in holding power over the people who are supposed to be in authority, especially when they screw up.

"Has he ever made a pass at any of the other girls?" I ask. I try my best to avoid gossip for the most part, but there's something weirdly comforting about it. It gives you the illusion you're sharing a secret—even if the secret is something everyone in school is talking about.

"Nah. Apparently it was true love with him and that one girl, or whatever. Guidance office." She points and it's reassuring to see the familiar "mountain climber with an inspirational quote underneath" poster that must be required decor for every guidance office in the country.

"That's crazy," I murmur as I poke my head in and peek at the out-of-date computers and dusty college manuals. "I'd probably quit if I were him."

"People 'round here are stubborn like that though." She shakes her braids out with her fingers. "My gram always says people have more pride than sense. They'd rather be miserable than admit defeat. I think some people just like being miserable, period." We stroll down a back hall. "Food science, shop, child care, music room," she ticks off.

"I definitely get that vibe from some people." I decide to test the waters. "No offense if they're your friends, but those two cheerleaders in our English class seemed pretty bent on spreading misery…at least toward me."

Khabria's pace slows and a blush warms the deep brown skin over her perfect cheekbones. "People sometimes forget we're supposed to be hospitable to newcomers, especially if we're on cheer. I know the other girls came off badly today, but their bark is definitely worse than their bite. They prolly thought they were being funny or something." She shrugs. "That whole pride thing. Don't take anything they say to heart. Maybe it's a side effect of being squad leaders every year since we were in peewee cheer—maybe they're just used to ribbing on the new girl."

"So they've always been the queen-bee types?" I can so imagine the Generic Mean Girls as preschoolers with pigtails and bows, lording over the snack table while they nibbled their graham crackers and sipped their juice boxes.

"Ain't *my* queens," Khabria bites out. She sighs and takes it down a notch. "Look, some people are really into cliques here. They have their friends, their jokes, their way of doing things… If you don't like them, my best advice for you is just stay away."

I realize I touched a nerve, and I get it. There are girls I would have counted as my best friends in middle school but haven't spoken a word to in years—girls I'd still defend if anyone else tried to talk crap about them. People—even people you care about—can change so fast, and loyalties get complicated.

"Sorry. I didn't mean to imply anything." By now we've rounded back to the main hall and Mr. Webster's class, all the initial closeness we shared over steamy gossip withered.

"Agnes, Khabria!" Mr. Webster pokes his head out the door, calls down the hall to us, and taps his watch in warning. "You're five minutes late. Let's hustle."

"Thank you for showing me around." I clutch my map in shaking fingers, off-kilter after possibly offending the first person who was actually nice to me.

"You're welcome. Let me know if you need help with anything else today." Khabria's voice runs as cold as the water around an iceberg. She hesitates, then says, "Look, most people here are good folk. We get along, we help each other out. Don't judge anyone too harshly based on a few minutes of knowing them."

I watch her skirt flutter as she flounces away before I can answer, and I slip into class. My classmates text on their phones, paint their nails, and chat as Mr. Webster robotically lectures, his body language limp with defeat. I wonder if he regrets anything. I wonder if staying here at Ebenezer was him standing his ground or giving up.

If I stay here, would it be standing my ground or giving up? Bells ring, classes move, and I follow my map like a pro now that Khabria's shown me the basic layout. For the rest of the day, I'm mostly ignored. Which is fine. I'm only enduring. Just a few months.

Just the rest of my *senior ye*—

It's like I accidentally pulled the plug on a hot bubble bath. I search under the suds to plug it back up because if I don't, every single emotion I've kept bottled up will drain, hot and wet and embarrassing.

No girl who grew up on the mean streets of Brooklyn (all right…fairly gentrified Crown Heights, but still) is going to cry on her first day of school in Nowhere, Georgia. I'd have to beat in my *own* ass. It wouldn't be pretty.

The final bell tolls and crowds press out of doorways and into the hall on every side of me, a tsunami of bodies. I don't care about being jostled, but it's weird to not have a solitary soul waiting for me by a locker or gesturing for me to sneak down a back hall and beat the rush.

I sprint alone to my little Corolla—a poor consolation prize from my mother to make up for the dissolution of my pretty rad life because of *her* screwup—and peel out. I choke on the diesel fumes from the line of lifted pickup trucks that leads home.

Home.

That's the word on repeat in my head when I veer the car to

23

the side of the road and pull the damn plug, unstop everything I've been holding in. I've felt seconds away from drowning all day, and now I weep and scream like a banshee on meth in the semiprivacy of my car, letting it all drain out.

"Vete pal carajo, Georgia! Concho hijo de la gran Yegua!"

I curse this godforsaken state at the top of my lungs and beat the steering wheel. I drum my heels on the floorboards. I scream curses over and over until my voice is hoarse. And then I wipe the mascara out of my eyes, blow my nose, take one deep breath, pull back onto the road. *"Coño."* Damn. There's nothing left to say, so I glare at the obstinate sun, and go…home.

God, it would feel good to spill my guts to Mom the way we used to, Lorelai and Rory–style, but the time for sitcom mother-daughter banter is long gone. When I look back at all the times I assumed she was doing something awesome, like tutoring one of her struggling students, and realize she was, in fact, doing something skeevy, like flirting with a married dude, a bone-crushing feeling of betrayal presses onto me. It's as if I was waiting at Luke's with my giant mug of coffee, but my mother never showed.

I wonder if I'll ever be able to look at her and forgive her for selfishly and systematically ruining my life. Ruining *our* life. All because of a skinny, kinky weirdo with a weasel face and my mom's very, very poor tech skills.

Word to the wise, kids: don't be a fat-fingered idiot when you're sexting with your married coworker. Because you just might accidentally send a pic of your naked ass to the HR secretary instead of your paramour. And said secretary just might be your weasel-faced sex partner's wife's yoga buddy. And then you and your innocent daughter will be unceremoniously exiled to the sweltering marshes of Nowhere, Georgia.

TWO

In the quiet sanctuary of my temporary home, all I want to do is forget the total disaster that was the first day of what's probably the biggest mistake of my life so far. Mom's teaching a class and won't be home for another two hours, so I have unsupervised time to kill.

There are very few perks that come with living in Georgia, but a big, refreshing one is the pool in the backyard. I can practically hear the pool pump hissing, *"Come swim in me, Nes."*

I tear to my room and rip open a box labeled Summer Clothes, then a box labeled Vacation, then, in a desperate last-ditch effort, I peel back the tape on one labeled Random Fun Stuff. I find a pair of denim overalls I don't remember buying, some really old family pictures from the summer we went on vacation to some hokey middle-America theme park, and three yo-yos from my brother's obsessive yo-yo-collecting days back when he was a nerdy middle schooler (instead of a nerdy college sophomore). I get nervous because I'm not sure where else to look for my lone piece of missing swimwear. I own exactly one bikini.

There's not an especially long swim season in New York, so

one will do. But it's January here. *January.* The time of post-Christmas blizzards and sticking to resolutions you made for New Year's, if you're all about that. And it's now hotter than it was when we arrived this hellish December.

I may need more bikinis. In the dead of *winter.* Unbelievable.

Our Realtor said this was an "unusually hot one" as she fanned her sweaty face and bemoaned every house we looked in that hadn't switched on the central air. I expect bikini shopping and sweltering heat in Santo Domingo over summer break; this is just madness.

I continue to frantically pick through the cardboard box ziggurat in my room and finally snag the stretchy material of my lone bathing suit in a box labeled Underwear. Fair enough. And I can't even blame the movers' crazy box identification because I packed that one myself. Just as I'm about to change, my phone rings and I realize I may have to pick up and talk intelligibly to another human being when all I want to do is dead man's float around the pool and feel sad for myself. The groan I bite back is a knife of guilt that twists in my gut.

Ollie wants to FaceTime.

My bleary, makeup-smeared image reflects back at me on the screen, and I want to sob. Again. But then I'll look even worse. It's all pretty chicken-and-egg.

"Olls, I look like a gargoyle!" I screech the second she connects.

Her gorgeous face, moon round and ethereally peaches and cream, takes up the entire screen, and my throat feels all clawed down both sides because I'm not sitting in her parents' modern, artsy apartment, gorging on the Vietnamese sizzling pancakes Ollie is a genius at whipping up and sneaking sips of rice wine from her parents' enormous collection before we get down to our homework and daily two-person merengue party.

"Shuddup! You look like a goddess." She gnaws on her lip. "Hey, I checked your Insta this morning…"

"Right." I shrug. "Call me melodramatic, but it was surprisingly hard to scroll through all those pictures of everything and everyone I was leaving behind." I take a second to steady my voice, the same way I steady my raw heart every time I flip through my winter photo folder—which is full of pictures of people and places that are a thousand miles away. "I promise I'll get a new one going soon."

I guess Ollie hasn't checked Snapchat yet, or she'd be calling me out about that too. I deleted my account late last night after getting shocked by another surprise Lincoln cameo in a mutual friend's post-winter-break video. If pictures are hard for me to look at, there's no way I can handle seeing and hearing video footage of everything I'm missing back home… Plus Lincoln would be like a ghost haunting every Newington clip.

"You really should. Your Insta pics were *goals*. Plus I want to know what things look like down there. Are there all those mossy trees like in *Scooby-Doo*? And plantations everywhere? Are they haunted? Did your mom buy you the Mystery Machine to drive around in? Are you wearing ascots and miniskirts? Did you get a Great Dane?" Before she can yell *zoinks*, Ollie's eyes dart over my shoulder and go wide with worry. "Wait. You *still* haven't unpacked?"

"It's 'asylum chic.' Like it?" She shakes her head and sighs, so I confess. "Truth? It's a reminder that I won't actually have to live here forever."

I wave a hand at the mattress on the floor, covers and pillows piled on it. That, my docking station, and a few choice boxes with the flaps permanently open make up my entire bedroom decor. The movers put all my boxes in my room for me, but I declined when they offered to put my bed frame together. That felt too permanent. Mom made several passive-aggressive comments about how she wouldn't have bothered to pay an arm and a leg to move all my furniture if I wasn't even going to set it up, but I stared at the ceiling until she left me to my misery. She was excited to finally have a space bigger than a couple hundred square feet to decorate, and she didn't get why I wasn't revved up to be in a new room that's almost triple the square footage of my old room.

Because I miss my tiny, cramped, perfect old room.

"I miss your old room," Ollie admits, echoing my internal thoughts with her freakish bestie ESP. Her shoulders slump, and my heart follows their lead.

"It's okay." No one brings out my reluctant optimist like Ollie. I hate seeing her down, so I put on a good game face no matter how crappy I feel. "Mom and Dad had been planning to sell our place when I moved to college anyway, and it went for way over asking price, like, the first week it was on the market. They were pretty psyched about it, and I…I'm trying to accept my fate at this point. You know I'm a 'rip off the Band-Aid' type when it comes to dealing with emotional stuff."

"Um, yeah you are!" she laughs. Then gets dead serious. Lecture-time serious. "Speaking of college…"

"I got all my applications in by the deadlines, I swear to God." I don't tell my best friend that I hit Send on my SUNY application literally two minutes before midnight on the last possible day. And I don't elaborate on the fact that I never took my brother up on his offer to proofread my personal essay. I didn't have the patience to be ridiculed on my native-tongue grammatical failures by my own trilingual flesh and blood.

"You'll tell me when you hear back?"

"Of course." I cross my heart with the hand that's still clutching my bikini, and Ollie freaks out.

"Are you going *swimming*?" The screen goes down for a second and her shocked voice floats through the speaker. "WeatherBug says it's eighty-five in Savannah. How is that *possible*?"

Her face pops back on the screen, and I roll my eyes. "Because Savannah is actually an outer ring of hell. Don't be jealous. I spent all day with sweaty pit stains. It's gross."

"It's actually not frigid here. Like we could have watched those hot Puerto Rican guys play basketball from your fire escape if we'd had a blanket. Or three."

"Are you trying to drive me to suicide?" My voice wobbles like the ankles of a first-time ice-skater.

"Sweetie." Ollie says it on the longest sigh. I know exactly what direction her lecture is going to take, because she's given it to me a few dozen times before. "Why didn't you stay here in the city? With me? My parents *love* you. Or with your abuela. Even if she would have welded one of those chastity belts on you...it maybe would have been better than getting trapped in Georgia. Right?"

"It's not chastity-belt bad here."

"No...?"

I think about how I can go to an Episcopal, Baptist, Lutheran, Presbyterian, Nazarene, or Seventh Day Adventist church if I walk five blocks from my house, but an Americano is an unknown species around here. I haven't found a single decent coffee shop.

"You have a point..."

"You could come back." She makes her voice small, like she's trying to disguise the hope so that I won't even notice it. Fat chance.

Not only do I notice it, big and comfy and bright as it is—it makes me ache.

"I know." I do. I made a huge, complicated pro-and-con list on butcher paper in my room and stayed up for a full twenty-four hours contemplating it the night before I made my final decision. "But she's still…"

"Your mom." Ollie nods.

"Yup." The word swings like a wrecking ball.

She chews on her lip and gives me space to be angry. I've needed the geographical equivalent of Russia and most of China in terms of anger space. But all that roaming anger is getting narcissistic.

"And he's still…" She lets the words hang.

"Olls," I beg, but she's relentless in her quest to make me face my emotions.

"He was your first love, Nes. And he broke your heart. He's a dog, but you can't beat yourself up because you miss him. You need to let yourself feel everything. Don't clam up."

The tears coat my eyes like a hot, glistening windshield. When they plop out and make their pathetic slide down my cheeks, I know Ollie won't say, "Don't cry." I tend to squeeze my emotions into a bitty ball I can ignore. Ollie is a "cry it out" advocate.

"I do miss him." It's hard to be honest when honesty makes me feel so weak and stupid.

"That's okay." The sound of her voice is a balm to my frayed emotions.

"I mean, he was my best friend other than you. I can't think about him without remembering how good the good times were—it's bizarre how it changed so slowly. How did he go from being the guy who could always make me laugh to the guy who pulverized my heart?"

"I know," she says.

"I was scared, *really* scared to leave home and Newington and you," I say as I lick a few salty tears off my cracked lips. "But I was more scared of staying and facing him every day, because what he did to me is unacceptable—but sometimes I forget because I'm busy remembering how sweet he can be. How can he be such a snake in the grass and legitimately one of the most interesting, caring people I've ever met? He messed up so badly, but I know he still cares about me. That's dangerous." I take a deep breath and look at Ollie's face, just a screen away. "I was scared of falling for him again after everything he put me through. Because a little part of me is always going to love the goofy, smart, sweet guy I fell in love with two years ago."

"Oh, Nes." I know Ollie would hug me if we were together, and I want to cash in on that hug more than I've ever wanted anything.

"I'm a coward." I close my eyes.

"Stop it. Right now. You're the bravest person I know. I love you."

"I love you, Olls. And I'm going to be okay, promise. I'm letting all the gross feelings come out, just in little drips and drabs. Did I produce enough tears for you today? Can I go back to pretending I'm hard-hearted and cool?" I joke. Or half joke.

I know Ollie still wants a full rundown of my first day of school, but I don't have any energy to tell her about all the crazy crap that kind of threw me for a loop today. It's childish, but I want to pretend I started the second semester of our senior year at Newington Academy with her. We met in the friendly halls of our Quaker school when we were in second grade and she yelled that she loved my glittery stockings and I yelled that I loved her heart necklace and our teachers shushed us as we tried to yell more compliments back and forth. We found each other at recess, and we've been madly, completely best friends in love since then.

"I miss you like butter misses popcorn," she mourns, and the sight of her tears firms up my backbone.

"Stop crying! Did Parson give you permission to run your bead-and-bracelet biz in the front hall?" I change the subject fast, and it works. Sort of.

"Yes! The middle school girls were all primped out in their Christmas/Hanukkah duds… Nes, they're crimping their hair! Why didn't I ask Santa for a crimper *too*? I both want to scorn them and buy a crimper with all the fat moneys I'm making weaving little unicorn beads into their hair. Advice?" She wipes the tears away with the tip of her fingers.

"No scorn. They're littles. Remember how much the scorn of the cool upper-class girls hurt our souls back when we were tiny? Also, no crimper. If you want your hair to look like Bride of Frankenstein's, just braid it when it's damp." I tap my finger on the screen, over her face. She opens her mouth like she's going to bite it.

Our laughs are sadder than I want them to be.

"And, I almost forgot to tell you… No, I'm going to make you *guess*. Guess how else my life is turning to crap," Ollie orders.

Her words stab more than a little. I know I'm one of the main reasons the tail end of her senior year is going to look nothing like what we'd been planning since elementary school.

"Thao is moving back across the hall." She rolls her neck the way she always does after a grueling bassoon session to get the tension out.

"And I'm not even there to help you booby-trap your house like we did in fifth grade! What kind of crap friend am I?" I laugh around the next words because the idea of Thao being anything but a nose-picking cretin is hilarious. "Maybe he's changed since you last saw him? Or maybe your parents won't make you two hang out every time they get together. I mean, you're not little kids anymore. You have a life. Thao probably does too. If you count sneak-attack farting on people a life…"

"That's right." Ollie nods enthusiastically. "I do have a life. A life that does *not* involve disgusting boys who think it's cool to squirt milk out of their eyeballs."

I gag at the memory. "I'm telling you, I became lactose intolerant right after that."

We both crack up remembering gross Thao.

"You know I want to talk to you for a jillion hours, but Darcy gave us a paper assignment. Already. I can't believe him. Will you be able to talk later?" She eyes the phone hopefully.

Darcy. My favorite teacher. Ollie's too. She's pissed because she can't charm him out of giving actual work-based assignments instead of the fluffy busywork so many other teachers tend to assign during the last half of senior year. Well, giving *her* actual, work-based assignments. *I* live in a Darcy-free world now. All I have is Ma'am Lovett.

"Love you, doll. We can chat all night if you call later." I don't cry when I disconnect with Ollie, I don't cry when I look around at the institutionally bare walls of my room, and I don't cry when I struggle to get into my complicated, strappy bikini, which is as frustrating as playing Chinese jump rope.

I walk through the echoey house. It's got all the mundane architecture and lack of character you can expect from a last-minute rental in suburban Georgia. The tiny amount of furniture we brought from New York didn't begin to fill this place, so Mom set up an order from the local furniture store. Even with a truckload of brand-new couches, coffee tables, rugs, and paintings, it's surprisingly hard to fill three thousand square feet of house with stuff when you're used to living in an apartment one-sixth that size.

Even though I know I could never call this place home, I wonder who might someday. And I feel bad for them. Though the future owners *do* get a pool. That's pretty rad, to just walk out of your house and—*blam*—there's a pool.

That you can swim in.

In *January*.

I guess this place isn't all bad.

It still blows my mind, because private pools are like unicorns where I come from. Mom tried to use the pool as incentive to get me to like the idea of coming here. Because leaving a city full of culture and art and beauty and ferocious ambition can *so* be made better with a concrete hole filled with chlorinated water.

I expect the backyard to be serenely empty when I turn the corner, and nearly have a heart attack when I run into a random stranger holding a hose.

"What are you doing in my backyard?" I yell, taking an aggressive stance and gripping my phone hard in case I need to chuck it at his head. Or call 911. I scan the yard for weapons and notice a pool skimmer the cleaning service left on the patio. Maybe I could smack this guy into the water if he tries anything funny?

"'Scuse me. So sorry. I didn't realize the renters already moved in."

The voice drawls rough, quiet…familiar. Where have I heard it before? The half-naked male attached to it is practically ripping new armholes in his T-shirt in an attempt to cover up.

I relax my stance and realize he's not some hulking intruder, but a freaked-out guy about my age, and the T-shirt he's putting on backward reads Rahn Lawn Care and Maintenance.

"Most days my grandpa and cousin'd be out here during the day, so as not to disturb y'all. I jest head out to the places where there's no renters in yet. Your house was on my list. Sorry 'bout the inconvenience, ma'am. And about working with my shirt off. Rahn Lawn Care and Maintenance strives to provide professional service, and I apologize if I made you uncomfortable, ma'am."

He sounds like he's reciting lines from the HR handbook I had to sign when I worked at the local Y last summer.

"I promise I won't report you to your boss if you promise to stop calling me ma'am." When my joke leaves him looking extra terrified, I snort, pull out my sunscreen—SPF 50—and plop onto the nearest lounge chair. "Dude, chill. Seriously, it's cool. I took my first life-drawing class when I was twelve. Trust me, I've seen my fair share of naked guys. I'm not a prude."

He manages to yank the T-shirt—neck all stretched from his crazy flailing—right side around and get both arms through the sleeve holes. "Uh, cool. I'm Doyle Rahn. Pleased to meet ya." He holds out a hand.

I shake it, and dirt from his fingers muddies my sunscreen. "Doyle? I've never met anyone with that name before. I like it. I'm Agnes. Agnes Murphy-Pujols."

"Pujols?" His wide, white grin contains just the slightest twisted tooth here and there, and it sends an electric pulse through me. Unexpected, but definitely nice. "Like Albert Pujols?"

"I don't have any Alberts in my family." I squint up at him, his head haloed in the sun. He has blond hair that's just this side of being strawberry, and freckles that have almost melted into a tan.

"Too bad. He's pretty much the best pure hitter of all time." Doyle squats down next to what I guess is supposed to be one of the many "shade trees" the real-estate woman kept squawking about. I hate when people say one thing when they mean another. Like, if you mean *shriveled, leafless sticks*, don't say *shade trees*.

"Ah. Baseball. My father is a Caribbean studies professor who lives in France, and my brother is hard-core into soccer. Like, he insists on calling it *football* when he's in the States even though he knows it's confusing." I think on that for a second. "Huh. I wonder if he does that *because* it's confusing. Jasper's a weird guy like that. Anyway, not much baseball watching going down at my place. But my dad's where the Pujols part of my name is from, and the DR is pretty famous for baseball players, so, who knows? Maybe I should pay more attention to baseball." Doyle's examining the dried-out stick so intensely, I swear he's doing it to avoid examining *me*.

"You should. Watch baseball, that is. Actually, you should *play* baseball. We get a killer game goin' most Friday nights in the far field back there. You could come 'round if you like. Your brother too." He nods over his shoulder, and, even with my amazing internal compass, I have no clue where "back there" could be. Someone's backyard? The empty woods that line the neighborhood? The community office lawn?

"Actually, my brother lives in Paris with my dad," I blab. It's weird how sweet it is to talk to a normal person about normal things in my life. Like what a jerk my irritating brother, who I miss a ton, can be. "My brother is one of those guys who ties a silk scarf around his neck like Freddie from *Scooby-Doo* because he thinks it's fashionable. He enjoys eating animal organs and watching really depressing documentaries—basically he's more Parisian than most French citizens."

"Yeah?" Doyle's gaze settles on me with a laid-back comfort. Like he could look all day.

I flap my hand in front of my face like a makeshift fan. Was there some kind of sudden solar flare?

"Yeah." I reach back and lift my hair, damp with sweat, off my neck.

"You ain't wantin' to move to Paris too?"

I cackle. "Nope. No way." I should stop while I'm ahead, but this guy is listening to me. Complete attention. Damn that's *highly* attractive. The most explosive arguments Lincoln and I got into before we broke up had to do with the way he seemed to look right through me, the way I felt like I had to fight for every scrap of attention he tossed my way. It really hurt because we'd been friends before we dated, so it wasn't like I was just losing my boyfriend. I was losing one of my best friends. But Doyle is one hundred percent invested in what I'm saying, so I ramble some more. "First of all my French is awful. Second, the French are, how should I say it…? *Les Français sont bites.*"

"Sounds fancy."

"I just said, 'French people are dicks.'"

The laugh catapults out of his throat so fast, he half chokes on it. It's nerdy to laugh at your own joke, but I do it anyway. There's been an alarming lack of laughter in my life lately.

"So, what about you? Do you have any siblings who irritate the crap out of you?"

When he chuckles, the skin over my ribs tingles like I'm being tickled. "I sure do. I got an older brother who's a marine. Proud as hell of him, but it ain't exactly easy living with a decorated combat vet." He dips the tips of his fingers into the soil at the tree's roots and stirs it into a shallow pattern of spiraling furrows that make me think of those Buddhist sand gardens.

"Does he have PTSD?" I'm not sure if I'm being direct or nosy. I hope I'm not overstepping. Ollie and I did a Civics project on PTSD at Newington, so I know the facts but have no real experience with the horrors of it.

"PTSD? Nah." Doyle scoops up a tiny mound of dirt and sprinkles it back on the roots. "Lee's one of them guys who was born a natural soldier. He's a leader, he handles stress real well, he's always got a plan, thinks on his feet. One time we got lost out hiking in the woods overnight when Lee was only 'bout ten or so. I was jest a little kid. Lee built a lean-to, caught us some fish to eat, made a fire... He near burned down half a nature preserve, but that's what led the rescue crew to us. I was crying so hard when they found us, but my brother was cool as can be. He got a medal from the sheriff, and, man, it blew his head up so big. He was... What's the word? A *bite*?"

I love the way his accent coils softly around the rude French word. "Brothers are annoying as hell, but Lee sounds like a great guy to have around in an emergency. My brother would have known every statistic about how close we were to death and had a panic attack."

Doyle's eyebrows, lips, and dimples all lift up when he smiles. I've never seen a smile change a whole face that way. "Problem is, Lee got used to being the boss, and he forgets I'm his brother and a civilian, not some jarhead in his platoon. But my grandparents won't hear it when it comes to him. They tell me to grab Lee's laundry, and if I decline, my granddad says, 'Your brother puts his life on the line for this great nation. You show some respect and pick up his dirty socks.' I don't sass my granddad anyway, but that's some hard logic to argue."

"So you live with your grandparents?" My guard must be way, way down because I swear I planned to keep that thought in my head, but there it is, sprung from the trap that is my flapping mouth. Maybe I'm relaxing after so many months of watching what I said around Lincoln. "I'm just asking because I considered going to live with my abuela in New York."

"Huh. Yeah, I've lived with them since I was in elementary school." He leaves it at that, and some instinct tells me not to push. "How 'bout you? Were you just so ready to come down here and soak up all this sunshine?" He holds his hands out at his sides like he personally ordered the blazing heat that surrounds us.

"Ha! No. The snow and ice of the north match my cold heart." I bat my lashes and am pleasantly shocked when his grin widens even more. "Her place was a super long commute from my school." I hesitate before I say more, but there's something about his face that I trust. For once I don't shut down and pull back. "She's also scary strict. Like, *super* Catholic, gets up at dawn to hit the rosary, full rotation, every morning, Bible class at her place every week, having Father Domingo over for dinner every Sunday night… Just not the end of senior year I was looking for."

"So you didn't want to sign up for the convent experience?" The laugh that starts from his mouth doubles back on itself. "I meant… 'Cause your grandmother is a Catholic… Not the whole vow of chastity thing," he says in a garbled rush.

I get the feeling Doyle's as uncomfortable tripping over his words as I am opening up.

"No worries, I get it. And, yeah, the cloistered life isn't for me. At all." The deep pink blush that's building under his stubble is adorable. "So it's just you and Lee and your grandparents?"

I'm employing polite conversation diversion to steer us into less embarrassing territory, but something in the question makes Doyle's features harden.

"And my little brother, Malachi. He's at Ebenezer too, but

you prolly won't see him around. He stays back in the computer lab with his friends all day every day. Think he might be allergic to sunshine and fresh air." The best way to describe Doyle's expression is *perplexed*. It's probably the same way my face looks when Jasper tells me he'd rather watch a documentary on spelling bees than the latest Marvel movie.

"So three guys in one house—wait, no, *four* if you count your grandpa—"

"Actually, it's five." When I greet that number with shocked silence, he explains, "Brookes, my cousin—his mama got remarried and he and his stepfather don't see eye to eye. And his stepfather gets mean when people don't see things his way. I guess my grandparents' place is kinda a home for wayward Rahn children. We all figured, what was one more bunk bed, plus Lee's only around when he's on leave, so it's a lotta…"

He waves his hands around like he's looking for the words to fill in the blank.

"Dirty boxers? Farts? Package adjusting?" I rapid-fire guess.

For a second Doyle stares at me, eyes and mouth wide-open. Then he starts to laugh, hard, and I join him. We both laugh until we're buckled over.

"Geez, I was gonna say, 'it's a lotta testosterone,' but I guess you got the point across your way jest fine." He balances easily on the balls of his feet despite his clunky boots. "People 'round here hardly ever come out and say the first thing that pops in their heads."

I wince. One of the last fights we had, Lincoln told me, *You know you don't have to say every thought that goes through your head out loud, Nes. You need a way bigger filter between your brain and your mouth.* I guess that's the consensus, then.

"Yep, I've heard that before." He tenses up at my tone like

he felt a chill in the air. "My big mouth gets me in a lot of trouble. Probably best if you steer clear."

"I never did have patience for people who play it safe."

The ice wall I was rapidly constructing around myself thaws.

"Fair enough. But now you can never say I didn't warn you."

"Most've my favorite things come with a warning." He clears his throat. "So, we're short a second baseman since Marnie Jepson moved, and we need someone like yourself. Someone who can call a whole country dicks in their own tongue. Whatta you say? You got a mitt?"

"Nope." And I plan to leave the discussion right there. Because, seriously? Baseball? It's very sporty middle school, and so not my thing. But I like the sloppy-slow way Doyle talks— I wonder if he plays ball the same way he speaks. And once I start wondering about something, I have to go with it until I know for sure. Damn my curiosity. If I were a cat, I'd be dead nine times over. "You have an extra mitt?"

He nods and smiles down at a jug of blue stuff he's now pouring on the roots of the "tree."

"I do. Wouldya like me to bring it over Friday night?"

For one cold thump of my heart, I think I shouldn't take this guy up on what might be a date. The last guy I dated messed with my head so badly, I wound up fleeing the state. Then I get annoyed with myself. Sure, Doyle is super attractive, but I'm a girl who's learned the hard way how to be careful with my heart. This is one single game of baseball, not a promise ring. And I'd like to have some fun with a guy—no, a *person*—who clearly likes me for myself, not some censored version of me.

I need a friend, and Doyle seems like he might be a really good option.

On top of that, this is all very 1950s' date-night adorable. "You know what? I would like you to."

He looks right at me, no smile, no niceties. Just a bald, hungry *look*. "Cool."

My guts pull in all different directions. "So, are you, like, the ambassador of Southern hospitality or something? Because you're the first nice Southern person I've met."

"What? You didn't like Lovett?" His long fingers cap the jug, and my arms and legs inexplicably tingle.

"You're in my English class?" It finally clicks, why I recognize his voice. "You schooled that guy, Alonzo, in geography."

Doyle rolls his eyes. "Hell, a preschool baby could school that ding-dong. He's a good guy though. Friendly." He screws his mouth to one side. "I know some people can be chillier than a Yankee winter 'round here." The way he chuckles when I almost sputter lets me know he's teasing me. "Not a whole lotta tolerance for anyone who don't fit in right away."

I'm not usually embarrassed by much, but I still feel like an idiot over the spectacle I made fumbling through that class. But Doyle seems like a good ambassador for all things Southern, so I straight ask him about something that's still bugging me.

"What's with the 'ma'am' thing?"

He squats back on his heels and cocks his head, owl-like. "You know... You say 'ma'am' or 'sir' when you speak to your teachers—to any adults. I thought you were jest raggin' on Lovett. She's all bark, I guarantee you. And she likes smart-asses better than kiss-asses, so you're gonna do fine."

"I never called any of my teachers 'ma'am' or 'sir' back home." I blow out a breath. "I thought that was military-school crap. Is that the rule, like, hard-and-fast? For every teacher?"

He nods again and pulls off his ratty ball cap to wipe the sweat off his forehead. His eyes are so blue, they're almost a light purple. Adorable.

"*Every* adult. If you don't want them to think you're a total punk. You lived in New York City all yer life?"

"Yep. Brooklyn, specifically. A haven for punks of all varieties." I smile when his face goes slack. "Is New York City, like, the scariest place in the world to everyone here? Because every single person makes that exact face when I talk about Brooklyn."

He puts the ball cap back on, shadowing those pretty eyes, and picks up the jug. "Jest exotic as hell. Most people 'round here've never left the Lowcountry. And don't want to."

"Yeah. I get that vibe." I probably shouldn't bring up the fact that, when I'm not at home with Mom, I'm at my father's apartment in Paris or my cousin's house in the Santo Domingo in conversation here. People might have heart palpitations and pass out.

"Not me though." His adamant declaration interrupts my stereotyping thoughts.

"No?" I'm instantly more curious about Doyle now that I know he might want to escape this place. It's like finding another inmate to help you chip a hole through the concrete walls of your cell.

"My grandparents took me with them to Maui last year. My granddaddy was stationed there when he was a marine, and he really loved it, so they took me and my brothers. It was pretty amazing. Speaking of them, I better get going. My grandmother will beat my ass if I'm late for supper." He stands up and brushes the dirt off the knees of his Dickies, and I feel a tug of regret.

Because I like talking to him. My FaceTime sessions with Ollie are always great, but I've been hungering for real-life human interactions, and Doyle's already twisted my expectations a few times. I like the way he's surprised me.

"See you in class tomorrow." I turn over and notice that he gives my cherry-red bikini a second and *maybe* a third look. I tip my sunglasses down and smile at him. "Aloha, Doyle."

His laugh is equal parts sheepish and pleased. "Aloha, Agnes."

"Nes." It jumps out of my mouth before I'm ready for it.

Nes is what my friends call me. My standards are dipping low if I consider Doyle a friend after only a couple minutes of conversation. But I guess desperate times and all that…

"Aloha, Nes." He hesitates, then points to the tree. "Do me a favor? Water her when the sun dips? Jest a trickle outta the water hose for fifteen, maybe twenty minutes to get a good soak going."

I slowly raise one eyebrow. "Doyle? I hate to break it to you, but that tree is *dead*. It's kindling. A lost cause. Have some mercy and let it die a dignified death."

His fingertips caress a clump of light green baby leaves barely clinging to life. "I like to root for the underdog. See you tomorrow in class."

Ah right. Before the awkwardness of baseball, there will be the awkwardness of school. Lovely.

I make a point to not watch Doyle's tall, rangy self saunter away from me.

I come so close to succeeding…

At the last second, I drink him in, then flip over and drag my phone close. My idiotic traitor brain actually thinks about calling Lincoln.

The boy who's been my best guy friend since we were twelve.

The boy who gave me my first kiss under an old oak tree.

The boy who broke my heart when we were seventeen.

Or the boy who only *loaned* me his heart so he could take it back eventually, while I *gave* him mine on a silver platter, free and clear so he could shred it into tiny pieces. Dumb. So dumb.

I toss my phone to the side and throw an arm over my eyes, wondering whose bed Lincoln will be in while I'm standing on second base this Friday. Guilt shoots through me when I remember Mom planned on the two of us going to Savannah on Friday after I got home from school so we could stroll through the art museums downtown and maybe check out the local performing arts college's production of *Grease*. I'm torn between wanting to hang out with my mother doing things we love together like we used to and holding tight to a lot of pissed-off anger over the way she screwed things up for us. The betrayal that still cuts deep won't magically disappear just because we're both excited to see some Helen Levitt photographs and bop along to "Greased Lightnin'." Everything is too complicated.

Except baseball.

Playing baseball is definitely easier than dealing with the whole sordid mess of a relationship I currently have with my mother. I roll back onto my stomach, and baseball and cheating and Hawaii and Sandra Dee all invade my dreams as I fall asleep in the oven-hot afternoon of my strange new life.

THREE

"**A**gnes!" Mom's on the patio in her favorite pencil skirt and silk blouse, her uniform for lecture days. "You're a lobster!"

"Wha—" I wipe the drool off the side of my face and try to push myself up, but my skin feels tight and puckered. "*Coño!* I actually used sunscreen, I swear."

"Honey, you're half-Irish. Sunscreen is nothing but a cruel joke." She runs her fingers over my tender skin. "Come in. I have aloe. And I picked up Chinese on the way home."

How many times have I had to explain to my more clueless pale friends that dark-skinned people can and do burn? What's that saying about heeding your own advice…?

"I don't get it. Why do my genes put me through this trial by fire every summer? Jasper can be out in the sun for hours and this never happens to him," I growl, limping in and sitting on a stool at the counter. Maybe my skin is reacting so badly because it wasn't expecting this kind of sun exposure in January. I say a silent prayer it won't be blotchy and peely tomorrow.

My mother pushes a carton of cooling Buddha's delight my way. We've already eaten at the one and only Chinese food place in a thirty-mile radius so often, they can recite our phone number from memory based on the sound of our voices when we call to order.

"You aren't in New York anymore, Aggie. As far as your brother's ability to endure the sun goes, I actually wish Jasper was more careful with sunscreen. Just because he *can* be out for hours without it doesn't mean he *should*. Skin cancer is nothing to play around with." My mother dabs aloe on my skin, and I suck air through my teeth to manage the pain that stings through the cool. "Plus you freckle."

I know the go-to image of an Irish lass centers on a redhead with alabaster skin and cinnamon freckles in a wool sweater standing by the Cliffs of Moher, but...

"Right. I'm Irish," I say through a mouthful of overcooked vegetables I just slurped off my chopsticks.

"But my family is bone-white pale, not freckly. I think your freckles are from your Dominican half." I look down at my mother's pale fingers tangled with my dark ones. I love that we have the same oval-shaped nails and double-jointed thumbs. I love what I inherited from her, and I love what's different about us. And that makes me miss how close we used to be. How close my whole family used to be.

When I was a kid I used to spill out my colored pencils and hold them close to my family members so that I could get the color of their skin just right in my drawings. After a long, dark New York winter, mine would mellow to a dark golden tawny, a few shades darker than my mother's at the end of summer. By contrast, after a summer spent at our communal family beach house in Santo Domingo, my skin would be a light sepia with a spattering of umber freckles. I'd admire myself in the full-length mirror in the bedroom I shared with half a dozen of my girl cousins, each one of us a different shade of gorgeous and proud to announce it. One of the first slang phrases I picked up in the DR as a kid was *hevi nais*, which my cousins said about anything and everything—cute new outfits, beautiful hairstyles, too-tall sandals, our sun-warmed skin. It basically means "very nice," and it's the kind of casually confident phrase that still makes me feel beautiful and strong in my own skin. I loved the fact that while everyone else in school had their twenty-four pack of Crayola colored pencils, I had my set of seventy-two Prismacolor Premiers with a range of russets and taupes and ochers for my family pictures.

"Can't a girl define her own cultural heritage?" I snap, annoyed that nothing feels easy with my mother anymore. Not even a conversation about something as simple as freckles.

"Oh, there's no denying you got plenty of my genes. Even if the freckles are open for debate, you have an Irish temper just like your mother." I want so badly to smile back at her, but my heart is a cold, congealed pile of old tofu. "You and Jasper might look more like Dad at first glance, but there's a lot of me mixed in there too."

"Huh, I'm kind of surprised you even remember how Jasper looks," I bite out. "We barely see him or Dad anymore."

"Ag, we were just in Paris this autumn—"

"About that." I interrupt before she can go into professor mode. My mother is a champ at talking for forty minutes straight at a clip and barely pausing for breath. "I thought you and Dad were making up or something. But you and that guy you worked with had...*whatever* gross mess going on, and you kept it up after we got home. I still don't get it."

Am I accusing my mother of cheating on my father? That makes no sense. They've been divorced for years...but the boundaries of their relationship weren't always crystal clear. I know more about their up-and-down, back-and-forth, off-

and-on relationship than I should because our apartment was tiny with very thin walls. Sure, I could have been thoughtful and put on headphones or something when Mom called her best friend, but sometimes I got tired of being surprised by my mercurial parents and their chaotic relationship.

"Okay, this is not a conversation I can have with you right now. Or probably ever, if you want the truth. I know you're not a baby anymore, but that doesn't mean you're privy to every detail about my marriage to your father, okay? Frankly, it's complicated and it's private, how your father and I—"

"What? Screwed up your marriage and all our lives in the process?"

My words skid to a stop like a dog that finally caught the car she'd been chasing for miles and has no freaking clue what to do with it.

The tendons in Mom's neck bulge when she swallows. She squirts more aloe on her fingers and rearranges her features until they're her best estimation of calm. I prime myself for her raging Irish temper, but she talks in this infuriatingly measured way.

"Agnes, I know you're angry. I know you blame me. I know you want answers that will help this make sense, but you're old enough to know that there aren't always easy answers in life. There are things you can't understand—"

"I bet I could." My knees knock under the counter because the little I do know has made me so angry. What if I find out more? What if things between us get even worse? "We used to talk. You used to let me know what was going on with you."

"It hasn't always been easy to know *when* to tell you things." Mom takes a deep calming breath, one her yoga gurus would be proud of. "Have you spoken to your father?"

"I missed his call from before. I'll call him later." I'll try anyway. I love my father, but our phone calls are always awkward and stilted. We communicate mostly through text, and that's basically comprised of sending each other funny memes or links to interesting *NPR* articles. Not exactly deep, but it works for us. "Why are you asking?" She's avoiding eye contact like it's her job.

"You…you just need to talk to him. That's all." Her words are like a judge's gavel hitting the bench.

"Why don't you just tell me?"

"There are some things that aren't open for discussion." The words are quiet but firm. "I try to respect your privacy, baby. But you have to understand that I need that back from you, even when it's hard."

"When respecting my privacy means you lose everything you care about, get back to me, okay?" I shift back and bump my shoulder on the wall behind me and bite back a scream.

"Let me see," Mom offers, sounding worried again.

I'm torn between wanting to soak up that worry and wanting to throw it back in her face.

"I'm good." I bite the words out and turn my shoulder, so she's left with a goopy blob of aloe dripping down her fingers.

"Sweetie, you're in pain. Let me at least spread this last bit—"

"I *said* I'm good," I growl, sliding off the stool, a carton of cooling Chinese food crushed in my fingers. I grab a bottle of water from the fridge and call out, "I'm going to eat in my room!" Any residual guilt I had about ditching Mom this Friday has evaporated completely.

"Agnes? *Agnes!* Please come here!" Her words shake, but she stands perfectly still behind the counter.

I stalk down the hall and slam the door to my room. I instantly hate being holed up in this still-unfamiliar space, alone.

When my mother's sordid tale first started making the rounds in her gossipy department after we got home from our annual Thanksgiving in Paris, it was just a rumble under the surface. TAs would stop whispering when I walked into the office, and I'd hear only my mother's name and the snapped-off end of a sentence that was definitely filled with dirt. When I went to the bookstore to grab an order for my mother, the snide clerk gave me major side-eye and suggested *Madame Bovary* as an add-on to the pile. I didn't get his passive-aggressive dig until a week later, when I realized it wasn't only the stress of grading fall semester research papers that had her so tense.

There were mysterious hung-up phone calls at all hours of the night. Staff meetings she came home from in tears. I found her laptop open with an updated résumé on the screen, and her friend from college had sent an email titled Unexpected Spring Semester Opening... You Are a Shoo-In! So the clues were blaring in my face like a full-blast neon sign for weeks, but I was dealing with my own drama.

Apparently Lincoln interpreted *I'm going to see my family in Paris for a week* as *Do whatever you want with as many girls as you can while I'm away,* and one of those girls contacted me as soon as she realized the guy she was falling for was already someone's boyfriend. A few hours before the call, Ollie had brought over dozens of nail polishes and painted intricate designs on my fingernails and toenails, then Lincoln's, then her own, then we rubbed every bit of it off and started all over again, the smell of nail polish remover burning our throats. My last coat wasn't even dry when the girl's voice cracked across the line. *There's something you need to know about your boyfriend.*

Lincoln.

Was it irony that, while I was loathing my mother for leaving some poor yoga-loving blogger home wrecked, my own boyfriend was screwing half the girls' tennis team?

He cried—actually he *sobbed*—when I confronted him and then, exactly three weeks later, *whoosh*, my mom threw our life into chaos with her announcement that she'd been Skype interviewed for a fantastic spring semester position in Georgia and she got the job. We were moving. Everything went really fast after that. Our apartment was almost empty in the weeks leading up to Christmas, and we had a tree so pathetic, it made Charlie Brown's look like the one at the Rockefeller Center. While the rest of the world was celebrating peace on earth and goodwill toward humankind, it was dawning on me that I'd really have to say goodbye to the only home I'd ever known and my best friend, beloved school, and Mama Patria. It wasn't so much that my mother forced me to go—it's that I had no other choice. Saying goodbye to the people I loved wasn't easy, but I took some comfort, knowing I'd dodged a big, emotionally draining bullet by not going back. I didn't have to figure out what to do or say the next time I ran into Lincoln because instead I'd put nearly a thousand miles between us.

So I made my decision and left Brooklyn, but I never really got to resolve…anything. About Lincoln, about life, about Mom's actions and her lies, about school and what I wanted from any of it. That's partially why I'm still directing so much fury at Mom. She messed up. So did Lincoln. But I have only her here, so she gets the brunt of all my swirling hate.

FaceTime beeps through on my phone. My pride has taken enough of a beating that it sits back and lets me sob openly to Ollie this time.

"Babydoll," she cries when she sees my face, already streaked with a few tears. "Grab Mr. Kittenface." She crosses her arms and waits for me to grab my old, sweet-faced teddy. "Hug him so tight." I do, laughing wetly at myself and us. "That's my girl. That's how hard I'd be hugging you if I were there. Tell me. Everything."

I nestle Mr. Kittenface in my lap, tugging on his ears while I blubber about Ma'am Lovett, the Southern kids whose shoulders are as icy cold as their climate is tropical, my mom fury, my Lincoln fury... I let it all stew and bubble until we're both crying.

"Whew. Holy shit." Ollie unleashes a shuddering sigh. "What a day. You're wrecking me, you know that, right? And you have every right to cry over every one of those things, but please never, ever speak that asshole Lincoln's name again."

I whimper. "Remember when—"

"No." She pulls the phone close to her face, so she's one gorgeous, blurry eyeball and a perfect swoop of winged liner. "No, no, no. We're not going down the LiNeOl road again."

LiNeOl. Ollie's nickname for the three of us since we were assigned to the same science group in eighth grade. After years of being our friend around school, I was scared dating him would be a disaster for everyone, but Lincoln was that amazing boyfriend who jumped from friends to more and never let it get weird. He never treated Ollie like a third wheel. He knew her favorite candy was Nerds when we went to the movies and got her purple tulips on Valentine's Day when she didn't have a boyfriend.

Ollie used to say she wanted to find the Lincoln to her Nes.

He had sex with five other girls. That I know of.

Five that he confessed to. And there had to be some times when he came back from one of their beds and climbed into mine, whispering about how much he wanted me, how beautiful I was, how we were so perfect together. He threaded his fingers through mine and pressed himself deep inside me, listening to me moan after he'd probably done the same things, heard the same things from another girl's mouth in another girl's bed.

Did I ignore the smell of other girls' perfume and the vague explanations of where he'd been that made no sense? Was I as dumb as the wife of the weasel my mother was having a torrid affair with?

"I…I just never got to really figure it all out. He's called. I haven't answered. Yet. But sometimes…I want to," I confess, hanging my head in shame. I'd never confess that to anyone but Ollie.

She blows out a long breath. "I know. He asks about you. Constantly. But listen to me—the truth is, he *is* sad he lost you. He is. Because he's not a complete idiot. But he used you, Nes. He disrespected you. And I will never, ever forgive him. He lied to both of us, and we can't trust him. Ever. Again." She tucks her shiny black hair behind her ears and gives me a hard, dark-eyed stare. "You are gorgeous, inside and out, and you deserve so much better. You hear me? He was your first, Nes. Not your only."

She looks so sad, like she thinks I'll get off the phone with her and call him. So I confess something else, something so new, I'm not sure how I feel about it yet. "I did get asked on kind of a date today."

"What?" she screams, almost dropping the phone. I watch her orange walls and Karen Geoghegan poster swirl in the background. "Are you kidding me? Tell! Tell me every damn detail now!"

I grab hard on the tail of her laugh and fly with that happiness. I don't skimp on details, and Doyle is even more attractive in my retelling. If that's possible.

"That's retro hot!" she gushes. "Baseball date? So adorable. I'm happy. I wish I could come and bat or umpire or whatever."

Her words cause a patch of thorns to bloom in my throat. I miss her so much. "Me too, Olls. Me too."

"Hey." She changes the subject before we get murky with sadness. "Just...don't compare him to Lincoln, okay? I know he was your first love and all. But Lincoln only *seemed* perfect—he was actually a huge, gaping asshole. Remember that," she warns.

I do. I will. I promise her three times, and I'm still not sure she believes me.

Later, after Ollie and I have gabbed late into the night and my Chinese food has congealed into a cold lump of tofu and water chestnuts, I creep out to the living room. Mom isn't sleeping on the couch with an empty bottle of wine rolling on the floor like she's been doing about once a week lately, so that's good. Her bedroom door is shut though, and I half want to go in and sit on the edge of her mattress so we can chat like we used to. There are four episodes of the stupid medical romance she and I are obsessed with rotting on the DVR, but neither one of us has invited the other to watch.

The last episode we watched together was the night before she got a barrage of intense and threatening emails, phone calls, and even a delivered package from the scorned wife, who was close friends with half the office staff my mother depended on to keep her department in line. My mom had a few options: stay and push back against a possibly unhinged woman whose husband she'd slept with, in hopes said furious woman would stop the harassment and not deliver any more "anonymous" boxes of shit (yes, literal shit, hopefully animal) to our apartment; endure "lost" memos, meetings that the scheduler "forgot" to mention, and general iciness from the office staff who were solidly loyal to the guy's wife; or hightail it outta Dodge.

Only a moron would have gone for anything other than door number three. Mom gave her notice the morning after

I found an obviously fake "STD Home Testing Kit" left on our mat, which I assumed was a lame prank that wound up at the wrong address.

I press a hand on her door and slide it to the doorknob, then stop and pad away. I should go to bed, but I head outside instead and drag the hose over to the sad little twig dying in our backyard. I turn the hose on and sit with my feet in the pool, swatting mosquitoes and looking at the fat pearly moon while the water gurgles. For the first night in years, I distract myself by thinking about a boy who's not Lincoln, and it feels like fraud. And maybe a little like hope.

FOUR

While Ma'am Lovett scrawls Bible verses that correspond to the old man's fishing trip in dusty chalk on the old blackboard before the bell, I palm a guava, working up the nerve to let it wobble in the center of her desk.

"Agnes?" She puckers her lips at the bobbling fruit.

"We were out of apples." I wave to her with my book, and she dusts the chalk off her hands and takes the guava.

She presses it to her nose and inhales deeply, eyes closed, lips pursed. "Heaven."

"Well, I *have* been called an angel. Now and then."

Ma'am Lovett shakes her head *somewhat* lovingly before she goes back to the blackboard. The Generic Mean Girls from yesterday snort and whisper on cue, like they're literally working off some D-list high school movie script on how to be total sociopaths, and then there's a laugh that sounds sweet and warm, like taffy left in the pocket of your shorts at the shore.

I flounce to my chair, my heart so light, I warn myself to pull away before I wind up like Icarus, too close to the sun and falling hard.

"Doyle Rahn. Fancy meeting you here." I smile at the familiar face sitting one row over, two seats back, and get an eyeful of daggers from every girl in between us.

Doyle either doesn't know he's the object of all the girls' wanton desire or he's so used to it, he doesn't notice anymore. Because the smile he tosses back is all for me. It's so magnetic, I wonder how I missed it yesterday.

"Guava, huh? Your yard would be perfect for a guava tree, y'know." He props his feet up on the crossbar under the desk. He's wearing these brown boots that are crusted with dirt, no laces, clunky and ruggedly attractive all at once.

Lincoln would have never been caught dead in dirty footwear.

"I watered that stick last night. Only because I don't kick a man when he's down, and that sad excuse for a plant is *so* down." I ball up a piece of notebook paper, double-check to make sure Lovett's back is turned, and anchor it on the pad of my thumb, then let my index finger trigger it right over some pouty girl's head.

Doyle catches it neatly without taking his eyes off my face. "It's gonna grow. It's gonna get so big, you'll be able to climb up in the branches. Maybe kiss. You know, like the song." The tips of his ears burn red, and I realize he's *flirting*. With me. And I'm game to flirt right back.

One half of the Day-Glo spray-tan twins huffs loudly. I notice her sending Doyle extra eyelash bats across the desks, which he doesn't pay a single second's attention to. It's always sweet when karma pops up out of nowhere and slams a dumb ass upside the head.

"Like Doyle and Nes sitting in a tree?" I laugh, then shake my head. "Uh-uh. Trust me, that version of the song does *not* exist. And here I thought you were a gentleman."

"I was raised with manners." His steady words scratch in my ears. "But I was also born with eyes."

"Smooth." I pull the word long so he won't hear my voice hitch around it. "Anyway, I don't plan on being around long enough for that sad little almost tree to hold up a humming-bird's nest, let alone two teenagers. I'm on a countdown to get out of here."

"Good riddance," Queen Bee Mean Girl mumbles.

I whip around. "Hello? Passive-aggressive?" She looks up at me with furiously shocked eyes. "Before you mutter anything else under your breath, let me introduce myself. I'm Agnes. Oh, but you know that because you made fun of my name before you even met me. The thing is, I prefer my fights in the open. So if you have something to say, don't mutter under your breath. It just irritates me and makes you look scared." The indignation on her face causes a pulse of happiness to rip-ple through me. "Do you have a name?"

I hear Alonzo snicker. "Hoo, *burn*. That had to sting."

"Ansley Strickland," she says through gritted teeth. "My daddy always says Yanks like to talk a big game. Don't think you intimidate me. You think you're hot shit, *Agnes*, but my family owns half this county. You better back on up, bitch."

"Ignore her, Agnes. Ansley thinks she owns this school." Alonzo rolls his eyes so hard, all I can see is the bright, ghostly whites.

"Of course *you* think she's funny, Lonzo. Just because some-one runs their mouth don't mean they're tough." She grabs the end of her ponytail and twists the shiny blond hair around her finger like a tourniquet.

"Look, maybe you two got off on the wrong foot." Khabria sounds like she should be narrating a meditation tape. "Agnes is new here. The Rose Court is supposed to be about *welcom-ing* people to Ebenezer."

Maybe it *was* all getting off on the wrong feet, and not the fact that Ansley is a heinous excuse for a human being.

"I don't have a clue what the Rose *Princess* is supposed to do, Khabria, but the Rose *Queen* upholds the traditions of this school." She flicks her now-curled ponytail back over her shoulder, and I watch Khabria's eyes go wild like her pupils are the swirling centers of twin hurricanes.

Nope. Definitely Ansley being heinous after all.

"You ain't the winner of that crown yet, Ansley," Doyle drawls. "You keep acting like you're too good for us peasants, you might have a Marie Antoinette moment on your hands."

"What are you even going on about, Doyle?" Ansley snaps. "You know, you're only embarrassing yourself showing off like that. You're the one acting like he's too good for the rest of us, goin' on about Marie Whoever like anyone even knows what you're even tryin' to say."

"Ah, hell no," Alonzo hoots. "Jest c'mon and admit you're the only one who doesn't know what happened to Marie Antoinette, Ansley. Admit it. Everyone knows you failed European history so bad, even your daddy couldn't help you outta that mess."

"Shut up, Alonzo," she hisses, but her blush is pretty convincing evidence that Alonzo's dropped the guillotine right on the neck.

"How does a guy who doesn't know where Brooklyn is know all these details about European history?" Khabria crosses her arms and shakes her head.

"Well, if some queen gets her head cut off by a bunch of pissed-off poor folk in Brooklyn, I guess I'll take notes," Lonzo shoots back.

"Really? That's what you think about me, Doyle?" Ansley's face has deepened from pink to maroon. "I know you're pissed about what happened between us, but you really think I deserve to have my head chopped off?"

"I meant it as a metaphor." Doyle leans forward and lowers his voice. "And I'm *not* pissed about…that anymore."

But Ansley is twisted in her seat, shredding her notebook paper into confetti. "So now you talk in metaphors? I remember the days when you just said what you meant. Funny you think *I'm* the one acting like e'rybody else is beneath me."

Before the stew of crazy comments can go any further, the late bell buzzes and we all swing around to face forward. Ma'am Lovett seems to sense something more than idle before-the-bell chatter was brewing, but she only gives us her no-nonsense face, and we respond to that look like a class of guava-bearing angels and stay on our best behavior. By the time the bell rings, my hand is cramped from all my Hemingway notes, and my brain feels buzzy.

As I rise from my desk, Doyle ambles over, wedges a hip close to mine, and leads me out the door. Up close, the way he smells makes me feel, I think, the way guavas make Ma'am Lovett feel. I bend my head so that my nose is close to his shoulder, and his scent is warm and rich, like hay in the sun, but with something crisp on the edge. I'd have guessed aftershave, but a blond prickle of five o'clock shadow covers his jaw.

"You're new here, so you couldn't know, butcha prolly don't want to mess with Ansley," Doyle says as we walk. He has one arm circled around my waist, held a few inches back. If either one of us moved closer, his hand would close over my hip and he'd lock me tight to his side.

But he doesn't, and I sure as hell won't.

"Thank you very, very much, but I think I'm well equipped to handle my own nemesis." I level him with a hard look and dare him to challenge my badassery. He cannot seriously think Ansley could take me in any form of a fair fight. She doesn't even know the basics of the French Revolution.

"She can be real spiteful is all. And she was—" He interrupts himself and rubs his hand over the back of his neck. "The thing is—"

When he doesn't finish his thought, I sigh and angle through the crowds, almost losing him over and over. He closes one hand around my elbow before I can go into my next class. I lean against the cinder block wall and roll my eyes when he pulls close. "Listen, I appreciate the concern and all, but I have no interest in listening to some big speech about Ansley or her little idiot friend—"

"Braelynn."

"Okay. Ansley and *Braelynn* don't intimidate me. I seriously don't care who anyone's daddy is or how much pull anyone thinks they have. Honestly, I think it's pathetic." I tug my arm out of his grasp.

"I know you don't. And I admire that about you. But Ansley really does have major pull 'round here, and if she has you in her sights—"

"Agnes?" Mr. Webster sticks his head into the hall.

"Yes?"

"Sir." Doyle whispers it as a soft reminder for me.

I bristle, but he puts his hand back on my arm, and his touch steadies me. Which is infuriating. "Yes, *sir?*"

Mr. Webster sighs and pinches the bridge of his handsome nose. "They'd like to see you in Principal Armstrong's office."

Doyle's mouth pulls tight. "Damn," he mutters when the teacher ducks back into the classroom.

"I'm new here. It's probably a schedule thing," I say with

way more confidence than I actually feel. "C'mon, you really think Ansley already ran to tattle on me to the *principal*?"

"Yeah, I do." Pissed is a strangely hot look on Doyle. I thought he was working it with the sexy smiles, but scowls? He's got this whole angry, tortured-youth vibe twisted around a sweet core that does it for me.

O'frescome, *what is this guy doing to me?*

"So, you're telling me that her family is so almighty, they've even got the high school principal in their pocket?" I tease.

But my joke obviously sucks, because Doyle grabs my hand and marches me to the main office.

"I just registered the other day. I'm perfectly capable of finding the front office on my own."

"There's something you don't get, Nes."

"More Ansley intrigue? You guys need to get a new obsession. I don't think—"

"The principal is her uncle," he finally grits out.

"Oh." My steps drop heavier. Slower.

"And she and I—"

"You and Ansley?"

"Yeah. We, uh…"

"You two…?"

"Um…yep."

"Oh."

Oh.

It all snaps into hyperfocus and my stomach churns.

I break the link our hands made and swing the office door open.

"Nes! Wait a sec," Doyle pleads.

"You're going to be massively late for class. And then your *ex-girlfriend* will run and tell her uncle, and we'll both be in detention together." I shrug at him, every muscle in my back and neck tight. "Just when I think this place might not be so bad, it gets sucky on a whole new level. Shoo, Doyle. I've got unjust punishment to deal with."

He thumps back a few steps, then jogs away, heavy on his boots.

I straighten and face the glass doors that lead to my possible doom. It's not like I'm unused to principals' offices. I love learning, but the rigidness of school grates on me. It was a problem even in my free-spirited Quaker school.

My easygoing Dominican father gave me his killer dance moves and quick smile, but I inherited my socially blunt mother's explosive Irish temper. I plod to the line of plastic chairs—the hallmark of the naughty corner outside every principal's office from Brooklyn to Backassward, Georgia— and announce my presence to a secretary, who shakes her head like she already knows my verdict.

Clearly guilty. Guillotine for me.

"Agnes Pujols?" a voice of manly authority bellows.

"Agnes *Murphy*-Pujols," I correct before looking up at the voice's owner.

"Excuse me?" A balding man at least seven feet tall with the crooked nose of a hawk glares down at me.

"My last name. It's hyphenated. Murphy-Pujols." We exchange a long, bristling stare, and I remember Doyle's whisper outside Mr. Webster's classroom. *"Sir."*

"Come into my office, Ms. *Murphy*-Pujols." My principal holds out his arm like he's some overlord, *el Matatan*, inviting me in for war talks.

I force one foot in front of the other and realize, with a sinking heart, that I'm treading toward my scholastic doom. I'm not afraid to admit I'm scared. I went to a Quaker school for my entire life. Quakers are people known for friendship and brotherly love. I'm now walking into a disciplinary office in a state that was founded as a penal colony.

Coño, this doesn't bode well.

FIVE

He busies himself with a thousand minute tasks while I sit and stare, the most basic technique in the campaign of intimidation meant to subdue me. I'm used to authority figures looking over their glasses, sighing, and telling me how disappointed they are. Armstrong is introducing a whole new set of tactics, but I'm nothing if not adaptable.

I just need to remember my *sir*s.

"Agnes, this is your…second day at Ebenezer High." His mouth sours.

"Yes…sir," I say, even if it makes the hair on my arms stand on end to say it.

"And I assume you got the student handbook when you registered." He folds his hands, desperate prayer-style. On his left ring finger he wears a plain gold wedding band. On his right he wears what looks like a huge class ring, with a sparkling ruby and a screaming eagle etched into the gold.

"Sure did, sir." I keep my voice chipper enough to set his teeth on edge. I got the fat packet in the mail, pulled out the few necessary papers, and forgot the rest.

"Then you know we have rules here at Ebenezer. I know

you don't come from around here, so you may not realize that we take pride in being the best high school in the area." His smile is smug.

I put a tight lid on the snort that nearly bursts out of my nose. *Best high school* in *this* area isn't saying much. The abysmal testing rates were one of the things I threw in Mom's face. She begged me to consider private schools, but I figured if I was going to have my life fall apart for a few months, I'd do it without the additional torture of a tartan skirt and knee-highs, thank you very much.

"No, I'm not from around here," I agree, zero hesitation. "And I understand that there are rules, but where I come from I guess we're a little more direct. So when I said what I did to Ansley—"

"Ansley Strickland has nothing to do with this situation, Agnes," Mr. Armstrong cuts in too quickly, his tone testy. I clap my mouth shut while he lies to my face. "Several of your teachers mentioned dress-code violations. I sense that there may also be an attitude problem."

"Dress code?" I echo.

Which teachers? Why didn't they tell me? My brain whirs, searching for answers, and then it all snaps together. This is like some John Grisham novel where they can't get the guys on murder, so they finger them for a million counts of petty mail fraud.

He can't let me know Ansley tattled, so he's going to invent other trumped-up charges.

"First of all, there's the problem of your piercing. The rule book clearly states two holes in each ear is the maximum allowed, and any other piercings are prohibited." He glares at the tiny diamond stud I've had on the side of my nose since I was a sophomore. I got it the day Ollie got her Monroe piercing and the studs we chose wound up so small, it was a pretty underwhelming rebellion. "It's also been reported you have a tattoo." In front of him is a paper that maps out a never-ending bulleted list.

"My tattoo?" I squawk the words like a repeating parrot, even though I clearly heard Captain Buzzkill the first time.

I do have a tattoo… A red *A* in fancy cursive, my own scarlet letter. On the *back of my neck*. Considering my bob grew out and my thick, curly hair now reaches my shoulders, no one would have seen that tattoo.

Except that I do tend to pull my hair up when I'm busy with classwork. Like Hemingway notes. But a person would have to be sitting behind me to notice.

Huh, isn't it funny that Ansley happens to sit *right behind me*?

"That tattoo is covered by my hair—" I begin to object, totally losing my cool, but my new principal's face is bland as he interrupts me.

"I'm glad you mentioned your hair. I hope that color is some kind of washout, Agnes—"

"This color cost a small fortune and was put in by one of the hair technicians who worked on *What Not to Wear*—"

"Speaking of 'what not to wear,' as a young lady trying to make positive first impressions in a new school, you may want to reconsider your wardrobe choices."

I yanked on this particular T-shirt this morning because my sunburn made my back and shoulders a tight, itchy swath of irritated skin. I dripped as much aloe as I could on it after sobbing through an icy shower. My choice in clothes was completely comfort based: Ollie and I organized a breast cancer 5k freshman year and completed it in our Save the Tatas shirts, and I've worn mine so many times since then, it's now tissue-weight cotton that doesn't cling or rub. Perfect for sunburned skin. And to raise awareness for breast cancer, of course.

Because who *wouldn't* want to save tatas? A man who's willing to play head games on a high school level would clearly be adverse to tata saving. Jerkwad.

Make that Principal Jerkwad, *sir*.

"I'll give you to the end of the week to sort your issues out, Agnes. We're not looking to pick on you here at Ebenezer High. We want to help you fit in and have a positive experience. Welcome to our school."

He says those last four words without a trace of irony. And just like that, I'm dismissed back into the cold halls of Ebenezer High, the school I thought I could take on. Now I realize those movies about clique-run, autocratic high schools that treasure conformity and beat down the slightest rebellion get made because those high schools *exist*, and the rebels survive to tell the tale on the big screen.

I think I've just become the president of Ebenezer's goddamn Breakfast Club.

Which is fine, except for the fact that I might also be the sole member.

I look at my pass and realize the secretary scribbled the time illegibly and a person could read the minute spot as a twenty *or* as a fifty. Which means I can hole up for half an hour and still use my pass.

Gone are the days when an understanding school counselor I'd known most of my young life would pull me into a cozy office, hear me out, and help me smooth things over. I'm on my own here. And with a so-obvious target on my back, I'll have to keep my eyes wide-open or I'll wind up smiling at a cheering crowd while buckets of pig blood get dumped over me.

And, with that macabre image in my head, I duck out a side door that leads to a sunny courtyard and feel the rough clamp of a hand on my shoulder. I open my mouth to scream, but a second hand covers my mouth.

SIX

"No, *shh*. It's me. It's jest me." I hear Doyle's voice and quiver like a plucked bowstring.

I beat my fists on his chest as he yanks me under the shade of some trees. Real trees with wide, glossy leaves so dark green, they're almost black, and white flowers that smell like rotting summer.

"You scared the crap of me," I hiss.

His chuckle mixes with the lazy, hooded look in his eyes and takes the wind out of my fury. "I was worried about you. Was it bad?"

"Armstrong just basically told me to buy a cardigan and join the cheer squad." I spit out the words as we hunker down on the soft grass, hidden in the hot shade.

"Are you into that? Cheer?" Close-up, I'm able to confirm that his eyes are almost a light purple, like a lavender. What a waste, for a boy to have what my abuela would call "Liz Taylor eyes."

Though, waste or not, they're throat-closingly beautiful.

"What do you think?" I walk my fingers along his hand because I can't help it. "And why are you here? You should go before your ex gives her commandant uncle stalker notes that detail your every move."

"I think I'd rather have you *on* my baseball team than cheering for it." His voice is all hungry and honey. "And I think Ansley might be targeting you because things didn't end well with us, so I'm feelin' kinda responsible for this BS."

"Great. Of all the boys who could have been landscaping half-naked in my backyard, it had to be the queen bee's ex. What are the chances?" I should feel prickly, but those eyes... looking into them is like sliding into a hot tub. Their warmth bubbles all around me like the jets are on high.

"I thought about what ya said. To Ansley. And about me and her. And you're right. It's time for her to get off her damn pedestal. I'm tired of how everyone jest lets her get her own way all the time." Fury must change his eye color, because they're a deep blue now, like the clouds around a full moon.

"There's a whole system stacked in her favor, Doyle. *I* should have listened to *you*. I should have kept my trap shut. Unfortunately, I suck at that."

He leans close, predator-like, and I feel very ready to be devoured. And equally ready to bolt.

"Goddamn, I *love* the way you can't keep your mouth shut, Nes. You're the first person around here in a long time who's had the balls to jest say what's on your mind to anyone, no matter who they are. It's sexy as hell."

My hand twitches, and he takes it in his.

He threads our fingers together like being this close is no big thing. And I guess I overplayed the whole flirty, badass NYC vibe...because my heart is a bird throwing itself against the bars to escape its cage, but he's looking at me like we're both cool with everything happening at warp speed in the secret shade of this tree.

I love the way our fingers lock together, but this is fast. On top of the dizzy feeling I get when I hold hands with Doyle, I'm upset about my idiotic trip to the principal's office, I'm miserable over facing Ansley, I miss Ollie so much it feels like I have a cough drop permanently lodged sideways down my throat. And there's Lincoln.

I want… I have no idea what I want. My vision goes grainy and Doyle's voice coils softly through the fog of my chaotic thoughts.

"Yesterday, in your yard after school, I was actually hatching this whole plot to get your attention somehow next time I saw you. Then you jest walked outta your house in a bikini. Hand to God, I thought I was bein' punked." His ears burn pink.

"Your ears are blushing," I whisper.

He leans lip-to-lip close. Every nerve in my face goes tight. I smell his warm hay scent mixed with the heady aroma of those heavy cream flowers sizzling in the morning sun.

The bell screams, and the courtyard fills with students. I jump up, my pass a congealed wad of pulp in my sweaty palm. "Crap! Doyle, I skipped. Like I'm not in deep enough trouble!"

"It's okay. Teacher'd have to remember to check when you left the office, and Webster won't bother. You're fine." His voice is laid-back as he reaches out to take my hands. I can see that he still wants to cash in on the promise of a kiss that was only barely possible when I was under his pretty-eyed spell.

"I'm not *fine*." I slap his hands back. "My life is out of control. You know what? I should never have left Brooklyn, but now that I'm here, I can't be some psycho debutante's target. I need to lie low."

"Meaning what?" Doyle's mouth twists with a disappointment he doesn't have any right to feel.

"Meaning, you and I should probably cool it, and I gotta

go *now* so I can make it to my next class on time." I brush grass off my butt.

"So that's it?" His eyes flash. "Nes, girls like Ansley have been gettin' whatever the hell they want since they were spoiled toddlers. No one ever stands up to her and her kind. It ain't right."

I shoulder my backpack. "Well, Doyle, maybe guys like you should stop giving girls like her whatever they want. She's *your* psycho ex. I'm not about to make this year any harder than it needs to be. I told you—my objective is to get out. Gone. Done. And I'll forget this place like it was a bad dream as soon as it's in my rearview."

"So you're going to sit back and take it? Let her and Armstrong and all the rest stomp on you? After standing up to her today? Seriously?" Doyle's mouth pulls tight.

Inside, the crowds in the halls are thinning already, students ducking into classrooms like I should be, and I have no energy left to stand here arguing. I'm not even halfway through my day, and I'm flattened with exhaustion.

"Seriously. Look, we hardly know each other, okay? Sorry if you thought I was going to be the badass rebel who'd shake up the end of your boring senior year, but I'm not here for your entertainment. Or Ansley's. This semester is my probation, and I'm just biding my time till it's over." I walk backward to the door and shrug. "See you around, Doyle."

I leave him standing in the middle of a last scurrying surge of students, and notice Ansley skip up, grab him by the arm, and stand on her tiptoes to whisper in his ear. A long shock of blond hair falls down her back and shimmers in the blistering sunshine.

It's so cliché, it hurts. And my jealousy is *extra* cliché. So I clamp down on it, head to US history, and grit my teeth when Ansley and Braelynn jostle against me on their way past, knocking me into a water fountain. Doyle sees me from down the hall and battles against the flow of traffic to make it to my side, but I slip into class before he can, my face hot, the tears so close to falling, I can taste the salt in the back of my throat.

I run my hand behind my neck, above my aching sunburn, and touch my scarlet *A*, the tattoo that was a fierce joke and a mark of pride.

"'Pride cometh before the fall,'" I mutter as I pull out my textbook and try to bleach my brain of this whole place.

By the time the final bell rings, I realize that I'm going to spend a lot of time trying to avoid Doyle at every turn because he's not letting our conversation drop.

"Nes!" Doyle sprints to my car as I throw my bag in the window, lean against the closed door, and cross my arms. When he's finally standing next to me he just stares, like he's not sure what to say.

For once in my life, I'm right there with him. But it's unnatural for me to say nothing, so I say the first thing that pops into my head. The thing I hope is the shortest path to getting him out of my life.

"Look, it's not personal, okay? I like you. I do. But we just met, and things are already too complicated, with Ansley and Lincoln and—"

"Who's Lincoln?" His eyebrows knot over his gorgeous eyes.

"My ex." My voice hiccups over those words, because they're strange. Deep in my secret romantic heart, I imagined I'd never have to say the words *my ex* and *Lincoln* in the same conversation.

"Oh. Was it, uh, recent?" He kicks at some loose gravel with his boot.

I nod robotically. "We dated for two years. We broke up just before I moved."

"Oh." This *oh* is totally different. And laced with pure shock. His eyes are a complicated mix of hard and soft. "Two years? I didn't realize—"

"What? That I had an ex?" My laugh is blasé. "There's a lot you probably don't realize about me. 'Cause we've known each other for all of... What? Two days? My life is pretty much exploding around me right now like crazy. And that's without adding in my whole insane backstory. I think it's better if we back up."

Clouds collect in a swollen gray mass overhead and the wind whips my hair around. When I tie it back, Doyle lays three fingers on my jaw. I startle, hold my breath, and let him turn my head and look at my neck.

"Hester Prynne?" His fingers trace along my jawline, under my earlobe, and stop just over the skin on my exposed neck.

"They let you read that book here?" I marvel. My veins pump carbonated fire, but I keep my voice on ice.

He half smiles as a light rain pelts down. "The book got taken off the sophomore curriculum 'long with a couple others. That's why I read it. Hawthorne's dry as hell, but the story's a good one." He pulls his one hand back slowly, then sticks them both deep in his pockets.

"I do like you," I admit. A fresh burst of light rain explodes around us and we squint into the damp. "I just have a lot going on, and I don't think my nerves can handle more."

"I get it." He watches as I shade my eyes from more rain, then pulls his cap off and tosses it on my head. I hold my breath, because it's easier to resist him if I can't smell his delicious fragrance. "And I like you. I know this feels quick, Nes, but like you said, you won't be here for long. I don't care if we're just friends or even just on the same neighborhood ball team. As long as we're not avoiding each other. Because I don't want to miss out on my only chance to get to know you."

I think about the way Ansley crowed like she'd won something in the halls and drag a cleansing breath into my lungs.

What did we learn from World War II?

Never back down from an aggressor.

I won't go out of my way to get in Ansley's face, but I'm sure not going to shut down the one and only friendship I've made since leaving Brooklyn on account of that flaxen-haired harpy.

"You're right. We should be friends. It's complicated, but nothing that's really good is ever easy, right?" I glance up at a sky rumbling with thunder that promises a full-on downpour. "I'd better go." I pull the cap off and attempt to hand it back, but Doyle shakes his soaked head as he jogs to his truck and gets in.

"Keep it. And get yourself a pair of sunglasses. You squint too much!" He yells over the roar of the truck's engine, attracting the attention of a dozen or so of our classmates, who pair up to whisper and giggle.

I wave and keep my head down and grit my teeth as Ansley flies by in her Jeep. Today I may have let her take Czechoslovakia, but I'll be damned if she marches on to Poland. If she wants a war, I'll lead her right into the bowels of Russia in the dead of winter.

Yes, I have only the foggiest idea of what my World War II analogies mean. But I do know that a confrontation with Ansley may be inevitable, and I'm going to fight smart.

Or get my cavalry rolled under by Ansley's tanks.

On a brighter note, even if I wind up committing social suicide, I'm definitely going to ace history this year. Mom would be so proud.

SEVEN

I scroll through Ollie's Instagram feed and try not to let jealousy eat me alive when I see yet another picture of her laughing with friends at the new chocolate bar she and I were supposed to check out together. I want her to have a great senior year, but here's another way moving sucks: I'm scared I'm losing Ollie.

Not losing her like we're not friends anymore. Losing her like our friendship is diluting.

Which isn't as dramatic as it sounds because we've always been a superconcentrated twosome, twined around each other for years. Conjoined, even. Ollie is pretty much reason number one that I dragged my feet over leaving Brooklyn.

Sometimes I feel like I should have just stayed.

But there was this whole other *thing*.

It revolved around Ollie's lifelong dream to go to Oberlin, this rad college with an intense music program located in the bowels of the godforsaken Midwest. The thing was, we'd also discussed staying close, geographically, so we could visit each other through college. Freshman year, our plan felt solid, but as high school went on and my life fell apart and my distaste for ever going to a college anywhere near Ohio became clearer, Ollie switched gears and started talking about Juilliard so she could be closer to me if I got into NYU, my dream school.

Now, no doubt Juilliard is freaking amazing and it's right in the city. But Ollie had done a million hours of research and *Oberlin* was her nest, not Juilliard. A few weeks before it all went to hell at my place I stumbled on her early acceptance letter to Oberlin hidden under her mattress. It had been stuffed there for over a month. She never said a word to me about it.

I wasn't sure if she thought I wouldn't be happy for her. I don't know if she thought I needed her too much, what with my life falling to pieces and everything. But, as far as I was concerned, Ollie and her bassoon were going to Oberlin, no questions. I pulled her mom aside and spilled about how I was afraid Ollie was settling and then I totally sold her on encouraging Ollie to go to Oberlin. Then I picked up and left for Georgia. I needed to show Ollie we could love each other from afar. That she had to go wherever she needed to go, and I'd be there for her no matter what.

Only I guess I kind of thought it would all stay the same. And that's exactly why it's so brave and noble to sacrifice for the person you love—because it hurts like hell. Things change. And they may not go back to the way they were before.

Ever.

My mother comes in from work as I'm simultaneously hashing through all of this, listening to angsty, dark music, and contemplating the intolerable stupidity of my day at school.

"Hey, honey." She cracks the door of my room open. "You want to grab a bite?"

"Nope." It's rude, but I have to put on a happy face for so many people all day long, and last night's spat left a dull ache in my head, like a hangover headache.

"You know, we have a couple episodes of our show waiting, and I'm kind of dying to see what happens with coma guy." She leans against my door frame, but I can tell she's working hard to look like she's at ease. "I finally read the article you tried to show me. The one about the fan theory where the coma patient is—"

"It was a dumb theory. So wrong. Spoiler alert—coma guy is one of the armed robbers who held up the bank across from the hospital. His crew dumped him because they thought he was dead and never told anyone. The head nurse helps him escape, but she doesn't make it to Mexico to meet him because at the last second they bring in the victims of the horrible car crash and her ex-fiancé is one of the patients."

My mom's face goes through a few expressions as she processes the information: shock at the twist, curiosity about how I know, disappointment over the fact that there's no reason for her to watch it now. I realize I'm the worst kind of troll. Only a very messed-up person spoils three of five episodes in a series's final season.

Part of me takes sadistic delight in hurting my mom like she hurt me. Part of me wonders what kind of terrible, petty jerk I'm turning into.

"I didn't realize you watched the episodes. Well, at least one of us got to enjoy them." She already looks sufficiently bummed. I could stop there. A good person would.

"I didn't watch," I blurt out. It's almost involuntary, like I'm possessed by the vengeful spirit of a chronic television drama spoiler. "I just read about it."

"You never look at spoilers." I try to interpret the wrinkles in my mother's forehead like fortune-tellers read palms. I realize there's no secret mystery, just the stress-induced skin creases that come from dealing with a belligerent teenage daughter.

"I do when I don't really care about a show. It was getting so stupid."

Eight seasons. One hundred twenty-four episodes. Three flus, a few dozen snow days, rerun marathons during heat waves and summer vacations at my maternal grandparents' lake house, episodes with pints of ice cream to forget boy problems, low-key birthday celebrations just the way we liked—*One Hundred Thousand Beats* had seen us through it all, and this is the way I honor my old faithful medical drama?

"Okay, enough." Mom presses her fingers to her temples like she's trying to ward off a migraine with her bare hands.

"Enough what?" I will her to fight, to explode, to *tell me why she chose that gross man over me.*

"Of this *attitude* all the time. I'm not some monster who ruined your life. You keep pushing me away, but—have you spoken to your father?" Just before she really lays into me for being a jerk, she flips and brings up my dad.

"I texted with him last night." It's not a lie. He sent me a bunch of screenshots from this site that puts witty text on famous art. I know it was just a ton of crying cat emojis from me and stupid art jokes from him, but it counts as talking. Sort of. "Why are you bringing Dad into this?"

"You…you really need to set aside some time and talk about what you're feeling with him—" Mom says in her best teacher voice.

"Why? Because it's too much trouble for *you* to have an actual conversation with me?"

"When are you going to stop punishing me, Agnes? I'm human, you know. I mess up too." She clutches the door frame with a white-knuckle hand, her hazel eyes blinking too fast because she's getting teary.

I debate asking. Or just telling her how I feel. Instead of vulnerable honesty, I choose caustic sarcasm.

"You sure do!" I exclaim with a big, fake smile. "And now here we are, in the middle of Nowhere, Georgia. I'd love to talk about how unfair this is to *you*, but I don't want to fail my classes on top of having the entire school hate me, so I better hit the books... You can go whenever."

I wait, breath held, for her to morph from the sad little rag doll's shadow she's been and fly at me like the raging Irish-tempered harpy she always turned into when I put a toe too far over the line before. I half salivate for her to come at me, my ears pricked to hear her screaming that I "better learn some respect" and that she's "not one of my little friends." I want it to be like old times, the way we were before, even if that means enduring a screaming fit.

But she doesn't raise her voice.

The hot mix of adrenaline and hope seeps out of me as she turns on her heel and pads back down the hallway. I'd bet a round-trip ticket to JFK that she's opening a bottle of merlot and flipping to the melancholy Celtic mix on her iPod. Boo frickity hoo.

Maybe she should have dated one of the thousands of nice, normal *single* guys who chased her all over the place instead of getting low-down and freaky with a married coworker whose wife aired their dirty laundry far and wide across the five boroughs. Maybe she should have told her only daughter what was going on instead of shutting her out until things were too screwed up to fix.

Just at the moment when my brain cannot handle one more pulse of confusing information, my phone rings and Lincoln's gorgeous, traitorous face lights up the screen. It's like he has a timer set to know when my emotions are most jumbled. I clutch the phone to my chest, and my body crumples around it.

I should have deleted this picture of him from my phone when my hate was surging and made me strong. He sent it to me long before I suspected him of screwing me over. His dark hair is plastered to his head and he's holding a surfboard. There's sand all over his dark brown shoulders, and he's smiling so wide, his eyes crinkled, his white teeth bright against his wet skin. His index finger points to the Saint Christopher necklace I gave him before he left.

He claimed that he sent me the picture because he missed me, and he said he was pointing at the necklace because he was telling his cousin about his *wahine purotu* who gave it to him for safe travels when he went back to New Zealand over the summer so he and his father could participate in a Maori leadership convention. Which was all so sweet when I thought I was his only "pretty girl." But now I look at that picture and wonder if he was with other girls on that trip—girls who could flirt with him in Maori, with sweet, sexy laughs, girls who could surf in water swarming with sharks without squealing with fear.

Girls who weren't *me*.

"Screw you, Lincoln," I whisper to his picture, which sweeps off my phone and disappears after the final ring, replaced by a generic voice mail notification.

My ears burn, wanting so badly to hear his cocky voice, even though I know it would probably be roughed up with his tears. My traitor heart pounds, wondering *will you, will you, will you?*

I pick up the phone and swish my thumb back and forth across the glossy black screen.

Will you, will you?

When I toss my phone on the bed, it lands in the navy bowl of Doyle's cap. I finger the rough canvas and rub a thumb at the frayed edge of the brim. Holding the hat works like magic to set my head straight, and it radiates goodness and confidence through me the same way finding a copper penny on heads used to when I was a kid. The hat helps remind me that I have no need for people who use and abuse me when there are people who like and respect me.

Decision made.

I will *not*.

But I *will* call Ollie to calm the last of my battered nerves.

"Did he call you?" she demands before I can say *hello*.

"Yes." I pace my room, which is an exemplary pacing space, since there's hardly any furniture in it.

"*Coño.*" Despite being crazy upset, Ollie's occasional DR swear always makes me smile. "He tried calling here too. And screw him!" I hear her pound her fist on her desk. I imagine all the famous composer bobble heads in her collection nodding along with her righteous anger.

"Should I just pick up? It's not like I can go see him, right? It's not like I'll get sucked back in, so why not hear him out? Right?" I feel jazzed up, like that time Olls and I sucked down an entire netted bag of those fluorescent-colored freezer pops that come in the plastic tubes.

"No!" She's ferociously adamant. "What will he say? What *could* he say that wouldn't be a complete waste of your time?"

"Okay. Can you...can you distract me? Tell me about anything. Your day. Not that that would only be a distraction. I mean, obviously I want to hear about your day anyway."

"Um, I bought these fierce-looking beads, the most beautiful pewter color, and they went berserk and the color all chipped off them before lunch. I had to refund twenty-five percent of my day's profits and redo so many seventh graders' bracelets, I wanted to scream."

"Damn those bead criminals," I growl sympathetically.

But from a thousand miles away, I can't see the shimmer of the beads or the intricate knot design, and I'm pissed at how unfair it is. I thought I'd take the gold in rocking my senior year, but it winds up I won't even get a participation ribbon.

"And the second chair cellist from Javier wrote a duet for his senior project. He needs a bassoonist, and, um, he asked me."

Even though we're not FaceTiming, my mind's eye imagines Ollie's smooth skin blushing pink, and I know she's twirling a piece of her long black hair like some hip Vietnamese American version of a Valley girl.

"Is this the skateboard guy?" I squeal. Ollie's had a revolving door of crushes the last few months, many of them from afar, so we don't always have names to work with, and I'm not always the best at keeping them straight. Name or no name, dissecting these crushes always takes top priority.

"No." I picture how she ducks her chin whenever she does that shy little laugh. "Skateboard guy is first chair, Thorton's. This is the guy with the pretzels at the fountain that time, remember? Before the symphony?"

"Romantic." The word floats out on a sigh. "You'll send me the demo? And some pictures of him? I think I'm thinking of skateboard boy but putting a pretzel in his hand."

"I will," she promises.

But I won't be around to sit on her bed while she practices her bassoon for a jillion hours and obsesses for twice that long over Pretzel Boy's every word and look.

Missing that will mean missing the meat of the entire experience.

Our friendship can get by on the scraps, but I would rather it was fat and healthy.

"So have you seen my idiot brother's Instagram?" The best way to feel better about anything, ever, is to rag on my brother with my best friend.

"You mean the dark, broody black-and-white pictures of half-eaten croissants and close-up eyeballs? I have no clue if it's an art project or real life, since he captions everything in French, and *mon français n'est pas bon*."

"He's so pretentious. I think he's embarrassed to let anyone know he ever lived in the United States, let alone that he's *a US citizen*," I say in a horror movie narrator voice.

"I'm not saying we have to, but a throwback pic of him might be a fun thing..." I hear what sound like thumps and grunts and am willing to bet Ollie is under her bed. "Ah! A little dusty, but I found that picture from the Fourth of July. The one where your mom bought Jasper and your dad matching American-flag shorts and they both had that weird haircut like the guy from *House Party*."

I howl. "The Kid 'n Play classic!" Underneath my unholy laughter at that memory is a little sting. Maybe it's partially that I brought the whole senior nostalgia thing on early by switching schools midyear, but bittersweet is my constant emotional jam. I miss the way things were—I miss my family being whole and unpretentious and happy. I miss my best friend. I miss having a boyfriend I trust.

I push through it because what else is there to do? Ollie is the best shoulder to cry on ever. She's better at long-distance best friendship than most people are at the one-on-one, everyday kind. I'm thankful our best friendship is still awesome and loving, but I'm pissed circumstances have forced it into a blurry copy of what used to be so sharp and bright, and that aches.

When we get off the phone, I feel hollowed out. If I was back in the city, tonight would be my life art class at Mom's college… The one we were attending together, the one where our folders with half-shaded legs and feet and *other things* are probably still leaning against the cluttered shelf. In the fall, I joked that the hot male model was kind of checking my mom out. But at Thanksgiving, I stopped making her blush by pointing out that kind of stuff (even though ninety percent of straight dudes check my mom out…that's just my life) because every sign pointed to her and my father reconciling. Maybe that's why the whole affair blindsided me so hard. Maybe I still feel cheated out of that naive *Parent Trap* dream.

Jasper *so* would have been London Lindsay Lohan in that alternate reality.

There are no art classes here. I could join a club, but every club has its hierarchy all set up by now, and it's not like I've made many friends. My Brooklyn neighborhood was full of coffee shops and bookstores I'd wander through with Ollie in our downtime. We prided ourselves on finding the best hole-in-the-wall food places. I went to musical reviews and art shows with Ollie and her parents, helped Mom organize student events at the college, rocked the vote, volunteered at soup kitchens, headed committees… My life back home was full to bursting, to the point where I'd dream about slowing down, taking time to do more *nothing*.

Now that I have all the downtime I could want, I also have a nasty case of be-careful-what-you-wish-for slap back.

In this new, boring version of my life, I do homework. I try to nap with no success. I scroll through playlists I instantly hate. I poke around in my unpacked boxes, but I find too many items that make me feel starved for a life that's washing away too fast. I decide to distract myself with a life-form more pathetic than I am in my current state, so I water Doyle's tree and imagine Ollie lounging on the beach chair next to me with a stack of paperbacks and a pitcher of her famous lemonade nearby. I imagine my abuela swatting flies, pruning the already-tended bushes, squatting down to save soggy, drowning dragonflies from the pool while we yell at her to relax a little even though we know she is physically unable to do that. I imagine my brother, dressed to the nines in a seersucker suit and poring over Mom's old copy of Simone de Beauvoir's *She Came to Stay*, impervious to heat and tedious literature. I imagine Mom and Dad, maybe fighting, maybe kissing… They did those two things so often, I'm having a hard time assigning them any other activity at this pitiful imaginary pool party.

And, though I fight it, my sappy brain imagines Lincoln, bouncing off the diving board, tucking his knees to his dark, muscular chest and flipping in a few tight circles before he breaks the calm surface with a splash so big, it disrupts everyone. We'd all be annoyed until his head pops up and he dazzles us with that irresistible smile.

That smile got him out of so much trouble. That smile sometimes made me scared I'd never be attached to another guy, because I'd never seen anything more beautiful in my life.

I know I was wise to put a thousand miles between me and it. Me and him.

"*¿Qué lo que carajito?* I feel like you're not even trying," I scold the sickly little tree to divert my attention. "Trust me, I get how hard it is to be a transplant, but you can't go down without a fight. You're here now. You might as well attempt to thrive."

So I'm talking to plants now. Doyle really is rubbing off on me.

Despite my pep talk, the tree looks zero percent better this mosquito-filled, muggy evening than it did yesterday, and I'm willing to bet that's a trend that will continue for weeks on end. The gusts of rain that blew through and chilled things for a nanosecond this afternoon are long forgotten, and the leaves sprouting out of this poor excuse for a tree look parched and overly delicate. While the hose soaks the earth above the tree roots, I wander to the edge of the pool and drop my feet into the still water, then lean back on my arms and tilt my head up. I'm attempting to untangle the few constellations I know when a voice on the other side of our white picket fence makes me jump.

"Stargazing?"

It's a romantic word anyway, but twisted around his drawl it sounds delicious.

"What exactly did you do before I moved here, Doyle? Because it seems like I take up a lot of your time." I watch as he climbs over the fence and jumps into my yard without asking permission, his legs stretched long and sure as he walks my way.

"You're gettin' ahead of yourself, Nes. I've spent a grand total of maybe two hours with you, not countin' English class, which is required." He kicks off his boots, throws his socks on top of them, cuffs his jeans, and slides down next to me so that we're shoulder to shoulder, our feet nearly touching under the water. "Know any constellations?" He juts his chin up.

We gaze at the black sky dotted with a few pale white stars, and I try hard to ignore how much I want his arm around me—both because he's got beautiful, muscled arms and because the reality of Doyle's arm will blot out the memory of Lincoln's.

"I know the big ones. The Dippers and Orion. And…that's all, I guess. Can you enlighten me?" I covertly side-eye him, but he's looking at me.

Coño. Caught!

"Nope. Now, if you wanna know the plants growing 'round here? Or the bugs? That I can help you with. But when I look up, I don't see nothin' in particular." His foot brushes mine under the water, and a chill swims up my back.

"You mean you don't know Shark Attack on a Half Shell?" I point, and he leans over to get a better look, his ribs pressing tight to my back. I move from word to word carefully, because my brain is mushy when I'm this close to him. "Those three, see, are sort of like a shell, if you squint when you look, and that kind of triangle—"

"Maybe more like Rabid Goldfish Attack on a Plank?" He wraps his arm around my shoulder and points to the left, pulling me closer as I tilt my face to the sky. "And that one? I'd say Four-Wheeler Running over a Hog."

I laugh because I'm supposed to, and I train my eyes at the stars in the sky, but I'm not sure all the beauty I see overhead is strictly astronomical. Some of that sparkle has to be because of my close proximity to Doyle. I swear the sky wasn't exploding with all this gorgeous light before he sat down next to me.

"Why are you here?" I blurt out. He drops his arm, letting it graze my side.

"My grandfather needed me to check up on the pecan orchard across the street. They've got weevils—"

"You're seriously trying to tell me that I'm just a side visit after you took care of pecan weevils?" His face is Norse-hero handsome in the moonlight.

"Hell no." His grin tentacles around my heart, squeezing tight. "Truth is, I don't think I'll ever run out of excuses to get over here and see you. The Dickersons think they might have a spider mite infestation in their cotton, but their fields are fifteen miles in the other direction. I convinced my cousin to take a look at them." He brushes the hair from my face with the back of his calloused hand. "I came here to see you, and I'll keep doin' it till you're back in New York City, forgettin' this all like it was a bad dream."

He slings my own words at me like the nasty slap of a rubber band on my skin. I pull back from him. "Don't."

"Don't what?" His voice never loses its evenness.

"Bring on the guilt. I mean…it's stupid."

We just met, he has no right. But if that were true, it would be simple to blow him off. So why isn't it?

The truth is, something stuck fast the second I met him. He walked up, and I had this feeling like, oh, there he is, that person I just met, but who I've been waiting for. Like I'd always known he was coming, and then—there he was.

Here he is.

But that's just a weird gut feeling, probably intensified because I'm so damn lonely and out of place right now.

"We don't even know each other," I muse, half-surprised to hear myself speak the words out loud.

"We could fix that. We should. Right now. We never even met properly, what with you bein' all flustered by my manly pecs the other day." My laugh skips over the pool water and echoes back at me in a friendly way. He faces me and holds out his hand. "I'm Doyle Ulysses Rahn. Pleased to meet you."

My mouth swings open like my jaw is set on faulty hinges.

He ducks his head and squints my way. "Yeah, it's weird, right? My granddaddy's side always middle-names every second son Ulysses after some Confederate soldier who saved our family farmstead during a Civil War battle… It's a long story."

I press my palm against his, squeeze hard, and shake. "Well, Doyle Ulysses Rahn, I'm Agnes Penelope Murphy-Pujols." I wait for it…

"Pretty."

"Pretty?" I shake my head. "Doyle, I'm middle-named after Penelope. From *The Odyssey*."

His face blanks, then lights up with recognition. "Uh, okay. I remember that one. Where he goes home after all those years, the bow, the crazy ladies who drive sailors wild with their singing, and the cyclops and the special bed, all that? We read that back in junior year."

"Ulysses is the Roman name for Odysseus." The look of pure adoration that splits across his face makes my skin tingle and itch all at once—hives of feeling.

"Holy hell. Your brain works overtime, don't it?" He rubs his thumbs over my knuckles. "So you're saying you and I have these weirdo middle names that connect us? Like maybe it was fate that we were meant to get to know each other?"

"Don't read too much into it. You didn't even get the reference until I explained it to you." My voice is too breathy to be convincing, but Doyle doesn't buy into my protest anyway.

"That's the beauty of it though. You teach me about things I don't know about, like old Greek books—"

"Roman books. You know the Greek version."

"Right. You teach me about the ancient Romans and all that nerd stuff, and I make this year better than purgatory until you're gone for good." He slides one hand over my knee, and my breath hitches. All I can see are his eyes, deep as wishing wells. "I get that you're gonna leave when this is all over. Hell, I respect it. But I think you might wanna reconsider forgetting everything just because a few people are total assholes."

"Maybe." The word is meant to be a lazy brush-off, but there's something about the starry sky and the quiet croak of the frogs that makes it hard to turn my brain on autopilot and go cold. "Can I tell you something weird?"

It pops out, before I can think it through.

"I love weird," he declares. I let the tips of my fingers brush over his forearm and like the way he sucks a quick breath in. "You gonna tell me you turn into a mermaid during a full moon or something?"

He looks so hopeful, I laugh. "Nope. Not like 'boy fantasy' weird. Weird like 'crap I don't talk about to anyone except my best friend.'"

I stop and reconsider my path. Once someone knows things about you—things you've never told anyone else—they can choose to use them against you. Not that I think Doyle would...but I'd have to move my trust in him from hypothetical to actual, which is a huge step.

"I know how to keep my trap shut."

He's not flirting or teasing. I bet Doyle is one of those true Southern gentlemen who lives and dies by his word.

"We moved to Savannah because my mom got into this crazy situation with her coworker—" I don't get any further because the words petrify in my throat. Before I can get up and flee back into the house, where I can safely avoid any more intimate human interaction, Doyle squeezes my knee gently, like he's steadying me. He speaks, quietly. Slowly. Like maybe it's as hard for him to talk about his feelings as it is for me.

"When I was in fifth grade, my mama finally came back again—she left the day before summer break my third grade year, and she was only around real spotty when I was in fourth. 'Figurin' her life out' is what she said she was doing. Never made sense to me, 'cause she had a life at home with all of us, so what the hell was she figurin' out?"

When he breaks off, I give the weakest verbal comfort. "That blows, Doyle."

It's a pathetic attempt at sympathy, but he gives me a half smile before he finishes.

"Back then, my father still had a job at the paper plant, but life was kind of fallin' apart 'round our ears. Lee and me and Malachi were goin' to school half-starved and stinkin', the house was always a mess. My parents weren't ever real great at the whole responsibility thing, but my daddy made money and my mama kept things pretty clean and took care of us, mostly. When she was gone, we were barely holding down the fort. Anyway, she came back, and I thought for sure life was gonna be all right. Maybe they'd let me get this pup I had my eye on that was jest born at the farm down the way from our place. But she only showed up to give him divorce papers."

His voice doesn't hitch or wobble. It's relaxed, like he's reciting a story that sort of bores him. Which is crazy because the frantic throb of his carotid artery makes me scared he's about to have a panic attack.

"When my daddy signed 'em, it was like he signed away the lot o' us. My mama walked out on us, and my daddy checked out. Wasn't a year later he was fired from the plant. Went in one day fallin'-down drunk and punched the foreman when he told Daddy he wasn't in no condition to operate big machinery."

Doyle dips his head and presses his mouth tight to the side, like that's the end of the story.

My own life problems suddenly come into harsh perspective. I've never been abandoned, hungry, or dirty. Sure, Mom drinks a little too much some nights, but it's nothing like what Doyle is describing with his dad. And my parents, though they're no longer a couple, have never stopped being there for me and Jasper.

"What did you guys do?" I realize a second after I ask the

question that I'm butting in where I might not be welcome. "Sorry. If you don't want to answer, that's cool. I didn't mean to pry."

"Nah. It feels pretty good to tell someone the whole story, even if it is all ancient history by now." His fingers squeeze my knee a second time, but now it feels like he's holding tight to calm himself down. I cover his hand with mine, and he attempts another weak smile. "Anyway, there ain't much more. Daddy lost his job and never has found any kind of regular work since. Child Services came knocking on our door when it was so bad our teachers were asking us all sorts of questions every day. That's when Daddy finally let my grandparents take us in. Pride'd been holding him back from asking for any kinda help, and by the time he bothered, it was too late. He was so far gone, and we were all done dealing with his crap anyhow. So trust me when I say I get what it's like when parents screw up."

He clears his throat, then gives me a nod, like it's my turn to spill.

"My story is *nothing* like yours..." I throw my hands up, guilty over whining to him about my life when his problems are so much bigger and scarier.

"I never figured you and me'd have identical stories." He licks his lips and takes a deep breath. "Pain's pain, and what hurts hurts, no matter if you think you got it better or worse than the next guy. It ain't a competition."

Doyle has a way of laying out the obvious so plainly, it can't be denied.

"Okay. So my mom and dad... They've always had a weird relationship." I lift one foot, then the other, watching droplets of water splash back into the pool. "And it got a whole lot worse when my father landed this huge book deal a few years ago—"

"Your daddy's a writer?" Doyle looks impressed.

I roll my eyes. "Not like Stephen King or something. He mostly writes boring academic stuff, but he wrote one book about growing up in Santo Domingo—he meant for it to be a cultural study, but it wound up turning into this really interesting memoir... I mean, I *guess* it's interesting. That's what all the book reviewers say anyway."

His eyes crinkle when he laughs. "You tellin' me your daddy wrote a book about his life and you never read it?"

I blow out a long breath. "Ugh, I'm the worst. I should, right?" I squint at him guiltily.

"You should do whatever you wanna do. All I can tell ya is, if my daddy wrote a book about his life, I'd be so curious, Satan 'imself couldn't stop me from tearin' through that thing. Don't you even wanna see if you're in it?" His eyes shine when he asks, like he'd be curious to flip through to those parts— if they existed.

Thank God they don't.

"The book only goes up to his undergrad years, so I know there's nothing about me in it," I say to definitively shut down any possibility of Doyle combing through my father's weird memoir for tidbits about me. "I guess I never read it because I kind of hate how it messed things up for my family."

"How's that?" Doyle leans in, intrigued like he's about to hear some twisted *Gone Girl* insanity. In fact, it's a boring story of a family that quietly fell apart.

"My dad got famous, in his own nerdy circle at least. And my mom got left out in a huge way. She took a hiatus on her PhD studies—which she'd been busting her ass on—so he could go on these worldwide tours and give lectures. Then he got offered a visiting professor position in France, which had been his dream job forever. When his guest semester was up, they offered him a full-time spot, and he wanted us to join him. But we had a life in New York, and I definitely didn't want to go. My brother did apply to college in France without telling our mother, and it sent her into this depression for a while when he left. She thought he was going to Harvard, so it was a huge shock when he told us he was actually headed to the Sorbonne."

I kick at the water, the silky splashes deeply unsatisfying. I want to break something, smash something, do anything immediate and violent to help me forget that bleak time when my family splintered apart quickly and permanently.

"That must've been hard," says Doyle Rahn, the guy who watched his mother walk out of his life before middle school and his father descend into violent alcoholism. When I snort, he raises his eyebrows in this no-nonsense way that would make Lovett proud. "Sometimes it's harder to deal with things fallin' apart when you feel like you had some say in it."

I never thought about it that way. I never considered that I might blame myself for dragging my feet about going off to France. I think Mom wanted to stay in New York City too, but what if I hadn't pitched such a fit? If I'd been down to go, would she have gone too? Would I be there right now, smoking a cigarette, dressed in black, scowling outside my beautiful French high school with my cool French friends because Mom and Dad wanted me to pick up fresh sheep intestines for our highly dysfunctional family dinner?

In other words, would my weird family unit have remained intact if I wasn't such a whiner?

"Some days I think if the boys and I'd been better at keeping house, kinda took up where our mama left off, would my daddy have gotten so bad so fast?"

Doyle muses his what-ifs out loud, while I keep mine locked in. But, where my what-if scenario casts me as a bratty villain, his is so noble, it dips its toe in martyrdom.

"Doyle, you know it's not your fault your mom left. You know it had nothing to do with how clean the house was or how you and your brothers behaved. Your mother's reasons for leaving had everything to do with her. And it was her fault. Her *loss*." I nudge him with my shoulder.

"That all makes sense to me now. But the little kid in me still don't listen to reason." He bumps me with his elbow. "So you were hell-bent on staying in New York instead of going to Paris, but you up and left for *Georgia*?" His laugh is rusty. "I mean, I like it here fine, but it's sure as hell not Paris."

I tilt my head back and direct my attention to the big, shiny moon. "It was more a lack of any other decent choice that landed me here. Like I was saying, my mom had this gross affair with a married guy she worked with. His wife found out, and it was basically hellish for my mother to go to back to work with all the office gossip. Everyone was giving her crap, all this stupid passive-aggressive high school drama BS. Which is kind of insane. I mean, *he's* the one who actually cheated on his wife. My parents aren't even…"

I stop short because it's easier to give up trying to explain than it is to untangle the knot that is my parents' crazy relationship.

"Married?" Doyle fills in, the word delivered softly. Helpfully.

"Yep." I was actually going to say "in love anymore," but I'm not sure whether or not that's a fact. It is *definitely* a fact that my parents are no longer joined in holy matrimony, no matter how lovey they acted during our Thanksgiving in Paris. "It's just… Their whole *thing* is complicated. Always has been. Sometimes I think about how much easier my life would be if my parents had managed to keep their crap together."

"I hear that."

Doyle's pain is on a different spectrum than mine, but our frustrations run parallel. A sweet relief spins through me as we sit side by side, our confessions laid bare between us. Ollie would be proud of all the sticky feelings I dredged out tonight.

"I don't hate it here," I confess over the rising chorus of frog croaks. "I mean, I wasn't excited about coming here, and I miss home, but this place isn't all bad."

"Not all bad?" He shakes his head. "Pretty weak. No worries though. I plan to pull out all the stops to make this year better than you'd ever have expected."

"What exactly does that entail?" I arch my back as his thumb arcs along the soft skin above my knee, inside my thigh. "Four-wheeling and hogs?"

"You wanna go four-wheeling?" He leans closer.

"Hmm. I've never been. Is it fun?" I try to rein my voice tight. It's just his hand. On my knee. It's just an invitation to ride an all-terrain vehicle. No big deal.

"I think you'd like it. You busy next Saturday?" His other hand cups my shoulder, pulls down to my elbow. His fingers are sparks, my skin is a river of ethanol.

"I'll have to check my planner. I'm pretty popular around here, you know." I slide one hand onto his leg, and I can feel the muscles through his jeans. It lights up something in me, and I want him. My breaths burst in and out, and my head spins as he leans closer.

I want to kiss him, just so I have one kiss notched in my belt from lips other than Lincoln's.

Ollie's warning about comparing Doyle and Lincoln flops around in my head. I bring my hand up to Doyle's chest and force us to keep those few inches of distance.

I lie back on the patio, and he lies next to me, silent.

The water laps on the sides of the pool, as measured as Doyle's breathing. It's peace.

I don't remember falling asleep, but suddenly Doyle is shaking my shoulder. "Hey. Nes. Hey. Your feet are all pruney. You need to get some sleep. In a bed."

"Okay." My voice is groggy. "Are you leaving?"

"Are you inviting me to stay?" The backs of his fingers brush my cheek.

"Mmm." I sit up and blink sleepily. "I kick in my sleep."

"I can take a beating." It's a joke, but something fierce in his eyes punches through the lightness.

My instinct is to stomp out that frantic look. Why? Because I'm protecting him? Or maybe it isn't that noble of me. Maybe I'm just avoiding anything complicated?

"I'm like a mule. On 'roids. Go home, Doyle. I'll see you in class tomorrow."

He stands, pulls on his socks, hops into his boots, and holds out a hand to tug me to my feet. "How 'bout breakfast first? I know a place, best cheese grits around, and they open at six."

"Grits, huh?" I wrinkle my nose. "Is this part of your plan to convince me stay? I *do* love breakfast foods…"

He raises his blond eyebrows. "I jest might be trying to convince you to stick around, and I'm willing play dirty. I'll use every weapon in my arsenal, cheesy grits included."

I poke a finger into his chest. "All right. Don't get cocky though. I come from a place where breakfast foods are like a religion."

He maneuvers so that his lips are a hair away from brushing mine, then boomerangs back, with a grin so adorable, I have to roll my eyes to fend it off.

"I'll pick you up." He walks over to the hose and turns it off, then braces one foot on the fence and gets ready to jump.

"I want to drive myself."

He looks over his shoulder and tilts his head like he's considering my statement.

"Nope. Tomorrow, ten to six, be ready."

"Ten to six? That's too early!"

"Breakfast is the most important meal of the day. I like to take my time over it." He jumps. I hear the thump of his boots and, a second later, the rumble of his truck's engine.

On my way in I pick up my phone and notice I have a new text from "Ulysses."

Penelope, thanks for watering our tree.

"Dork," I whisper to my screen, but something deep in me flutters so hard, I'm vibrating.

I flop onto my bed and sink into a sleep so deep, the world is soundless and pitch-black until the blare of my phone alarm drags me into the early dawn light.

I have fifteen minutes before Doyle gets here. I sprint to the bathroom and take a GI shower, goop on some mascara and lipstick—this *is* a date, sorta kinda, after all—scrunch gel into my dripping hair, decide I look *hevi nais*, especially considering my limited time frame, and get ready to grab some clothes. But Mom blocks my bedroom door, her face more stricken than usual.

"Aggie, sweetheart, I have to tell you something." Her eyes

are puffy, like she didn't get much sleep. Or like she has a wine hangover. She twists her hands tightly. "It's Lincoln. His parents just called. He was in an accident."

EIGHT

"What?" My fingers bite into my towel and my eyes swim. "Is he...is he..."

"He's at the hospital right now. He'll be okay. He fell from a fire escape, honey. His mom and dad wanted you to know."

My mom looks at me like she doesn't know what to do, and I know we have this entire moat of complicated, bubbling anger and resentment separating us, but this is *Lincoln*. My Lincoln. Lincoln, who patiently showed me how to play pool like a pro and bluff through many hands of poker. Lincoln, who stayed on the other end of the phone until 3:00 a.m. whenever I felt like talking about anything and everything under the sun, no matter that he had to be up at five for soccer practice. Lincoln, who taught me one of the hardest lessons of my life so far—that growing up sometimes means growing apart and losing someone you thought would be by your side forever. I press myself into Mom's arms. She smells like vanilla and musk, scents that are netted around all my childhood memories.

"He called me." My voice is dull. I should cry, but I can't. It feels unreal. "He called me, and I ignored it."

She smooths her hand over my damp hair. "This has nothing to do with you. From what I can gather, he's been drinking more than he should. His parents have been worried, and they're committed to getting him help. He's going through a lot right now, I guess."

I stiffen against her. My mother knows Lincoln and I broke up, but she doesn't know *why*. Before this winter she would have been the first person I told after Ollie. Now I'm choking on this acidic hatred because she doesn't know, and even though it's my own fault for not telling her, I can't damn up my anger and redirect it.

"He's been drinking for months. His parents never took it seriously when I tried to talk to them about it."

It had gotten so bad, I'd had to lie to my mother so that I could stay at random houses where he'd passed out so completely I couldn't shake him awake. I'd be huddled next to him, worried he was going to choke on his own vomit in his sleep or just never wake up. I'd keep my eyes screwed tight and pray no one messed with me while I shivered the night away under a thin throw blanket on someone's couch or curled on the floor next to his sprawled body, my arm pillowed under my head. Of course, Lincoln usually apologized when he first opened his bloodshot eyes, confused about where he was and how he got there. Every single time that confusion scared him, but when I suggested he cut back, he morphed from sorry to nasty and said I should drink more—enough so I'd stop being such a nag.

His parents always treated him like an adult, always let him do whatever he wanted. They thanked me a million times for taking such good care of him, but they never seemed to notice or care that I was scared at all the ways he was changing: drinking and drugging more, hanging out with random people I didn't know, disappearing for hours or even days on end with no word. By the time I found out he cheated, I wasn't very surprised…and I was almost even *relieved*.

It proved that I wasn't making things up in my head about how he acted, and it gave me the push I needed to finally walk away. I'm glad his parents have been scared into finally getting him the help he needs.

"I know you two had problems—" my mom starts, but the doorbell interrupts her.

"Coño." I bang my head against the door frame.

"Are you expecting someone?" Mom sounds surprised.

"Yeah. A friend from school." I have no reason to feel this hot grip of guilt, but I do.

"Do you want me to…"

"Can you tell him…tell him I need five minutes, okay?" I run to my bedroom and close the door. I don't even want to know what she'll think when she opens the door to six feet three inches of tan, muscled Southern gentleman with gorgeous cornflower blue eyes.

I pull on whatever clothes I grab first and sling my backpack over my shoulder. When I skid into the foyer, Doyle's eyebrows are pressed low over his eyes.

"Nes." His voice tiptoes around the tension in the air. "Your mom told me Lincoln was hurt."

Mom wrings her hands, and I resist flinging out some stupid retort she doesn't deserve. It wasn't her business to tell Doyle, but I don't think there's any normal way to react to all this grief and anger and ugly, painful regret. It's not like there's a "Someone You Loved Who Broke Your Heart Is Hurt" manual after all.

"We don't know too much yet." My voice is as cold as the

egomaniacal surgeon's on *One Hundred Thousand Beats* as I concentrate on putting on my shoes.

They watch as I shove my feet into my sneakers a tad too aggressively.

"We can stay here," Doyle offers. "Or you can, if you'd rather I take off. I'll let 'em know you're not gonna be in today at school. Whatever you need."

"I need breakfast." Mom and Doyle trade looks of concern that make me feel irrationally pissed. And defensive. "There's nothing I can do for him, okay? I'm here—he's there. How the hell is my not eating going to help him?" Tears prick behind my eyelids, but I'm not about to let a single drop fall. Not even if I have to bite my tongue off to stop them.

"I have late office hours after lecture tonight, but I'll keep my phone on me, Aggie. Call me if you need…anything…" Mom's words fade as I brush past her and march to Doyle's truck.

He jogs ahead of me and helps hoist me four feet up and into my seat before he gets in and drives his monster truck onto the road to the sound track of our awkward silence. When the tires finally crunch on gravel outside the Breakfast Shack, neither one of us makes a move to get out.

"Did you call him?" His question punctures the heavy silence.

I shake my head, the static buzz of my mounting panic leaving me tongue-tied.

He runs his fingers over his jaw, prickly with golden stubble. "You only get one chance to call as soon as you hear 'bout something. Once that window closes, it's closed for good."

"You think I should call?" My voice accuses Doyle of crimes he's not remotely guilty of.

"I think you should take your time and do what you need

to do." His lips attempt a smile. "I may not like it, but he was your boyfriend for a long time. There's nothing wrong with wanting to know he's all right."

"Is there anything wrong with feeling like he maybe got what was coming to him?" I croak. I put my face in my hands, the air choked in my lungs, and feel a telltale wetness against my palms. "Oh my God. I can't believe I said that. I'm so sorry. I don't know why I—"

Doyle's arms are around me. He drags me across the bench seat, and I breathe in the smell of his skin through the warm cotton of his T-shirt, shielded from all the crap life's pelting at me right now.

"It's okay." His lips press against my hair. "You can love people and hate them at the same time. Trust me, I know how that feels."

"My God. Oh my God, you must think I'm a monster." I mean more than that. I mean, *you must* know *I'm a monster* because it doesn't matter what Lincoln did to me. He didn't deserve to fall off a damn fire escape.

"I think you're scared and hurt. I think you need to know what's going on with him." He unsuctions me from his chest and trains his gaze on mine. "I had a helluva breakup with someone I thought I loved too. I get it. I get how you can care for somebody…and then have a hard time thinking Christian thoughts 'bout 'em." He swallows hard. "After I broke things off with Ansley, I said some things… I'm not proud of 'em. I was hurt, bad. And I wanted her to hurt too."

"It sucks," I whisper. My imagination isn't strong enough to conjure what Doyle—the most perfect gentleman I've ever met—could have said that would still be filling him with regret today. His confession does go a long way in justifying my seething contempt for Ansley Strickland though.

"It does." He blows out a long breath. "I don't spend a lotta time focused on it, but it still stings. I nursed a serious crush on that girl forever… I'm talking since we were barely outta elementary school. When I finally got the guts up to ask her out, I was so pumped she agreed. Felt like Christmas morning and getting my new truck and winnin' the lotto all rolled into one."

I attempt to hide my grimace over Doyle's excitement about dating a cretin like Ansley. Even though I know their story ends in catastrophe, it still bugs me to acknowledge that, of course, there were good times.

"You know she was the lucky one." The curve of his grin files down the jagged edge of my jealousy. "Don't let your ego overinflate, but you're obviously a pretty great guy. She's a moron for screwing things up with you."

What did that idiot do to pulverize Doyle's good, strong heart?

"Winds up our whole relationship was all some big scheme. Jest Ansley's version of an Ebenezer reality show, with me cast as the dumb redneck boyfriend she was gonna remake how she saw fit and parade around like her little rescue puppy." He shakes his head. "I was jest too deep in puppy love to open my fool eyes and see it for what it was. She dragged me to the barber to get my hair cut how she liked. Wanted me to quit my family's business and get a job at her daddy's office, wanted me to play baseball even though I'd decided I was done. I always got the feeling she wanted me to be like my brother Lee, join the military and wear a uniform all the girls'd drool over. But that's jest not me. She bought these expensive polos and khakis, said I had to dress nicer when I went out with her parents, then wanted to dress me up all the time. Her parents seemed to like me for myself, I think. Her daddy said he thought Ansley could use someone with a level head around."

"I guess her entire family isn't comprised of morons then," I mutter begrudgingly.

"The Stricklands're an old family, and they like that I'm from an old family too, even if mine don't have anywhere near the money and power theirs does." He closes his eyes tight. "I have no clue how long I woulda followed her lead. I was so convinced she was exactly what I wanted, I never let myself think too hard about how we never really had much to say to each other. I didn't want to face she wasn't the perfect girl I thought she was. Who wants to admit his girl is mean and shallow? Or that she judges everyone based on their looks, their bloodlines, and their bank accounts?"

His girl. I have to hog-tie my bucking jealousy.

"Sounds like you're describing the Ansley Strickland I met on day one, minute one," I can't help quipping.

He gives me a sheepish smile. "Hey now, go easy on me. She was my childhood crush and the town's little princess. There's a lotta deep brainwashing involved in the whole setup."

"Fair enough. Besides, I clearly have no room to talk." I get the feeling we're almost to the meat of the story, and I'm salivating for it, so I throw Doyle a bone by telling him the still-mortifying story of how my own relationship ended. "So... what finally changed things? For me, it was when one of the girls my ex cheated on me with realized he was a liar with a girlfriend and called to let me know what he'd been doing behind my back. In humiliating detail."

Doyle balls his hand into a fist. "Damn dog."

"Yeah, he was a total pig. But knowing for sure was a relief. Things hadn't been all rosy for a while, and I could finally make a decision based on real evidence."

"Yep, I get that." He slides his phone out and rubs his thumb on the screen. "Ansley'd always accidentally add me into these stupid group chats with her cheer squad minions. I hate my phone blowing up unless it's important, so I jest dropped out of 'em. I left my phone in Brookes's truck overnight once. By the time I charged it up the next day, I had over a hundred notifications."

"Holy crap."

"The last bunch were Ansley telling me to call her, saying she had an explanation for everything, to ignore the texts from her friends. It was all jest 'girl talk.'" His face goes a mottled shade of crimson. "I don't go lookin' for trouble, but this time I had to see what had her so panicked."

"Oh God." My heart fractures at the pain and humiliation that registers on Doyle's face.

"It was like reading all the ugliest things you ever thought about yourself and your kin. The stuff you pray nobody else sees, even though you know that's a real long shot." I'm sure he's going to leave it vague, but he keeps going. "There was the fact that I talk and dress and act like a redneck. Ansley told her friends she knew I was so in love with her, she could get me to jump off a cliff if she snapped her fingers. That crap didn't bother me too much though. It was the stuff 'bout my family. That my grandparents were white trash who had a bunch of loser kids, which is why they gotta raise their grandkids. There was stuff 'bout my daddy bein' the town drunk, how Ansley saw him digging through the garbage behind Randall's Liquor Store—I never seen him do that, but I guess he might've. And my mama—"

My fury is at its peak now. "What kind of scum breaks the cardinal rule of *life*—you *never* talk bad about anyone's mother."

"Problem with Ansley is, she don't think the rules apply

to her." He blinks hard a few times and his voice cracks a little. "I'm not tryin' to make excuses for what my mama did, but she got pregnant and married real young. She'd already raised her own brothers and sisters, dropped outta school junior year. Once Malachi went to preschool, she got a job at a gas station. It was her first taste of freedom, working for her own money and all. She started to hang out with some shady people… My mama was always kinda naive. She was livin' a real wild life, partyin' and stayin' out all night like she was a high schooler instead of a mom."

"That must've been rough." I put a hand on his arm and squeeze. I know how much it hurts when you think your mother is choosing other people over you.

"I guess she never really had a lotta choices, so she never realized till it was too late that she wasn't cut out for the life she got. Anyway, I know full well my mama screwed up, and I don't know that I ever sorted out how I feel 'bout all that. But when I read the hateful things Ansley said, I realized I could never be with someone so small hearted. I could never be with someone who judged the people I loved like that."

"So you broke it off with her?" I watch his mouth move back and forth.

"Not before I told her all the ugly things people said about her. All the things I closed my ears to when we dated. It shook her up pretty bad. I'd been her biggest supporter, and she really expected we'd pick up where we left off like I'd never seen her true colors. She was cryin' the whole time I laid into her."

"I bet it felt amazing." Deep in my rotten heart I'm shaking my black pom-poms and cheering Evil Doyle on like the bad influence I am.

"For a minute." He shrugs. "I shoulda been honest. But

dragging her through the mud the way she did with me and my family means I sunk to her level."

"You could *never* sink to Ansley's level of evil. She's like the prototype for a fairy-tale villain. You're a way better person than her. And you're a way better person than me, Doyle Rahn." I tap my phone's dark screen. "I'm going to call Lincoln. I can't promise I'll be super nice, even if he's in pain."

"Aw, that dog don't deserve anything close to 'super nice,'" Doyle says with a wicked smile. "I'm gonna jaw with the guys at the tire shop. Half an hour, all right? Then we can do whatever you want." He jumps out of the truck and lands with a hard thump.

"Doyle!"

He holds the door open. "Nes?"

"You'll be back in half an hour?"

Because I don't want him to just…leave. Which makes no sense. He's not going to walk away from his truck. Even if someone as messed up as me is sitting in it.

"Half an hour. Then we'll discuss those grits." His smile isn't a total put-on this time.

His boots are heavy on the hot asphalt as he crosses the parking lot. My palm leaves a damp bloom of sweat on the back of my phone and my reflection stares back from the blank screen. I nearly jump out of my skin when it rings to life.

"Ollie?"

"Nes, you heard?" When I say yes, she bursts into tears. "I'm sorry I told you not to call him! I had no idea. Did you talk to him yet?"

"No." I can barely hear my own voice.

"Oh." The pause is long and full of questions I'm glad she doesn't ask. Instead she thinks the best of me, like always.

"When you do? Can you tell him…tell him I hope he gets better fast."

"Okay."

Ollie untangles herself from our stilted phone call, and I slowly—so slowly—go to my recent calls and press my thumb over his name, half hoping he doesn't pick up. Before I have time to prepare, his voice vibrates through me like thunder before a storm.

"Nes? Nes, baby, is that you?" His voice slurs. Probably pain meds.

"Lincoln."

The second his name slips out of my mouth, he gives a relieved sob. "Holy fucking shit… It's you. Baby, I thought I lost you for good. I miss you so damn much. I deserve everything, I know, believe me, I really do. But you gotta hear me out. I've been so screwed up without you. I need you, I need to feel—"

"Lincoln." I freeze the emotions that warm and swirl up from deep in my heart when I hear his voice, the voice I used to fall asleep to on the phone every night. "What happened? Are you okay?"

"Me? I'm fine, babe." He laughs like it's old times, like nothing has changed. "Sprained wrist, concussion. I'll be out by tomorrow. It just sounds dramatic, you know? Falling off a fire escape and all that. Forget me. How are you? When are you coming home?"

Home.

Mom in our cramped galley kitchen with take-out menus spread across every inch of countertop. Ollie's bassoon's mournful wails punctuated with colorful swear chains whenever she flubs a note. The smell of concrete and exhaust fumes, the screams of kids swinging high in their caged-in parks during recess as we munch on some chocolate-covered frozen key-lime pie to follow up heavenly grilled Mexican corn slathered in *cotija* cheese and lime.

Home.

Lincoln sitting with his back to my locker and a new mix to share, one earbud for each of us, hands locked, heads bent together.

Home.

Where my heart was broken. Twice. Where my life fell apart. The one big, crazy, beautiful city people flock to for their second chance at life is the one place where I couldn't have mine.

Home is where the heart is. I guess I'll figure it out once mine starts beating again.

"You know I'm here for the rest of my senior year." I sound like a robot about to short-circuit.

"C'mon, there's no reason for that. You can stay at your abuela's. I know she'd love it if you came back."

It's been less than two minutes, and he's already bossing me around the way he had been doing more and more toward the end of our relationship.

"Mom is here. I just started school and—"

"People transfer in and out all the time, baby. If you don't want to stay with your abuela, my parents said you can move in with us. To tell you the truth, I'd love that."

The only sound is our breathing, off rhythm and quick. I close my eyes and picture his spacious room, the king-size bed, the midnight blue walls, modern and understated. I was always uncomfortable in it, even wrapped in Lincoln's arms. Maybe my gut knew what my brain was too chicken to face.

"I'm not moving back to New York now." The words are calm and sure.

The silence is finally interrupted by Lincoln's temper. "What the *fuck*, Nes? What did my mother say? I asked her to keep her mouth shut. This is the truth. I swear to God, I swear on my grandmother's grave, Nes. Hear me out, okay? I was just hanging out with her, okay? I barely knew her, and I definitely wasn't screwing her. I left by the fire escape so I wouldn't wake her parents, and I lost my footing. That's all—"

"What?" Hot sunbursts of rage flare up and keep my brain from putting the pieces together. "You got hurt leaving some girl's place?"

He swears under his breath. "Look, just tell me what my mother said *exactly*?"

He's scrambling to get his story straight.

"I honestly hope you get well soon, Lincoln." I recite it like it's a script written for a more decent person than I am. What I want to tell him would melt the ears off a trucker. Even Ollie's most screwed-up bassoon solo couldn't dredge hateful words like the ones I'm biting my tongue to hold back. "Ollie sends her best wishes. I need to go."

"Nes! Don't you hang up on me! I love you! I want you back. Do you hear me? I can explain. Hear me out—"

I end the call and power off my phone, imagining his rage when he attempts to call again.

I lean my head back on the seat and wait for the tears that feel so close, but they never come. When Doyle taps on the glass next to my ear, I don't even jump. He swings the door open and waits on me to speak first.

"I'm starving," I announce.

"All quiet on the northern front?" He drops his eyes like he's trying to let me know he isn't prying.

"Mild concussion and a wrist sprain." I don't bite my tongue fast enough to keep the rest back. "That's what you get when you're sneaking out of some girl's bedroom."

Doyle's eyes burn hot and wild, and his smile is unapologetic. "Sounds like he got exactly what was coming to him. Milady?"

NINE

"Okay, I have no idea why people worship grits down here. They taste like farina—"

"What's farina?" Doyle flips a toothpick into his mouth.

"A breakfast food no one eats unless their mom says, 'Eat your farina.'" I lean back and pat my full, happy gut. "But the biscuits and gravy? They were *amazing*." I reach for the last bite of salty bacon on my plate, but I'm too stuffed. "In the DR we have a word for being this stuffed—*jatura*."

"*Jatura*," Doyle repeats. "Sounds like it means 'stuffed.'"

"Exactly. Only my abuela's *tostones* have ever made me feel this *jatura* before. I wish I could bring you some, or one of Lou's bagels. Or a waffle from Five Star. Food of the gods."

"Y'know—" Doyle arches one blond brow high on his forehead "—roads do head north, contrary to what most people in this county believe. I could make a trip to New York City sometime."

I let the legs of my chair drop with a thud as loud as my surprise.

"You? Doyle Rahn in New York City?"

He flicks a balled-up straw wrapper at me. "I went to Hawaii. I've been places."

"Can't argue with that."

Doyle grabs the bill with freakish quickness the nanosecond the waitress drops it. I insist on leaving a substantial tip before leaving. Our waitress was unsmiling but efficient, and I like to imagine her finally cracking a smile over the big wad of money on the table. Or shoving it in her tip bag and going on to the next customer. Whatever.

"Thanks for breakfast. I'm suitably nourished for Lovett's Hemingway quiz. Do you think she'll quiz on dates? I suck at dates." I can't read Doyle's thoughts based on his facial expressions alone.

"You sure you wanna go back to school? We could skip," he offers.

"Great idea. Since I got reamed for my tattoo, my nose ring, my hair, *and* my clothes after I flirted with the princess of Ebenezer High's ex and told her to go scratch—skipping school seems like the logical next step. I don't want to get expelled. Plus Lovett will never let us make up that quiz unless we can prove we were on our deathbeds or something. So…"

He turns the key in the ignition. "All righty, Miss Goody Two-shoes. We still on for baseball Friday?"

"Yep." I poke him in the ribs across the seat. "Bring me a mitt, remember."

"And four-wheeling next Saturday?" He pulls out and we bump onto the road to school. "Though I gotta warn you… coming to opening weekend at the mud pit basically baptizes you as a full-fledged Georgian. That mud gets in your soul."

"Geez, Rahn, you're clogging up my social calendar." I roll the window down and breathe in the morning air, sweet in the golden light of the early sun. "Do I *want* this Georgian mud christening?"

"Of course you do. You can't leave this place without getting your feet muddy." He goes quiet for a few long seconds, then clears his throat. "I also might want to keep you busy so you stop thinking 'bout running away. I gotta say, when I heard your ex was in the hospital, I kinda expected you to up and bolt home. You know, nurse him back to health or whatever." He drums his fingers all over the top of the steering wheel.

"I think you have some serious misconceptions about me. Let me educate you. If you get rocked in the head by a baseball or choke on some beef jerky, I'll administer emergency lifesaving procedures. And then hand you over to the people who are trained to care for you. I'd be a useless nurse. Unless you need someone to play with the controls on your hospital bed and eat all your Jell-O." I like the way he's smiling, like he's thinking something he shouldn't be. "What?"

"Nothing." The word filters out through a huge-ass grin, which clearly tells me that his *nothing* means nothing about as much as my mother's *fine* means fine.

"Not nothing. You're smiling about *something*. Spill."

His shrug rocks his shoulders. "I was jest thinking of you in a little nurse's uniform, playing in my bed and eating my Jell-O." He doesn't look the least repentant about his dirty thoughts.

Which make me bubble over with laughter. "You're pushing your luck, Rahn."

"You make me wanna live on the wild side, Agnes." He lets his arm graze my stomach as he pushes my door open once we park. "Positive you don't wanna skip?"

"I *want* to," I assure him. "I'm just not dumb enough to go through with it. C'mon. We've got an authoritarian establishment to stick it to. Speaking of which, do you have a rubber band?" Doyle shakes his head. "Binder clip? Two pencils?"

He roots through his pocket. "Two pieces of gum, a marble, and a bootlace."

I pop one piece of gum in my mouth, toss my hair over to tie it up with the bootlace, and eye the marble. "What do you have a marble in your pocket for?"

He rolls it back and forth on his palm. "My granddaddy's been collecting them since he was a kid, and this one was jest rolling around like a death trap, so I scooped it up. I guess I pocketed it because it reminds me of the color of your eyes." His ears burn red and he laughs at himself. "You know, I can be pretty romantic when I put my mind to it."

"Let me see." Doyle drops it, cool and heavy, into the curve of my fingers. The green and gold twists at the center of the glass ball look nothing like my dull, hazelish eyes. "I'm unconvinced."

He takes back the marble, throws it, and catches it backhand. "You see your eyes every day, so you're used to how gorgeous they are." Just when I'm melting right around the edges, he adds, "Also, you don't get to see them when you look at me. Isn't there a thing about how your eyes change color when you're looking at something you want real bad?"

"Does your neck hurt from holding that big, fat head up all day?"

We waltz into school so early, the halls are empty except for a few eager beaver students mingling around debate club notes. Doyle skids to a stop in front of a sparkly vote-for-me poster for some random high school contest, squinting like it's one of those 3-D pictures that pop out when you relax your eyes.

"What's this for?" Context clues aren't getting me anywhere.

There's a big red glittery rose encircled by a glittery crown. The school logo is done in—guess what? *Glitter!*—along with Khabria Scott's name and "Ebenezer's Next Rose Queen" written in fancy cursive.

"'Rose Queen'?" I read aloud. "Wasn't that what Ansley was getting all 'let them eat cake' about? Do I even want to know?"

Doyle's eyebrows press all the way up to his hairline. I'm not sure if that facial expression communicates shock or admiration. "Holy hell. Khabria Scott is running for Rose Queen."

"Again—do I even want to know?"

This time when Doyle looks at me, he seems almost embarrassed. "Naw. You really don't. C'mon. We're wasting time talking when you could be soaking up my good looks."

"No, seriously, are you not even a little worried that your arrogance has crossed some kind of sociopathic line? I think you may be full-blown delusional."

He heads to the courtyard where we sat yesterday, and I follow like a pull-toy on a string. "A healthy dose of confidence is a good thing. Around a girl like you, I'd say it's pretty damn essential." He flops onto the grass and pulls his cap low over his eyes.

I sit cross-legged and resist the urge to pull his brim up and look into those purple-blue eyes. Violet eyes, especially on a guy, sound ridiculous, but, in reality they're a blink of soft, hidden beauty that reminds me not to assume I ever know everything about anyone. And especially not to assume I know nearly enough about Doyle Rahn.

As if he can read my thoughts, he crooks a finger, trying to lure me closer. I shake my head.

"You're sittin' on an anthill. Come sit here. I'll protect you from them little bastards." He pats his lap, right over his thigh, where the denim of his jeans is worn so thin it's fraying.

"I'll put up with the ant bites, thank you very much."

Then an ant crawls down my ankle and clamps its jaws into my skin. At first the pain doesn't register. We had our share of gross bugs in New York, but ants? Since I got here, everyone from the real-estate lady to the pest control company that won't stop calling has been making way too big a deal over them.

Or so I thought, until the pinch and burn radiates along the lower portion of my calf. I hop up and swat at my ankle, brushing my legs frantically because I'm *positive* an entire army of these deranged mutant monsters are scampering all over my skin with their poison jaws.

I'm screeching and dancing around and flailing my arms, but Doyle comes to my rescue, hoisting me up, one hand on each side of my rib cage. He wraps an arm around my waist and runs me to a picnic table with green paint peeled back from the blistering heat. He pulls my leg straight and tries hard not to laugh.

"I told you you were sitting on an anthill." He uncaps his water bottle and douses the tiny bites swelling up like an ugly anklet.

"You didn't tell me they were killer mutant monster ants!" I try to collect the shreds of my tattered dignity.

"Or fire ants, as they're called 'round here." He reaches into his backpack pocket and pulls out a tin. "Lucky for you, you got bit while I was around. This is something my gram makes for us. You get bit by all sorts of crazy things in the wild, and this? Magic." He dips two fingers to collect a scoop of waxy yellow stuff that smells like old herbs and whiskey.

"What's in it?" My ankle twitches with pain as the bites swell.

"I know better than to ask my gram 'bout her secret recipes.

I'm not as dumb as I look." He rubs a thumb over my ankle and massages his finger along my calf.

The shallowest thought flits across my brain: *I'm so glad I shaved my legs yesterday.*

"So this will help? Because it feels like I have hot coals around my ankle. I can't believe *ants* did this." Doyle smears the salve on as I whine. As soon as it touches my skin, I breathe a sigh of relief. "Oh, this is definitely working. I can feel it already."

"It don't work that fast." He twists the lid back on the tin. "It's probably my nursing skills."

"So you'd do more than eat my Jell-O and play with my bed settings?" My heart attempts to dance a messy merengue.

"Hell yeah. I make a mean chicken noodle soup. I'm not squeamish 'bout changin' bandages or cleanin' wounds. And I give an amazin' sponge bath." He waggles his eyebrows, and I laugh so hard the pain shrinks to a distant echo.

"Holster your sponge bath fantasies, my friend. I'm good as new and perfectly capable of bathing myself." I turn my ankle back and forth and scoot over when he jumps up to sit next to me.

"Totally unrelated to seein' ya naked, but I was thinkin' you should mebbe bring that little bikini when we go four-wheeling." The way his eyes crinkle lets me know he's aware he's playing with fire, and he doesn't care.

"You just keep pulling me deeper into these plans of yours. First it's baseball, then you get me to agree to breakfast. I say yes to four-wheeling, now you want to swim?" I tap the sole of my sneaker on the toe of his boot, and he looks totally happy to have me playing featherweight footsie with him.

"Do you have any idea how much mud we're gonna be coated in after we four-wheel? We're gonna need to rinse off.

My uncle's got this little house on the river with a rope you can swing off over the water."

"Won't it be cold?" It's been hot as Mordor here, but it's still January. The water must be freezing.

"You scared of a couple chill bumps?" He leans back on his arms and grins.

"Is it even safe to do that? Swing into a river?"

His jaw drops. "You never jumped off a rope into a river?" When I shake my head, he rubs a hand over his face like he's barely able to process this information. "It's safe as can be. And I'll be there to nurse ya back to health if anything happens."

"Hmm. Not sure if that makes me feel any safer." I jump up when I notice the halls filling with students. "Thank you for breakfast. I need to get my butt to class."

"Let me walk you."

It doesn't feel like a sweaty-palmed, thundering-hearted endeavor. So why are my hands slick and my cardiovascular system in overdrive?

It may just be my sensitivity to being new here, but I swear people everywhere stop and stare at us, before whispering behind their cupped hands.

"Am I being crazy, or are we all anyone here wants to talk about this fine morning?" I crane my neck and find people looking away before they meet my gaze, pretending to trade notes or adjust their backpacks. Something is definitely up.

"It's jest that some people can't keep from yappin' 'bout what ain't their concern!" Doyle announces loudly enough that he sends a few of the gossipers scurrying. His scowl is fierce. "It's leftover from when I was with Ansley. She was always broadcasting our business like she *wanted* people stickin' their damn noses in it. Irritatin' as hell."

"That sucks." We're near my classroom and I want to stall.

123

I also want to get to class on time, but I don't like losing the few minutes I get alone with Doyle at school. "My ex was big into PDA, but I was never a fan."

"Ansley considered making out a spectator sport." He leans against the lockers outside the classroom, tall and lanky, arms crossed. "It wasn't all the PDA so much as the girl. Now, if there was a girl I had a mind to kiss, I'd kiss her wherever she'd let me."

"Or maybe you have the attention span of a gnat. I don't think any hot-blooded male would have a hard time paying attention if they were doing anything physical with your ex." I sound cucumber cool, *mansa* even, but I'm gripping the edge of my binder to avoid tearing it in half. "Anyway, I thought gentlemen didn't kiss and tell."

"I'm as much a gentleman as you are a nurse." He leans so close, I can see the spatter of freckles next to his ear. "Trust me, I got plenty of hot blood. Jest takes a fiery sort of girl to turn me on."

I suddenly can't wait to see what kind of sparks Doyle and I can make fly when we get together.

TEN

"Headed out?" Mom's voice rings with hope, like I'll echo friendliness back to her if she projects cheerfully enough.

Too bad we're too far in for those kinds of charlatan tricks.

"I'm going to play ball." Just to be an asshole, I grab the back of my T-shirt and knot it tight halfway up my back, the way she says looks trashy.

"Basketball?" She's delicately sipping Perrier with a twist of lime through a striped paper straw while she reads an issue of *The New Yorker*.

I should ignore my mother and the whole little ridiculous tableau, but it makes me burn so hot, my blood feels ashy.

"No. We're not in Brooklyn anymore, though I see you're doing an admirable job pretending nothing in our life has changed at all."

My mother blinks slowly like she's coming out of her hoity-toity daze, then follows my glare to her pretentious drink and magazine.

"Do you reckon I should get myself some sweet tea and a copy of *Better Homes and Gardens*?" she faux-drawls.

The sneer in her voice is a garnish—like the lime in her

drink—and it helps settle my irritation. *Here's* the feisty mother I remember: the one who actually functioned as an in-control parent instead of a lame character in some erotica cheating scandal. Here's the woman who would have smashed the DVR in a fit of hot temper if her jerk of a daughter spoiled eight seasons of loyal television show devotion.

"Maybe you should stop pretending our lives haven't been screwed beyond recognition." I sound more melodramatic than I mean to. Her smirk alerts me to the fact that she agrees.

"Sweetheart, I have tried everything to make up for this, okay? Let it be known—your mother screwed up. I'm only human. I was lonely. I was more open than I should have been to—"

I slap my hands over my ears, but it only muffles her words.

"—people and situations that weren't in my best interest. And now here I am. Here we are." She waits until I take my hands down. I keep waiting for one of us to do something überirritating to tip the scales either way, so I can decide if I should leave now or stay for another minute. "I have self-flagellated long enough—"

"Really? A bottle of pinot a night is suddenly the equivalent of beating yourself up over everything that happened?" I dare her to hold my stare, but she can't.

"I know what you think you know. But trust me…" Her voice cracks. "It's infinitely more complicated than that. I know you understand what a broken heart feels like. Let me tell you a sad truth. It gets harder the older you are. The longer you love someone."

"Are you talking about Dad?" My parents have a strict policy of never, *ever* talking crap about each other in front of me and Jasper.

"Your dad has some things he needs to talk to you about,

Aggie. In his own time. It's not my story to tell." Her dark hair slides out of its bun, and she looks so much younger with messy pieces hanging around her knife-blade cheekbones.

"You can tell me *something*." I love my dad, but he's a distracted phone talker, he can't write an email that isn't professional, and he refuses to use emojis when he texts. I'm not asking him to get on Snapchat, but he could edge into the twenty-first century. I hate that I feel relieved when I remember I have a science lab to finish, so I might have to push off a call to him for another few days. "I came here with you, but I barely know what went down. Tell me how we wound up in this bog of eternal misery."

For a few seconds I hold out hope she'll let me in.

"Is it really so bad, Aggie? A fresh start for both of us, is that so terrible? I would understand if you were being bullied or ostracized, but you're going out to play baseball for God's sake." She flaps her highbrow magazine at me.

The scales have definitely tipped. "Right." I swing my fist in a golly-gee arc and put on a big phony smile. "I'll go play some baseball, and maybe you can bake a nice pot roast and an apple pie, and then I'll come home and we can totally pretend like life in this backwater hellhole is a-okay."

She sets down the glass—without a coaster…things must be about to get serious—but I'm out the door before she can say another word.

Doyle is sitting on my backyard fence when I storm out.

"I'm calling the neighborhood watch to report a suspicious hooligan hanging around my house!" I yell.

Even though he doesn't look, I can tell he's smiling when he answers, "Dontcha dare. This ain't highfalutin New York City, with all their PC warnings and police interventions, Nes.

This is shoot-to-kill country, and your neighborhood watch is Jonesy Whittle."

"The nice guy with those cute concrete bulldog statues in his yard?" I hop up next to him, and he eyes me from head to toe.

I shift to give him a better view. My cousins in Santo Domingo would say the look he's giving me means he'd like to make me his *jeva*—his girlfriend—but I can't entertain that thought right now. What Doyle and I have between us is too complicated to explain in any language I know.

"Jonesy Whittle's got a gun collection that could arm every soldier in a second War Between the States, and he's a steady shot." He hops down and holds a hand out.

I refuse his hand and land sideways on my ankle, correcting it just before it buckles under my weight.

"The War Between the States, huh?" I squint. "Is that an adorable Southern term for the Civil War?"

"No, ma'am." He takes one step closer to me. "The *adorable* term is the War of Northern Aggression."

I pop an eyebrow and a coordinating hip. "You're kidding me."

"Never would." He stoops to grab the mitt lying next to the fence, and the smells of cut grass and warm leather rise into my nostrils like a whiff of pure, all-American summer. "My favorite's the War for Southern Independence. It's got a nice rebel ring to it without soundin' bitter. The War of Northern Aggression sounds like some crybaby Southern kid tattlin' on the North to his daddy."

The mitt has been so lovingly oiled, I can practically see my reflection in it. "That is some certifiably crazy crap, Doyle."

He shrugs and tugs on my curly ponytail. "Didn't you steal my cap? How're you s'posed to play ball without a cap, Yank?"

"Oh, so now the story is that I *stole* it, huh?" I whack him with the mitt, and the leather makes a satisfying *thunk* against his arm. "I forgot. I guess I'll have to run back in and—"

I'm afraid to go into my house and see whether my mother traded sparkling water for something stronger. I prefer imagining her pissed instead of pathetic.

"No worries. My truck's at the field, and I got so many caps, even a thief like you'd never be able to steal 'em all." I stick the mitt over my hand when he reaches for it, and he chuckled. "Aw, I get it, I get it. You need to wear that big ole mitt 'cause touching me gets you so wild, you don't know if you'll be able to control yourself. I see how it is."

I tug the mitt off and toss it up, watching it spin before I catch it. "Honestly, I have no idea why I hang out with you."

"My charm's pretty well documented 'round these parts," he says. "Want some advice 'bout the game?"

"Don't." I toss the mitt again. "Please. I do *not* need whatever advice you're about to give me."

"Jest as well." He swings a lazy arm around my shoulders. "It'll make it that much easier to trap you in my web if you ain't prepared for what's coming."

I glance down at our feet, sinking in the asphalt that's so hot, it's liquefying. What kind of cursed place is this hot in the dead of winter? "We're playing ball. Don't you think sneakers would've worked better than boots?"

He takes inventory of his scuffed boots and shakes his head. "I can run circles 'round you in these," he brags.

"Really?" I tuck the mitt under my armpit and rub my hands together. "Let's race."

"Race?" His eyes shine with blood-boiling, competitive excitement, but he sighs. "Sorry. It jest doesn't feel gentlemanly."

"If you win...you can kiss me." It pops out before I can

think it through. Those violet eyes of his darken with excitement. "I don't want a pity race, and I sure as hell don't want you trying to say you let me win. You want a kiss, right?" It's a declaration, like I know he does for sure, even though I don't, really.

Know, that is. If he wants to. Kiss me. My brain fuzzes like radio static.

I do have a firm grasp on my feelings about kissing Doyle, but I'm mostly ignoring them. Except when I'm playing with fire making bets I shouldn't be making.

"A real kiss?" He steps closer and rubs the backs of his fingers against the backs of mine. And I imagine racing him, but slowing down just short of the finish line, so he can claim his kiss. Ridiculous girly fantasies. "We ain't talkin' some li'l peck on the cheek, right?"

"Fine. A kiss on the lips." I try not to stare at *his* lips when I utter that mellifluous phrase: *kiss on the lips.*

"Tongue?" He holds his arms wide, an open target for my scorn.

"Pushing your luck, Rahn! You win, you get *one* kiss, on the lips. *No tongue.*" I crouch into starting position and point to the chain-link fence at the end of the street and across a field. "To the fence?"

He crouches next to me. I'm staring straight ahead, but I see the sunlight glinting off his bright hair in my peripheral.

"And what if you win?" he asks.

I straighten and ponder what I want. What I can realistically ask of Doyle Rahn anyway?

My brain skips like a broken record over one word: *kiss.*

"If I win…" I weed through different ideas—a week of him being my personal servant or buying me dinner, doing my English homework—but I dismiss them as too stupid or too likely to make him attempt to lose on purpose. "If I win, you leave me alone for a full week."

I say it because it's the one thing he maybe wouldn't want, and also because I have no clue what I *do* want. Dread churns in the pit of my gut when I realize how blanketed in loneliness my life will be without the only friend I have down here.

I realize it also sounds unbelievably childish and petty, but Doyle doesn't look remotely insulted.

"You'll still go muddin' with me next weekend, right?" he checks. "Jest in case we start this race and enter some kinda parallel universe where you're faster than me or my legs fall off in the next two minutes. 'Cause I don't plan on losing if circumstances're fair."

"I guess I can bend the rules for you this one time." Our pride and dares spin out fast and furious in the subtropical heat.

He hocks from low in his throat. When I recoil, he draws even deeper before spitting on his palm.

"C'mon, you lived in the big, bad city. You must've seen plenty worse than a little spit." He holds his hand out vertically, and the lugie doesn't budge.

"I *saw* all kinds of gross stuff, but I never *stuck my hand* in any of it." I turn my face away as bile laps at the back of my throat.

"This is embarrassing. For you. Come on, tough nuts. Don't be such a wuss." He thrusts his hand my way, and I have no choice.

But if I'm going to do this, I'm going to do it right. I snort as hard as I can and don't spit until I manage a sizable contribution, but Doyle shows zero disgust; he just slaps his palm against mine and we shake, our bodily fluids squishing between our hands.

"I'm going to puke," I moan when he releases my hand.

He crouches in starting position. "You wanna quit? Jest say,

'I'm a big ole whiny quitter and Doyle Rahn is the fastest, smartest, best-looking guy in the world,' and we'll call it a day."

"I'd rather die." I crouch next to him and wipe the remnants of our handshake on the leg of my shorts. "No cheating."

"You offend me." His voice flattens. "I'm a joker, but I never cheat."

"On three then." I inhale and flex my legs. "One." He leans low. "Two." We both rock forward. "Three!"

I forget that I made a stupid bet I probably don't even want to win the second I scream the last number. We run like two kids at recess who don't have a single twisted worry in the world to anchor us. Neither one of us holds back: we pump our arms, jerk our knees high, throw our torsos so far forward, one misstep, and we'll both wind up bloodied with road rash.

It's clear from the heavy *thunk-thunk* of Doyle's boots that running in sneakers would've been easier for him, but he's long-legged and adapted to this tropical heat. I lag one step behind, then two, and, before I can catch up, he crashes into the fence. He shakes the fence and hoots, but I can barely hear him or the clank of the metal over my ragged breathing.

"I won!" he crows. He grabs my shoulders and pulls me up until I stand tall. Our faces are slicked with sweat, and our shirts stick to our chests in moist blotches, but I'm not thinking about any of that.

I'm thinking about how this prize kiss is going to feel, delivered under the blistering sun with my dignity sweating in crazy rivulets down my face. He tugs on my hand and pulls me close.

"So. You ready?" Doyle asks like he's got this situation on lockdown, but his body language conveys nothing but nervous twitches suddenly. "Fair warning, this moment'll prolly change your life."

"You sound pretty sure of yourself. How much data do you have on this? Are you some kind of serial kiss stealer?" It pains me to imagine Doyle kissing anyone else, but my need to rib him is stronger than my jealous streak.

"Quality, not quantity," he informs me. His heart races under the thin cotton of his T-shirt. "Trust me, this kiss'll be a game changer."

"Hmm, you think?" I edge closer, and he raises his eyebrows in alarm. "I don't want to brag, but I've had some pretty great kisses in my time. Even if this kiss is *amazing*, I'm not sure it'll even make my top ten."

"This one'll take first place, no contest." One tug and our bodies lock tight. I can't figure out if it's my heart hammering or his. "Ready?"

Our lips are so close I can almost taste him. I'm a plucked guitar string, vibrating and anticipating the next notes, the whole, beautiful song. "I guess I have no choice," I whisper.

A second later I'm puckering into the muggy Georgia air, and Doyle Rahn is standing too far away, his brow furrowed.

"What's wrong?" It's like I just jumped off the playground merry-go-round. The world around me swirls and dips, and I can't trust my equilibrium. "Why didn't you kiss me?"

"That was a decent race. You almost had me. I don't feel right claimin' the full prize," he declares.

"Like my grandpa always said, '*almost* only counts in horseshoes and hand grenades.' You won. Fair and square." I move a step forward, and he takes one back.

"Look, the truth is, it ain't gentlemanly to kiss a lady who's got no choice. Doesn't sit right with me."

Damn my clumsy attempt at flirting!

"That's not what I—I mean, you were bragging about your

kissing prowess…" I sputter because I can't yell *I was joking, kiss me! Kiss me right now, you gorgeous idiot!*

His eyes light up like he had a eureka moment. "I'm man enough to admit when I'm wrong."

"Maybe you just know your kiss wouldn't live up to all the hype." I hold my breath. He narrows his eyes.

He leans dangerously close, and I'm sure I've got this kiss in the bag…

But he bypasses my lips. His mouth hovers next to my ear. "Trust me, our kiss will be epic. As for when it'll happen? Lady's choice." His ticklish breath breaks goose bumps out on my arms.

"But…I don't want you to accuse me of wimping out later!" I yelp.

He wraps one arm around my waist and cocks an eyebrow. "We'll compromise then. No lips." He pulls my hand up to his mouth, sticks out his tongue and drags a long, hot lick across the top of my hand. "All tongue."

"Disgusting!" I yank my hand away, but it's all for drama. My nerve endings scream awake, and the boundaries of my imagination expand to include all the places Doyle might lick if he bests me in another contest.

Game. On.

He howls with laughter. "You're jest sore I did whatcha asked without you getting your way." He's bent in half, hands on his knees, cracking up. "Admit it, you wanted me to kiss you."

"You wish," I hiss, rolling my eyes at him.

"Aw, don't be put out, now. All you gotta do is ask me for that kiss you want so bad."

"You have zero chance of getting a kiss from me." I shrug

like I'm not light-headed with pure *want*. "Should've taken your chance when you had it."

"If a lick on the hand got you so riled, imagine how it'll be when you ask for that kiss."

I order my wild, yapping, excited imagination to heel. "Never gonna happen," I snort.

"We'll see."

He winks and sticks his boots into the diamond-shaped fence links. Doyle climbs as nimbly as a cat. When he's at the top, he jumps and lands in a cloud of dust, presses his back to the chain link, looks over his shoulder, and crooks a finger. "Climb. When you get over, put your feet on my shoulders, and I'll help you down."

I don't have a snowball's chance in hell of vaulting that fence without help, or I'd try. I haven't hopped a fence since middle school and never one this big, so I climb slowly. When I finally make it over, I hang from my hands, kicking my sneakers until I balance on Doyle's wide shoulders.

He reaches up and lowers me by the waist until I'm tucked in his arms. "Was this some kind of plan?" My mouth presses against his neck as he cradles me.

"Mebbe. Gate's over there."

I whirl around. Two girls with bats and mitts slung over their shoulders swing a gate open and walk through like normal humans.

"Doyle!" I beat his chest with the mitt as he cackles.

"It was fun though, right? You can't say hangin' with me ain't fun." Before I can argue, he takes me by the hand and we run to the far side of the field where his truck is parked. He leans into the window, then pops back out with a hat that says Ebenezer Rebels.

"What's that?" I grab the bill and stare at the vaguely familiar symbol.

"You pullin' my leg?" He narrows his eyes like he thinks I'm playing babe in the woods. My brain shoots through every image in its arsenal, searching for where I've seen it. "Front hall of our school, Nes. You don't recognize our school mascot?"

The giant *E* in our school's hall comes into focus in my mind's eye, but I guess I never put together that it had Ebenezer *Rebels* plastered underneath.

"Our mascot is the *rebel*? I thought it was that giant *E*. I guess that would be a little weird...but *Rebels*? Is that even legal?"

Doyle tips his cap off his head, chucks it through the window, pulls a Yankees cap out of the truck, and presses it low over his eyes. "Is it illegal to have a team called the Yankees? With its weird giant *NY* symbol?"

"That's different," I argue. "Technically they also have that red, white, and blue top hat. Also they're pro ballplayers. And it doesn't mean—"

"Anything?" He raises his eyebrows and half smiles. "'Cause *rebel* ain't jest a Civil War thing, y'know. I never met a bigger rebel than you, and I grew up smack in the middle of Sons and Daughters of the Confederacy Nation." He tugs down on the edge of my shirt, and his fingers graze the quarter-inch slice of bare skin.

"Yeah, but *here*? I mean, doesn't it get people...riled up?"

I want to ask if it gets *black* people riled up, but I don't know how to ask that question. Back home I knew my classmates really well, and we had tons of conversations about what it meant to be whatever we were—for me, that was mixed race, but also black, European American, Latina, and Afro-Caribbean. Dozens of my classmates and teachers had cultural backgrounds just as complex, and we tried hard not to avoid discussing race and culture just because it was complicated—in fact, we talked about it openly and often in my school, so it never felt like a taboo subject. It was so commonly addressed, it barely registered on my daily radar, and I didn't give it much thought outside of the occasional heated class discussion. Down here, I'm too new to know how people see me and too culture shocked to know how to start any kind of conversation about that.

I especially don't know what to do about the fact that some people see me as black—as I am, proudly so—but assume that means I'm African American. Especially in the South, being African American comes with its own complicated set of experiences. It's confusing and strange, to be seen and assigned a history at a glance by people who might not bother to take the time to get to know me. At least it makes me remember that I should never assume I know everything about anyone, but that's a minor consolation in the face of a big, complex issue.

When Doyle pulls the cap off his head, he inspects it like it's a foreign object he's never seen before. "Does it get *you* riled up?"

He asks an honest question, and he wants to know my honest answer, but I don't know *how* I feel.

"I only meant to joke with ya. Rebels and Yanks. I didn't mean... I never meant to offend you, Nes."

Watching Doyle search for words is like watching an expert juggler fumble. I nab the hat by the bill and throw it on.

"I guess if I never even noticed the stupid mascot the dozen times I passed it in that hellhole of a school, I've got no business crying about it now."

His face droops with relief, and I'm happy to let it all go and sink into some good old-fashioned fun fit for all races and regions. Doyle grabs a cooler out of the back of his truck and explains that anybody with real skill plays on the school's official team. This is just a bunch of "slackers who like to horse around and drink the beer Lonzo's small-time crook cousin provides for a steep finder's fee."

"Sounds perfect." I crack open the can he hands me and drink a few swallows.

"Everybody!" Doyle yells as we approach the diamond. A few people already have cans of beer in their hands, some have cigarettes, all wave. "This is Nes. She's new here, but she comes from Brooklyn and her last name is Pujols."

"You sure we want a Yank on the field?" asks Alonzo from English. Now that I see him standing at full height, I realize he's at least six and a half feet tall. His dark skin shines in the blaring sun, and his teeth are so white, they look almost blue. I gulp for words like a fish out of water, trying to decide whether or not he's teasing. "Nah, nah, I'm just messing with you, all right? Wanna be on my team?" He holds out his hand. "I never introduced myself all formal-like. Pleased to meet you, ma'am. I'm Alonzo Washington."

"Don't you dare try to nab my star player, Lonzo." Doyle throws an arm over my shoulders, and I know a pretend-casual stake on a claim when I feel it pull me tight.

"Are you any good?" I ask Alonzo.

He presses his hand to his chest and his mouth is a perfect O. "Me? I'm not just good. I'm the *best*."

"How can I turn that down? You better have the moves to back up all this swagger, Lonzo."

Doyle's mouth steels in a grim line. "All right. Desert me in my hour of need, then."

"Be on our team too," I suggest.

"Nah. Me and Lonzo're the only two who can hold our liquor. These fools'll be sloppy by the third inning." He turns and calls, "Teams!" And I'm not remotely shocked when two pretty girls flock his way first. He introduces Amanda and Destiny to me like they're the reigning queens of backyard baseball.

"Who we waiting on? Braelynn coming, or she still butt-hurt I called out Queen A?" Alonzo yells.

Khabria walks through the fence, face bent over her phone, and swats at Alonzo's arm without looking up. He yelps and pouts, but when he can see she doesn't give a rat's ass, he stops.

"Runnin' your mouth again?" Khabria slides her phone into her pocket and shakes back her hair.

"Just tellin' it like it is." Alonzo makes a big show of looking over both Khabria's shoulders. "Where's your barnacle?"

"Shut up." The words are fierce, but she chuckles around them. "Delivery runs. And if you give him an ounce of hell, I swear I'll poison your chow mein next time you order."

"Ice-cold." Alonzo pretend shivers.

I suppress a groan when I see someone familiar making her way to the field. It's Generic Mean Girl Number Two.

Alonzo waves his arms over his head. "Braelynn! Did Ansley let you outta your closet tonight? You ain't gonna turn into a pumpkin, right?"

"Real funny, Lonzo." Braelynn's scowl is so intense, it's blinding. Then she turns to me, and I realize I ain't seen nothing yet. "Oh. You're here."

"This is our homegirl *Nes*, and if you don't wanna play with her, *you* can leave." Lonzo crosses his arms and stands at my shoulder.

"Me?" Braelynn jerks a thumb at her peach Simply Southern tank top, a few shades lighter than her orangey spray tan. "I don't intend to mess with no one tonight." She pulls out her cell phone and taps away.

"Secret messages to your handler?" Lonzo stage whispers.

"Screw off," Braelynn hisses as she and Khabria mosey to right field, heads bent close.

Doyle jogs back over to our huddle. "Ansley gonna show?" His mouth twists.

"Naw." Lonzo waves a long arm. "She's waiting for you to call and 'pologize for hurting her feelings."

"Yeah, she can go on and keep waitin' for that." Doyle's expression sours into a frown.

"Forget her. I never got what you saw in that chick anyhow." Lonzo winks at me. "C'mon, Nes. Ready to watch me strike this joker out?"

"I'm beyond ready to see Doyle Rahn taken down a peg or five." I slide the mitt over my hand and try not to worry that it swims on my fingers. This game is fun… I remind my competitive edge.

"Ooh, hear that, Doyle? Your sweetheart wants to see you eat clay!"

Doyle practice-swings a bat like he's starring in a Powerade commercial. He points it to the distant gray patch of woods.

"Can you pitch?"

"I've played baseball once every gym cycle since third grade. I'm probably not the person you want as your pitcher." I throw my hands up, and the leather mitt arcs into the air. Alonzo tucks and rolls, sticks one hand up, catches my mitt, then jogs back and hands it to me with a low bow. "Holy crap. I think Alonzo should pitch."

Doyle scowls in the face of Lonzo's physical prowess. "Damn show-off. Imma make you run."

"Do your worst, Rahn." Alonzo swaggers onto the improvised mound, tossing and catching his mitt without taking his eyes off Doyle's. "If you spent half as much time practicing ball as you do running your mouth, we'd all be watching you at Turner Field."

"Nes, go center. I'll hit one right to you." Doyle winks. "Lonzo, get ready to duck, 'cause this ball's makin' a beeline for your fat ole head."

"Come at me, beau." Lonzo claps. "Khabria, Braelynn, double up in left. You know Doyle can't keep straight!"

"I'm always center!" Khabria yells back, sloshing beer from her red Solo cup onto her hand.

"Aw, don't ruin Doyle's date any more than he already did. He wants his girly center!"

"I'm not his girly!" I wave arms over my head like I'm signaling for a plane to land. "I'll go...wherever."

"Doyle, you serious?" Khabria drinks several swallows from the cup, tosses it aside, and burps. The field erupts into laughter as she wipes her mouth. "Hell, son, you never heard of dinner? Or the movies?" The cackles grow louder and Doyle rolls his eyes.

"Seriously. I'm not... We're not a thing!" I'd might as well be screaming into the abyss.

"C'mon, quit raggin'." Braelynn hikes her tank up and knots it in the back, sweeps her long red hair into a high ponytail, and slides on aviator sunglasses. "Maybe they just wanna play some ball."

It's on the tip of my tongue to thank Braelynn for defending me against all this third-grade "Doyle and Nes sitting in a tree" ribbing.

"We all know what Doyle's like when he really cares 'bout a girl. Remember how he filled Ansley's Jeep with roses last Valentine's?" Her announcement is met with awkward shuffling.

And I'm glad I held off on the thank-yous.

I march to the cooler, grab another beer, and toss it back

faster than Khabria chugged hers. "How about we quit running our mouths and play some ball?" I crush the can, toss it, and stalk back to center.

"I love that idea." The heat of Doyle's eyes burns me from across the field.

"Play ball!" The catcher yells the words around the wad of gunk tucked in his bottom lower lip and lets off a fine spray of dark brown mist as he does.

In the center of the diamond, Alonzo contorts himself into all kinds of yoga-inspired shapes. Doyle shuffles his feet over home plate and taps the bat against his boot soles impatiently.

"When you're done with the gymnastics, we got a game to play," Doyle gripes.

"All right, all right." Lonzo shakes his shoulders out and palms the ball in one full rotation before he turns to me. "Keep that mitt up, Nes. I usually strike this clown out, but Imma let him take a taste today. Seein' his girl take him down on this sad excuse for a date's gonna make my weekend!"

Doyle adjusts the brim of his cap and adjusts his stance, then narrows his eyes at Lonzo, who pulls back and whips the ball straight down the plate. At the last second, Doyle straightens up and yawns.

"What was that?" Lonzo's goofiness melts away as the ball smacks into the catcher's mitt with a clean thump.

"Strike one!" The catcher spits into a jagged-edged can that's just begging to give someone tetanus.

"Doyle, you better hit the next ball." Lonzo points his mitt and waits for Doyle to return to position before he lets another ball sail, this one a little wobbly, but still clean over the plate. Doyle stands and leans his weight on the bat like it's a cane. His smug grin elicits a scream of frustration from Alonzo.

"Strike two!"

Some members of the outfield boo and chant, *"Struggling!"* and "No batter, no batter, *swing*, batter, batter!" in various states of drunken slur.

"You asshole! Imma throw you a curveball that's gonna knock you on your conceited ass, you hear me?"

Doyle rocks his neck, points to his eyes then at me, and blows a kiss. I blame the tingle that floats up my spine on the fizzy beer I chugged.

Alonzo doesn't need to yell directions to any of the disorganized boozehounds scattered across the outfield. Doyle's flagrant disregard for the sanctity of this admittedly ragtag game leaves everyone hungry to see him go down. The intensity directed toward home plate is nuclear.

The ball sails out of Lonzo's hands on an impossible-to-hit curve, but Doyle swings like it's all in slow motion for him. The crack of the bat shudders through the air, sending a flock of roosting birds cawing into the orange sky. Every outfielder stampedes, desperate to ensure Doyle's out. But that damn ball sails straight for me.

I'm fairly athletic, but I have no stomach for high-stakes situations involving missile-like projectiles. Panic forces me to shut down. I raise up my mitt to prevent traumatic brain injury, duck, and close my eyes. The thwack of the ball against the leather palm is more shocking than a concussion would have been.

Everything goes completely still, then the field ignites with cheers and whoops. Even Braelynn high-fives my mitt. "*Girl*, that was badass!"

"Woo, baby, that's one way to pay that fool back for not taking you to Red Lobster. This girl earned herself some cheddar biscuits!" Khabria hoots.

My legs shake like a newborn colt's. To my horror, the ball

rolls out of my glove with a thud. I swoop to grab it and wonder if I'll lose the goodwill my surprise catch earned me…

I zero in on Doyle.

Leaning against the chain-link, jawing to the catcher, arms crossed, winner's smile on his loser face.

"Hey!" I bypass Alonzo's high five on my march over the mound to home base. "What the hell was that? Why didn't you run?"

"'Cause I knew you'd catch it." He pulls his hat brim up. "And looky there." He tugs the ball out of my hand and spins it in his fingers. "You did it."

"You didn't know I would though." But I'm not sure.

"Yeah." He tosses the ball back to Lonzo without looking away from me. "I did."

My desire to kiss him mud-wrestles my desire to punch him in his smug mouth.

"Cheater."

"A cheater'd be 'a person who acts dishonestly to gain advantage.' That's Webster's words, not even mine." His pupils grow dark and wolfish.

I bare my teeth. "You're going down, Rahn. Don't underestimate me."

"I never do." He leans close and swoops back the second my breath catches, then strolls to the bench.

The next few batters don't hit any balls in my vicinity, so I mostly stare down Doyle from across the field, plotting his demise.

A steep incline in alcohol consumption leaves my team stumbling to the bench for our second turn at bat. I follow the herd and combo smile/nod at everyone, because I can't keep track of names. The alcohol has left me floaty. I'm second at bat, following a quiet girl with buckteeth named Kelwanda

144

Smith, who Lonzo tells me will be Ebenezer's valedictorian. Doyle pitches an easy third ball to her, then takes his time catching so she can make it to first. When I step to the plate, his eyes gleam with pure evil.

"Bring 'em in! C'mon, clowns, come in. Easy out!" He waves in the couple flirting at center field, the daydreaming left fielder, and the first baseman who alternates between squatting low and ready and tipping over drunkenly.

I practice swing and, encouraged by Lonzo's cheers, point with my bat into the indeterminate distance. "Quit yapping and pitch already, Doyle!"

"Woo hoo!" he hoots. "You hearin' this, Lonzo? I was jest gonna deal with this Yank, but I figure your whole team needs to be taken down a peg." He nods to me, crouches low, snaps his arm back, and hurls a ball so twisty, it knocks the catcher and his can of sticky brown muck into the dust.

I hop back before that pitch comes near me, and Lonzo screams at Doyle, but I shake my head. "Forget it, Lonzo. I can take this fool. Don't hit me, Doyle! I wanna knock it out of the park, not limp to first."

My teammates stomp and chant my name. Between Solo-cup slurps, Khabria and Braelynn even improvise a cheer dance that's surprisingly polished. The catcher tosses the ball back, and Doyle winds up to shoot a second blip of a pitch, which curves slightly left. I nick it with the tip of my bat, and it pops in a high arc that would have landed directly in the second baseman's mitt if she was anywhere near second base.

Luckily she was chain-smoking and practicing handstands, so she's scrambling while Kelwanda books it past second to third, and I'm hot on her trail. She's already rounding home while the outfield fumbles the ball in the general direction of third base, and I try to determine if I should nab third.

I'm halfway between second and third when Handstand Girl scoops and tosses, so I slide. This isn't the soft orange clay I'm used to. My outer thigh skids along a patch of uneven sand, and my toe catches on a grass lump before I roll and...

"*Safe!* Damn, girl, that was a helluva slide!" The catcher screams around the lump of chew in his cheek.

Doyle bolts my way, mitt, beer can, and ball cap abandoned on the mound. "You okay? Nes?" He turns me back and forth by my hips, and our fingers knot as we swipe at the dirt on my legs.

"I'm fine, Doyle." I hold out my arms and turn around. "Just a little bruised. I'm not made out of sugar."

His twilight eyes sweep over my grass-stained shorts and shirt, and he runs a hand through his golden hair, wavy from the sticky Georgia heat. "Don't know 'bout that. I had a lick. Thought you tasted pretty damn sweet." He grins and points back to the mound. "Lonzo's up. He's gonna pop it outta here." He jogs backward, his grin pure cockiness. "I'm tagging you out."

My left big toe barely touches the edge of third base as I stretch my right leg as close to home as possible. "I hope you don't mind disappointment."

"Don't know. Got no experience with it." He calls for a beer. The catcher tosses him one, which he tosses to me.

"I'm half-Irish, Doyle. You're not gonna win this by getting me drunk!" I crack the beer and chug it defiantly as my teammates cheer, stopping only when I hear Doyle's low whistle.

"You sure you know which direction you're headed if Lonzo actually hits this?" he teases. He holds out a hand to catch another beer, drinks this one, crushes it, and drops the crumpled can. I'm swimmy, but his words burn clear and bright. "Leveling the playing field. Jest me and you." He winks at me like a cocky idiot, and I stick my tongue out at him. Childish? Yes. Satisfying? Deeply so.

I want to focus on the game, but I have a sudden urge to pee that's so intense, my thoughts are sloshing around between my ears. I promise myself that when I round home, I will find somewhere—anywhere—to go.

Doyle winds up and throws a clean pitch, and Alonzo's bat cracks the ball with thunderous force. I can't count on the out-field fumbling this ball. They're out to prove themselves after their last disastrous performance.

Handstand runs the ball down like she's in flames and that ball is her icy bucket of water. She scoops it up smoothly, and Doyle waves for her to throw it as he hops in my path. I run like my life depends on getting to home base. The ball sails over my head, and Doyle positions himself in the path directly between me and home, his mitt up and ready.

I attempt to pass him, but the alcohol has dulled my coordi-nation, and I wind up bashing into his side. He twirls around and pivots back in front of me. I hear the thwack of the ball against his mitt as I knock him off balance and topple on top of him, my fingers stretched out to brush home just as he's grazing my ass with the tip of his mitt.

"Out!" The catcher spits a long, sticky stream of tobacco juice to punctuate his call.

Alonzo screams from second base. "Are you kidding me, Walsh? Are you for real? Rahn didn't smack her ass with that ball till *after* she touched the base!"

Handstand Girl jumps in to holler that she *clearly* saw Doyle tap me before, and Kelwanda throws down her mitt and tells Handstand Girl she would punch her in the face, but she has a rule against hitting blind kids. Braelynn records the two of them on her phone, and Khabria giggles as she tries to stay upright against the chain-link, a few of her braids stuck in the diamond cross sections. Another girl heads over to untangle her.

Doyle laces his arms around my waist. "So, how you doin'?"

"Just fine, hanging out safe on home, fair and square." I bat my lashes.

He presses the bill of my cap back. "Walsh called you out, girl. Don't you know when to quit?"

"Never." I wiggle to get off him. It's hard to ignore how good our bodies feel pressed together. "I need to pee in the worst way."

"Breaking your seal this early? Sure you wanna do that?"

"Who says this is early?" Once I stand, all the fluid in my body rushes to my bladder. I need to find a place five minutes ago. "Maybe I'm on my way out."

"We're jest going into the third inning," Doyle argues, and we both look at the field. A few seconds ago, it sounded like a vicious brawl was about to break out, but it resolved itself fast.

I'm no detective, but I'd say the quick resolution had something to do with fresh cans of beer and Handstand Girl getting everyone to trade their mitts and bats and balls for a clumsy impromptu gymnastics exhibition.

"Looks like baseball has been trumped by cartwheels." I fix my cap and bob up and down like a toddler.

"Cartwheels," Doyle scoffs. His scorn doesn't stop him from admiring the girls turning cartwheel after cartwheel in the prickly grass.

"I should head home."

"Hell no. The night's young. Even if those fools don't wanna play ball like good 'mericans, you and I gotta do something. At least till the streetlights come on. You can't go in before the kiddies do." He tilts his head. "C'mon. I know a bunch of bushes you can go behind."

"No way." I'm no prude, but I will happily walk the couple hundred feet to my street and use a toilet. "It was fun. I left your mitt right by Lonzo's on the bench."

"All right. Lonzo'll grab any stray balls and mitts and keep 'em till the next game. There's a nice as hell bathroom right back there." He points to a building that's no closer than my house, but no farther either. "Whadda ya say... You wanna take care of business and watch the sun set with me?"

It's a simple question, and it demands a simple answer.

But the longer I'm around Doyle Rahn, the more complicated even the simplest things become.

ELEVEN

"**L**ead on."

I'm not ready to leave him yet. Plus who doesn't love watching the sun set?

When we get to the low building, Doyle looks in both directions before he takes a key out of his wallet and opens the locked bathroom door.

"You have a key to the neighborhood bathroom?"

"And pool and weight room. And conference center. It's all in the same complex." He tucks the key back in his wallet and tosses me a shameless Artful Dodger pickpocket smile. "What? I like a clean restroom when I'm done tryin' to keep all these scrawny suburban trees alive. The idiots always leave the key under the mat. Practically begging me to steal it."

"Criminal," I declare. He bows like I gave him a compliment.

In the bathroom I catch a glimpse of myself in the mirror, my dirty face streaked with sweat, my hair exploded out of my ponytail holder and hanging loose over my forehead, the little bit of mascara I gooped on this morning streaked under my eyes.

If I'd been with Lincoln, I would have rushed to fix myself. With Doyle, it feels like this dirty version of me is just fine.

That said, I still take a few paper towels and wipe the grit from my face, then rub my fingers under my eyes to smear the mascara into something resembling smoky eyeliner. And I pinch my cheeks the way my abuela always does to get some color.

Because *I* like this reflection better. *Hevi nais.* I smile as I push open the door.

"Ready?" Doyle offers me his elbow and we walk past the ball field full of amateur gymnasts. Half have devolved from cartwheels to forward rolls, the other half sip beer and watch the sun turn the sky rose gold.

"You need another beer?" I ask to open the possibility of going back to his crew.

"Nah. Two or three are okay, but I'm not about getting bombed." He leads me around a turn and we walk past elaborately gabled brick-faced houses with dark windows and waist-high weeds, for-sale signs pitched in the yards. He motions for me to sit next to him on a porch railing. There's a perfect view of the sunset from here. "This was pasture when I was a kid."

"Like cows?" I let my hair down from the ponytail, even though the air is still sticky. The slowly setting sun tricks me into thinking the unrelenting heat will let up. It never does. Day is like an oven with the light clicked on, night is the same oven with the light clicked off.

"Like *herds* of cows. And some chickens. Not many trees though."

We look at the grass, stained setting-sun orange, and I try to imagine the idyllic presubdivision pasture scene.

"Pretty stupid that they got rid of the pasture to build houses no one wants to live in anyway." I flick my eyes over the rows of gold-hued houses, still clean and neat, but leaning another fraction of an inch toward decay every passing day.

"To accommodate the Yankee swells." He gestures to the neglected homes with a sweep of his hand.

"Seriously with the Yankee stuff again?" I knew there was a whole Southern pride thing before I came here, but this is crazy. "When I told people I was moving to Georgia, no one talked about rebels."

Granted, the few people I did tell warned me about shitty school systems, poverty, and racism, which—honestly—seemed like accurate worries to me.

"Maybe I should've said it different," he amends. "They got built for the *people from the North* looking for cheap houses when the economy tanked. Guess no one sent them the memo that it tanked down here too."

"It may have tanked here, but it's still way less expensive than New York City."

"Makes sense." Doyle kneels down and inspects what looks to me like a weed. The gentle way he touches it makes me wonder if I'm wrong or if Doyle just loves things that grow so much, no green thing registers as a weed to him. "E'rybody knows city life's expensive. Guess I never really thought about regular people living in big cities. Jest imagined lots of doctors and lawyers and stockbrokers."

"It's not easy." I grimace. "Our apartment wasn't too bad because my parents bought it when the neighborhood was still up-and-coming. But jobs at my mother's university were super hard to come by, and she kind of had to take what she could get. Down here, she's the head of the American studies department. She was only an adjunct in the city."

"No kidding?" Doyle massages the leaves of the little brown

plant like he's trying to do plant CPR. "I didn't know your ma was a professor. No wonder you're so smart."

"I'm smart because I'm smart."

Guilt twists in my gut. I've been so busy being furious at my mother for uprooting us, I never considered what an amazing career move this was. We honestly haven't talked about details a ton, but she mentioned the other professors are friendly—though it wouldn't be hard for them to be nicer than the total jerks she worked with back home. She drives a car to work instead of battling crowds on the subway. Our generic house is so much bigger and nicer than our drafty, cramped apartment. We even have a *pool*. Talk about moving on up.

I've been consumed with whining about how I've gone from heaven to hell (or at least purgatory), but this move has been the reverse for my mother.

We wander off the porch once the horizon swallows the last pink rays of sunset, and I kick at some loose sidewalk cement, sidling so close to him, I can smell the tang of aftershave mixed with the sharp burst of sweaty guy and a general good, clean scent that's just Doyle.

"I guess people down here are bummed by so many transplants. I get how it could be weird."

"People here've been bummed 'bout change for the last three hundred years." Doyle leads me through a backyard to my own fence. "Screw them if they say a Brooklyn accent's like listenin' to nails on a chalkboard."

"Who said that?"

But he's already hopped the fence. I guess this is what we do now. Avoid kisses and jump fences all day long.

He gives me a hand getting over and we weave around lawn chairs and potted palms to sit at the edge of my pool.

"Nobody who knows what good-sounding really is. Now, me? Can't get enough of that accent, myself."

His undeniably romantic statement hangs in the air as he peels off his shirt, unbuckles his jeans, and kicks off his boots. He's in one sock with his belt loose in its loops when I finally snap out of staring at all of him, tanned and strong and surrounded by the buzz of tiny insects that must be biting him, though he's not swatting them away.

"What are you doing?" I ask around my suddenly fat tongue.

"Swimmin'. Finally made a rich friend who has this big ole pool. Let's use it." He slides his belt off and drops it on his clothes pile as he nods to me. "Your mama won't mind, will she?"

I wonder if Mom's in a wine coma. "Wait here. I need to get my bathing suit." I don't look when I hear the drop of Doyle's jeans, even though I want to.

Unfamiliar shadows spook me when I open the door and walk through the living room. I call out, "Mom?" My distorted voice echoes back off the vaulted ceilings.

I'm primed for another confrontation. Worst case, Mom's sprawled on the couch, an empty wine bottle twisting on the floor in a lonely game of spin the bottle. I rush to the kitchen and am temporarily blinded when I flick the light on. A Post-it is stuck to the fridge. "Went to the movies with the girls in the Italian department. Be home late. Love you. Mom." She signed her name with a sloppy heart.

"'The movies'?" I mutter, fingers pressed to the note. "'The girls in the Italian department'? Random. Guess I should be glad your date isn't a kinky married freak."

I head to my room, wrestle into my red bikini, and ignore the empty couch and vacant kitchen as I fly out back and swan dive into the pool. Underwater, the fury of my racing thoughts is muffled into bubbles that erupt silently out of my mouth. I float to the surface just as Doyle cannonballs next to me.

We tangle around each other underwater, his fingers jabbing my eye accidentally, my heel kicking his stomach without meaning to. Then we both push to the surface and break through, gasping out laughs and pressing our hair away from our faces.

"You wanna race?" His voice is all cocky sweetness.

"Again?" I bluff uncertainty to throw him off my scent, because I'm *so* winning this round.

My abuela lives next to an apartment building with a gorgeous pool, and the doormen (who loves her *and* the fresh-baked *deditos de novias* she brings over) always let us use it while they gobbled up every single powdered-sugar-covered cookie.

I am an *exceptional* swimmer.

"Two laps?" he offers, like he's afraid I'll be winded after that.

Snort.

I bite my lip. It's a total farce, and his self-assured smile tells me he buys it…hook, line, and sinker.

Our fingers curl on the pool's edge and we brace our feet against the wall as he counts back from three. I even give him a second's head start because that's how sure I am of my body slicing through this water like a hot knife through a big stick of yellow butter.

The water caresses me, up and down, under and over my limbs until I'm part of every bubbling molecule. My strokes break through the water, strong and focused. When I pull out in front of Doyle, I'm jostled by his splashes, a last-ditch effort to gain on me.

He can't.

I win and wait with my arms resting on the edge of the

pool, cheek on my hand like I popped out of the water hours before him instead of seconds.

"You some kinda mermaid for real?" Doyle ducks back under and tunnels through the wavering water until he's close enough to grab my ankles and drag me away from the ledge. I have just enough time to hold my breath before I plunge down with him into the silent, cool underwater world where I'm strongest.

We circle each other, splashing until I'm surprised the pool's not half-empty, and brush up, silky wet skin on silky wet skin. It's got to be exactly what swimming in a pool of electric eels feels like: disarming, jolting, and a little scary.

When Doyle finally drags himself onto the concrete patio, he's gasping. "Holy hell, Nes. You're not tired?"

I shake my head, catch water between my hands, and squirt him right over the heart. "I could swim for hours."

"I could watch ya swim for hours." He links his fingers together behind his head and lies in a half-crunch position he has to know shows off every ab.

And he has many.

Six at least, each more glorious than the last.

Even submerged in water, my skin burns and tingles like I'm standing under a heat lamp. "So, do I get my own four-wheeler next week?"

His wide smile suffocates a full laugh. "Not ATVs, Nes. We're going mudding. Trucks."

"You're taking your truck out?" I swim between his legs. His boxer briefs are drying fast in the hot night, and, even though it's ridiculous and rude to look, look I do. It's hard not to when there's a lot to see.

"Sure am. Me, you, my truck." He wraps his legs around my back, heels just above my tailbone, and tugs me so close, my arms rest on the hard muscle of his thighs. "Lots and lots of mud. Basically it's as close to heaven as I can imagine."

"So, what's the point of this again?" My voice is admirably even, considering how my heart attempts to kickbox out of my chest.

"Point?" Doyle scoffs. "What's the point of two innings of drunk baseball?"

"That's an excellent question, actually. What *was* the point of that?" I nestle against him and suck in a breath when his gaze drops down and follows the stray water droplets that skim underneath my bikini top.

"The point? *Fun*, Nes. Damn, you need so much fun education, it ain't even funny." His heels pull against the small of my back and his knees squeeze my sides.

"I know how to have fun." It comes out as suggestive as I was afraid it would. I want to keep going, suggest we get wild, peel off our swimsuits, and jump back in the water where we could swim until dawn.

I stop myself from making those suggestions.

Lincoln pulverized my heart, and Georgia is just a blip on my timeline before I go home. The pulpy mess of an organ knocking around in my chest doesn't need any more trauma at this juncture. I lock both feet against the side of the pool and push off with all the strength in my legs, breaking Doyle's hold on me. He flops back like I shot him through the heart, and I do two laps, breaststroke, then kid myself into believing my heart is thundering from cardio, not Doyle.

I drag myself out of the water after the third lap, my muscles on fire. He's already fully dressed, his damp hair still pushed off his forehead.

"You're leaving?" My heart sinks like a stone chucked in the pool. He can't stay here all night. I can't sneak him in the way I used to sneak Lincoln in, and let him do things to me I used to let Lincoln do…but better. Possibly.

Probably.

The possessive way he looks at me, the honest things that spill so easily from his mouth, the way he touches me—respectfully, but with a wild undercurrent—all make me think being with him would be everything I never realized I wanted.

My brain is a basketball dribbling against the inside of my skull.

"I got some stuff to get done before we head out next weekend. I had to pull some major strings to get so many weekend days off, and my cousin's making me pay." He twists the Yankees cap so the brim is backward and looks at me like he wants to say something. At the last second his eyes shutter like he changed his mind. "C'mere."

I'm a puppet on his string. I don't care; I just *want*.

He wraps his arms around me and hugs me tight. We fit against each other—bumping knees, damp hips, freckled shoulders. "You wish on stars?"

"Just look at them. And make up constellations that don't exist." My voice creaks.

His blond lashes tangle at the corners when he closes his eyes. He leans in and rolls his forehead against mine. "I'm gonna wish."

"Okay." I let my nose brush the prickly stubble of his cheek. "Isn't it bad luck to tell?"

"Nah." He drags his lips slowly along my jawline until I whimper. "I wish…" He takes his time nuzzling the sensitive skin under my ear and whispers, "I wish I thought you lost that race on purpose."

"I didn't," I stutter, eyes closed, head tilted back, wanting to feel his mouth on my neck.

"I know that. I wish I didn't know, 'cause I'd've kissed you. But you got this plan to leave, and I don't think I'm gonna be okay gettin' left by you. Goddamn, I never wanted a single thing in my life the way I wanna kiss you right now."

Are my lungs processing air? Are my veins transporting blood? Are my organs functioning the way they should be, or are they failing me? All my body registers is the feel of Doyle's hands, one spread wide on my back, his calloused palm warm and rough over my spine, and one tucked around my neck, his fingers laced through my hair, his thumb rubbing that tingling spot just under my ear.

His hands pull away. His mouth follows. And I ache.

My eyes flutter open as Doyle vaults the fence, and I listen to the thump of his boots as he runs back to his truck, away from me, toward the next time I wish was right now already.

TWELVE

I need to hash out every detail of this whole date/not date with someone I trust, but there's a problem.

I've been calling Ollie since Doyle left almost an hour ago, and she hasn't answered me yet. Which is weird. No texts back, no videos of kittens stuck in tissue boxes or impromptu collaborative orchestras arranged by Austrians in old-world squares. *Nothing.*

My secondary fear—which I fully realize is based on binge watching too many crime dramas—is that Olls is dead and no one knew how to give me the news gently, so it went undelivered.

My primary fear—the one that claws me raw because of its probability—is that Ollie's just busy. Too busy living her life. Without me.

I know she's doing normal stuff: making out, wailing on her bassoon, drinking her parents' wine with Toni or Lotte—girls who were fine subsidiary friends when Olls and I were a unit. They're now competitors who are encroaching on my Ollie territory.

Which I'm reluctant to admit may not be very *mine* anymore.

Then, like magic, my phone rings, and I'm excited…

Until I see the picture on the screen.

"Jasper!" I whine over his laugh.

"Bonjour, petite soeur. Où est notre mère?" Jasper is a full-fledged Parisian, every twist in his accent is *parfait*. My Spanish is decent, but my French is spotty at best. Any other teen would be applauded for bilingualism, but I have to come from a family of linguistic brainiacs.

"Je ne sais pas. Je ne m'inquiète pas." That sums up my present truth: I don't know where our mother is, and I don't care.

"Ne sois pas une enfante," Jasper chides. My brother thinks I constantly act like a toddler, but I think he's been acting like a curmudgeon since he was in elementary school.

"Pas plus de français," I bite out, asking him to switch out of French so we can communicate in the language I argue in best. I'm not about to be aggravated *and* searching for the right French word to use against my aggravating brother.

"Fine," he sighs. "Your accent is terrible. You need to converse more, Aggie. How's your Spanish? Is Mama Patria still letting you answer her in English?"

"No te preocupe, to'ta frío," I say, imitating our aspiring-DJ cousin, Antony, from DR, who manages to drive Jasper crazy every time he opens his mouth.

"Tu si eres baboso," he says, accusing me of talking crap.

"Y tu hiede a chinchilín." Yes, it's immature and inaccurate to tell him he stinks, but Jasper truly brings out the bratty little sister in me.

"You really need to work on something other than insults and slang, Ag. Our baby cousins could speak better than you when we went to the Santo Domingo last year."

"When did you become the commandant of languages?" I gripe. "Do you know how many Dominican friends I had who spoke no Spanish? Stop acting like I'm bringing shame on all Dominican Americans. Isn't it, like—" I pull my phone back and check the international clock "—two in the morning your time? Is something wrong?"

"You really have moved to the backwoods. I didn't even eat dinner yet here. Nothing's wrong. I just missed my *maman* and baby sister. Is that okay?" Jasper clears his throat. "So, you're really going to graduate from high school in Georgia?" He says the state name with the same horror people use when they say *Gulag labor camp* or *Siberian prison*.

"What choice do I have?" I fall back on my bed and kick my heels on the mattress like I used to when I threw a tantrum as a kid. I'm too old to do that kind of crap anymore, but sometimes I wish I wasn't.

"You could live with Mama Patria, like we all thought you were going to. Finish at Newington."

"That was an impossible commute, Jasper. Everyone's saying this is the worst winter in decades. That means spring storms too. I wouldn't have gotten back to her place until after dark… Not safe. Trust me, if there was a way, I'd be there. I would've loved to have finished at Newington. It just wasn't possible."

"I know you think Newington's just some artsy little school, but competition to get into that place is pretty fierce. A diploma from there would mean a lot."

I actually check to see if I accidentally put my phone on mute.

"Right, but I *can't graduate from Newington.*" *Plunk, bounce, plunk, bounce.* My ankles hit the mattress and bounce off the springs over and over. "Don't worry. A diploma from Ebenezer High won't tank my bright, shiny future."

I wish Jasper would accidentally put *his* phone on mute.

"Aggie…" My brother wears his older sibling responsibility like an albatross around his neck. You'd think getting himself through one of NYC's premier high schools, then getting accepted into the Ivy Leagues, and *then* to the mythical Sorbonne would have been enough for one crazy overachiever, but no. He's got to take the rudder on my life too.

"Jasper, I'm going to be fine. I'm not even sure I'm *going* straight to college. Maybe I'll backpack through Europe for a year or something."

I was wrong. There *is* something that relieves stress better than kicking my mattress: poking at my big brother.

"*Jésus*, you're not serious? If you want to be a Euro-trash bum, just shack up here. We have an extra room and Dad misses you, Aggie. You've barely called since the move."

"I can't come to France unless I'm enrolled in school. I asked Dad about using his place as a base for a gap year of traveling, and he shot me down cold."

"He worries that if you take a year off, you'll never wind up going to college." Jasper pauses, sighs, and says, "You really need to call Dad. There's something he needs to tell you, and he's stalling."

A stab of panic jolts through me. "Is Dad sick?"

"No, nothing like that... Just, trust me, you need to have a talk with him. Please, call."

"I will." I wonder what the thing Dad needs to talk to me about is, but I'm willing to bet it has to do with college, and I can't listen to that endlessly looped conversation again. I never told him that I didn't apply to any of the Ivies like he asked me to. What was the point when I knew I'd never want to go to any of them?

My father has never accepted that I'm not the academic star Jasper is. Dad truly believes that I'm so much smarter and more capable than I am. I hate to disappoint him, so it's easier to avoid him.

"Good. You two are overdue for a talk. He misses you and Mom. She hasn't been calling much either."

This time, Jasper doesn't even dive into a lecture about what a crappy daughter I am.

He probably knows I'm well aware.

What Jasper seems blind to is what happened between Mom and Dad after our big Thanksgiving trip to Paris. A few weeks before the trip, a guy Mom really liked showed up at the apartment with a bouquet of hydrangeas—her favorite—and she shooed him away. The week before we left, she bought a sexier wardrobe, got her hair done at this incredible salon, and had a new batch of Dad's favorite perfume made. While they were together in the City of Lights, it seemed like… things were going well. Really well.

And then, when it all fell apart for reasons I'm still not clear on, that weasel was waiting. The night our plane landed she went out with some faculty. I thought it was crazy she'd go out that jet-lagged, but also kind of badass. And good for her.

She didn't come home until morning. Wash, rinse repeat for a week…and then one fat-fingered digital mistake and… *bam*. Life unraveled fast and hard.

What happened between Thanksgiving and New Year's? What part did my father play? I don't want to call him and find out I have reason to be pissed at him too. It's exhausting enough being so furious at Mom.

"Right. Well, with the time difference and all…"

He keeps his mouth shut, but the guilt gnaws at me.

I think about all the rage I'm directing at my mother. I don't want to get all armchair psychologist on myself, but it occurs to me that she might not deserve all the anger I'm throwing her way.

People screw up. Daughters who love their fathers don't

reach out and call. Best friends don't keep in touch like they should. A girl might be falling head over heels for a solid, good guy, but she pushes him away instead of opening up, because it's all so damn scary.

"You know Dad's a night owl. That's one of the only things the four of us have in common." My brother takes optimism to stupid levels.

"Right. Only there isn't any 'four of us' anymore." I attempt to deflate his stupid shiny happy bubble, which is only fair since he's always trying to get me to "wake up," "live in the real world," "get my head out of the clouds," yada yada.

"Of course there is," he insists. "It doesn't matter that they're divorced or with other people or whatever. They'll always be our parents. We'll always be a family. And we're lucky our parents actually acted like adults when they split. That's pretty rare."

"You've got some crazy rose-colored glasses on, Jasper."

"You need to get out of this emo stage you're in. It's getting old fast." I hear a female voice in the background, all sex, cigarettes, and whiskey, telling my brother something about a reservation and a dog.

"Are you going on a date? Do you have a girlfriend? Do you have a dog?" I demand.

"*Chêne*, not *chien*. *Jésus-Christ*, Aggie, bone up on your French. And your Spanish, while you're at it. And try not to pick up a drawl. You're not some Southern belle."

"*Baise ton chien,*" I singsong.

"Right. But I don't have a dog to fuck, so no can do, sis. As always, it was lovely talking to you. Maybe next time you can leave out the bestiality, and we can have a nice conversation. Also..." He lets out another long sigh.

My brother is fluent in four languages: English, Spanish, French, and dramatic sighs.

"What? What's wrong now?"

"Make *sure* you send information about your graduation so we can book flights. I assume they do that, right? Have graduation ceremonies? They *do* do the whole cap and gown thing?"

It's like I can see Jasper rolling his eyes across the world when he asks that.

"You better believe it, sugar. It's just the biggest ole celebration with lots of peach cobbler and collard greens and sweet tea. Y'all should come see." I lather the Southern accent on as thick as I can. It still sounds way too Brooklyn, but Jasper gasps on the other end.

"Don't *do that*. Even joking." He pauses. "I'm excited to see you. I miss you. Are you still coming to Santo Domingo this summer with Dad and...me?"

For a second I could've sworn Jasper was going to say something else. Maybe Mom? "I'm going to Vietnam with Ollie this summer, but I'd like to go to Santo Domingo too."

"Mama Patria's going this year," Jasper informs me.

"What?" Our grandmother hasn't been back to the Dominican Republic since her mother's funeral. She's deathly afraid of flying. "Really?"

"Titi Josefina named her new baby after her, so she wants to come for the christening. Dad told her to get some anti-anxiety pills. It would be great if you could fly with her from New York. Think about it. And seriously, call Dad, please. Remember, what you do now matters later, Aggie. Be good."

It's always when he's just about to leave or get off the phone that I miss my brother most. And wish we weren't always bickering. "I'll try. Right back atcha. You and your little dog too."

He chuckles. "Brush up on your language skills while your brain is young and malleable. *Buenos días*."

"*Buenas noches*, Jasper."

I hang up and scroll through my contacts. I come across the smiling face of my father. Seeing a photo of him makes me feel even more guilty for not calling, and it makes me miss my four-person family unit.

When we got home, it was obvious Mom and Dad weren't going to chuck those divorce papers after all. Mama Patria, her dark hair rolled in tight curlers so she'd be ready for midweek mass, growled about Dad's obliviousness as she washed her dishes, clanging the bone china into the wire rack recklessly. At that point she had no idea we were only a few weeks away from leaving the city and our close vicinity to her.

"Emilio obviously still has eyes for your mother. I just don't understand why a nice, hardworking man and a nice, hard-working woman with two gorgeous children call it quits because they need to 'find themselves.' Damn that book! He should have written a boring one no one would have read. A man shouldn't write a memoir until his golden years. *I* should write my memoir. *I've* lived."

I rubbed the dishes dry with a soft old towel decorated with roosters. "I guess Dad missed Paris. He's wanted to go back since he moved to the States before Jasper was born. And Mom said she was happy staying there back when she was finishing her master's, but she loves New York too much to leave for good now."

I had *no clue* then how ironic those words would be a few short weeks later. Or maybe I had no idea how little I actually knew about my mother.

"Paris, New York?" Mama Patria stared at the water streaming out of the tap, her parchment-soft hands a deep, shiny brown against the tiny white sink. "What's the difference? Sometimes I wake up and expect to see the shutters of my abuela's house in Santo Domingo. She had a pomegranate tree right outside with fruit as big as your head." Her voice softened with this longing, then she snapped her head up and clipped back to business mode. "But what good is some fruit if my son and husband can't enjoy it with me?"

"Are you upset Dad moved back to Paris?" I put the dish I was drying aside and reached over to turn the tap off, but Mama Patria swatted my hand.

"I thought you'd all move *together*." She ran a finger over the resin statue of Saint Jude, perpetually blessing the kitchen sink. "Sometimes I think, 'Well, you old witch, you got what you prayed for after all.'"

"What?" I'd never noticed there were tiny pomegranates on my abuela's old plates before.

"I was very proud your father got the department head position, of course, but I was so sad to see him go, and I cried to Jesus about it." She crossed herself, dripping soapsuds down the front of her dress. "Stupid, stupid. You complain about good in your life, you get half-baked answers to your prayers. Now I get to have my beautiful granddaughter and daughter-in-law here with me, but the family is ripped apart." She plunged the clean cups back into the suds and rewashed them just to keep her hands busy.

"Mama Patria, you don't honestly believe your prayer did that, do you?" I leaned on the counter.

"Get off the counter, Aggie. And, yes, I believe in the power of prayer. I also believe God sees." She pointed at the ceiling like He was floating on His cloud above us. "He sees when you're too stupid to accept the blessings you have, and He opens your eyes."

I should have listened instead of laughing it off. Maybe this whole move is my eyes being opened when I want nothing more than to screw them shut.

I flop back on my bed and allow the reality of my own friendless state to wash over me when Ollie fails to answer another attempted call, and I don't get up until I hear my mother's keys in the front door.

Without thinking about it, I skid into the hall. She steps out of her heels and rubs the arch of one foot as she rolls her neck. When she looks up and realizes I'm lurking, she nearly falls over.

"Aggie! Sweetheart. It's late." She clamps her mouth, like she's not sure what to say next.

"I talked to Jasper. He misses you."

Mom's face glows softly. I'm a little jealous that the mention of my brother brings such brimming happiness to my mom when lately, I've seen her look at me with only angst and worry.

"I need to call him. How is he? How's…" Her voice hitches, but she levels it. "How's Dad?"

"I didn't talk to Dad." I lean against the back of the couch as Mom unpins her hair and shakes it out around her pale shoulders. "Jasper just wanted to lecture me. He thinks I'm an idiot for moving down here."

Mom gnaws on her bottom lip. "Aggie, you know I would have been happy if the commute from your abuela's hadn't been impossibly difficult. I *wanted* you to be able to finish at Newington."

"I know." This conversation was implied, but never spoken out loud before.

"I know there wasn't another plausible choice, but I hope this move hasn't been only awful for you." Her voice wobbles as she concentrates on placing her bobby pins up in hyperneat lines around the fallen tulip petals on the entrance table, like some tiny found-art project.

I clear my throat. "I'm happy here."

"Yeah?" Her eyes widen with cautious hope. "Aggie, I never expected it to happen like this, but I always hoped we'd have a home somewhere calmer than New York City. You know how much I loved our old place, but this has been a really peaceful experience for me. I actually have friends at work—interesting women who like me and want to see girly movies and drink sugary pink cocktails."

She's glowing with happiness, and I can't remember the last time I could say that. It dawns on me that my mother's been putting on a brave face while she drowned in stress and, I guess, sadness.

"You look happy." I'm embarrassed I didn't notice before.

"I never expected to want to live somewhere other than New York City. But there's something about the sun, the friendliness, the pace that just makes me…" She closes her eyes. "It just makes me feel *good*."

Something hard and icy cracks inside me.

"Hey, *One Hundred Thousand Beats* had such a huge surge in viewers this last season, they're renewing for another eight episodes. Probably that's, like, really truly it. I heard the head nurse and the slimy neurologist already have parts on other shows. But maybe, if you want…we could catch up on the episodes we didn't watch. I know we, uh, know how it ends up," I mutter, hoping she won't point out *why* we know. "But—"

She abandons her bobby pins and wraps her arms tight around me. "I'd *love* that."

Before anything can unravel or slide back into nastiness, she kisses my temple and tells me she's going to bed. We skip over the usual *sleep tight*s and *I love you*s—it's still a huge step forward.

I sleep more peacefully than I have in a long time and wake up the next morning to Ollie's face on my phone. My heart fist pumps with happiness. There's my bestie, ringing through, and I accept her call like I never doubted her commitment in the first place.

"Morning, sunshine!" she singsongs. "I'm sorry I missed your calls yesterday. Had the phone switched off to rehearse. So, how was baseball? Did you get to second? Did you get to third? Did you get a *home run*?" She cackles and shakes her head. "Damn, those were easy but ultimately unsatisfying jokes. Spill."

"Okay. In literal bases? I made it all the way home!" I'm aware this isn't what Ollie's asking about, but the heady victory of my slide to home—never mind the stupid catcher calling me out—still feels like a cause for celebration.

"Are you seriously talking about the actual sport of baseball right now? No. You shut up about all bases *except* romantic ones, Agnes."

"The closest I came to metaphoric bases was barely first, and that was only on a bet. He backed out." I try to hold back my sigh, then remember who I'm talking to and let it burst forth because Ollie knows tangled-love pain better than anyone.

"He backed out of first?" Ollie's eyebrows dip with worry. "Shy? Gentlemanly?"

"I think…I told him the kiss wasn't my choice if it was a bet, and he told me he'd never kiss a lady unless he was sure she wanted him to. So…it wound up being bad timing, I guess." I flop onto the bed and hold the phone in my outstretched arms.

"That is so feminist and *woke* of him! *That* is the most incredibly romantic thing I've ever heard in my life." Ollie hugs herself. "It's like Hercules completing all those tasks."

"Olls, did you pay any attention in our mythology unit? Hercules did those to atone for slaughtering his six sons."

"Oh right. Not as romantic then. But this example so clearly illustrates why you and I have divergent budding romantic lives. You take a perfectly good love metaphor and twist it back to death, while I take a horrible story about filicide and make it romantic."

"*You* are completely nuts. That's what you are," I tell her, my laugh edged in the pain of missing her with all my heart. "I miss you. Also, did you mention a budding romantic life of your own? Are you and some cellist making beautiful music together?"

She hides her face in a pillow. "Sorry. Romance metaphors really *are* lame. Maybe. Yes. Maybe."

"So, was it like a symphony? Or was it just a few off-key notes? God, yeah, you're so right. Metaphors suck. Did you make out like crazy?"

"Yes!" She rolls on her bed and drops her phone, so I stare at her paisley quilt until she digs it out. "He played me like he was Yo-Yo Ma and I was a cello."

"Worst metaphor yet," I groan. "But I'm so, so happy for you."

"When will I get to be happy for you? What are you doing on your next date?"

"Driving trucks in the mud."

Ollie looks confused, and it's actually a relief. I'm tired of being the only one totally caught off guard by what passes for a good time around here. "Driving in the mud? Why?"

"Fun, of course." I drizzle sarcasm all over that explanation. "What are *you* doing? Are you two lovebirds hanging out today?"

"I have some, *ahem*, music to make. Sweet, sweet music. Seriously though, I can't make out with him all day. This project is killing me, and the crazy making out helps me de-stress, but it doesn't help me practice. I have so many glitches to work out."

"Well, work them, lovey," I command.

"I will. Now," she says, sighing.

"Love you." She tells me she loves me back and we hang up after we kiss our screens. As always, my longing for her is worse right after I listen to her voice.

I don't just miss Ollie. I miss Brooklyn. I miss the city and its constant noise. I miss my school, where I had teachers who stopped me in the halls just to hug me and tell me they enjoyed my passionate comments in their class. I miss going places and having people excited to see me, instead of whispering about me behind their hands.

I even miss stuff I shouldn't. I miss the way it felt to walk into a room with Lincoln at my side and have everyone know and accept that we were a couple. When I didn't know it was all a sham, it was like the blanket I carried around as a toddler: mine, all mine, claimed by chew marks and slobber.

I didn't tell Ollie about the rebel mascot thing, even though that's the kind of news we're usually happy to exchange. Why? I feel embarrassed. Even though it has zilch to do with me. I'm embarrassed because I know Ollie would want me to *do* something about it.

I flop back onto my mattress and watch the sun move across the gray cobwebs on the ceiling, wondering why I feel guilt and embarrassment and raw need and what exactly I'm going to do to help myself stop feeling it all.

I also think about mudding next week.

"I'm thinking about mudding," I declare to the ceiling, and

marvel at what a strange mess my life is. "Enough is enough. I need to find something more productive to do with my time."

And I will. As soon as I get through my big mudding initiation. My cousins in Santo Domingo would howl with laughter if they knew I traded nights of dancing the merengue for driving trucks through the mud. In Santo Domingo, we say you're *enchivarse* when you're stuck in the mud on the road, and it's not considered fun at all. It definitely wouldn't be their idea of a romantic *chercha*. And it wouldn't have been mine either. But Doyle is changing the way I define a good time, and I can't lie—I kind of love my new perspective.

THIRTEEN

The entire bog area varies between slick and pitted expanses of reddish, sandy mud. A dozen other Jeeps and trucks are parked around, and people talk high and quick, laugh loud with excitement, steal each other's cigarettes, and chase each other through the mud like they *want* to get coated in it.

"Um, is everyone here wearing white?"

I feel like I'm in the "after" shot of a laundry detergent commercial. Blindingly bleached caps and T-shirts and bikini tops are everywhere, and even Doyle's wearing an old white Hanes shirt with holes in the collar.

"It's kinda tradition." He maneuvers his words around a grin. "It's like a point'a pride to see how dirty you can get."

"Why didn't you tell me?" Even if it's ridiculous to want to wear a white shirt I'm just going to destroy instead of the perfectly good navy one I have on now, any subtle detail that helps me fit in is comforting.

"You wearin' your bikini?"

I tug my shirt down and show the red ties. "You said we were going swimming after."

"I didn't want to tell you to wear your bikini *and* wear white and have you only do one or the other. It was a calculated risk." He drives over a particularly raised mound of mud and presses me back in my seat with his arm as if I'm not wearing a seat belt.

"You could've just told me that you wanted to see me half-naked," I gripe. I'm irritated that—as usual—I'll be the one who doesn't fit in because I never even thought to ask what the rules were.

I've never broken so many rules I had no clue existed.

He lowers his arm and his goofy smile fades. "You're pissed."

I know from the flash of my reflection as we crest another hill that my scowl reads all hot belligerence. I have zero game face.

"No, I'm not."

Doyle rests one hand on the wheel, lifts his hips off the seat, and roots his free hand in the back, finally pulling out a pristine white T-shirt.

"My extra gym shirt. It's clean." He hands it over. "It wasn't jest about the bikini. Though—I can't lie—that was high on my priority list. I never thought you'd wanna match with us dumb rednecks. That was stupid of me. You're not the kind of girl who does anything by half. Why'd mudding be any exception?"

I pull off the shirt I'm wearing and enjoy the bob of Doyle's Adam's apple as he watches. I know how good white looks against my skin, and I can tell from the hungry look in Doyle's eyes that he agrees. "Thank you."

I love how his shirt smells like the detergent he uses and also like dirt, leaves, starlit nights, and pool water.

Maybe that's just Doyle.

Or maybe I'm turning into a pining romantic, because I even think the air smells better when he's around.

"So, what's the point of this?" I need a distraction before I start mentally writing him love sonnets.

"The point?" He grins like a fool. "The point's to hold on tight and embrace the mud." He leans half out the window and lets loose a wail that sounds straight out of the throat of a Lost Boy or a delinquent.

Screams, hoots, and cheers puncture the air as Doyle guns the engine, bumping us up and down the soft mounds of mud that squelch under our tires and spray in globs and mists and waves over the roof and into the windows. I'm so mud-flecked after we crest the first hill, I look like my freckles have tripled in a few seconds. By the third hill, I closely resemble a Dalmatian. By the time we're on our second lap, I have no clue what we look like, but there's too much mud caked on the rearview mirror—and the rest of the truck—for us to be anything less than complete bog monsters.

Doyle screams out the window and spins his tires. The guys behind us lay on their horns and scream back.

"You're mighty quiet." He leans over like he's going to kiss me but doesn't. I'm tired of this lip-over-lip tug-of-war. I have no intention of asking for a kiss, but I might take one.

I smile and grip the side of the window when he glances over.

"It's fun!" I insist.

Maybe too emphatically.

His eyes glint the exact way my brother's do before he gives me a wet willie or tickles the crap out of me until I can't breathe.

"You can't jest *say* you're havin' fun. You need to produce evidence."

I raise my eyebrows as we get sucked down into the sinking mud and rock from side to side.

"Are we stuck?" I wonder what protocol is when you get trapped in this pit.

"We are." Doyle leans out to check how bad it is and shakes his head in defeat. "I only know one thing that'll get a rig this stuck outta the mud."

"A tow truck." I can't even imagine how they'll get one back here. Doyle's truck is twice as big as any tow truck I've ever seen, with huge, gripping tires. "Do you have AAA? Does AAA cover this kind of stuff?"

"AAA can't help us now." His bright blue, flame-like eyes are hot and disarming all at once. "What we need is a hot girl—I mean, like smokin' hot, hot as hell, *blow-your-mind hot*. This girl—who's crazy hot—jest has to lean out the window and scream her pretty head off."

I narrow my eyes at him and fold my mud-flecked arms over my mud-splattered shirt. "You're *insane* if you think that's happening. I'm not going to act like an idiot so you can laugh at me."

Doyle puts a hand over his heart, gasping like he's deeply wounded by my words. "Are you serious? You really think this is some put-on?" He leans out the truck and yells, "Guys! I'm deep in the muck, and Nes don't believe me when I tell her what she gotta do!"

The one-word chorus spreads from the inhabitants of the few vehicles in our vicinity to every single mud-flecked soul in the pit, all shouting with pure, crazy joy.

"Scream!"

Doyle looks over at me smugly and shrugs. I hear his un-spoken triple-dog dare loud and clear. And I open my mouth.

I open as wide as I can without actually hurting my jaw. I pull from low in my gut, from deep in my bowels, from the pit of somewhere I haven't wanted to face in a long time, and I *scream*.

The accompanying screams from the pit get louder until it's all a dull roar so intense, I swear it blows my hair back. My throat protests, stripped ragged and raw, but I push on and scream louder, harder, until my vocal chords vibrate and my throat starts to go dry. Doyle joins in, and we must sound like maniacs, like banshees. I couldn't care less. Since my life started falling apart, *nothing*—not snarkiness or kicking my heels against the mattress or laps around the pool or vodka— has felt as good as this guttural, primal scream.

I stop when the truck springs forward and flies over the next mound, spraying mud into my mouth and Doyle's. We both lean out our windows and spit. No matter how much we do, there's still grit crunching between our teeth, but we're laughing too hard to care.

"You wanna turn at the wheel?" Doyle asks, pulling to a less muddy area.

"What if I get you stuck?" I ask. Before he can recommend screaming again, I cut in, "Really stuck. Not stuck just so you can trick me into acting stupid."

"That wasn't a trick. That there was harnessing somethin' pure and wild."

"I trust you," I tell him.

His eyes are blue as the twilight sky reflected on a summer lake. He slides close to me on the bench seat, so close I can hear his every breath and smell his minty gum. So close I could wrap my arms around his neck if I wasn't the world's most co- lossal chicken.

He tugs me over until my jean shorts glide across the leather seat, the sweaty backs of my legs sticking slightly. He lifts me and, for one quick beat of my hammering heart, I'm sitting on the strong muscles of his upper thighs. My back is to his chest, his breath is hot on my neck, his fingers are locked high enough on my ribs that they brush just under my breasts.

I imagine all kinds of soft touches, tickling whispers, sweet and shocking kisses, but all I get is plopped in front of the steering wheel. Doyle runs a rough hand over his hair again and again.

"Damn, girl. That was no joke when I said you were hot enough to scream us outta that mud."

I can't control how erratically I'm breathing, or how hard my heart punches in my chest, so I get busy buckling my seat belt and starting the engine. I say a silent prayer of thanks for the summers I spent with Mom at my grandparents' summer cabin in upstate New York. City kids don't get to drive much at all, let alone drive stick—unless their grandfathers sneak them lessons behind the wheel of an old beater truck. If Mom knew Gramps taught me to drive before I graduated eighth grade, she'd have a fit.

"Mud." I focus on that single dirty word to tourniquet my dirtier thoughts. Thoughts about Doyle and the hard muscles in his legs and how completely right his arms felt around my waist. "The point of this is mud, right?"

"Yup." He doesn't say more, and his hand shakes when he tries to clip his seat belt.

"I'll be careful," I promise.

"The point is *mud*, not *careful*." He clinches his belt tight. "C'mon. You don't scare me, Yank."

I shake my head, laughing all the impure thoughts of Doyle to the back of my brain. "You're on, Johnny Reb."

I gun it, flying over dirt mounds and propelling us directly into mud pools. We rock but never get stuck, because I know from watching Doyle that in order to get coated, you need to avoid the sticky half-dry stuff on the edges and stay to the wide, shallow, murky puddles. Fountains of mud spray over us, explosions on every side of the truck, until it's sluggish and hard to handle.

"Bein' a beast?" Doyle asks as I fiddle with the stick.

"It feels off suddenly. Like it's—"

"Heavy?" When I nod, he explains, "Mud's drying fast today. There's a truckload caked on the chassis, I bet."

I pull over alongside a group of Jeeps and trucks. I don't want to risk breaking Doyle's main form of transportation.

"Hell, Doyle! That yer girl at the wheel? I was gonna say, you ain't never gone so crazy before! She's a wild one, boy." A guy claps his hands on his protruding beer belly and laughs deep and long.

It's aggravating that he talks about me like I'm not sitting right in front of his face, but he's bragging about how completely my skills outdistance Doyle's to anyone who will listen, so I let it go. Doyle nods and points for me to pull farther up and park. We hop into a puddle, not giving a damn about adding mud-caked feet and ankles to the list of coated body parts, and strut around the truck, ludicrously proud of all the filth we kicked up.

"That's Critter. He's all right, but he's making eyes at you," Doyle says softly when we're perched on the tailgate of his truck, segregated from the crowd.

"Weren't you just going on about how hot I am? How can the poor guy help himself?" A rush of warmth singes through me, which is irritating. I should know better than to be bowled over by macho possessiveness.

Apparently the part of my brain that's still hardwired to pick whichever mate beats his chest the hardest is stronger than the part of my brain stuffed with reams of Mom's feminist-theory literature.

"He can help himself far away from you if he knows what's good for him." Doyle's usually teasing tone is all business. He ignores my eye roll. "Maybe you'll never date me, and I'll cry in private over that. But I'm sure as hell not gonna stand by and let Critter Sharkey come out of the deep and steal you away."

"How chivalrous," I drawl, my words heavy with sarcasm. "So do I get a say in this, or do you just clunk me over the head with your club and drag me back to your cave after you scare Critter off?"

He starts with a series of chuckles that make his shoulders shake, but soon he has to rip off his hat and cover his face. It's difficult to keep stony during an argument when the person you're trying to school is laughing his ass off.

"Stop laughing." I hiss the words so there's no chance my lips will mutiny into a smile. "I mean it. This whole thought process freaks me out."

His laughs water down to occasional chuckles until he turns to face me, dead serious. "Don't be freaked out. It's jest, y'know, you're mine. Forever." He drops his voice theatrically low. "And I might watch you sleep at night. Also, I might be a vampire."

"Ass." I smack his arm, and might *possibly* use this gentle abuse to angle my body closer to his. And I might be supremely annoyed when a familiar feminine voice breaks through what might have almost been an attempt at a kiss.

On his part.

Not mine.

"You let her drive your truck?"

"She has a name, Braelynn," Doyle growls. "And, yes, Nes tore it the hell up out there."

"Thought the Gospel of Doyle was that you never let *anyone* drive your truck. Hoo, boy, Ansley's gonna shit a brick." She giggles behind her hand.

"Lovely imagery." I lean around Doyle to face Braelynn directly. "I guess you should go report to Ansley right away, while it's all still fresh." I flash a toothy smile. "PS—she's super lucky to have you watching her back."

I feel a microscopic glimmer of pity for Ansley. I'd never be giddy over anything I thought might hurt Olls.

Braelynn rolls her eyes and shakes her silky red ponytail. "Whatever, Yank. Obviously we've got a different sense of humor here than y'all do."

"I don't think 'sense of humor' means what you think it means." I stare her down, and she half bares her teeth. "I think the word you're looking for is *backstabbing*."

"Y'know, I was kinda feelin' bad for how Ansley tattled on you to her uncle and how she's been talkin' shit on you all over the place, but now I'm starting to think you deserve it." She flicks a disgusted look in Doyle's direction. "I don't even know who the hell you are anymore. I'll tell you right now, I ain't a backstabber, Doyle, and you should know enough to stick up for me and say so. When she dumps your ass and goes back to her precious New York City, your real *nonbackstabbing* friends'll be waiting for ya where ya dropped us."

"Go bother someone else, would'ya?" Doyle glares as she flounces away.

"With friends like those…" I mutter, but he leans his head against the side of the truck, and a frown chisels away at the happiness that lined his face preconfrontation. "Ignore her."

"Her voice is particularly difficult to get outta my head," he mutters. "Might be that screechy pitch. Might be she's a backstabbing asshole, but she shoots from the hip." His look levels me. "She right 'bout you?"

"About me what?" I pick flecks of dried mud off my arm and rub at the grayish spots left behind. "Me dumping you? 'Cause, I hate to break it to you, but we're not dating, Doyle. About me going back to my 'precious New York City'?" I do my best imitation of her drawl, but Doyle doesn't even attempt a smile.

"You know damn well I'm going back. I never made a secret about that. Because, even though I can be an asshole, I *also* shoot from the hip." I pop one foot on the edge of the mud-crusted tailgate. "By the way, I'm serious when I say I'm not a backstabber. Ever. I'm just saying, assholes and obnoxiously honest people are kind of par for the course if you want friends who aren't total wet blankets. But backstabbers? I'd rather be a hermit than hang around with someone who has zero loyalty."

When I'm done, there's still no smile from him, but he's through pouting, apparently. "You know what would make me happy?"

"What makes you think I care what would make you happy?" But I let my grin grow.

"You, swinging over that river, screaming your head off, in a little bikini." He raises his eyebrows like he loves how much he's testing me.

"Sounds like a really bad country music video." I grimace. "You like me screaming, huh?"

"Girl, you got *no idea*." He lays the drawl on thick, smiling so hard his eyes are slits of electric blue.

I refuse to go to mush. *Refuse.*

But I can't help if I run hot and my heart rocks around my chest like a truck in a mud pit.

Ah, the metaphors I'm picking up living in the Deep South…

"Such a pervert. You're wrecking every stereotype I had about gentlemanly Southern guys in white suits, smoking corncob pipes," I gripe.

I listen to the adorable echo of his laugh as we jump down and stomp off the dried mud. "Looks like they're 'bout ready to head to the river." Doyle helps me into the driver's seat as the engines around us start up. He takes a second to just stare my way before going around to the passenger's side and getting in. "You're crazy, girl, you know that?"

"You know what would make *me* happy?" He quirks an eyebrow, not even trying to pretend he doesn't care. "If you swung out and your trunks came undone."

"Damn. And you call me the pervert? I could oblige right here." He lifts his hips and flicks his belt buckle open.

I scream out an adamant *no*, cover my eyes, and stamp my feet. "Put it back on! I meant I wanted to see you publicly humiliated, not that I wanted a private showing of your bare ass!"

"You say potato…" I don't open my eyes until I hear the clip of his belt buckle. "If you're nice, I'll flub the tie on my trunks."

"I'm never nice." I bump my shoulder against his, start the engine, and drive according to Doyle's verbal directions. "I actually like driving this beast."

"Yeah?" He lets one arm dangle out the window. "I was wondering if you'd freak 'cause it's so much bigger than that windup car you drive."

"My car is midsize," I protest.

"Midsize my ass. That car's a roller skate, and it's gonna make you feel small and sad after you drive this big boy 'round for a while." He pats the door like he's petting a beloved dog.

I feel like I'm driving from three stories up and it gives me a prime view of the turquoise sky, the low, flat salt marshes choked with reeds, and glimpses of the snaking muddy river that winds alongside the road. "You must get, like, a half mile to the gallon. Your carbon footprint is tragic."

"I plant things for a livin'. And I recycle. It evens out." He closes his eyes and the sun glows gold on his face, making his hair look plated.

Doyle directs me to a clearing near the riverbank where someone already dragged a hose from behind a shed.

If I thought jumping in the river sounded like a cheesy backdrop for a bad country video, I had no clue what a few Southern kids in mud-splattered clothes with hoses could do—CMT would lose its mind. Squealing, screaming, soaking wet, half-dressed teens run back and forth, sprawl down in the mud, jump into truck beds and roll underneath them, getting dirtier by the second and then blasting the hoses nonstop until all the mud runs clear... The entire scene couldn't have been more *Southern Teens Gone Wild* if it had been scripted and choreographed.

We finally all drip and shiver in front of our clean vehicles, and Doyle points to the river. "I'll jump first, but all y'all fools better follow!"

He winks at me, strips his shirt off, drops his jeans, loosens the ties of his swim trunks—every single female catcalls for more naked Doyle—and takes a running leap off the edge of the bank. He barely grabs on to the frayed rope that looks like it's been hanging off the branch of the Spanish moss–draped tree since the dawn of time, but he manages to hang tight and swing back and forth.

The shorts do come down. Halfway.

His ass isn't tan with freckles like the rest of him.

It's bright white. That detail aside, it's a fine-as-hell, muscled, gorgeous ass. A few girls clap me on the back in envious congratulations as Doyle lets go and sails, bare-assed, into the water.

"Damn, girl, you're a lucky one," a tiny brunette wearing head-to-toe camo sighs.

The whooping peters out when Doyle doesn't pop up from the murky depths after half a minute. All conversation comes to a dead stop after another agonizing thirty seconds tick by. We stare at the waves lapping the bank and eye the flotsam whisked downstream by a current that could drag a submerged body fast and far.

Critter gives an overloud laugh fueled by nerves. "Shit. It's jest Doyle playin' on us. He done it every year, and we always fall for it and get scared as hell."

Everyone murmurs and nods, but the big group fractures into little comfort knots, two or three friends holding each other or standing shoulder to shoulder as they wait.

I press both hands hard over my breastbone because I have no one to hold except the one person everyone on the bank is afraid we lost. Weird that it hasn't even been five minutes since we cheered on the crazy way he embraced life, and now...

No.

No, no, no, not Doyle, not today.

I can't even process the possibility that...

No.

My fingers hover over the screen of my phone, and I'm just about to send a call through to 911 when his idiot head explodes out of the water. I rush the bank ahead of the herd, my feet kicking up furious sprays of sand.

"What the hell was that?" I scream, because it's still too real and raw. I can't join the laughter that's already canceled out everyone's worry. "Are you *crazy*?"

"These fools all know I can hold my breath for three straight minutes if I want. They jest like being scared is all. Stop fussing at me and jump, Nes!" Doyle reaches his arms out of the water like he's offering to catch me. "I let you see my ass jest like ya begged!"

I try to explain that he's a raging idiot, but the hoots and whistles drown me out. I shuck off my shirt and shorts, drop my phone on the pile, run as fast as I can and leap out, grabbing the rope like it's a lifeline. My stomach bucks as I swing. When I'm right above Doyle, I cannonball into the scary, glistening river that churns far below me, screaming the whole way down.

The river is several degrees colder than I expected. I don't pinch my nostrils, so I get a stinging noseful of silty water. There are a few frantic seconds where I'm not sure if I'm up or down, but Doyle's hands reach for me, and he pulls me up and spins my sputtering self around.

"That was a hell of a jump!" He yells so everyone can hear. The sun shines off his wet skin, and his light hair sticks up off his forehead. Droplets of river water cling to every ridge of his muscles. He pulls me close, so our bodies twine against each other.

I go tight between my legs, and my body opens to a want I haven't been able to feel since I found out about Lincoln and his menagerie of girls on the side. Before I think it through, I let my body float right up next to his and pretzel my legs tight around his hips, the way we were in my pool. This time there's a crowd of girls who admire this incredible guy, and an animal need to claim him as mine rises up in me. He's tugged his shorts back up, but they still hang dangerously low, and I can see the white sliver of his very fine ass over his shoulder.

"I couldn't let you show me up." I brush my hair back while his hands cradle me at the small of my back.

"Then you should've let your top fly off." He closes his eyes and nods like he's imagining it. I unwind my legs, kick back, and splash him full in the face, cackling as he sputters. "Sneaky!" he roars in accusation.

I shrug and cup my hands at the water's top again. "Sneaky? We're in a river. It's full of water. And you have a face that looks like it needs to be splashed."

He raises his eyebrows in warning, gliding his arm across the surface of the river to create a surging tidal wave I won't be able to escape.

I use my hands as a defensive shield, a pathetic attempt to catch my breath before he's got another wave missile crashing over my head. His friends start to jump and dive into the water, one human splash explosion after another, and I give up dodging the chaos and let Doyle wrap his arms around me.

I press my forehead tight against his chest to create a pocket of breathable air, and listen to the laugh thunking around in his chest. He runs a hand over my wet hair. "Now, now, there's nothing to be afraid of. Doyle won't let the mean ole river rats get you."

I wiggle out of his arms and contemplate pantsing him, but change my mind fast. That's definitely one of those ideas that seems super funny, but will probably escalate to me taking an involuntary public skinny-dip while Doyle holds my bikini captive over his head.

"You have too many inches on me. And your hands are like skillets. Unfair splash advantage." I pout.

He floats on his back and clucks his tongue. "And here I thought you were someone I had to fear, Northern Aggression."

I snort and float alongside him. "Well, I'm waving the white flag. Consider this your Southern independence from my Northern scourge."

A few giant black tubes get thrown into the water. Doyle nabs one and pushes it my way. When I struggle to get in, he hoists me up easily and tickles the bottom of my feet, ignoring my screams of protest.

"No mercy!" His laughs slide across the water and send me shivering like the soft nibbles of the guppies darting with the current. "You jest surrendered, so I guess that means you're my prisoner now."

Shackle me, Doyle Rahn. I'm all yours.

FOURTEEN

Doyle flops into a second tube and yells, "Critter! Send the beer cooler this way!"

Critter shoves out a tube with a red cooler bungee-corded to it. Doyle paddles us closer, opens it, and pops a tab, then passes a silver can to me. A million dazzling fragments of sunlight reflect off the river, each one dancing directly on my retinas.

"Jest shut your eyes." It's like he can read my mind. "Sun won't set for a while yet."

"I'm going to get burned," I lament. It took a full week of aloe slatherings to get over the last burn.

"Nah." Doyle takes a long drink and leans his head back. "You got a base now. You'll be fine."

"I don't think it works like that." I love the silky suck of the current against my fingers and toes.

"You'll look like you're from Brazil or something." He lifts his head. "Did you tell me you were Dominican?"

The question hangs like a heavy picture frame on a wobbly thumbtack.

"My family came to Georgia from England as indentured servants. Prolly a bunch of criminals. So we been right here forever."

I think he offers his backstory so I'll know he's asking for mine because he's genuinely interested in me, not just idly digging for information about why I'm kind of black, but kind of white, and maybe something else mixed in.

"My mother's family came from Ireland through Ellis Island." The cool river water drips off my fingers and runs in streaks down my stomach, pooling right next to my belly button. Doyle glances over, then can't seem to break his attention away. "My father's family comes from the Dominican Republic. He was born there. My grandfather moved to Brooklyn when my father was a baby, and he worked for years until he could send for my grandmother and father."

"But your dad lives in France now?"

"Yep. He and my older brother live in France because Dad got a professorship and my brother goes to college there. My abuela's father was French, so she's fluent, and my dad and brother are too."

"You fluent too?" His voice is as lazy as the river that's barely moving us.

"Sort of. My dad traveled a ton when I was little, and I cried whenever he came back after a long trip and spoke French to me. He didn't want to add to my mental torture or whatever, so he stopped. My brother is completely fluent though. My grandmother speaks Spanish to us, so I'm way better with that." I siphon a tiny sip of beer that's gathered in a warm puddle around the lip of my can, and Doyle fishes a second can out of the melting ice.

"Every single thing 'bout you's different. You ain't like any other girl I've ever known." Doyle's smile makes the harshest sunlight feel like shade. "God, I'm glad you showed up this year."

"So I'm like your own personal zoo freak? Like the swimming polar bear in Central Park?" I kick water at him hard enough that it gets in his beer can and makes him sputter.

He claws at the rubber of my tube, fighting to grip the curved side. "Not at all. You're like this real smart, sexy girl who makes me realize that it don't really matter if my family's stayed here for three hundred years, 'cause there's a whole world out there I gotta go see."

"There are plenty of other smart, sexy girls out there in the world, Doyle," I point out. "One day you'll go to New York, and you'll see that I'm pretty average."

"You? Average?" He shakes his head. "There's a helluva lotta words I'd use to describe ya, but *average* ain't one of them."

It might not be the most romantic thing he could have said about me, but it's the most romantic *way* he could have said it, his accent thick like white biscuit gravy, his voice crunched like gravel under truck tires. He only drawls that heavily when he gets so worked up, he forgets himself.

I lay my neck on the warm tube and relax, hoping the sun doesn't roast my skin. I doze a little until something brushes against my foot and jars me into full panic mode, flailing around to get a better look at what I'm sharing the water with. The cool comfort of the river is a mirage. It's too murky for me to see if what brushed my leg was an innocent river fish or a turtle that might snap off my toe with one strong-beaked bite.

The distant echo of the other tubers screaming with laughter carries our way. Doyle cranes his neck, and his eyes bulge before he settles back, jaw set.

"What is it?"

My internal alarms sound off one by one. I can't decide if the screams are fun or panic based. Paranoia and the look on Doyle's face make me think the latter.

"Nothing for you to worry 'bout." But he hooks one foot over my tube to keep me close.

"Doyle?" I drag his name out in a desperate plea for information, even though I get the feeling I don't want to know.

"Jest a teeny, tiny, miniature, little gator."

Gator?

Alligator?

Images of primordial hunters with ancient scales, slitted gold eyes, jaws that can rip a limb off your body and leave a few bubbles of blood on the surface while they pull you down and drown you in the muck send my amygdala into overdrive. My elbows and knees flail as I beat against the current in a desperate effort to eject myself from this watery grave. My beer can burbles gold liquid into the river like a bitter sacrifice.

"Whoa, what're ya doin'?" Doyle yells.

"A fucking *alligator*?" I strangle back a screech. "Doyle, I don't want to die today, thank you!"

"Nes, I been floating on this river since I was in diapers. Never had a problem." He jumps out of his tube like some agile merman and follows me into the shallows, beer can in hand. "I'm telling you, you're safe."

I stand with my toes squishing in the mud and crane my neck to see past the bend those screaming tubers curved around, trying to catch a glimpse of evil reptilian eyes or a slashing tail.

Doyle stands by my side. "I promise, there's nothin' to worry 'bout."

"Except alligators, Doyle. *Alligators*. We're not talking snapping turtles here. These are certified man-eating apex predators." I drag my tube onto dry land and examine my mud-smeared toes, never more glad to see all ten of them, attached and wiggling.

"That gator was two feet, max. It'd choke on your pinkie finger, I swear. Come back in."

I nearly dislocate my neck shaking my head. "Uh-uh. There's no way *in hell* I'm getting back in that water!"

He shades his eyes with his hand. "The hike back to the house is too far without shoes."

"What was the plan in the first place?" I squint at the tubes that are now nothing but black specks bobbing along the alligator-infested river's curves.

"We were gonna float down to Critter's aunt's place and take her boat back. My uncle borrowed the tubes from her anyway. C'mon. I promise you, you'll be fine." He holds his arms out invitingly.

Sure, those arms protected me from a splash war. There's no way I'm fooling myself into believing they'll protect me from blood loss and drowning when some gator decides to take me for a death roll.

"Even if it's a gator so tiny it could choke on my pinkie, it's still big enough that it could *bite off my finger.* I'm pretty attached to my fingers. All of them. And my toes. And, you know, also my life. I have no plans to bleed out in a Georgia river from a gator bite. Even a baby gator bite." I lift one foot, then the other, checking the pale pinkish soles of my feet. They look especially tender, all pruney and soft from their soak in this river of terror.

He shakes his head like I'm some hysterical Victorian lady lying on her fainting couch, smelling salts clutched under her nostrils. "Hell, girl. You're making this day much less relaxin' than I planned, y'know that?" Though the words are barbed, his tone has zero edge. "Wait here, okay?"

"Where are you going? Doyle? Be careful!" I scream as he

dives back into the river overflowing with alligators and slices through the water with clean breaststrokes.

I keep to the place where water melts into the sandy dirt, and follow the rhythmic gleam of his back in the rushing water until I can't see him anymore. My hot, itchy feet are being preyed on by an army of ants. I beat them away, hop from foot to foot, and chew on my cuticles, while I wait for Doyle. It's not only that I have no shoes: I have no phone, no purse, no idea where I am, and I'm freaked out.

There's a word we say in Santo Domingo when you're finally used to your surroundings and just soaking it all in: *acotejar.* Some days I feel like I've reached that place here in Georgia. Then things like this happen.

I took my first solo subway ride at eight. I flew overseas with Ollie to visit her grandparents in Vietnam when we were sophomores. How could I have felt so brave then, managing international travel at fifteen and the maze of subway lines at eight, but now, standing next to a soggy river in some backwoods swamp, I'm scared to death?

The bile at the back of my throat recedes when I hear the reassuring slap and pull of a rowboat's oars. Doyle navigates my rescue vessel against the current and onto the shore with nothing but his very impressive upper-body strength.

"I'll be weeding Mrs. Winslow's garden till doomsday in exchange for borrowin' this rickety thing. C'mon, girl! I gotta row against the current the whole way back, and I intend to beat the rest of 'em—point of pride." He crooks a finger at me. "Don't be scared. That water's barely over your ankles."

I wade out and throw my tube in the boat on top of his, my heart thudding sickly in the pit of my throat. "You laugh." I moan. "You laugh, but it's no joke. You're all crazy, doing this for 'fun.'"

"Crazy's our way of life." He helps me balance as I step into the tiniest, leakiest rowboat in existence. I sit fast and hold tight. "You good?"

I double-check for life vests. I'm unsurprised to find there are none. My nod is a quick, let's-get-this-show-on-the-road gesture. "I'll be better when we're safe on dry land."

Doyle pulls at the oars. His back and arms stretch and his muscles bunch, then release, long and smooth.

It's a beautiful thing.

"You got a curfew?" he asks through his teeth, his brow beaded with sweat.

"One on weekends. You want me to take a turn?" I offer.

"Nope. I gotcha into this danger. I'll getcha out."

The sun arcs toward the rushes, and the river awakens with croaking frogs that plop heavily into the water and buzzing insects that hurtle in crazy flight patterns through the purpling twilight sky.

"It's beautiful." I keep my voice soft, afraid to disturb the peace.

"It sounds pretty. I got too much sweat in my eyes to know for sure."

"Poor Doyle." I brush back the hair that's caught in his lashes. He startles at my touch, and his face goes hungry.

"We'll be all alone when we get to shore." He says it like a warning.

"We've been alone before." My voice quivers as I state this obvious fact.

"This time somethin' feels different." He braces his foot against the bench I'm sitting on and pulls hard. We're close to the house now.

"What's so different?"

He leads us to the shallows, jumps out, and drags the boat

up. When he takes my hand, electricity startles from his body through to my marrow.

"I'd never seen you scream in a mud pit before." He walks me closer.

"I never thought I'd have gone to one willingly." The friction between our bodies ignites every cell inside me.

"I'd never seen you jump off a rope into a river." Thoughts glow and extinguish like the yellow blink of the lightning bugs swirling around us. His mouth zeros in on my jaw, like he wants to trace that same frustratingly hot trail he started blazing the night of the baseball game.

"Enjoy the memory because that was the first and last time." My voice wobbles around those saucy words.

"I never believed I had any kinda real chance with you." He nuzzles his lips close to my neck. "But I heard a rumor you stared at my bare ass like it was somethin' you wanted bad." His laugh moves my hair, and I slap the flat of my hand on his shoulder.

"You're an idiot, you know that?" But my lips tilt into a smile, and then they're hovering close enough that another fraction of an inch will close off everything in the world and leave Doyle and me, alone, together, feeding a need I don't think has anything like a bottom.

FIFTEEN

Just before his lips slide over mine, a boat motor purrs close to the bank. Doyle steps back, his hand gripped so hard on the back of his neck, the bite of his fingers leaves white marks on his skin.

"Doyle! Ya crazy sonabitch! We were looking for ya all over the place! Thoughtcha drowned for real this time!" Critter stands at the prow, a can of beer clutched in each hand. "I swear, I was 'bout to call and ask them to dredge the river for y'all!"

"Naw! Nes got spooked by the gator! I borrowed Winslow's rowboat and brought her back!"

"Winslow let you take that boat? What's yer penance?" Critter would definitely fail a road sobriety test. He nearly staggers off the dock a dozen times trying to walk a straight line to us.

"Enough weedin' to kill a weaker man." Doyle claps Critter on the back and takes a beer off him. "It was worth it."

"Hoo-yeah, boy." Critter checks me out from the crown of my matted hair to the tip of my mud-caked toes. I ball my fists at my sides.

"Gotta get something from the truck," Doyle announces

abruptly and turns me by the shoulder. We snatch our now-dry, crumpled clothes from the riverbank as we hightail it.

"What do you need to get?" I whisper.

"My temper back under control," Doyle mutters. I glance over my shoulder, and he says through his teeth, "Please don't tell me if he's starin' at your ass like he's never seen one before."

I don't. But he is.

"He seems pretty harmless." I'm still glad to get back into my slightly mud-encrusted clothes.

"He might be jest a li'l touchy when he's got a few in 'im, and he's got way more than that now." He takes my hand. "I'm not tryin' to play caveman, but I brought you to this den of fools, and I feel responsible for you. Promise you'll stay by my side tonight?"

I can't tell which one of us is more surprised when I say, "Okay."

We head to the fire being set up in a cleared section by the old river house, and Doyle takes care to make sure I'm tucked close to his side. We smush into the circle and laugh along to stories that get progressively wilder as the pile of empty beer cans stacks sky-high. There's a plan to noodle for catfish dinner (Doyle just grins when I ask what that even means), but I've gone too long without sustenance to wait.

"You hungry, Nes?" he asks guiltily when my stomach makes an audible rumble.

"Starved. How about I run into the nearest town and pick us up some food?" It's a little laughable how worried Doyle looks at my suggestion.

"Ya don' mind?" His words are so slurred I need to use context clues to decipher them.

"Not at all. But no more beer for you. You're gonna feel like crap in the morning." I'm relieved to find the can I ease out of his hand is still more than half-full. He didn't drink much, but baking in the sun and rowing upstream along the South's version of the Amazon must've lowered his tolerance. I brush his hair back from his forehead. His eyes have drifted shut, but his hand shoots up and grabs mine when I try to stand.

"Take my wallet." He fumbles through the pockets of his crumpled jeans.

"I have money." My mom would never let me leave the house without cash, just in case. I press his hand back when he holds out the brown leather wallet.

"I haven't even worn a white suit or smoked a corncob pipe. What kinda Southern gentleman've I been? You gotta let me pay, or I'll bring shame on my kin." He shakes the wallet, and I'm kind of shocked at myself when I take it.

Doyle's sleepy, beer-soggy directions aren't exact, but my phone is almost dead, and Critter warned my GPS would just "turn me circlin'" way out here anyway.

When I don't see the pecan orchard Doyle told me I'd pass, I make a jerky U-turn in some scrub grass on the side of the road. Just as I get going again, a set of blue and white lights flash in my rearview.

Coño.

I didn't drive much in New York, so I've never been pulled over. Thank God Jasper and my father are both obsessed with police procedurals. Times like these are exactly when half watching marathons of *Law and Order* come in handy.

The lights flash again, and I lurch the truck to the shoulder, stomach bottomed out, hands clammy. I miss the latch on the glove box twice before I manage to spring it open and rifle through napkins and Taco Bell sauce packets and even a box of Trojans like a frenzied maniac, pawing everything onto the floor, looking for Doyle's registration. When the glove box is empty, I duck down and sift through what debris I can reach.

The officer cocks open one door of his crusier. I bite on my lip to dam the tears and wonder if I should call Doyle. I slide my flattened hand in the lost space next to the driver's seat, and my elbow bumps the center console trip button. My blood pressure shifts out of overdrive when I see the card lying in there. Now I'm biting my lip to stymie tears of relief.

I grip the card like a talisman. The heavy thump of the officer's boots on the pavement raises the hair at the base of my neck.

"License and registration," the officer intones, shining his blinding flashlight into the window.

I hold a hand up to battle the glare as I hand over the paperwork, trying to convince myself that the officer's thick drawl is a sign of friendliness. Laid-back easygoingness. He speaks slowly because he thinks things through, doesn't jump to conclusions, doesn't ticket lost high school girls on swampy back roads.

For half a second I wonder if I could fake an accent, just a stretch of my vowels and a drop of end consonants to make me seem a little more...*likable*. I've noticed the raised eyebrows, pursed lips, and tightened jaws when my choppy Brooklyn accent rears its head—it's a very suspicious-sounding accent around here.

"Ms. Pujols." It's on the tip of my tongue to correct him, to say *Murphy-Pujols*. But I'm not *that* stupid. "This vehicle isn't yours, is it?"

Well, obviously not. It's not registered to me.

I bite my tongue.

"No, sir." If my *sir* carries the faintest Scarlett O'Hara inflection, it's unintentional. Mostly.

And then I panic. Is it illegal to impersonate the spoiled fictional daughter of a Southern plantation owner? Is it okay to tweak your accent when an officer has you pulled over on a deserted stretch of road and asks you questions he already has the answers to?

He flips the registration card in his fingers, and I notice how young he is. I'm not sure how long it takes to become a police officer, but this one doesn't seem like he's much older than I am.

"People who drive this kinda vehicle tend to be a little more…country. I trust you aren't driving a vehicle you don't own because you stole it, right, Ms. Pujols?" I can't tell if he's teasing or mocking me.

"I'd never steal a car." Maybe I should try to banter with him, but I'm so shaken, all I can do is try my best to convince him I'm an upstanding citizen who did not engage in grand theft auto.

"I'm sure you wouldn't." He smirks. "Not this big ole truck anyway. Now, a Bentley? Or a Range Rover? Those might be a temptation for a girl like you."

Should I tell him I own a Corolla? Should I keep my mouth shut? Am I doing this wrong? I think I might be.

"I borrowed it," I blurt.

"I happen to know who owns this truck." He stops flipping the card and taps the edge against the door. "Thing is, the guy who owns this truck ain't real nice about letting people…*borrow* it. Do *you* know the owner of this truck?"

The accusation is as heavy as the night is dark, as loud as the incessant whine of the insects, as fierce as the thump of my heart. My first instinct is to crush the gas pedal to the floor and fly off this road, into the farmland that rolls alongside it, jumping over muddy streams and through wire fences and away from this situation I don't know how to handle.

Which is idiotic. The cop has my license and Doyle's registration. My deranged plan would only work if I were actually the kind of criminal he's insinuating I am.

"I do know Doyle." My words jerk out. "He's a…friend."

The cop crosses his arms over his chest. A wide chest. Strong arms. A belt hangs off his narrow hips. I notice the dull black gleam of his gun, a baton, a taser, the silver clank of handcuffs.

Not that I think he'd need more than those arms to restrain me if he decided he needed anything.

I plan to give him *zero reasons*.

Stay calm, speak respectfully, don't be confrontational, I remind myself, my sweaty hands twitching in my lap.

My breath rattles in and out, so loud I know he must hear. My body is its own lie detector test, screaming *guilty* over and over in traitorous gasps.

"You claim you're a…friend?" His voice twists and breaks to mimic my hesitation.

"I go to school with Doyle. I just… We just moved here. My Mom and me." I'm stitching together all these stupid words, hoping they'll clear me so I can go.

"No daddy at home?" He puts a question mark on the end, but he's not fooling me. It's a fact in his book.

"My father lives in France." The words rattle out.

He lets out low whistle. "France, huh?" He chuckles like he thinks I'm telling a great joke. "So your daddy's not around because he's doing time—'scuse me, *spending* time in…*France*? Never heard that one before."

When I inhale, even my breath stutters. "I just moved here, and Doyle invited me out tonight. He…he let me drive his truck to get food. I swear. Doyle is my friend."

"Doyle knows lots of people at his school, sweetheart. That doesn't mean he's friendly enough to lend his truck to all of 'em." He peers into the window. "You don't look much like the *friends* Doyle usually drives around with on a Saturday night. Those *friends* are usually a bit more...blonde." His eyes glint in the moonlight and words like *werewolf* and *vampire* snap through my brain, but they don't scare me because I'm too busy being freaked out by words like *cop* and *man*.

"I am. His friend." My words are weak and small.

"I know Doyle's got one *friend* I can imagine him lettin' borrow his vehicle... Her name's Ansley. Maybe you go to school with her? Real sweet, long *blond* hair, daddy's the mayor. If she and Doyle Rahn are the ones who are such good *friends*, I'm wondering why you're the one driving this truck?"

I'm in trouble because I'm not sweet and blonde with a daddy who's a big shot in local politics? I'm in trouble because I'm dark and he thinks I'm a liar who says her daddy's in Paris when he's in prison and that she borrowed a truck from a friend when she really stole it?

Is this legal? Can he ask me these things? Did he tell me why he pulled me over in the first place? I can't remember. I can't think. *What do I do? What do I fucking do?*

I clench my fists around the steering wheel, praying for someone to come by, to help. As if fate is giving my wish the finger and laughing, a car drives by, barely slowing down, its headlights illuminating the officer so that I see he doesn't even have a five o'clock shadow. His name tag flashes. It says Hickox.

I search my brain for a reference, someone else I know who might know him, but I know no one here other than Doyle and the handful of people he's brought into my life. It's right then that I remember I actually have Doyle's wallet on me.

Relief fills me up, but it's replaced just as quickly with heart-stopping panic.

If I show the officer Doyle's wallet, won't it look suspicious? Why would I have his wallet and his truck when he's not here?

I know the answers to my own questions, and they're normal, rational answers, but I get that sick feeling that always overwhelms me when someone accuses me of something—even something I didn't do. There's this instant rush of guilt and doubt—like maybe I *did* do something wrong.

"I… Uh, we were at the river and, uh…" I'm dangerously close to blubbering. I funnel air into my lungs in quick gulps. "We took Jeeps into the mud. And went to the river. I was going out to get some snacks. Doyle had a few—" I stop because Doyle is eighteen: it's illegal for him to drink. I feel like my words and Officer Hickox's narrowed eyes are tying me into knots that are tightening into nooses. "Doyle was really tired."

"Tired?" He finally smiles, but it isn't a nice expression. "At the river?"

"It's his uncle's place," I stammer.

"I know it." He rubs his jaw. "All right. I'll let you off this time, Ms. Pujols." I wonder for a second what exactly he's "letting me off" for, but relief clamps down on my tongue before I go all stupid and ask.

I barely nod. My fingers are coiled around the steering wheel so tight, I'll need a crowbar to get them unclamped. Sweat rolls off my temples, down my neck, and soaks into the cotton of my T-shirt. I bite back sobs that keep rocking against my lips like boiling water rattling at a pot lid.

"Be careful 'round here. There's some areas that aren't real welcoming to…strangers." He hands me my license and Doyle's registration and saunters back to his cruiser.

When he doesn't leave right away, I realize he's waiting for me to leave first. There's no way I can drive, no way I can stop my body from spasming and curb my need to vomit. My nerves are too frayed. But before I know it, I'm driving, my eyes flipping between the windshield and the rearview mirror every other second.

By the time he pulls off a side road, I can just make out the lights of a town glowing up ahead, and I shudder with relief. I spy the neon purple-and-pink Taco Bell sign, and since I found all those hot sauce packets next to Doyle's napkins and condoms, I pull up at the drive-through window and order anything. Everything.

When they hand my bag out, I don't even wait until the truck comes to a full stop before I tear it open, cramming greasy, fried gorditas and sour cream–loaded chalupas down my throat like I haven't eaten in weeks. And just when I'm sure I can't stuff another bite in, I feel it all knock back up so quickly, I almost don't make it out of the truck. I retch hard, doubled over, my palms and knees biting into the gravel under me. I coat his front tire in puke, along with the curb and the prickly grass outside the parking lot. I hear a car door slam and the rhythmic thump of feet headed toward me.

"Hey, ma'am, you all right?" a man's voice calls.

I sit up and wipe the side of my mouth with my wrist. "Yes. Thank you. Just something I ate."

"From here?" A girl eyes the glistening puddle of puke and gags a little.

I shake my head, unwilling to implicate Taco Bell in my puke-a-thon. "No. Lunch, I think."

I hear the girl whisper that the guy should offer me a ride. He whispers back that I'd think it was weird, and she argues that her being there would make it okay.

I attempt to stand, but my knees buckle like they're made of a bunch of rubber bands balled together.

"Ma'am, do you need a ride?" the girl asks, her voice high and worried.

I paste on a smile. "Thank you so much, but I'll be okay. Seriously, thank you."

I hear the word *drunk*, but she whispers it with such sadness, I don't have the heart to get offended. They walk over to her truck slowly, looking back to make sure I'm okay. I manage a reassuring wave to let them know they're not being Bad Samaritans.

I rinse my mouth out with my soda, dust the gravel chunks off my knees, and climb back into the truck. I drive slowly, carefully, making two wrong turns and taking twice as long as I should, but I find my way back to Doyle without attracting the attention of any other cops. One look at his crooked, relieved smile brings the urge to sob roaring back, but it also feels like home.

He feels like home.

I hand over the food, collapse into his arms, and press my face to his side. He runs a hand over my soft curls and croons off-key country songs about pretty women and heartbreak, and my panic slowly sinks to the pit of my gut. I stop shaking; my muscles relax; I breathe easier. Maybe it wasn't such a big deal after all? Maybe being alone and lost magnified the craziness of the situation.

"Hey, you all right?" His fingers strum my ribs softly, like I'm some instrument he's learning to play by ear.

I swallow a few times before I answer, to clear the tears out of my throat. Luckily he's a little too sleepy and buzzed to notice. The entire horrible story is on the tip of my tongue, but I'd rather just forget it.

"Yeah. I'm good. We should head back. I can drive to my house. Can someone pick you up?"

"I'm good," Doyle slurs. Instead of debating with him, I get up and search out Critter, glad to have something to worry about other than my run-in with the law.

Critter's had his fair share to drink and is shooting the breeze around a roaring inferno. I ignore the drunk catcalls as I drag him away, rolling my eyes when he says, "Hoo yeah, maybe dreams do come true!"

"Critter, do you know who I can call to come get Doyle from my place?" I ask when we're far enough away that no one can overhear our conversation.

His beer-wet mouth droops. "Shoot. I really thought you might be pulling me over here to tell me I'm the best-lookin' guy at this party."

I cock an eyebrow at him, cross my arms, and pop my hip.

"So you ain't gonna rip my clothes off and have your way with me?" He levels such a dopey grin my way, I can't help smiling.

"Nope. This will be a sexual harassment–free night for you. So who can I call?" I repeat.

He pushes his ball cap up and scratches his matted hair. "His cousin Brookes is prolly home and sober. It's his night for emergency runs. You know, the family business."

"Emergency runs?" I repeat, trying to imagine what exactly constitutes a horticultural emergency. A Venus flytrap rebellion? "For bugs and trees? What would count as an emergency?"

"Swarm of locusts?" Critter guesses. I'd tell him he has a great laugh, but I'm afraid it might rekindle the whole do-bad-things-with-you vibe he's been pushing all night. "If you can't get Brookes, his younger brother, Malachi, got his farmer's license."

"Right." I wonder if I'll have to drag-down fight Doyle to call. But when I get to him, he's snoring softly, and his phone is sticking out of his pocket.

I'm not a snoop. I respect privacy. Everything in me screams that I have no business going through Doyle's phone. I close my eyes and imagine what I'd do if this was one of those videos they show in health class.

I grab the phone, slide it out of his pocket, take his hand, and use his finger to unlock it. Quickly, before I change my mind, I press the contact list and scroll through, trying to keep my eyes squinted so I don't see anything other than the names Critter told me. I'm caught off guard by two things.

One, for a guy as adored as Doyle Rahn, his contact list is pretty bare.

Two, I'm the only *A* in his list. No Ansley.

Lincoln is still in my phone. So what does my turn as a reluctant amateur Sherlock allow me to deduce about the situation? Ansley didn't mean as much to Doyle as Lincoln meant to me? Doyle goes through life with a fully functioning backbone and I don't? Maybe I'm just looking for drama in the absence of her name to avoid thinking about this crazy night.

I find Malachi and Brookes. I don't want to call the former, because a farmer's permit sounds sketchy, legally speaking, and I'm committed to staying on the right side of the law, even by acquaintance. I don't want to call the latter, because technically he's working and might be pissed. But he's probably legal, so I bump his name with my fingertip and wait through the rings with my eyes screwed shut.

"What the hell, Doyle? Ya callin' to cry 'cause she ditched you after all? Don't tell me I gave up a night with Skylar just to hang out with your dumb ass." I guess even vocals can be genetic, because the voice on the other end is deep and gravelly, but with that friendly confidence that makes listening to Doyle so addictive.

"Brookes? Hi. You don't know me, but I'm a friend of Doyle's." As if he heard me say his name in his sleep, Doyle rolls over so his head is cradled against my legs, his scruff rough on the skin of my bare thighs.

"Sweetheart, I know that's a Yank accent, and those ain't exactly common 'round here." The way he says it isn't unfriendly, but I cringe anyway. "You Doyle's New York City girl?"

How the hell do I answer that one?

"I'm Doyle's friend. And, yes, I'm from New York." I lift my tone a few huffy notches, like Brookes shouldn't assume things, when all the while I'm the jerk calling from his cousin's phone at midnight and running my fingers through Doyle's overlong hair. Not that Brookes knows that last bit.

"He drunk?" The two words unwind on the tail of a long sigh.

"Not like alcohol-poisoning bad, but definitely too far gone to drive."

"Hell. All right, all right. Y'all down at the river?" Brookes speaks with the take-charge resignation of someone who's used to getting other people out of screwed-up situations.

"We are, but I can drive him to my house and you could pick him up there, if that's closer for you." Guilt over annoying Brookes is outweighed by my relief at finding someone to help me end tonight on a blessedly boring note. My goal is to go to sleep tonight thankful I won't be waking up in county lockup.

We spend the next few minutes on logistics, and I thank God Brookes seems to know every backcountry road in the area, because I have no chance of giving anything like decent directions. He even tells me how to get to my house from the river before we hang up.

Critter wanders over and offers to help hoist a tipsy Doyle into the truck. After I almost take a boot to the face twice, we manage to get him in.

"Thank you," I gasp.

"No worries." Critter bends at his thick waist and examines me up close. "What's a matter? You drink too much too? You guys can bunk here."

I realize I must look rough from all the panic and vomiting, but more than anything in the world, I want to go home. And, though I'd never admit it to anyone, I want my mom to tell me everything will be okay.

"No, it's…uh, it's just that I got pulled over. Before. When I ran to get food. And the cop acted like—" Instead of being righteously pissed, I do this weird little half shrug, because in the fragmented retelling, I'm afraid maybe I'm making a big deal out of nothing.

"Was he a dick to you?" Critter asks the question with such genuine concern narrowing his eyes, the back of my throat prickles exactly how it used to when I was a little kid and I'd hold back tears all day because something bad happened at school, but the second I saw my mom—the floodgates just exploded open.

So…things have been bad with my mom and kind of bad in general, if I'm being honest with myself. And this beer-bellied, overfamiliar, half-drunk Southern boy isn't the person I expected to be my surrogate mommy, but screw it. I'm sad and pissed and confused as hell, so his sympathetic shoulder gets sobbed on. Possibly snotted on too.

Through the whole weepy tale, Critter pats my shoulder

awkwardly like the nice guy he is, then he takes me by the hand and says, "Look at me, all right? Some people are small and stupid. It makes 'em feel big to scare people they know they got cornered. Fuck 'em. I don't want you cryin' over that crap. You got friends. We take care of ours, and we'll take care of you. Hickox was it?" He shakes his head. "Un-fucking-believable."

I dip my head to the side and wipe a salty sludge of snot and tears on my T-shirt. "Thank you, Critter. Seriously, thank you. But don't go all vigilante on my account, okay?"

He grits out an obviously reluctant okay, triple-checks that I'm good to drive, and wraps me in the kind of brotherly bear hug that makes me miss Jasper. I drive slower than my grand-mother on a Sunday while Doyle snores away at my side.

When I pull into my neighborhood, there's a lone truck parked at the end of my street. A guy in a ball cap with Doyle's rangy frame leans against it. Doyle opens one eye, then the other.

"Nes?" His voice is dry and groggy.

"Hey." I turn off the engine, and the sudden silence is jar-ring. "You okay?"

"Jest beat. I guess from rowing you back to safety from that gators plus being out in the heat…and the beer." He yawns and rubs his eyes. I feel like I'm watching him do something private, and I like that. "I coulda drove."

"Why risk it?" I clear my throat and fill him in on how he's getting home. "Critter told me to call your cousin." I point out the windshield. "Is that him?"

"Yup. That's Brookes." Doyle studies his boots and rubs his neck until it's brighter red. "Hell. I wanted to take you on a date. Kind of embarrassing you wound up havin' to baby-sit me."

I tug on a piece of hair that keeps falling from under his hat. "I should ask your parents to pay me. And my fees are *high*. I can't stand snot-nosed little rug rats."

"Lucky I'm such a charming snot-nosed rug rat." He hooks a finger in the belt loop of my shorts and drags me his way. "I always had the biggest crushes on my babysitters." His skin radiates this cozy warmth, like it stored a little of the day's sunshine.

"Your cousin is waiting." Even a whisper feels overloud right now.

"Damn Critter, hooking me up with a chaperone. Got half a mind to call and—" He pauses to check his phone. "Speak of the devil. Weird." He looks up at me with furrowed brows. "Everything go okay while I was conked out?"

"Yes." Doyle's eyebrows edge up as my vowel stretches long.

"You sure?" He drops his voice and leans in like there's someone else in the truck who might overhear us.

It feels like I crammed a year's worth of stress into this never-ending day, and my eyes have that grit-caked pain that comes with extreme exhaustion. "Look, we can talk tomorrow. Okay?"

His face scrunches and tightens as he scrambles through a thousand different possible intrigues and worst-case scenarios, and I hate that this whole stupid little thing is already rippling beyond my control.

"I just got pulled over by a cop who was kind of a dick, and I kind of freaked out, I guess. I cried to Critter a little, and then I got over it. No big deal."

Doyle rears back and squints at me, then speaks with a slow, icy calm. "You ain't the type to cry over nothin', Nes. Seems like a big deal as far as I can tell. You weren't gonna tell me?"

"You were zonked out." I nod at Brookes, now pacing in front of his truck. "For real, your cousin is waiting."

"Screw him," Doyle lashes out. "Dammit. I shouldn't have letcha go on your own." He rubs his hands on the thighs of his jeans, then pounds his fist on the dashboard.

"I'm not some damsel in distress. I took care of the situation just fine. Let it go."

"Why'd you get pulled over?"

Obviously, he's *not* letting it go.

"He didn't really say why," I mutter.

"You can't pull someone over and not give a reason."

He's not saying it like he thinks I'm lying or guilty, but like he wants me to say the thing he and I both know I don't want to say.

I don't want to believe some police officer saw the color of my skin and took it upon himself to judge me a criminal. Sitting helpless in the truck while he questioned me made me feel like I was at the mercy of things exponentially out of my control.

When I was a kid, some of my cousins' friends came to visit our little beach house in Santo Domingo, and they got pretty tired of hearing me talk about my life in New York City. Eventually, the most obnoxious little boy branded me a *jablador*, a liar. I cried and told him he was a stupid head (I was only seven at the time), but that feeling of having my truth questioned with no way to prove myself really stuck with me. I'm always a little nervous that people will accuse me of stretching the truth even when I'm being honest.

"I… Just… Nothing. Nothing I can fix."

"We can. With your brains and my Rhett Butler charm, we're one unstoppable force."

I love that he can make me laugh, even when my bones

feel like quicksand in my longing-to-be-kissed, sunburned, racially profiled skin.

"Honestly, there's nothing we can do. I was lost, and this cop pulled me over and questioned why I was driving a truck that didn't belong to me…and then he kind of implied that I stole it. He also implied my father was in prison, and I was lying about him being in France. And he warned me there were places I wouldn't be welcome around here. It was weird and gross, but he let me off without a ticket. He didn't even make me get out of the truck. What am I supposed to do?"

"A police officer treated you like that? When you were lost?" He shakes his head in disgust. "What the hell's wrong with his head?"

I slam my palm on the steering wheel in frustration. "Why am I Ebenezer High's bad seed when every teacher at my old school loved me? Why was it so damn easy to make friends in Brooklyn, but I can't get anyone to talk to me here unless they know I have the Doyle Rahn stamp of approval? The fact is, nothing makes much sense since I moved down here, and tonight…" I lean my forehead on his steering wheel and breathe slowly. "Tonight was just one more stupid thing that proves I probably should have never come here."

"Don't say that." He grabs my hand like he's offering a lifeline. "People down here don't like change. Folks can be a little prickly at first, but no one who spends any time with you could help fallin' for you. Head over heels."

I roll my head to the side and smile at him, even though I'm so freaking tired. Of everything. "I don't even think you're saying that to get in my pants. Which is sweet. But you're very, very wrong."

"I've been waitin' my whole life to meet someone honest and brave like you." He stares out the windshield at the moon covered with thick, gray clouds. His voice is as dim as the night. "Don't give up on this place jest yet, Nes. I know it's so selfish, and you got friends back in Brooklyn and a great school and a whole life, so I should be telling you to go. As your friend, that's what I'm supposed to do. But I gotta face the truth. I don't want to lose you yet. Not when I barely got a chance to know you."

Now would be the right time to kiss him, with everything rising and converging around us, and the universe basically pushing us into each other's arms. Just as we begin to give in to the undeniable magnetic force, Brookes beats on the side of the truck. For one beautiful, terrible second, I mistake Doyle's sigh for the brush of his lips.

"Thomas farm's irrigation system backed up, and I gotta run out and take a look," Brookes announces when Doyle rolls down the window with a vicious jab of his finger. "You don't seem too bad at all. Wanna give me a hand?" He glances at me, swipes off his cap, and nods his head. "I'm Brookes, by the by."

"Nes." We exchange uncertain smiles/waves before I turn back to Doyle. "You should go help Brookes. I'll drive over to your place tomorrow and pick you up so you can get your truck," I offer, not even wanting to think about tomorrow until I sleep for about fourteen straight hours. Even my blood feels tired, like I went anemic overnight.

Doyle jumps out of the truck, sticks his hands deep into his pockets, and rocks back on his boots while a smile creeps over his face like molasses in December, as my abuela would say. "I was gonna say I was fine to drive, but I ain't stupid."

It should annoy me when he lays his good ole drawl on thick, but Doyle oozes this very specific kind of charm I find frustratingly irresistible.

"If you call before noon, I will delete you from my life forever," I vow, popping open the truck door. Doyle and Brookes both race over to help me out, but Doyle speeds ahead and shoves his cousin back.

"You ain't even serious right now, cuz," Doyle warns, his hands firm and possessive on my hips as he helps me down.

"Just jokin' on you, son. Hurry up with your girl, we gotta get going." Brookes jogs back to his truck, and I shimmy from side to side, twisting out of Doyle's grasp.

"Southern hospitality," I gripe. "I'm either being chased down by a mob with pitchforks or I have two guys knocking each other over to prove how chivalrous they are. Y'all gotta make up your minds."

"Damn, a twang's hot on you, girl." He leads me to my door and lays his hand flat on it when I reach for the knob. "You okay?"

I pop a shoulder against the frame. "I'm fine," I lie.

"Liar." He reaches out and traces his thumbs under my dry eyes like he's searching for the memory of tears.

It's sweet. God, it's so sweet. But I don't want to need his help to get through every little thing because it means I won't be able to separate wanting to be with him from needing to. And that makes all the difference.

I loop my fingers around his wrists, pull his one hand from my face and the other from my door.

"Talk to you tomorrow." I deliver the words firmly, to mask the jelly of my uncertain feelings about this sweet and dangerous thing we're volleying back and forth.

Doyle reholsters his hands in his pockets and tromps backward away from the door and onto the street. His shuttered gaze locks with mine until I close the door and force a break.

My eyes flutter shut for a second, and I acknowledge I'm

hard-core tempting fate. I might fall asleep standing up in the front hall.

My mother pads out of the kitchen in an old tank and a pair of comfy sweats. Her dark hair is growing out of its bob, so it swirls in soft waves around her neck. She's wearing her librarian glasses and has one hand wrapped around an I Heart NY mug of steaming tea. How does she hold it without scalding the skin on her hands? I asked her once. She said, "Thirty-seven hours of back labor with your brother, and I think I developed a superhuman tolerance for pain."

"Do you want a mug?" She holds up her tea, and I inhale. Mint. My favorite.

This is a substantial olive branch. "No." The word nearly extinguishes the flicker of peace. I blow gently on the embers until they grow orange. "No, *thank you*. I'm really tired."

The words, carefully free of any obnoxious tone, warm the air between us, and Mom stiffens like she might be afraid to make a move and break the spell.

"Fun day?"

A lot of culture shock and a little racism aren't exactly my definition of fun. I'm relieved when it hits me that I probably wouldn't have told my mother about being pulled over even if we were still as tight as we'd been before a few months ago, when everything fell apart.

The things out of her control—middle school mean-girl cliques, a broken arm while I was on a skiing trip with Dad in Switzerland, my heartbreak when Ollie's dad was seriously considering moving to Vancouver for work—those always hurt her the worst. And there's this whole thing with her where my being half-Dominican means I'm going to face things she can't anticipate. To make up for that, it's almost like she went into worry overdrive. Like if she couldn't predict what might hurt me, she'd assume everything would.

"Really fun. Doyle's friends are great."

It's a gray lie. Some of them are. Some of them hate me. And it may seem like I'm putting another wall between my mother and me, but that's not it at all. I'm shielding her from unnecessary hurt.

"You two seem to be getting pretty serious pretty quickly. Maybe you can have him over for dinner sometime." She's pushing her luck, and she knows it.

I'm too tired for hate or peace or anything but sleep. Deep, sweet, merciful sleep.

"I don't know. Maybe. Look, I'm going to…" I point to my room.

Mom nods. "Right. Okay. Good night, baby."

I've already started walking down the hall. I turn my door-knob and am about to march into the dark and collapse on the mattress and into oblivion. But—

"Good night, Mom."

A few pounds of weight slip off my shoulders after I utter those three simple words, and I start to tumble down the deep-est rabbit hole of sleep with one fuzzy thought dominating my brain: anger is too damn heavy to keep lugging around.

SIXTEEN

For the next few weeks my life revolves equally around pretending I'm not falling hard and fast for Doyle Rahn and praying the end of term comes quick enough that I can tap out of all this convoluted emotional craziness and go back where I belong. The problem is, by the time Doyle is through being my personal tour guide in this wild, crazy, beautiful place that's sort of slowly growing on me, I'm not sure how I'll feel about leaving.

"Hey, slugger, how you feelin' 'bout that old man and the ocean and the fish...?" Doyle's popped up next to me in the sardine-can halls of Ebenezer High, and I seriously wonder if he's a ninja. How does he always manage to appear out of thin air?

Not that I'm complaining.

"Like, a swordfish dinner would be delicious right now." I moan. "Eating fish is cool. Swimming with fish is cool. Going fishing might even be cool. Reading an allegory about a fish? I'd rather sleep with the fishes."

"Hear that. I'd much rather deep-sea fish for a giant, killer marlin than read about some old dude doing it." He stays protectively close to my side, which has been his default stance since the night I got pulled over.

We walk to class in a comfortable tandem, grinning like fools whenever our shoulders bump. Ansley sits at the spirit club table, legs crossed, smoothing the pleats of her navy cheer skirt. Her corn-silk ponytail whips around the second she catches sight of Doyle's golden hair, and she immediately throws her head back, laughing hard and long while the three guys in football uniforms crowded around her stare at each other with a mix of confusion and pride.

Sadly, it appears these lug heads actually believe they made an unintentionally hilarious joke. It doesn't seem to dawn on them that Ansley is using them as gorgeous, muscled props in her quest to make Doyle jealous. Even more sadly, Ansley notices Doyle didn't hear the first cackle and goes for round two. The guys around her puff their chests up, probably contemplating their future stand-up comedy careers.

"Are you ready for Lovett's quiz? You know it's going to be intense."

"I hope. I read by flashlight in the back of my pickup while Lee checked a field for cotton fleahoppers—"

"You are lying!" I interrupt. He keeps striding along, using his elbow as a kind of rudder to direct me around the crush of our classmates.

"Why would I lie about cotton fleahoppers?"

"Because that has *got* to be, like, a *Yu-Gi-Oh!* character or something. No way is that an actual insect." I study his face, positive I'm going to see him crack a smile and tell me he's just kidding. But nope. Apparently cotton fleahoppers are a real thing. "So, are they, like, a plague of locusts?"

"Naw. They're brats when the cotton's young, but they eat bollworm eggs when the cotton gets older, which is a blessin'.

We're way past cotton crop harvest now. This was an experimental plot at Armstrong we been monitoring. Trying to see if we can use fleahoppers instead of pesticide to control bollworms. They done ate the crap outta last year's crops *bad*."

"So you were collecting data about cotton fleahoppers who might become fierce predators of the evil bollworms? Exciting stuff. You might give Hemingway a run for his money, Doyle."

"Funny you say so, smart-ass." He reaches up and undoes my hair clip, holding it hostage above his head. He finally takes pity on my short-stack height and lets me have it back. "I was lying there, tired as hell, wonderin' which I'd rather—be stuck on a boat deep out at sea, fighting storms and a bunch of sharks to bring in a monster marlin, or stuck in the bed of a truck figuring out how to fight a million crawlies with another million crawlies in a sad-lookin' cotton field."

I reclip my hair and look at him from under my lashes. "So which scenario won out? Because, honestly, they both sound so crappy in their own ways."

"The truck and the field. I hate some of the pesticides they gotta use to keep the crops up, so I like knowing we help. It ain't glamorous, but it makes a difference. Some of them pesticides hang in the air like a kinda sticky cloud. I breathe 'em in and think, 'Nah, this can't be good.' So I like bein' a cog in the machine run by the smart guys makin' changes. Plus I knew I'd finish my chapter and get some shut eye, then come here and get to jaw 'bout all that *lit'rature* with you."

"You know, I get you're a cog right now, but you're smart. Get a degree in botany and you can run the machine."

"You ain't saying it jest 'cause you think it'll give you a better shot at getting in my pants?"

"Stop making this a joke," I warn, and his smile loses some of its court-jester urgency. "You have some pretty amazing ideas in that overinflated head of yours. There are tons of ag programs at schools with rolling admissions. Oh, look what I found!" I tug the school list I printed for him out of my messenger bag, write *APPLY NOW* in capital letters, and pop the pen into my bun as I hand it over. "You're welcome."

Doyle pinches the paper between his fingertips like it's coated in cotton fleahoppers. "Rolling admissions?"

"Yep. It means they don't have a deadline for enrollment. You took your SATs?"

"ACTs." A worried frown puckers his mouth.

"That's fine. If you don't show me *proof* that you actually applied, I'm cutting you off cold turkey. No more breakfasts, no mudding, no baseball, no nothing. I'm not playing with you, Doyle Rahn," I warn, channeling Ollie.

"Hey now, we're supposed to be friends. What you're proposin' sounds a whole lot like extortion," Doyle mutters.

"Consider yourself extorted then." We step into the classroom.

"Whelp, I better get to my desk so I can study s'more. Can't get some fancy college diploma without finishin' high school." He holds his hand out so I can slide into my seat and winks. "Best'a luck."

"You too, Rahn."

Ansley flounces in and surveys the room, trains her laser gaze on me, smirks as she sits primly on her chair, then turns to Doyle. "I think it would be really cute if our class started a tradition where the senior Homecoming King and Queen gave out flowers *together* on Valentine's Day."

Doyle doesn't look up from his paperback when he answers. "Homecoming was way back in the fall, Ansley. What's that got to do with Valentine's Day?"

"It's got to do with *you*, fam," Alonzo interrupts. Several of the guys around him snicker, and several of Ansley's cheer-leader cohorts scowl.

Ansley snorts and neatens the perfectly aligned books on her desk. "That's plain stupid, Lonzo. Everybody knows me and Clint Fulton are a couple now, so I'm gonna go ahead and ignore you." She flicks her fingers his way dismissively. "This is about our school and our senior year. I got to thinking that Ebenezer's been lettin' go of too many traditions lately, so why don't we start some of our own?"

"Right, but why not some that actually make sense?" Alonzo presses.

"I'm not even talking to you, so mind your business!" Ansley snaps.

Alonzo sits back slowly and shakes his head. "Girl, the only one you're yappin' to is your fool self. Like it or not, we're *all* Rebels, whether we got crowned in some dumb pageant or not. No one here cares about all this high school–royalty crap 'cept you."

"Funny you claim you don't care." Ansley tries a nasty smile on for size. It's a perfect fit. "You're the one who decided to run against Doyle for Homecoming King as some sort of joke."

Ansley cuts her theatrical laugh short when Alonzo's face clouds over and his nostrils flare. "I was *elected*. It's not like I put my own name on the ballot or something."

"Bless your heart, Lonzo. So it wasn't a joke after all? But you didn't really think you'd win, right? I mean, no offense, but *you*? Homecoming King? Against Doyle?"

"Back down, Ansley," Doyle warns. Alonzo gives Doyle a silent nod of thanks.

"Alonzo only lost by a few votes," Khabria chimes in coolly. "My best friend's the student council president, and they had to do a recount to make sure."

"I heard the race for Homecoming Queen was just as close," says Braelynn, her face as red as her hair. She and Ansley are locked in a furious stare-down that definitely hints at intrigue in the Mean Girl ranks.

"I don't know why everyone is jumping down my throat for making a suggestion," Ansley huffs.

"I got my own booth to run for Ag Club anyway," Doyle announces, staring back down at his book. "So we can forget about homecoming."

"You can wear your little plastic crown when you sell carnations if it makes you feel better, Ansley," Lonzo says, sticking out his bottom lip as her eyes bug out.

"Just shut up, Lonzo! You act like you're Ebenezer's elected senior class mouthpiece. And I'll remind you that it's a free country, Doyle Rahn. I'll talk when and about whatever I please."

"There's a big difference between talking and stirring the pot jest to cause trouble. You should know that better than anyone," Doyle says in a low voice.

There's a chorus of oohs, but the bell rings before Ansley can retort. Ma'am Lovett breezes in and drops quizzes still hot from the photocopier on the first desk of each row. Quiz time means silence in Lovett's class.

I turn very slightly in my seat so I can see Doyle bent over his paper from the corner of my eye. I love the way he grips his ballpoint pen too tight, like it's a fishing rod with a monster marlin at the other end. When Ma'am Lovett calls for the quizzes back, I'm pretty sure I did fine, but I would have gotten a perfect score if I'd given the questions the kind of attention I gave checking out Doyle Rahn.

And it's like that for days. The sound of his laugh, his addictive smile, the way he leans against the lockers with this effortless cool—it all has me distracted and more head-spinny than ever.

So when a unique opportunity to *do something* other than ogle this guy I think I'm falling for presents itself, I grab it... even if it's a Valentine's mission.

Just because it's Valentine's Day tomorrow doesn't mean it *has to* be romantic. In fact, I have a history of activism aimed at downplaying the romantic social stigma of this greeting-card "holiday." To combat the idea of Valentine's as some couples-only romantic shindig, Ollie and I developed the Sisters Before Misters Valentine's Day project as part of our feminist club at Newington. We basically ran a campaign by ripping off memes with cute sayings that made sense, like Fries Before Guys, and had girls buy each other little flowers-and-candy packs. They became the must-have Valentine's accessory, and Ollie and I were able to buy a cake on March 15 with the proceeds. (To celebrate Ruth Bader Ginsburg's birthday.)

I'm unsurprised to find Valentine's Day in the South causes just as much angst as it did in the North.

"Wanna see somethin' cool?" Doyle asks me on the way to lunch just before the big day. The cafeteria is already overfull, since no one is opting to brave the seventh-circle-of-hellfire temperatures outside. To add to the general sense of misery, fish sticks are on the menu, so there's a decidedly unpleasant piscine aroma that mingles with too many deodorants, body sprays, and perfumes as well as some good old-fashioned BO.

I'd take a hard pass on eating in the cafeteria today anyway, but the fact that Doyle wants to show me something secret makes following him wherever he wants to take me the logical choice.

"All right." He leads me to a large glass building that looks jungle hot through the condensation-laced glass. "Ready to see as close to heaven as you're gonna get on Earth?"

"How can I say no to that?"

He sweeps open the door and we enter a hot, sticky room that's impossibly bright from two distinct sources. One is the ever-present sun, baking the glass with a white-hot light. But the second is gorgeous, blooming pink flowers with delicate petals and a bright orange…

"What's this thing called?" I point so I don't have to play botanical Mad Libs based on the plant unit I completed back in fourth grade.

"The stigma." He runs the tip of one finger across it, and the whorls of his fingertip are dusted in gold pollen.

"These are gorgeous, Doyle. What are they? Did you plant them?"

"They're swamp hibiscuses, and I did. Usually the Rose Court nominees sell carnations for Valentine's Day—"

"Not roses?" I ask.

"Too expensive, I guess.

"Other than that, there's always a bake sale table for the Daughters of Georgia. The drama club does these romantic fortune cookies, and there's a dunking booth run by the captains of the guys' sports teams—"

"A dunking booth?" I interrupt.

"Yeah. Sports are pretty big 'round here, in case you didn't notice—"

"You don't say," I drawl as I roll my eyes.

His grin is laced with evil. "Think for a second 'bout all the girls who've been burned by these guys who think they're God's gift to women jest 'cause they have decent hand-eye coordination. Now imagine what a girl'd pay for tickets to toss baseballs at 'em and watch 'em get half-drowned on Valentine's Day."

"That's so sexist and crazy and—"

"Genius?" He waits for my reluctant nod before he informs me, "Dunking booth always makes a killing."

"You didn't want to run a kissing booth? I bet you'd have a line out the door." I smile like I love my joke, even though the thought of Doyle doling out his kisses drives me insane.

"Would'ya buy a ticket?" He waggles his eyebrows. "Mebbe *all* the tickets?"

"In your dreams, Rahn." Or mine. But he doesn't have to know that…

"Ansley and the cheerleaders usually corner the flower market with the Rose Court's carnations 'cause they sell 'em so cheap, but I wanted to do something a li'l different this year." He tugs my hand and we stroll up and down the rows. Delicate pink petals nod as we pass and release an intoxicating perfume. "Anyway, kissing booths ain't really my thing. Now, flowers…?"

"You have more than a green thumb. You've got…like, a Doyle and the Beanstalk thing going here." I drag my fingers along loamy dirt and across terra-cotta pots. "This…this is definitely your thing."

"What grows is, yeah." He stops and examines one wilted-looking flower with the care a doctor would lavish on a preemie. "If I could live in the dirt year-round, I would. It's like my whole world can be crumbling 'round me, but I get to digging, bring something to life from dirt and seeds, and I feel like a whole man. You know what I mean?"

"I do." Theoretically. It's been a while since I've done anything I feel that passionate about. "So what's the plan for these bad boys?"

"They're on the buy slips for Valentine's, and the proceeds'll go to more greenhouse equipment for the Ag Club." He draws the edge of this thumb along one thin stem, and I find myself feeling jealous of a flower.

"Very noble. I'll make sure I buy one for somebody." I turn and pretend to be engrossed in a flower.

"Somebody? You got a sweetheart?" He leans back with his hands on the table behind us, lifting himself on his arms. Every muscle in his upper body bulges, and I flip-flop between the urge to roll my eyes and taking a long look.

"Maybe I do. A lady never tells." I peek at him from the corner of my eye. "How about you? Do you think you'll be getting a carnation from someone special? A dozen some-one specials? The Doyle Rahn fan club has to be reaching maximum membership at this point. I mean, you *are* the reigning Homecoming King..."

He rolls his eyes and turns to the flowers as I giggle-snort over the same joke I've been softballing at him since Ansley's little theatrical stunt in English.

"You're never gonna let me live it down, are ya?" he sighs.

"I just feel so *misled*." I snicker. "I mean, if I knew I was in the presence of the all-powerful Homecoming King, I might have shown some proper respect. You're Ebenezer royalty after all," I tease. "Lonzo seemed bummed about losing. We didn't have homecoming at Newington. Was it that big of a deal here?"

"More stupid traditions people take way too seriously is all." He stops arranging the leaves under one flower and says, "Tell ya the truth, I don't think I won fair and square."

"Wait. *What?*" Doyle has this "knights of Camelot" sense of honor and justice. I cannot imagine he'd throw that out the window for a stupid high school popularity contest.

"Ansley honestly and truly thought if she and I paraded around with those goofy crowns on our heads and danced in the school gym as Homecoming King and Queen, I'd forget she thought I was trash that needed fixin'." He sinks his fingers into the dark soil and his face instantly relaxes, like the soil is calming. "Like Lonzo says, you don't run. You get nominated. Ansley made all my posters and talked her cronies into voting for me. I wanted nothing to do with it, and I was pretty sure I'd never win. When they called my name and led me up to the stage, she whispered that she 'made sure it happened for us.' That it was 'part of our fate.'"

"Well, *that* makes sense, at least for Ansley. I'm positive corruption will be a huge part of her fate." I can't help a little dig. "But did she think you'd be happy she… What did she even do? Stuff the ballot boxes?"

"I don't have a clue, but I hate that I got up there and accepted what was probably Lonzo's crown." He balls his soil-dusted fingers into a tight fist. "If I had any way to prove it wasn't legit or figure out what Ansley coulda done, I would've blown the whole thing wide-open. But she's sneaky, and the last thing I wanted to do was show more interest in the whole homecoming mess."

"That's crazy." I lean closer to him.

"Yeah. E'rybody thought I was the one'd be broken up when Ansley and I weren't a couple, but the truth was, I prolly coulda gotten a restraining order. Ansley Strickland's not used to hearin' the word *no*."

"Definitely noticed she doesn't give up easily." I give him a wicked grin. "Do you think you'll wind up with an unwanted bouquet of carnations from a persistent ex?"

"Nah. Ansley ain't gonna send me crap. Never did when we were together. Ansley's of the opinion that men give presents and women receive, period. She'll get Clint and a few of her 'secret admirers' to buy a whole flat. She'd never dare walk around with less than a couple pounds of flowers on Valentine's." There's a soggy bitterness to his retelling, like he's both disappointed and bored by it all.

"Well, I'm perfectly happy knowing I'll probably be flowerless tomorrow."

I cringe. I meant to say it with this kind of swagger, a badass-single-lady-feminist vibe but I gave off more of an I'm-desperate-for-you-to-buy-me-flowers jam. Gross.

Doyle doesn't seem to overthink it though. He stops showing off his impressive pecs and leans close to me. "No way in hell you won't get a flower tomorrow, Nes."

So, yes, I'm a little giddy when ballots are passed out at afternoon homeroom, and I see people scribbling down the orders they'll pick up at the booths tomorrow. It's only when I actually read the form that I get a sick feeling. I find Doyle by his truck when the bell rings, but he doesn't look freaked out, and I relax. Maybe I misread?

"Hey, you're a sight for sore eyes." His grin is so happy, I'm sure I made a mistake.

But the pessimist in me wants to double-check.

"I tried to order one of your flowers, but they weren't on the form."

His smile collapses. Dammit. I was right.

I hold out the red photocopied order form, and it lists the four other items that can be purchased for Valentine's Day and the clubs the money will go to—but Doyle's Ag Club swamp hibiscus is missing.

"I was in the greenhouse during homeroom, so I didn't see this. I don't get it." He flips the paper over, like he's expecting to find something hidden in the fine print. "I put the paperwork in weeks ago. Never even thought to check it. I jest assumed… Dammit! What am I gonna do with all them flowers if nobody ordered any?" He half crumples the form, but I pluck it from his hand.

"Who runs off the forms?" I demand.

"I don't know. School spirit club?"

"Spirit club?" I cock an eyebrow. "So cheerleaders?"

He smacks the flat of his palm to his forehead. "What the hell did I ever see in that snake of a girl?"

"Maybe she's trying to force you to share a table with her any way she can."

"All those weeks spent growing all them plants for nothing." He looks exactly as crestfallen as he looked excited in the greenhouse.

"Not for nothing. So you're not on the paper ballot. Okay, it's not like people leave school and go milk cows and read by candlelight. They have phones. And laptops. And social media."

His face brightens for a nanosecond before it falls. "But we're so behind already. Do we have time to do this? Plus it ain't jest sellin'. The spirit club helps with distribution and money and all that. I was planning to be at school by four to get the flowers all cut fresh, but I don't have time to do the rest."

"If there's one thing I'm gifted at, it's figuring out an emergency plan B when my original plan falls apart."

"You'd help me?" His gives me a shameless puppy-dog grin.

"Just because I don't believe that stick in my backyard will grow doesn't mean I'm a plant hater. I like flowers."

His smile pulls wider. "So, what do we do, boss?"

I embrace the heady power of organizing. It's strange to not have Ollie running interference for me like she usually would, and I recognize that will mean details will fall through the cracks. I'm okay with that. In the immortal words of Mark Zuckerberg, "Done is better than perfect."

And, holy crap, do Doyle and I get it *done*.

"Meet me at the greenhouse in five, no shirt, with a marker."

"What was that now?" Doyle's expression is half pleased, half terrified.

"You. Biceps. Flowers. Marker. Five minutes. Go!" I shove him away and head to the cafeteria, where I notice some of the cardboard milk-delivery trays lying around. After batting my lashes at a friendly custodian, I walk away with my arms full.

"Shirt off." I nod to Doyle when I reach the greenhouse, and he tugs his shirt over his head from the neck, his face pink as a hibiscus. "Marker," I demand, telling myself to stay professional while I ink his skin. "What are you charging for these?"

"Two bucks each." He holds his arms straight out on either side, and I neatly calligraph *Southern Hibiscus for Your Belle, $2 each, All Proceeds to Support the Ag Club* on his warm, tanned skin. I have to press a palm to the hard, flat expanse of his pecs to steady my hand.

"Done. Pose." I point my camera phone.

"Pose?" He looks over his shoulder, like he's hoping a troupe of male models is behind him.

"Yes, Doyle Rahn. You. Pose. Now." I sigh when he freezes, stiff as a statue. "Do that thing you did before."

"What thing?"

Now it's my turn to glow pink. "When you leaned. With your arms…and the muscles." I sigh with impatience and demonstrate.

"Aw, that?" He slides back on his hands and gives me a suggestive smile. "So you were eyein' me before?"

I snap clusters of pictures. "Well, it was hard to ignore your shameless posing. Yes, you got my attention for all the wrong reasons. I hope you're proud."

"As a peacock."

I flip through the shots. Once he stopped posing like a spooked ice sculpture and started flirting with me, the camera ate him up. Choosing one shot isn't easy, but I do the hard work and send him the best picture.

"Who would be happy to get a sexy Doyle Rahn picture they could share on their social media?" He opens his mouth to protest, but I shake my head. "Don't get all pretend-humble. Send. Now. To as many people as you can. And when you run out of Doyle admirers, send to Ansley haters."

After twenty nonstop minutes of texting and messaging across social media platforms, Doyle says, "Done. That all?"

"Not quite. Rose Court, drama, sports, Daughters of Georgia, and Ag Club have booths. Who else is there who's has never had a role in this whole Valentine's mania but wants one?"

Twenty minutes later, he has the glee club, the dance club, the majorettes, and the band geeks enlisted in his scheme. A posse agrees to get to school early, glitter in hand, and decorate.

"You'll be there, right?" Doyle's dragging his shirt back over his head as we walk to the parking lot.

I'd be proud for resisting the urge to sneak one last shirtless peek…if I didn't have those pictures of him saved on my phone. "I'm going to see this campaign through," I promise. When I get to my car, there's an awkward moment where I feel like we both want to say or do something that's probably not a good idea…

It's the flowers. The partial male nudity, the muscles. The single-on-V-Day blues. That's what makes me think telling him he's adorable and planting a kiss on that handsome mouth is a good idea when it's obviously not.

"See you in the morning," I say instead. If I burn a little

rubber leaving the lot, it's all in the name of attempting to make good choices.

I'm pissed about my choices when my alarm goes off at an ungodly hour the next morning. I try not to put too much thought into what I wear because this is just me helping a nice guy, not some whole *thing* where I'm buying into the Valentine's Day romance machine.

I do select a very flattering pink V-neck and some lipstick Ollie swears makes me look ten times hotter instantly. It is a *holiday* after all. I listen to an old Fernando Villalona CD Mama Patria made for me years ago, and my feet tap out the unrushed step movements of the merengue I wish I could practice with a certain lavender-eyed partner.

I get to school and am surprised at how full the parking lot is. When I push through the main doors, I'm doubly surprised to find Doyle standing in the middle of some serious controlled chaos, calling out orders and compliments like a jolly foreman.

"What's up?" I ask Doyle as I try to get a grip on all the crazy activity going on around him. The drab cardboard boxes I grabbed yesterday have been given a glitter-and-paint make-over. There's an assembly line of hibiscus arrangers, a small section of the band practicing what sounds like Frankie Valli's "Can't Take My Eyes Off You," a dance troupe arrangement, and a hibiscus face-painting station.

Khabria is clapping her hands and shouting, "Okay, listen up for your duty station. I'm only telling you *one* time!" Groups of students scramble to their feet.

"Your ideas, in motion." He gestures at the sea of giggling students. "You're a genius."

"I guess I am." I've never had a campaign go so well so quickly… Doyle's charisma is a powerful tool. The two hours to homeroom fly by because there's glitter to sprinkle and signs to make and cash boxes to set up.

A full-service dunking booth goes up outside the main entrance doors. Trays of fortune cookies with heart-shaped red paper slips are arranged. A huge table of sweet baked goods with lacy napkins and wax-paper wrappings is like a Pinterest dream. The saddest table by far is for the Rose Court's carnations. It's clear they've spent many years getting by on popularity instead of effort.

Khabria holds a wax paper–covered treat out to me. "I saved you a lemon bar. Thought you'd be hungry after getting here at dawn to help Doyle."

"Khabria, this is *amazing*." I nod to the Daughters of Georgia table. "So you didn't want to sell with the other cheerleaders at the Rose Court table?"

"Nah. My granny's been on me to join the Daughters of Georgia since forever. Plus the Rose Court table's always full. I'm just an extra there. Here? I'm kinda like a celebrity." She waves at the group of beaming girls who are clearly over the moon that Khabria Scott decided to join their club.

"And Ansley didn't mind?" I ask, but back up when Khabria glares at me.

"Ansley Stickland is *not* my keeper." She grimaces at the table full of sulky cheerleaders, jealously looking at the fun going on around them while Ansley barks orders to try to last-minute resuscitate their anemic table. "Let's just say I'm not too good at following rules, so I'm on the outs with my squad at the moment."

"I hear that. Thank you for the best freaking lemon bar in the world." I'd rather be struck by lightning than admit this to my abuela, but these lemon bars are almost as good as her *mantecaditos*. Almost.

Khabria smiles and heads back to her table, and we wait for the crowds with our breaths held.

When students stream off buses and out of cars, Doyle's Darlings (*not* my idea) get to work hocking their flowers with an enthusiasm that would've made Eliza Doolittle proud. Soon the halls bloom with pink hibiscus flowers tucked behind ears and stuck in buttonholes, on makeshift wrist corsages, or clutched in fists. Apparently the spirit table was a little elitist to potential shoppers. Our man-of-the-people advertising strategy gave Doyle a serious leg up. Everyone has from bus arrival to the end of homeroom bell to enjoy the festivities, and the atmosphere at Ebenezer feels distinctly carnivalesque.

I watch a girl with an awesome arm hurl baseball after baseball at a target outside the dunking booth, dropping a tall, panicked-looking guy into the sloshing water over and over.

"This is for standing me up last Friday! And this is for the Snapchats you sent that girl from Screven! And this is for saying I throw like a girl!" she screams as baseballs fly.

Everyone cheers like it's any other fun activity, and I hustle over to the fortune cookie table before I witness any more dunking booth drama. I grab one cookie for charity's sake and crack it open to read my fortune.

"'The very essence of romance is uncertainty—Oscar Wilde,'" I read as I crunch on the cookie. Doyle *does* make me question everything I thought I knew… Is that how true romance begins?

Didn't Oscar Wilde die lonely and unhappy?

I meant to nab Doyle a flower, as a symbol of our platonic friendship, but the hibiscus blooms are gone before homeroom is over, and I can't even find a ratty carnation after first block.

Ansley bounds into English with a clutch of assorted flowers, laughing and tossing her ponytail.

"Are you freaking out that Doyle made more money than you? They announced the totals raised, and Ag smoked Rose Court, hands down!" Lonzo hoots.

Ansley's bright smile stalls for a second, but she forces a laugh. "Freaking out? It was all for charity, Lonzo. Plus I *adore* hibiscuses. If I was mad, I wouldn't have accepted all of these, would I?" As Ansley humble-brags about her flower-based popularity, she sends me a pitying look. "Guess nobody clued you in 'bout our Valentine's tradition, Agnes? Bless your heart, don't worry. It's just some flowers." She smirks, and I come up with nada on the crushing comeback scale.

It's no big deal.

It *isn't*. If I'd gone to Newington this morning though, I'd have exchanged gifts with Ollie.

But I didn't.

No biggie.

Khabria turns in her seat and rolls her eyes. "Ansley, she could've had her pick of flowers. When *someone* forgot to put Doyle's flowers on the order forms, Nes is the one who got Ag Club organized. She's probably just flowered out by now."

I smile at Khabria and would have called it a pretty successful Galentine's based on Ansley's furious expression alone. But jest then two underclassmen come in carrying a glittery box loaded with the most gorgeous blooms. They beeline past Ansley, who was clearing her desk to make room, and place the box of flowers in front of me. One of them opens a card, clears his throat, and reads:

"To Penelope,

"Thank you for all your help. We made enough for the greenhouses. I know you probably wanted a carnation, but there were none left.

"Hope these are okay.
"Ulysses"

"Her name isn't Penelope," Ansley announces in a panicked squeal. No one is listening.

Everyone cranes their necks to see the garden on my desk. Doyle had to be eavesdropping outside the door because he saunters in like he knows exactly what kind of entrance he makes.

He heads to me with a large pink flower, kneels down, and says, "Happy Valentine's. Thank you for saving my ass." There's a chorus of *aws* that's so saccharine, the air tastes sweet.

"I meant to get you one," I tell him quietly.

He winks a violet eye and heads to his desk. "I prefer live plants. Jest water that tree and think of me, and we'll call it even."

"Doyle?" He pauses. I finger the soft pink petals. "Thank you."

"You're very welcome. You and me? We make a good team, Nes."

If my heart flutters a little, I'm blaming it on allergies from all this pollen.

SEVENTEEN

A rhythmic tapping jolts me awake, and I grab my field hockey stick, ready to bludgeon whoever's stupid enough to bother me this early. Outside the window, I see a familiar truck. I drop my weapon and bury my head in the covers, not sure if I want to laugh or cry or murder Doyle Rahn with my bare hands.

I text him after the next tap, because I don't trust my willpower if I see his face.

I WILL KILL YOU IF YOU DON'T GO AWAY!

Short, sweet, to the point.

He taps again.

"Dammit, Doyle!" I croak in something between a sob and a scream. "I'm tired!" I pound my fist on the mattress, then jump up and raise the window sash.

Doyle leans in and surveys my room. "Sparse. Wanna swim?"

Dawn is not my favorite time, but Doyle convinces me to give sunrise a shot. I make sure my sigh is audible, but the sound just cracks out his smile. I'm shockingly defenseless when it comes to that smile.

"Five minutes," I grumble.

I slam the window shut, root around for my bikini, brush my teeth, and avoid the mirror. Doyle's waiting, feet in the pool, proper swim trunks on, smiling like he's just seen the answer to all his problems.

Which is impossible, since I'm nothing *but* problems right now. I start to drag the inflatable lounger out of the shed, but I step back and yawn when Doyle intercepts. My feminism is still asleep at this hour. I'm tired enough to let chivalry win this hand.

Once it's in the water, I fall facedown on it, fingers trailing in the water. He does quiet laps around me like a seal circling a boat.

"How the hell are you so chipper?" I gripe as he dives and rolls. "Didn't you have to help your cousin babysit fleahoppers again last night? You should be like the walking dead."

"I don't need a lot of sleep." He cups water in his hand and squirts it at me.

I turn my head and glare. "Force my hand and I *will* jump into action and drown you so fast, you won't have time to beg for your life. Stop."

Just like that, the wind collapses from his fun sails and I feel like Comandante Buzzkill.

"Talked to Critter. 'Bout the night you got pulled over." He zeroes in on me, waiting.

I groan and fling an arm over my eyes. I start to get hot and think about how cool the water would feel on my skin, but my laziness wins out over my discomfort. "You seem calm about it. I'm going to guess you agree it wasn't a big thing?"

Doyle cracks every knuckle on both his hands in immediate response, which kills that wet dream.

"You never mentioned his name when you told me 'bout that night." He sets his mouth in a grim line.

"He did say he knew you." I left that out in my abridged retelling. "I assumed he meant he knew you the way cops in small towns just know everyone?"

"He's my cousin," Doyle admits.

I vow then and there to *never* say a word about anyone to anyone else *ever* as long as I live in this one-horse town, because I'll never be able to untangle the knotted web of family and friend and lover and former lover and enemy and whatever-the-hell else that ties every person to everyone else in this place.

"Okay." I slide into the water to cool my skin and this conversation. "Maybe he went hard on me because he wanted to make sure nothing shady was going down—"

"My cousin's a dickhead," Doyle declares. "And a fucking racist." The last word shoots out and rattles us into silence.

I tilt my head back and feel the cool of the water spread over my scalp. "Maybe that too. I don't mean any offense by this, I swear…but racism's kind of a thing down here, right?"

He gapes at me like I just blasphemed all over the noble truth of his existence.

"What?" I reach up and squeeze the water out of my hair a little too aggressively. "C'mon, I don't mean it like that. Trust me, New York has tons of racists too. I guess I just never experienced much firsthand, like, directed at me before. And, it sucks. It does, no doubt. But that's just what things are like down here, right? Like you said, change isn't exactly high on anyone's agenda." I try to do this flippant shrug, but my heart isn't in it.

Under all the bravado, I'm still pretty shaken up.

"You're wrong." Doyle's eyes meet mine, looking like two flames burning dangerously hot. "Change is on *my* agenda."

"Okay." I try to tread lightly. "You know, I don't think you're a racist or anything."

"How's that possible, if I see things happen and jest keep my trap shut?" he counters.

"Fair enough. But you can't go up against the police force, right?" I repeat the last word with a little more insistence. *"Right?"*

"Not the cops. Though my cousin's gonna be sorry he messed with you," he says darkly. "I guess I gotta start with somethin' I can change."

"Like what?"

My interest flares up immediately. I know nothing about mudding, tubing in rivers, drunk baseball…but activism? Not to toot my own horn, but back at Newington I was treasurer of SPARK, the feminist club, *and* cotreasurer with Ollie of the Random Acts of Kindness Club, all of which I am proud to say I was part of. Admittedly, I was the worst treasurer ever, and we always had to throw together last-minute bake sales or chili cook-offs to make up for the deficit.

Doyle opens his mouth and chooses his words carefully. "So I'm not sure if you know? 'Bout prom?"

"Prom?" I try to picture a Southern prom and nearly drown myself belly laughing. "Holy crap, I bet you guys go crazy over prom down here, don't you? Girls get all dolled up for gym class, so prom's probably like some ball straight out of *Gone with the Wind*, right?" I stop the chatter.

Doyle's expression is hard to read, but if I had to, I'd say it's embarrassment.

"Oh. Do you not have prom?" I've heard there are schools

that can't budget proms. But considering Ebenezer has a football field with stadium bleachers and state-of-the-art lights that look like the ones used to light Beyoncé during the Super Bowl, I don't think money can possibly be an issue.

"We do." Doyle cups water in his hand and dribbles it along the back of his neck, avoiding my eyes. "We have two."

"Like a prom and homecoming? Or do you mean like junior and senior prom?"

We had a fall fling at Newington, since our football team was kind of pathetic and technically played for the nearby Catholic school since there were only enough players for a team when we combined schools. Everyone else played soccer, which made sense since thirty percent of the students had parents who were foreign nationals and soccer fanatics.

"Not exactly like that." When the French doors open, Doyle's head jerks up and he sighs like he's relieved.

I swivel as my mother walks out. I may be seriously annoyed with her, but it's not shocking she got caught up in a love triangle. My mom is the kind of mom people constantly mistake for my friend. People routinely compliment her perfume/smile/outfit/hair. The mystery isn't *why* my mother had an affair; it's *who* she chose to have it with. She could've chosen anyone.

"Doyle, right?" My mother sashays across the patio in a black pinup-style bathing suit.

My mother has amazing style. We used to raid each other's closets all the time. Since she took a jackhammer to our life and I took one to our relationship, my wardrobe has never been grungier.

Doyle Rahn is too much of a gentleman to greet my mother while he floats in the pool like some wet rat. He hoists himself out of the water, wipes his hand on his dry shirt, and shakes her hand while making eye contact. He's pure manners.

"I never got a chance to introduce myself properly before. Doyle Rahn, ma'am. Pleased to make your acquaintance, officially."

"The famous Doyle. It's nice to *properly* meet you."

I close my eyes and wish they'd both let me nap.

My mother uses the pool for laps, not for leisure, so I know we're cramping her style, but I'm too exhausted to drag myself off my float.

"It's nice to meet you, ma'am."

I wonder if my mother finds the soft, rolling way Doyle speaks as charming as I do. Even half-asleep, that voice makes my body prickle with goose bumps.

"I don't want to crash the party—"

"Not at all, ma'am," Doyle exclaims like the prince of proper behavior he is. "We were jest talking."

My mom makes small talk with Doyle—mostly answering his polite questions about the classes she's teaching and discussing weather and trees and other topics that are basically making for the world's most boring conversation lullaby—and I appreciate how cool around my friends she is, never trying too hard, but never tiptoeing around us.

My social isolation has made things worse for the two of us. We're marooned in this house like two gnarly castaways, clawing at each other's throats for survival, and there's no one to keep up polite appearances in front of, so our worst floats to the surface like the grimy slick of oil on top of dishwater.

I nod off to the sound of my mother and Doyle chatting and wake up to Doyle leaning over the edge of the pool, jostling my shoulder as my float bumps into the side. "You wanna go inside to nap some more? Your mama invited me to stay for lunch, and I don't turn down food. I was gonna help her make it. Somethin' called puttanesca?"

I groan and unstick myself from the raft. I wait to feel the awful tingle of early onset sun poisoning, but someone pushed me under a big canopy-style umbrella Mom and I eyed a thousand times but never figured out how to set up.

"Mom didn't know how to work that."

"It's tricky," Doyle's smile makes it clear it's not. Not for him at least.

"So." I slide off the raft and drift to the stairs. He comes over to join me. "Plants, baseball, umbrellas, cooking—is there anything you *aren't* amazing at?"

"Not so fast on the cookin'. I mean, I can grill, of course. Imma Southern man. And I mastered my gramma's secret biscuit recipe. Fair warning—I may use it on you in case of emergency." He nudges my shoulder. "I don't cook real fancy though."

"Stop worrying," I say with that kind of chuckle that's meant to be the opposite of reassuring. "Puttanesca loosely translates to *whore pasta* in Italian. It's definitely *not* fancy."

"What's it made with?" For the first time since I've known him, there's fear in Doyle's eyes.

"Are you afraid it's made with whores?" I'm giddy over seeing überconfident Doyle Rahn ill at ease. "You'll just have to get in the kitchen and see."

If I had any thoughts about upending this little repast or catching a few more z's, that's all back-burnered by my desire to catch a glimpse of Doyle in an apron.

By the time I've pulled on a pair of cutoffs and a tank top, Mom has Doyle in a black Kiss the Chef apron. He stands at the counter clutching a knife and frowning suspiciously at a can of anchovies. The oldies station blares and Mom shakes her hips, singing into her wooden spoon about stopping in the name of love.

"You swim with gators. Are you seriously afraid of these tiny canned fishies?" I whisper as I slide up alongside him.

His smile is weak. "I don't know if I ever ate one before." He pokes at the can with the tip of the knife like he's ready to use the blade in self-defense.

"It's nothing a big, strapping lad like you should be scared of." I peel the top off the can back, hold it under my nose, and inhale deeply. "Mmm. Delicious." I pinch one out by the tail and dangle it over my open mouth.

Doyle's eyes bug wide. I give a commercial-grade smile as I drop the miniature fish in and chew ecstatically.

"Aggie, please don't eat all the anchovies," Mom scolds.

It's more playacting than actual discipline, but we both pause. The tension in the air creates an atmospheric shift intense enough that Doyle notices, and he shifts uncomfortably.

My mother gathers herself like a gladiator in the arena. She squares up, not about to back down. It's not the most dramatic coup, but I've been waiting for this, for the return of my mother the *parent*. Now that she's showing signs of blooming, I decide not to screw it up.

I slide the tin across the granite countertop to Doyle and meet my mother's gaze. "Sorry. I guess I should be in charge of the capers or something gross?"

Doyle's laugh slices through the tension. "Grosser than tiny dead fish in a can?"

Mom spins toward the stove like she's afraid to say anything, but she belts out the next lyrics so loudly, Doyle jumps.

"Cooking makes her a little crazy," I whisper, and, damn, it all feels *good* and *right*.

Not like I'm ready to forget everything that happened in

the last few months, but being a constant bitch wasn't exactly a peaceful way to exist. A new calm settles over us as we move toward getting back to our version of normal. We chop and mix and sing along with the sweet songs that play on the radio. Doyle's rendition of "Stand by Me"—belted out in part on his knees, arms raised, eyes closed, like the words are coming from his soul—turns me and Mom into whooping fangirls. While the sauce simmers, Mom hums along to "Earth Angel."

"My father used to come home, stinking drunk on whiskey, and dance with my mother to this song in our little yellow kitchen in Belle Harbor." She closes her eyes, and I feel like I can see what's inside her mind: Grandma and Grandpa's galley kitchen with the big blue ceramic fruit bowl on the wooden table and the stained-glass sun catchers winking in the window. I imagine Grandma, young and pretty like my mother, her arms around my charming grandfather's strong neck, rolling her eyes as he clomps around, drunk and so in love.

When I look over, Doyle is holding out his hand to me.

I'm not sure any words have ever sounded more amazing than the two that fall from his lips right in the middle of my kitchen.

"May I?"

"Right here?" I'm not prone to blushing, but a hot rush of blood tingles up my neck and cheeks.

"I don't think we oughta put on airs." He crooks his finger. "It was good enough for your gramma and granddaddy," he teases.

My mother turns to check on things that don't need checking. I step into Doyle's arms. I'm guilty of having a serious Cinderella-at-the-ball secret fantasy. I'm barefoot in our sunny kitchen, but the way Doyle looks at me makes me feel like I'm decked out head to toe.

He looks at me like looking is only the beginning of what he wants to do. Like his eyes are searching out beautiful things no one else has ever bothered to notice about me.

I've never had such a visceral reaction to being looked at before. My heart seems to pirouette in tight, quick circles, and I go dizzy. He folds his arms around me, one hand anchored at the small of my back, one tangled around my fingers, locking my hand tight to his chest.

How can someone have such a loose, easy way of walking, but be so graceful and sure-footed when he dances? In his arms, I don't have to think about how to move. I allow my body to melt against him and follow his lead.

"I'm just a fool," he croons, tugging me a step closer so the space between us erases.

"You sure are." It doesn't come across as light, the way I mean it to. It scratches like my words are about to tear open something dangerous.

He doesn't sing the next lyric.

"For you," he amends, his smile kicking up a notch.

He takes advantage of my stunned silence, and gets creative with his dance moves, spinning me around with sure fingers, and dipping me so low, his hand is the only thing saving me from a collision with gravity.

Mom's applause clears the hazy spell Doyle put me under. "You two would put Ginger Rogers and Fred Astaire to shame."

I want to dance with him to the next song and the next one after that. But we're in my *kitchen* with my *mother*. There's also the danger of being swept up in feelings that once led me to complete heartbreak.

For so many solid reasons that don't hold a candle to my desire to be near him, I push away.

"Doyle's definitely a smooth operator." We stand a few inches apart, and I fight the urge to put my hands all over him by knotting my arms across my chest. "Is the sauce done?"

Mom quirks an eyebrow. "Don't you dare even think about it, missy. That sauce needs to set." She tugs off the floral apron my father's mother made her with bright fabrics she had shipped from the Dominican Republic. "You two scoot. I'll call you when the food's ready."

Doyle waits for me to lead the way, and I practically have to drag him to my room. He follows right up to my doorway, then hesitates.

"Is this more Southern manners? You may enter, Master Rahn," I say with a flourish of my hand as I flop onto my mattress.

"You sure it's all right with your mama? For us to be in here?" He clears his throat and says *alone* in a hushed voice that makes me giggle.

"My parents are pretty liberal. When I started dating Lincoln, my mom sat me down to tell me about how I shouldn't be worried if I didn't orgasm vaginally from sex at first, then handed me a box of condoms. Ribbed. *For my pleasure.*"

I'm the only one laughing at the story.

"Sorry. TMI?" I pat a messy spot on the bed where he can sit. He takes a single cautious step into the room.

"I don't like thinking about you with your ex-boyfriend." His voice loses all of its usual warmth and comes out so icy and clipped, he sounds almost Northern. He flips open one of the cardboard box flaps at the base of my room's storage ziggurat.

"Hey, I never said you could root through my stuff. Isn't that, like, Manners 101?" I'm irritated at how, suddenly, my perfectly comfortable mattress pokes me with previously unnoticed springs. Or maybe I'm reeling from how quickly the lovely giddiness I felt in Doyle's arms spirals away, like dirty dishwater down the drain.

He digs his hands deep into his pockets and leans against the wall, looking at me with hooded eyes. "You got a nice room." It's more accusation than observation.

"It's pretty cookie-cutter."

"Better than what a lot of people got."

"I guess your room is pretty crap if my messy hovel impresses you."

"I share with my brothers and cousin, remember?"

"Wait, you share a room with both of them? *And* Brookes? That's gotta be tight."

"When Lee's home on leave, both of them. So there's sometimes four of us in a room half this size. Two sets of bunk beds and a whole lot of elbowin' for an inch of space." I raise my eyebrows in sympathy and he explains, "Helps make sense of why I roam so much, I guess. Need more space than I got at home." He shifts his eyes around my room. "Maybe you should do something with this place."

"Why bother? I'm not—"

"Planning on sticking around for long?" he finishes for me, and it comes out sour.

I flip facedown and thump my fist on the pillow. "How'd we go from slow dancing to lectures? Can't we go back to talking about crap that doesn't make us fight? Like...prom! You were telling me about prom."

There's nothing more generic and safe than prom. It's one of those cliché traditions that unites horny teenagers across the nation, bonding us all by our love for formal wear, crappy food, schmaltzy music, and nostalgia.

Doyle pushes his shoulders off the wall and sits on my bed, finally losing that stiff-limbed, disappointed look I bring out in him every so often. But it's strange, because instead of looking judgmental, he looks guilty.

"So…'bout prom?" He scoots back so his knees don't knock against his jaw. It's hard to sit this low to the ground, especially when you're a giant like Doyle.

I hook a hand around his elbow and force him to trust fall back. We stare at the plaster swirls on my ceiling.

"You *sure* this is all right?" His strawberry blond hair curls on my pillowcase, and I fight back a lump in my throat over how beautiful it is.

"It's not like we're humping each other." I turn on my side and let a devilish smile curve over my lips. "Unless…"

"I don't *want* to get your mama chasing my tail with a shotgun." Before I can protest the likelihood of that happening, he holds up a hand. "I'd rather imagine it going down that way to keep us from fallin' into something we might not mean to fall into jest yet."

There are so many baseline feminist, sexually liberated problems I have with every ideology he's spouting, but there's also the weird but true fact that his insane philosophies make me feel protected. So, no matter how my brain protests, my mouth stays shut.

I scoop up his hand and lace our fingers together, then position our joined hands between our chests like a barrier. "As long as we just lie here, we're okay."

I mean it in the way it sounds on the surface plus a level deeper, and wonder if Doyle knows that. He rubs his thumb along my index finger, knuckle to fingernail, in answer.

"Prom ain't a topic that'll put things at ease." His face is so close to mine, I can see every spoke of purple blue and pale lavender in his eyes.

"Why not?"

"It's complicated." He squirms when I don't give him the out he so clearly wants. I'm intrigued. *Why* does the always-chatty Doyle want to let the whole prom thing drop? "It's… not official."

"So, like a rebel prom?" I mean it as a joke.

Doyle never misses an opportunity to smile at my jokes. He doesn't smile at this one. "Nah." It's crazy, the amount of bitterness he infuses in that one word. "More like a coward's prom. Two of 'em."

"You mentioned that. Two proms," I say. "That's not that weird, Doyle."

"Two proms." He darts his eyes down, staring at his big hand caged around my smaller one. He says each word like he's pulling it out from somewhere deep inside himself. "One white, one black."

For a second, I think he's talking about our hands. Our skin. *Us.*

Gentle as his voice is, that stripped-down description of the two of us—which is just the truth—presses a jagged knot of emotion into the back of my throat.

"What?" I croak out dumbly.

"Proms. Two. Black. White." He goes monosyllabic and tightens his fingers around mine.

Once it all clicks, a cyclone of thoughts roars through me so fast, I drag Doyle with me when I sit up.

"What?"

"I know it ain't right. Lots of people hate it, but lots don't. Tradition's a strong thing down here. ''Cause it's always been that way' is everyone's favorite way to explain anything they know ain't right—"

"Like…segregation?" My words hop between his, a fierce one-two punch.

Doyle hangs his head and nods like he's personally responsible for all this.

I tug my hand away, because I need to get my whirling thoughts landed, but Doyle takes it as evidence that I want to be nowhere near him.

"Right. I should probably see myself out—"

"What the hell are you talking about?" I stand on the mattress and push him back down with one bare foot. "Why would I want you to leave? Why are you not *freaking the hell out*?" I demand, pacing back and forth on the squeaking mattress.

Doyle reaches out his hand and lets his fingers graze my calves as I sweep by.

"I guess you can adjust to even a real batshit-crazy idea once you live with it long enough, but I swear I nearly puked having to tell you, Nes. That's not freaking out enough for ya?" He runs his fingers through his hair until he looks like a ginger Einstein and rubs the back of his neck raw. His skin is flushed and his are eyes overbright, like he's got a fever.

I stand so that my feet straddle his body, and I look down into his upturned face. "And everyone's just like, 'Oh, it's not like we had a Civil Rights movement or anything. This is totally fine'? I know things are backward around here sometimes, but this is… *Seriously*, my mind is *blown*, Doyle." I pace away and rush back, pointing in his face. "Mind. Blown."

In case he didn't catch the sentiment the first time.

"It's always made me sick," he says shakily.

"What *is* prom? Just a fun party with fancy clothes and crappy catering and uncoordinated dancing… Oh, and what am I missing?" I throw my hands up and let loose a maniacal evil-villain laugh. "Racism! Of course. *Racism* is the key ingredient to any successful social gathering down here, right?"

"Nes, it's not like everyone thinks it's right—"

"Just *most* people?" I interrupt. "And let me guess. The people who agree with it are the people in charge? Crooked cops, principals, queen bees…the people *nobody* bothers to stand up to?"

I should take the innocent-until-proven-guilty high road, but putting probable faces to this lunacy makes it personal. Under all my rage I'm sad, pissed, and grossly disappointed.

"Nobody bothered to stand up to them *before*," Doyle amends.

I'm too furious to listen to technicalities. This is some screwed-up bullshit, no matter how it's worded. I refuse to go limp with tears, so I rev my anger into high gear.

"So what about me?" I demand, staring at him like it's not a clearly rhetorical question.

He shrugs, but I'm being vindictive even though this isn't his fault, and I know that.

"Don't shrug at me, Doyle Rahn! Do I get to choose which prom I go to? Or do *they* get to decide my race? Oh my God, do they whip out the 'one drop' rule? How 'bout the old 'paper bag' test? How about other people of color at Ebenezer? Huh? Asian kids? Native Americans? Pacific *goddamn* Islanders?"

I make a fist and think about how satisfying punching a hole in the wall would feel. I also think about how much broken knuckles would hurt.

But what's a little more hurt? I hurt right now. Badly. I ache.

I think about what Jasper and Ollie and even Lincoln said. About going home. To Brooklyn, where there are problems, of course, but nothing remotely like this. Isn't relocating to choose a better, easier existence over a crappier one what my families did—my Irish family *and* my Dominican family? They left places that were unjust to come to America, a land of freedom and equality and opportunity.

"What a crock." I collapse on the mattress and loosen my fist, suddenly sapped of all my strength.

Doyle sits with his legs pulled up, chin on his knees. "I want to change it."

"Yeah? Good luck, Doyle. People around here haven't gotten over losing the Civil War, and that was two hundred years ago." I scowl, not at him, just for the sheer satisfaction of letting my face twist into something ugly.

But he takes it personally. "Please, Nes, hear me out. I been thinking on so many things since I met you. I know you ain't planning to stick it out here for the long haul. I don't blame you for that, not at all. But maybe we can do this now, while you *are* here, while we have the time. Change this one thing, you and me."

"Change *what*?" I look out the window, at the wall, anywhere but into Doyle's hopeful eyes. "News flash, Doyle—the rest of the country at least *attempts* to keep their bigotry under wraps. Is this even legal? And if it's such a long-standing tradition, who do you think will want to fight this other than you and me?"

He hesitates.

"People will," he insists.

But he hesitated.

"People like who?" He can't come up with a single name. "Doyle, it's a lost cause. I want you to know I'd never look down on you for going to your own prom, even if it is a racist travesty. I get that it's a big rite of passage or whatever."

Doyle gives me a blatantly irritated look. "I ain't plannin' on goin' to prom without you, and I ain't plannin' on skip-pin' either. So, you do what you like, but I'm finding my way 'round this mess."

I'm ready to keep arguing, but my mother calls us in to eat. I block the doorway. "Look, my mom is sensitive about the way people treat me…about race and stuff. So shut your trap about this, okay?"

He nods and keeps his mouth pressed in a tight line.

We march out to the dining room, where my mother has set the table with her mother's shamrock-adorned Belleek china. I'm going to smile when I eat her food because it's time to call a truce. I can't be at war at school and out in the world and at home. I need a safe haven. I think about how quickly digging in your heels becomes a habit you can't break.

It becomes your own little *tradition*.

I refuse to do that anymore. To show Doyle there are no hard feelings directed at him, I link my pinky around his under the table and appreciate the tiny smile he crooks my way. We will eat and pretend things are good because lying is how I'll shield my mother from the ugly truth facing me.

Taunting me.

Daring me to do something, even though the odds of my winning are microscopic.

Dammit. I was never good at walking away from a dare.

EIGHTEEN

Off and on for the next few weeks, Doyle bothers me about the prom business.

That's not all he does, of course.

He drives me to a deserted beach with white sand dunes we run to the top of, then slide back down, screaming until our mouths are full of grit. When we're tired and sun pinked, I drive his truck on the beach. Once the stars speckle the sky, we park and lie in the bed, our heads pillowed on rolled-up sweatshirts. The radio is stuck on the oldies station, and Doyle sings "Brown Eyed Girl" to me even though I don't have brown eyes and I'm not Doyle's girl.

"Your voice is so beautiful," I sigh as he croons along to Van Morrison.

"Hush now, you're gonna make me blush," he says, but he's clearly pleased with his talent and even more pleased with my admiration. He continues to sing the song in a way that makes me think those "hearts a-thumpin'" might be all about us.

One random Saturday morning he knocks on my window with a bundle of hangers and tells me to shut my piehole as he digs through a box from the pyramid in my room without asking permission.

"You need to make up your fool mind 'bout whether you're staying or going." He points the hangers at me like a judge's gavel.

"I'm here, aren't I?" I snap.

"Are you?" He tugs out some long-sleeved shirts that are too hot for this sauna state. "If you're stayin', commit. I'll help you dip your baby toe in, chicken."

"I'm not a chicken." I *bok*.

"Really? Prove it." He holds a bare hanger out to me, but I swat it away.

"Later."

"Now." One more shirt, one more hanger. "You don't wanna dip your baby toe in, I can always straight toss you into the deep."

"I wish you'd find someone else to bother." I negate my weak threat by grabbing a hanger and zipping my leather jacket onto it. Another thing I can't wear here, but I couldn't wear it in Brooklyn in March either. It's practically summer here, and they're getting another freak spring snowpocalypse back home.

"You'd cry a river if I found someone else to bother." He hangs the next shirt with arrogant determination.

"Would not," I mutter, but not too loud.

By the time we're done unpacking that single box, there are a couple shirts hanging in the closet, an owl sculpture on the windowsill, a few pictures stuck to the once-bare walls, and a tin of violet candies on the bed between us. Doyle grins at me as he sucks on a candy only he'd like, and when we almost kiss but don't, his eyes brighten to lavender and his lips smell like tiny purple flowers. I'm hungry to know if they'd taste that way too, but I'm too gutless to find out.

On other days, he picks me up for school too early, and we sit with our legs draped over each other's in the grassy school courtyard. Doyle crowns me with tiny flower wreaths. We scout new breakfast spots and share ice-cream sandwiches at lunch. I make him Spanish flashcards and teach him to dance the merengue on the cement patio next to the pool, my hips rolling with his, the relaxed movement of our feet forming pretzel patterns on the bricks as Rubby Perez's "Volveré" keeps our steps and hearts in sweet rhythm. He traces the red *A* tattooed on my neck and it's not quite enough, but neither one of us knows how to ask for more.

A thousand times our lips almost touch, a thousand times we go quiet and lean close, but…nothing. All the chances we had to kiss and never took have webbed us into this sticky friend zone.

My ongoing quest to navigate the ins and outs of Ebenezer High has also been as successful as I could have hoped. Which means I'm almost entirely ignored.

The only time I'm noticed is when Doyle bounds down the hall to meet me, when his friends extend me an obligatory greeting, or when Ansley attempts to make my life hell. I've managed to dodge Armstrong's office, but I feel like Generic Mean Girl One's dogging me, waiting for me to slip up so she can march down and file her report.

One random Tuesday, Doyle has a dentist appointment, so I'm alone in English when Ansley takes the seat behind me, claws out, ready to pounce.

Her smile's triumphant, most likely from some "win" she imagines she scored against me. "Hello, Agnes. I see you're not attached to Doyle's behind for once."

"Don't you have some puppies to kick or babies to steal candy from?"

She brushes her fingers over the gold cross that dangles from her neck and gives me such a smug look, I have to sit on my hands so I don't punch it off her face.

"I'm coming to you on behalf of Doyle's friends. We're real worried about him. He's not spending time with any of his old crew. He's skipping church and didn't try out for baseball this year, even after he promised Coach he would. His family asked me if I knew where he was running off to. They're hoping he's not getting in with the wrong crowd."

The snide comeback I had loaded jams in the barrel. Does Doyle usually go to church every Sunday? Did he want to play baseball?

I'm half-sure she's lying, but if she's not, I'm hovering at the border of worried and offended. Did Doyle's family really reach out to her? Is he hiding the fact that he's hanging out with me? Am I Doyle Rahn's dirty little secret?

My jaw clicks tight and my shoulders start to shake, but I choke my rage back. I need to check with Doyle before I swallow this girl's crap.

Ansley's main objective is to get these kinds of thoughts sprinting through my brain. I refuse to give in to her mental terrorism, and I will *not* let her know she's got me panicked.

"Doyle Rahn is a big boy. A *very* big boy." I roll my eyes up and bite my bottom lip, letting that innuendo flap out in the breeze for a few seconds. Unlike me, Ansley doesn't have a Texas Hold'em game face. She presses her lips together until they're bone white. "I'm sure if he needs to be somewhere, he'll be there. And if his family is so worried about him, they should ask him. Or someone he *actually chooses to spend his time with*."

She sputters before recovering. Her next barbs sink in deep. "You think you can waltz in here and do whatever you like, dontcha? Sure, you're this hot new thing that spreads your legs and got his interest, but you'll be gone soon. People like you don't belong here *and never will.*"

"Maybe people like Doyle don't belong here either. Maybe he's hungry for something better than this racist one-horse town."

Ansley tugs at her cross with so much force, I expect the chain to snap. "Doyle's family's been here since Georgia was just a colony." Spittle flies from the sides of her mouth. "His people got pride in where they come from. He's lost his way, but he'll find it again." She fumes for a few beats, then flips her expression and smiles like a sociopathic Cheshire cat. "I talked to Doyle's cousin."

"Brookes?" Betrayal slaps me upside the head, which is crazy. Brookes met me for a few minutes that night after Doyle took me mudding, but that doesn't make us friends. It's hard having so few people on my side.

"Reginald," she corrects. She searches my face like she expects more of a reaction. "Or maybe you know him as Officer Hickox?"

My blood pressure rockets so fast, it's impossible to hide my reaction. Ansley smirks in genuine satisfaction in the face of my distress.

"You remember him then? Oh good. Reginald Hickox's a respected officer in the Ebenezer PD. I know you think you're above the rules, Agnes, but there's a reason we live in such a God-fearing place when the whole rest of the country's going down the drain." She thumps her fist on the desk, rolling with this whole good ole gal, Tea Partier monologue.

"It's because people here know it's important to keep things the way they've always been. We know how quick one rotten peach can spoil the whole basket. So my advice for you would be to keep your head down, 'cause a lot of people have their eyes on you." Like a switch flipped, she goes from TV evangelist to calm and collected beauty queen smearing lip gloss over her wolfish smile. "Though I don't expect you'll stay long past graduation *if* you even make it that far."

"Ms. Strickland?"

I never noticed Ma'am Lovett enter, but there she stands, fists planted on her hips, glowering like she caught us smoking a joint or fist fighting.

"Ma'am?" Ansley's hateful mask melts away, and she's all glossy, innocent smiles. Holy crap, is she some kind of demon? I can't compete with her supernatural level of treachery.

Even my mortal powers are useless here. My wit comes off as sass. I can't tell the truth because the lies around here run too deep. My character won't carry me because I can't change the way people see and judge me—or stereotype and prejudge me.

I've never had a panic attack before, but I think I may be popping my nervous-breakdown cherry.

"Ansley Strickland, I need to have a word with you about your final paper on Hemingway. *Now.*"

The smile smears off Ansley's face. I should be able to enjoy seeing Ansley squirm, but I'm busy figuring out how to keep the walls from folding in around me. I throw my hands on the desk and breathe in and out as slowly as I can. But it's not slow. It's so fast, I start to get a little light-headed.

"Agnes?" Ma'am Lovett leaves Ansley, rushes over, and presses a hand to my forehead. "You don't look well at all. I'm writing you a pass to the nurse. You need to stay there until I come for you. Do you need an escort?"

"No, ma'am. Thank you."

At Newington, it wouldn't have been a question. Ollie would already have her arm around my shoulders.

"Hey, Nes, you look like you saw that girl from *The Ring*." Lonzo says as he walks into the classroom.

"I, uh, feel bad," I manage to say.

"'Scuse me, Ms. Lovett, you want me to take Nes to the nurse?"

Ms. Lovett gives a relieved nod. "Don't dawdle, Mr. Washington. You have a quiz to make up."

"Yes, ma'am."

Lonzo's arm keeps me steady as we make our way to the nurse's office, but I have to grip the wall every once in a while so I can catch my breath.

"You okay, Nes?" If I had to guess how crappy I look based on Lonzo's expression alone, I'd say "death warmed over."

"I'm just exhausted. Or maybe dehydrated." I laugh at my own ridiculous excuses. What am I, some celebrity on a bender?

Lonzo drops me off in the nurse's office and tells me to get better soon—the World Series of Drunk Baseball is right around the corner, apparently. Before I can tell him I may be retired from semi-intoxicated ball, the nurse breezes in, glances at my pass, looks me over, and directs me to a cot with a curtain around it.

I sit, put my hands on my knees, and squeeze them hard, willing myself to breathe evenly. Away from Ansley's accusations, the full classroom, and Ma'am Lovett's watchful eyes, my heart slows down and my breathing evens out.

I haven't been sleeping all that well, so, even though the cot is lumpy and I can hear other students coming in to complain about sprained ankles and strep throat, I decide to lie down and close my eyes. Just until my mounting headache loosens its vise grip on my temples. My little doze turns into the kind of sleep people get only after pricking their fingers on spinning wheels, and I stay that way until I wake up to Ma'am Lovett shaking my shoulder.

I spring up, panicked. "Damn. Sorry. Excuse me." I wipe the drool off the side of my mouth with my wrist. "Did I sleep through class?"

"Yes, you did. Thank you, Nurse Hathaway. I'll catch her up on what she missed and see her to her to next class."

The nurse offers a distracted wave as she administers ointment to a huge guy with a tiny scratch on his elbow.

Ma'am Lovett and I walk shoulder to shoulder, my shuffling rubber soles and her clicking heels creating a soft cacophony. "I'm sorry, ma'am," I begin. "I swear I didn't even feel sleepy until I got—"

"Come in," she interrupts, gesturing to her empty classroom.

Feeling brave, I pick the chair next to her desk. The one where she isolates people who are in trouble and need a stern talking-to. The one Ansley was planted in before I mentally wrecked.

"I overheard Ms. Strickland threatening you." Her eyes are deep brown, fierce, and reassuring. She's someone I'm glad to have on my side.

Theoretically anyway. The last thing I need is to blow this whole Ansley thing even more out of proportion.

I immediately protest. "She's kind of a monster, but I swear, it's just your average mean-girl crap—"

"I heard her reference Reginald Hickox." It's like Ma'am Lovett's raised eyebrow is her own Jedi mind trick. It goes up, my mouth shuts.

I do this whole throat clearing, nervous tic thing that probably makes me sound guilty before I say a single word. "Right. See, I was driving Doyle Rahn's truck—with his permission—

and I got lost. Officer Hickox pulled me over and questioned me. It wasn't a big deal."

The events of that night goose-step through my mind. I'm desperate for the privacy of the nurse's office cot…and maybe a paper bag to breathe into.

Do not lose your cool, Agnes. Enough panic attacks for one day.

Ma'am Lovett whips her glasses off her face, leaving her features naked of authority. "Officer Hickox has a reputation. You aren't the first person of color he's pulled over without reason." She shakes her head like she's clean-slating a mental Etch A Sketch. "Officer Hickox was rough with my grandson a few weeks ago. He claims Malcolm was belligerent, aggressive, but my grandson isn't a troublemaker. He has a clean record at school, work, church, and he says he was pulled over for no reason, harassed, then charged with resisting arrest. We're in talks with the station, but I doubt there will be any disciplinary action taken."

"I'm so sorry," I whisper.

I remember the billy club, the cuffs, the gleam of the gun on his belt. How relieved I was that I didn't have to get out of the truck. How worried I'd been about what would happen if he used force. Now I realize that night could have ended up much worse than it did.

Was I pulled over because of the color of my skin? Was I let go because of my gender? My age? The fact that there was nothing to book me on? Or was it because intimidating me was enough for Officer Hickox that night?

Trying to make sense of it feels like drowning slowly.

"There are so many people fighting hard to do right, to make things good. But there is still so much power in the wrong hands." She opens a drawer in her desk. "Have you ever read Nella Larsen, Agnes?"

I shake my head and she hands me a book. *"Passing."* I read the title out loud.

"It's about two women in Harlem in the '20s. Both are mixed race, but one chooses to 'pass' as a white woman. This book is supposed to be about an America of the past, but there are quite a few relevant themes. I think…it's important for us to remember where we came from, to remember that old battles only matter if we acknowledge that they were fought and why we had to fight them."

"I'm not…I'm not actually African American." I admit this kind of sheepishly, like I lied, even though no one ever asked, and I never offered. "My father is Dominican."

"Race is getting more beautifully complicated by the generation, isn't it?" She raises both eyebrows, but this time it's like a surrogate for a smile. "My daddy swears we're half-Cherokee. My mama swears great-grandaddy escaped slavery with the help of a Creole woman he fell in love with." She shrugs. "I've decided to respect their oral history and embrace all the intricacies of my ancestry."

I flip the pages of the book against my thumb, listening to the whip of stories I'll know soon. "My grandmother claims we're descended from the Taíno Native Americans who were settled on our island before any European settlers came along and African slave rebels who escaped and formed their own Maroon colonies. That's what her abuela told her anyway."

We laugh a little awkwardly. Then Ma'am Lovett's mouth pulls flat. "There are too many people who see two colors and an easy division right down one line, black and white. And they like it that way. On both sides. People like you…" She shakes her head, but her mouth has pulled up into a smile I think might be proud.

"Are pains in the a—butt?" I fill in that blank.

"And challenging. And inspiring, Agnes. This old town needs to shake some of the dust off. I know full well that you're only here for a few months. I bet I'll be able to smell the rubber burning off your tires the second that diploma is in your hands. And I know you probably want to keep your head down." She puts her own head in her hands. "It's my job to tell you to do exactly that."

When she looks up, her eyes shine with the same kind of daring that convinced me I'd love her right off the bat.

"So it's your job to tell me that. Fine. I hear that, officially. But what if we weren't in school right now?" I let my voice drop low. "What would you tell me?"

"I'd tell you things I have no business saying. I'd tell you to be braver than I ever was at your age. To not let the things that bother you go unchallenged. To call out the people in charge when they misuse their power." She pinches her lips together. "At the same time, I think about you and Malcolm and all the young people who are brave in the face of ignorance. And I worry that your principles might cost you too much."

"It's not like I never thought about being mixed race in Brooklyn. I guess it was just that everyone was almost, like, competing to be unique or surprising. By comparison, I was boring, seriously. Really boring."

"*That* is something I just can't imagine." She tears a single sheet from her mint-green pad of hall passes. "Where are you headed?"

I'm being dismissed and once I leave, Ma'am Lovett will transform back into the tyrant of English she always was, never acknowledging this wrinkle in reality.

I'm not ready to have it end.

"Computers doesn't end for five more minutes. Maybe I can sit with you until the bell?"

She purses her lips like she's not sure whether she's going to say anything. But then she says it all.

"I'm not sure why you left Brooklyn, but I'm glad you did. Maybe you thought you were boring. Maybe you blended in in a way that felt comfortable. I'm sorry your time here has been a trial so far, but know that your passion, your truth, can be a catalyst for change. You're not alone in wanting to challenge the things you don't agree with. You could be one of the first to speak up. And if you did, you'd certainly be one of the loudest." She leans forward, her eyes narrowed to slits. "Don't hide what you have under a bushel, Agnes. Let all that light come out and shine."

When the bell rings, I think I should hug Ma'am Lovett or shake hands, something to acknowledge all we've shared. But the strange veil that lifted between us falls back into place in an instant. She puts her glasses on her nose and raises her eyebrows. I wonder if this is what it's like to see a member of the Illuminati after a secret meeting.

When I hesitate, she flaps her grade book my way. "Scoot. I don't want you to miss any more classes."

"Okay. And...thanks. For everything." I hold up the book and walk to the door backward.

"Agnes?" She stares intently at the neat columns and rows of her grade book.

"Yes, ma'am?"

She never looks up. "I'm rooting for you."

I stumble into the hall, wishing for Doyle's steady presence with my entire pathetic heart.

I leave Ma'am Lovett's classroom with the kind of glow people radiate after river baptisms, like I got anointed by some wise, tough guru...but I think she chose the wrong person. I'm pissed about a ton of what's happened since I've been here, but I'm not eager to pin a bull's-eye to my back and hold my breath, waiting to get taken down.

Ma'am Lovett herself pointed out that, in order to get out of this place, I need to keep chugging forward.

But the sugary poison of Ansley's words jitters in my brain and distracts me all day.

I squint in the hot sunshine of the parking lot after the final bell and realize I could've stayed in a panic coma on the nurse's cot because I didn't absorb a single fact all day long.

"Hey, pretty thang."

I shake off my daze and notice Doyle leaning against my car, one cheek swelled and a little pool of pink drool leaking out of the side of his mouth.

"Holy crap, you're a sight for sore eyes." I borrow one of his favorite phrases as I fling myself into his arms and sink into the tight pull of his hug.

"If this is the way you're gonna act every time I get back from a root canal, Imma start snackin' on sugar cubes." He swings me around, lifting my feet off the ground.

"Don't." I slap his chest when he puts me down. "Idiot, you'll make your heart pump and you'll start bleeding. Lemme see." I peer into his mouth. "Was it horrific?"

I've never even had a cavity—thank God, because I'm scared to death of a drill coming anywhere near my mouth.

Doyle shrugs. "I got a high pain tolerance." He touches two fingers to the side of his mouth. "Nes, why you lettin' me drool all over myself?"

I grin as he mops his drool with his sleeve. "You're gonna be doing that for a while. Want to stop at the Dollar General and get a bib?"

"Wanna hide out with me till I'm presentable again?" His

voice toes over the line of friendliness and dances right into flirtatious territory. "Nurse me a bit, maybe?"

"I don't have the kind of time that mission demands." He tries to stick his tongue out and winds up licking his chin. "Okay, you're pathetic. I guess I'll keep you company and hidden until the Novocain wears off."

"That's my girl. Your place cool for a couple hours?"

I shift my backpack on my shoulders. "Right. My place. That's fine. Also, I've never seen *your* place." I draw in a deep breath. *Just ask him. Don't let Ansley play you. There's nothing to worry about.* "Is there a reason for that?"

"You got a pool. You got a new house that's mostly empty. You don't share a room with three slobs. Your mama is sweet and her cooking's pretty amazing. Did I mention how much I liked that…uh, the, um, the whore—damn, I hate that word—"

I save him from his gentlemanly humiliation. "*Puttanesca.* And yes, you've told me a million times. I promise I'll get you the recipe so you can try it."

He shrugs. "Gramma's kitchen's hers. Period. She don't take kindly to anyone poking 'round in it without her permission. Every egg and slice of cheese's rationed. Guess that's the way it's gotta be, seein' as there's five men with bottomless pits for stomachs livin' with her."

I raise my eyebrows. "You're sure she doesn't want your help? Who'd *want* to cook for five hungry dudes every single day?"

"I swear if she'd let me in, I'd help. I think cookin's her way to destress. She makes magic in the kitchen. You gotta try her brown-butter greens sometime."

"I'd love to try them. Sometime. I mean…if you wanted me to." The quiet between us speaks volumes.

"I know you're probably curious to meet my family. You better not be thinking I'm ashamed of bringing you around or somethin'."

I stutter, thrown off guard by how accurately he reads my embarrassing insecurities.

"N-n-no! If I thought you were ashamed to be around me, I'd have kicked you to the curb a *long* time ago, Doyle Rahn."

He raises one eyebrow high, but lets it go. "Jest so you know, in case you ever have to meet 'em, my brothers are kinda dicks. And you met Brookes. Not the most fascinating person in the world. My grandparents are nice folks. Just old-school."

I wonder, by *old-school*, does he mean "adorably confused and hokily out of touch" or does he mean "very, very tied to the way things are and have always been, which does not include saucy, dark-skinned Brooklyn girls hanging around their grandson"?

"So, you're *sure* it's not about me?" I ask to double-check.

He points at me, wagging his finger. "*I knew it.* You don't trust me. Fine. Decision made. We skip swimming and your mama's delicious Italian, and I take you to my place. But I'm warning you—it's chaos. I know it might seem excitin' when you imagine it, but trust you me..." He leans close, so close I tilt my head back, lick my lips, let my eyes flutter shut. "It ain't." My heart lurches as he pulls back. "You wanna follow me?"

I nod and press a hand over my palpitating heart.

He's right.

Excitement really isn't all fun. And I have a distinct fear that the excitement I'm dredging up every time Doyle Rahn gets too close might just kill me.

NINETEEN

We pull up at a house a quarter the size of the one Mom and I rent. It's white with a broad gray porch and tons of beautiful plants growing all over outside and up trellises, arches, and lattices, with twisting vines and flowering blossoms everywhere.

It's not so much a house with nice plants as a miniature Garden of Eden with a domicile in the middle.

"Wow." I stare, mouth gaping. Doyle takes my hand and drags me to the door.

"Yeah, a green thumb runs strong in the Rahn family. Would be pretty embarrassing if we weren't able to grow some nice stuff on our own plot."

I dig in my heels as he tugs on my wrist. "C'mon," he insists.

"I'm looking."

"You're stalling."

"You're being pushy."

"You're chicken."

"That's not very gentlemanly of you."

He presses a finger to his lips.

"Shh. My gramma catches wind I'm screwin' 'round when

it comes to manners, she'll take a switch to my backside."
He points to a low, old tree with far-reaching branches. "We
picked our own switches, from that oak. Never grew quite
right. Stunted or something. Those thin branches down low
cut like a whip. The thicker ones leave black-and-blues like
you been clubbed."

He shares this like it's some fond and hilarious childhood
memory. It makes my guts clench. My parents did *not* believe
in spanking or any form of corporal punishment.

"Doyle," I hiss. "That's, like, *child abuse*."

His smile falls. "Ain't nothin' but good old-fashioned discipline, trust me. A whippin' smarts enough to leave you thinking over what you done wrong. A real beating?" The shake
of his head is knowing. "No rhyme, no reason, and you don't
get the luxury of thinking *anything*, 'cept that you wish you
could sleep a week and wake up outta pain."

It's like Doyle's speaking a language I'm not fluent in. I'm
unconvinced there are gray areas to beating on a kid, and his
description of bad versus unspeakably worse doesn't convince
me violence is just a different form of discipline. But I obviously hit a sore spot, and I don't press him.

"Wanna go in?" He nudges me toward the door.

I know exactly how Gretel must've felt standing outside the
cute little house made out of gingerbread and marzipan. Am
I about to walk into a place where the adults are lunatics who
cage and eat children?

Metaphorically, of course.

Literally, they just beat them with switches.

"Okay." I step over the threshold, relieved to see there isn't
a giant walk-in oven dominating the place.

All the walls are white and the floors are lemony polished
wood. My room at home is light on decor, but this place is

Spartan and so clean, you could perform surgery in the living room. There are two big brown couches and a plaid La-Z-Boy, plaid curtains, a wooden coffee table with a glass dish of fancy marbles, and a fireplace featuring a mantel crowded with pictures of boys: boys fishing, boys hunting, boys covered in dirt and grime, boys standing at attention in freshly ironed button-downs and staring at the camera with grim, cornered looks.

Doyle's easy to spot. He's the one with the hair that looks like it's on fire. The other boys are darker and lighter blonds. They all share identical cheekbones and only slightly varied smiles. Doyle's is the biggest by far.

Banging from the kitchen interrupts my portrait inspection. Doyle drags me toward the noise, and I catch a glimpse of a small, sharp-looking woman, with tired eyes and teased hair dyed butter yellow, standing over a counter dusted with flour. She glances at the two of us and puts down her rolling pin slowly.

"How'd the dentist go?" She gestures for Doyle to lean in and he opens wide for her without being told.

"Good enough. Still got most of my teeth."

"You brought company for supper."

It's not a question or an accusation, she's just announcing a fact. I sense it's a big deal, her acknowledgment of me.

"Gramma, this is Agnes Murphy-Pujols."

"It's nice to meet you." I say polite words, but my brain is consumed with figuring out how she gets her hair that shade of neon yellow. Maybe she uses highlighters… Doyle elbows me in the ribs, and I glare, then immediately shout, "Ma'am!" so loud his grandmother jumps a little.

She sighs. "There'll be plenty enough to eat." She looks at me pointedly. "I *always* cook plenty."

"Thank you. For the food. Soon. I mean, thank you in advance. Because you're cooking. For the—" Doyle drags me to the back door before his gramma can smack me upside the head with the rolling pin just to shut me up.

"Gramma, Imma go tend to the pumpkins!"

"It's a fool's errand, Doyle. Pumpkins spoil in the sand. Too hot, too wet," she warns, but Doyle's already heading to the backyard.

The backyard is a denser, more colorful Eden than the front. Birds perch on the edge of stone birdbaths and flit between budding branches, tweeting and squawking and chasing each other. Rainbow-winged butterflies and swirls of humming bees nuzzle inside bright flowers in a twirling rhythm that feels like modern dance choreography.

"This is like something out of a fairy tale," I marvel. Doyle takes a knee next to a patch of dark earth and rotates each of several tiny pumpkins like he's handling baby dragon eggs.

"Like Grimm?" He pushes his hat's bill back off his forehead so he can see more clearly.

I consider the ethereal settings and the strange, dark details that lace through every Grimm fairy tale and nod. "Yup. Like a Southern Gothic version of Grimm's fairy tales."

"My gramma likes you." He glares at what looks like a tiny green watermelon as he says those moronic words.

"Uh, *nope,* you couldn't be more wrong. Your grandma definitely thinks I'm a moron. Makes sense, since I acted like one in the kitchen." I plop down on an overturned bucket and watch two birds in vicious combat over what looks like a stick while Doyle fondles squash gently. I feel jealous. Of squash. I'm officially out of my gourd. And punny. "Did she like Ansley?"

"Why would you ask that?" His words are even, but Doyle's lips pull down a quarter inch on each side.

"Inquiring minds want to know."

"Ansley Stickland ain't worth the headspace you're giving her."

"I asked *one* question. You don't have to answer." I stretch my leg out and tap his hip with my toe.

He stands and brushes the dirt off his knees. "I'm not gonna lie—my grandparents were excited when I brought Ansley home. They thought I was finally rubbing shoulders with the right people, and they liked that she's a Southern girl to her marrow. But Ansley's self-centered and small-hearted. They weren't surprised when I stopped bringing her around, and no one wondered why."

I'm embarrassed for being so reassured by his words. "Can I tell you something? But you've got to promise not to get pissed."

"I promise," he lies. I narrow my eyes, and he loops an arm over my shoulder. "You can't ask me to make a stupid promise like that. If you tell me something that pisses me off, Imma get pissed off."

"Why did you promise then?" I demand.

"Because I can jest act like it don't bother me."

"Which would make it a double lie." I snort. "Anyway, I can read you like a book, Doyle Rahn."

He leads me to a wrought-iron bench, and we sit so close our knees knock. "Go ahead. Hit me with your best shot."

"Ansley had a little chat with me before English." He just finished bragging he'd be able to hide his reaction, but he's already failed. A spark flares in his eyes.

"Yeah?"

I nod. "And before she talked to me, she talked to your cousin." I pause. "Reginald."

He pushes off the bench with unexpected force and kicks

at a clump of thin-stemmed flowers. I wince as their lazy yellow heads go flying. "What was their talk 'bout, exactly?"

"Keeping an eye on me." He swings his head toward me, his face twisted with rage. "She's trying to play me, Doyle. The weird part was, Lovett overheard."

"What did she say?" He stalks back to the bench and flops down too close with such force I almost wind up on his lap. He reaches for my hand and links our fingers like he's reminding me we're in this together.

I take in the contrast of our hands, the dark and the light.

"All kinds of 'keep your chin up' and 'fight the good fight' stuff," I tell him. "She said your cousin harassed her grandson, roughed him up when he didn't go along with some bullshit questioning. She gave me a book about a mixed-race lady back in the day who passes."

"Passes what?" He shoves his pissed-off-ness aside in favor of curiosity.

"Passes for white. She was mixed race, but light enough that she looked white, and she chose to walk away from her black family and friends and live a more privileged life as a white woman. But it was a huge risk, because if she ever had kids, they could be dark, and the white community would ostracize her for lying."

"So what happens in the end?" he asks, eyes wide.

"I don't know. I only got to read it during study hall. But Lovett recommended it, so it's probably depressing." I sigh. "She said even though it's about the Harlem Renaissance, there's a ton about it that still holds true today."

"I'm sorry, Nes. I hate that things haven't changed more. I hate that my own blood treated you like crap." His shoulders buckle over his chest.

"You don't get to choose who you're related to." I rub a hand between his shoulder blades.

He presses his forehead to mine and brushes the tip of his nose against mine. "I'll fix this."

"I'm not asking you to fix anything. It isn't fixable. It just *is*." I pull back and laugh when I get a good look at him. "Your pissed-off face isn't as convincing when you're leaking drool."

He swipes the back of his hand over his mouth. "Dammit! It *feels* better."

"It *looks* fine. I think you're just a drooler."

"Doyle! Dinner in five!" A tall guy flings open the back door and holds up his hand, all five fingers spread out. His features mirror Doyle's except there's none of Doyle's laid-back good humor.

"That's Lee, my older brother. We better hustle. Gramma'll blow a gasket if we don't have our butts in our chairs in five." He stops short at the door, dips his head close to mine and kind of growls out the next words, "It's true things are what they are 'round here, but I'm still not lettin' this go."

He navigates me inside and down a hall to a small bathroom where Lee, Brookes, and one more Doyle clone I assume is Malachi elbow each other, a bar of Irish Spring jumping from soaped hand to soaped hand.

Lee rinses his hands and backs up when he catches sight of me in the mirror, then glares at the other two. "Hurry up. Lady's waiting."

I flutter my fingers in a nervous wave as the guys rinse and file out, the faucet still running, the green bar of soap abandoned in the basin. The three guys linger in the hall, staring, until Doyle snarls, "Take a damn picture, it'll last longer."

Lee, clearly the alpha, barks, "Move out," and they all march down the hall.

"You could have just introduced me." I breathe in the scent of the soap. It's very…masculine. My mother and I are shameless soap snobs. Everything we use is French milled and delicately scented.

"They coulda not been a bunch of apes." He passes me a clean hand towel.

"I think you need to prepare yourself for the fact that your family might hate me." Doyle escorts me out the bathroom, his damp palm flat on my back.

"They won't." It's a little weird how he says the words so confidently, as if he actually thinks he has some control over whether or not they do.

"I can't help it anyway," I say, and then I square my shoulders and march to the table.

Meeting Doyle's family is extra hard because everything was too easy with Lincoln. His parents were impressed that both my parents are professors, they loved that I'm bilingual, that my name was stamped all over the *Newington Gazette*, that I knew what colleges I wanted to apply to.

Lincoln's mother once said, "My boy needs to spend time around people of quality. He needs someone refined, grounded. That's you, Agnes."

Someone of quality. Refined. Grounded.

Me.

Me?

We head into Doyle's grandparents' dining room, where a long, distressed table is loaded with so much food, the legs have to be wobbling. Five pairs of eyes survey me, and I don't get the sense anyone feels like they're looking at someone refined and grounded.

I'm well aware I give off a different vibe down here—rebellious, smart-alecky, underdressed, cocky. And that's *before* I open my mouth and my Brooklyn accent comes clanging out.

Doyle's grandfather smiles at me, and there's a twinkle in his eyes—pale blue with hints of lavender, a slightly faded version of his grandson's.

"Hoyt, would you say grace?" Doyle's grandma watches me out of the corner of her eye.

I'm aware they're probably not Catholic, but it doesn't feel right to pray unless I make the sign of the cross first, so I do. Doyle's grandfather asks Jesus to bless the food we're about to eat.

My stomach rumbles in answer. *En el nombre del Padre, del Hijo, del Espíritu Santo, amén.*

The guys chow down in ravenous silence. Doyle's grandmother's biscuits are incredible—buttery, featherlight, and mouthwatering. When there's only one left, Malachi reaches for it and Lee raps his knuckles. I think back to Doyle's earlier threat to use his grandmother's biscuit recipe against me and seriously question my ability to resist.

"I know we ain't had a lady other than Gramma at the table in a while, but I can't believe you'd forget your manners so quick." Lee snatches up the basket and offers it out to me. "Nes, please, take it."

This is about more than a tasty biscuit. This is hospitality. Chivalry. A peace offering dripping with butter and wafting its fragrant aroma into my nostrils.

I'm not rude. I'm also not made of biscuit-hating stone.

"Thank you, Lee." I make sure I eat like a lady, but I feel like I'm in a den of wolves and the pack leader tossed me a juicy bone.

Once every morsel of food has been devoured, I expect them to jump up from the table, but only Doyle and his grandmother stand, and they won't accept my offer to help clear. I look with panic at Malachi, who still seems to harbor resentment about the biscuit resting comfortably in my belly; Lee, whose stone face is unreadable; and Brookes, who's endless yawning is contagious. Only Grandpa gives off a remotely friendly vibe.

Doyle darts back into the dining room and whispers, "I don't want you to freak out...but Gramma made homemade peach cobbler with peach ice cream." He waltzes into the kitchen, a stack of plates balanced on his forearm, whistling.

Like a dwarf on his way to the gem mine.

I guess that makes me Snow White, and Happy just left me sitting with Sulky, Broody, Sleepy, and Grandpa.

"You the gal lettin' your tree die?" Grandpa accuses.

"Guilty as charged." I try to laugh, but my attempt at revelry goes over like a lead balloon. "I get it. Trees are people too." Crickets. You'd think I'd have learned to quit while I was ahead. Nope! "Sometimes, being with Doyle, I feel like I'm hanging out with Johnny Appleseed's brother."

Malachi finally snickers. "He's like one of them flower-child hippies."

"Don't make fun." Grandpa shakes a warning finger. "You should be following your brother on the job, learning a thing or two. But you're always at that damn interweb. I told your grandmother getting you that laptop was a mistake."

Malachi stares at his hands, which he curls into fists and relaxes flat, like a pulsing heart. They're the exact same shape as Doyle's, with the same long, strong fingers, but Malachi's are soft and pale, unlike Doyle's, which are calloused and caked with dirt he can never seem to wash away entirely.

"Computers are the future, Granddad." Malachi locks

those hands into frustrated fists. "Doyle *likes* the work you do. Brookes too. Me and Lee ain't like that."

"Leave me outta this," Lee mutters.

"Lee serves his country as a marine. That's a man's work, proud work. There's nothin' proud 'bout sittin' in your briefs playing soldier on some screen all hours of the night."

"That game takes strategy and skill, and I've got one of the highest scores outta hundreds of thousands of players all over the world, Granddad. The *world*." Malachi raises his chin at his grandfather like he's daring him to refute that cold fact.

"Don't surprise me none. There's a whole world full of fools doing like you do. Jest means you're the king of the couch potatoes is all." Their grandfather's hoot wakes Brookes with a start and deepens Malachi's scowl.

"I have a friend—" I begin, but stop short when everyone turns to stare at me with narrowed eyes, like I'm traipsing into territory I may want to avoid. I may be making a huge mistake, but what the hell? I decide to march into no-man's-land and tell my little antagonistic story. "I have a big gamer friend, and he started to do some development. Dragged me to Comic-Con once, which was actually pretty fun, just kind of weird with all the slave-girl Princess Leia costumes. Like, dozens of them. Anyway, that's not the point. The point is, instead of getting together a résumé and portfolio for college, he submitted a preview of the game he'd been working on. He got accepted to a ton of top-ranked schools and was scooped up by Riot once he graduated from MIT."

This last bit of information means nothing to any of them other than Malachi. The smitten grin he sends me officially morphs him from Sulky into Dopey.

"Riot is a video game developer. They were voted one of the best places to work in technology a few years in a row."

"And where is this video game place?" Granddad's voice is gravelly with suspicion.

"Um, Santa Monica? I think. Or is it LA? I'm not sure, but I could text Piotr and ask him—"

"Well, that's all fine and good for city dwellers." Granddad puffs out his chest like he's trying to regain some of his footing. "What would Malachi want with all that?"

"I might *like* the city." Malachi slaps his palms on the table and stares his grandfather down.

I hold my breath, but his granddad waves a gnarled hand dismissively.

"You'd get eaten alive. Takes a certain type for big-city life. You move to one of them concrete jungles, you wind up changed, *not* in a good way."

I interrupt with a snort. "I've lived in some of the biggest cities in the world, and I'm doing okay."

The twinkle Granddad had for me sputters. "Malachi can't just be flyin' off, willy-nilly, far away from us. We won't see him for months, won't be with him the way we are now."

Brookes sits ramrod straight, totally at attention. Lee still has his arms crossed over his wide chest. A Semper Fi tattoo curls around his massive biceps.

"But Malachi would have to travel if he was a marine." I know my logic won't be met with a standing ovation, but I'm not anticipating the glare leveled my way by the family patriarch. I sink low in my chair. "I mean, just to weigh pros and cons."

Malachi's eyes flicker like kindling's been stoked inside him. I'm nervous it might blaze into an inferno. "That's a real good point."

"It's a real lopsided point, is what it is," Granddad lashes out, lips curled. "Thing is, a marine is a marine and that's a whole 'nother ball game. There's no comparin' a marine and a guy who sits on his ass making up computer games, and that's that."

Just as things are escalating to early-explosion Pompeii levels, Doyle arrives with plates and forks teetering in one hand and a bulbous glass pitcher of what's probably sweet tea in the other. His songbird whistle gives a death warble as he sets everything down.

"What have y'all been chattin' 'bout?" He narrows accusatory eyes at his brothers and cousin.

I clear my throat. "The marines. And video games."

Doyle winces at me with one eye squinted shut, like a migraine instantly gripped his brain. "Now that we've covered ultimate evil and ultimate good, how 'bout some—"

"Peach cobbler!" His grandmother sets the platter down on the table with a proud flourish. Before anyone can say a word to ruin or salvage the moment, she hurries back to the kitchen and returns with ice cream.

Doyle doles out plates and forks like a madman, then slides next to me and whispers, "What the hell's been going on out here?"

"Just more of my irresistible Yankee charm," I mutter through clenched teeth like a ventriloquist.

Dessert is a great distraction from the smoking ruins of our conversation, but it doesn't clear the air entirely. Gramma is fine with silence for the first few bites, but when the only sound is forks scraping her good china, she eyes us with undisguised suspicion. As she spoons second helpings of steaming, heavenly peach dessert onto everyone's plates without asking if we want more, she snaps, "Cat got all y'all's tongues?"

"These sweets're so good, seems a shame to ruin 'em with conversation," Granddad proclaims with glares for everyone except his wife.

"Oh man," Doyle breathes.

"It *is* a good batch." Gramma's lashes flutter with pride. "But we've got company tonight. I don't want her to think we're a house full of barbarians." Her glare, even scarier than Granddad's, lasers around the table.

Before I can offer a polite compliment about Gramma's flowers/cooking/hospitality, Malachi torpedoes any chance at armistice. "Nes said a friend of hers is doing jest fine makin' video games for a living."

She glances at her husband, who's spearing his cobbler with more aggression than is really necessary, and then she asks me, "Did this friend of yours have to take a job far away?"

"It was in Santa Monica." I'm still not sure if it was LA, but what does it matter? California might as well be Mars as far as Granddad's concerned.

She gives a little shoulder shrug and side-eyes Granddad. "Well, Santa Monica is a heck of a lot closer than Afghanistan, and a sight less dangerous. And we'd be able to have regular email and phone time." Granddad huffs, but Gramma ignores him. "Malachi, why don't you ask your guidance counselor for more information? What we can do right now is gather all we need to know while we focus on gettin' you graduated."

Everyone nods, and I realize I underestimated this yellow-haired lady. She is the captain of this vessel, and her word is law.

"Agnes, Doyle tells me you two are gonna try your hand at a prom for all the students at Ebenezer?" She looks at me expectantly. I glance at Doyle, but he's pretending to be consumed with shoveling cobbler into his mouth.

Coward.

"We've been thinking about it, ma'am." I wait for her

ruling on this particular topic, encouraged by her coolness about West Coast video game careers.

"I'm not from this county, you know." I nod like I do, but, seriously, if she named twenty other counties, I wouldn't know a single one. "When I was a girl you wouldn't think twice about seeing separate drinking fountains and bathrooms, right along with pools, buses, eateries, the whole thing. But our county was very forward thinking. There were only a few colored kids at my school, but they were nice as could be, and *of course* they came to prom, our school's *one and only*. We all went to the same school, we all played on the same sports teams and had the same teachers. Why in heaven's name would we have different proms? I've always thought the whole separate prom idea was just plain ridiculous, especially in this day and age."

"It's not like it's white folk telling the blacks not to come to their prom." Lee darts his eyes at me apologetically. Oh, he *looks* sorry, but it doesn't stop him from plowing on like a big, bumbling idiot. "I mean both sides got their own things they like and want. So they have two proms and there's that much less arguin'."

"What the hell does that even mean, Lee?" Doyle half stands in his chair. "That don't make no sense."

"Quit it." Lee tosses his fork down, then flicks a look my way. "Look, I don't mean no offense to you. I'm not saying rap music is better or worse than country. I'm not saying collard greens are better than…fried okra. I'm saying certain people like certain things and sometimes the best way for everyone to get what they want is to separate 'em."

I squeeze my hands together in my lap so hard, I'm afraid I might snap bones. But I will myself to relax and say what needs to be said.

"Oh, I'm not offended," I say before Doyle can flip the

table, which will be his next move, judging from his white knuckles. "I guess I'm confused. I'm mixed race. So do I like fried okra? Or collard greens? I guess I should like both, right? Weird, because I've never even had either."

Lee's face pinks. "It's gettin' twisted now. You can debate it so it sounds like I'm ignorant and being a racist or whatever, but the truth is, people are different."

"What the hell are you trying to—" Doyle begins, but I link a finger through the loop in his jeans and tug him down onto his chair the same time his grandfather reaches over and presses on his shoulder.

I will myself to speak around the choke of frustration tears. "You're right, Lee. People are different. Your brother and I are so different, sometimes it's kinda weird how well we get along." I grab Doyle's knee under the table and squeeze hard. He lays his hand over the top of mine. "But I'd be happy to listen to country music—which I always figured I didn't like because I grew up in New York, where not many people listen to it, but who knows? Maybe it's because of the color of my skin? Anyway, I'd be more than happy to dance to Reba or Dolly or whoever—as long as it meant I was dancing with Doyle."

It's a little more romantic than I actually intended. Things with Doyle are tricky and, even if I wanted him as much as every other girl in our school, I wouldn't blurt my feelings out at his grandparents' dinner table.

Except I kind of do and just did. Doyle's smile is so wide, it must ache. I lace all five of my fingers with all five of his, and the world shrinks to just him and me, holding on to each other for dear life.

But ignorance can't seem to leave the bloom of romance be.

"Do whatcha like," Lee snaps like he was just trying to

be reasonable until I stomped all over his "logic." "All I'm sayin' is you two might be the only ones on the dance floor."

Gramma derails the conversation immediately, but her overeager questions about the McCullaghs's orchard and Pastor Mike's daughter's bronchial infection are just filler noise.

They don't stop Doyle from gripping his knife in his fist like he wants to use it on his brother while Lee shoots him fierce glares between mouthfuls of cobbler. Their grandfather scowls at his melting puddle of ice cream, Brookes nods off in his chair, and Malachi sports this defiant grin that I bet will land him picking his own switch before this night is done.

The second it's socially acceptable, Doyle says, "Gramma, dinner was amazing, but I gotta get Nes home. Big test tomorrow to study for." He picks up a few plates, and I follow despite his emphatic head shaking.

Hell no, I am *not* interested in headlining the second Civil War by staying at the table with the men of his family. But I'm as unwelcome in the kitchen as I was in the dining room. Gramma doesn't even seem to like *Doyle* being on her turf, so I hover near the back door, trying not to look like I'm eavesdropping.

"I jest want things to be nice between y'all," his grandma pleads. "Fightin'? Over a girl? That ain't the way you been brought up. Y'all should know better."

"I didn't think we were brought up to be a bunch of bigots and morons neither." Doyle lowers his voice, but I can still hear it rumble through the overwarm kitchen. "She means a lot to me."

"Your blood should mean more than any girl," she bites back, letting her voice carry on purpose. "You seen your daddy lately?"

"Not since Reginald called me to pick him up after the brawl at the Wild Pony." Doyle gnaws on the edge of his thumbnail. I've never seen this nervous habit before. "Why?"

"Jest ain't right. I don't know what I ever done wrong raising the lot of you, but it must've been something real bad. I got fathers and sons not talking, cousins fighting, brothers can't get along. I pray to Jesus about it, Doyle. I ask him what I did wrong and how I can do better." She tugs off her yellow rubber dish gloves—the exact same color as her hair—and slaps them against the counter.

Doyle wraps an arm around her shoulders. "Wasn't nothing you did, Gramma. We got bad blood, I guess. Every generation seems like it gets a little worse. But better too, in some ways mebbe."

She leans her head on his shoulder. "Malachi's gonna be moving to that damn California. They're always saying on television that it's about to fall into the ocean, you know. Too many fault lines all over. What will I do when he goes? When all of you go?"

"Don't worry," Doyle says, pulling away. "I ain't going nowhere."

His words are purely bitter.

She pulls him to her level and whispers urgently against his ear. Doyle's expression goes darker and darker the longer he listens. I hold my breath waiting for an argument as his jaw tightens like a vise, but all he gives her is a quick, tight nod.

Doyle kisses his grandmother, walks over to me, grabs my hand, and leads me out the door so fast, I'm left calling out my goodbyes and thank-yous over my shoulder.

We get in the truck, he starts the engine, looks at me, and grinds out, "Like I told you. *Chaos.*"

TWENTY

"We shouldn't stop here. This is a stupid idea." Doyle puts the truck in Park anyway. He jerks his leg up and down and leans half out the window, then sits back hard on the seat. "Before we left, Gramma asked me to leave these damn papers at his place so he'll sign 'em for her. That was his truck at the Wild Pony. I'm sure of it. Otherwise I wouldn't be caught dead anywhere near here." He tugs off his hat and combs his fingers through his hair, his eyes a little wild. "You mind stopping for a second?"

We left his grandparents' house and drove for a while in silence except for the squall of bugs and the steady whip of the wind rushing through the cab. Doyle didn't ask me if I wanted to come wherever we were going, but I was glad to keep him company. We drove past the saddest dive bar on earth, and Doyle pointed to a truck that was more rust and duct tape than metal and told me it was his father's. He looked spooked just seeing it. Now we're parked at the end of a long, dusty dirt road at the edge of his dad's property.

"You're sure he's not around?"

"A truck as ugly as his kinda sticks out." Doyle steadily devours his thumbnail. It has to hurt, but he doesn't seem to register any pain. "He spends a good ninety-nine percent of his life at that bar."

"If you want to drop the papers, we can. I know you want to help your grandma out." I don't get why a grandmother would force her grandson to do something that so clearly freaks him out, but maybe it's because she wants to figure out a way to stitch back together the bloody tatters of her family.

I watch his profile and look where he looks, trying to see what's in front of us through his eyes.

The grass in the yard is burned black in wide patches around a rusted burn barrel, and there's a dilapidated double-wide with a sputtering air conditioner hanging from one of the three tiny windows. The other two have black trash bags for curtains. The door is crooked on the hinges and when it flies open, Doyle slams his palms into the steering wheel, startled. A thin, heavily tattooed older guy, naked from the waist up, stands in the doorway and stares. He pulls a ratty shirt over his head and stomps down the steps, barefoot, toward us the way a bull charges a matador.

"What the hell's that asshole doing here?" Doyle's face goes bone white. He throws the truck into Reverse as the man I assume is his father bolts across the yard.

We're fifty feet away, a hundred, when his father trips or falls—I'm not sure which—and hits the ground hard. Doyle stands on the brakes, and we both lurch forward.

"Is he...okay?" I crane my neck. He looks scarily lifeless.

"Yeah. He passes out a ton. He's fine." But it comes out with an edge of uncertainty.

"Should we...check?" I will the prone figure to move, just a twitch. But there's nothing. I remember what Doyle told me the day I found out about Lincoln. How you only get one chance to call as soon as you hear something. The same has to hold true times ten when it comes to seeing something. What if his father is dying? Will Doyle be able to live with the guilt if he doesn't help? "Do you want to check on him?"

"Damn. I better. Yeah. I guess. I better jest do it." I hate seeing him so tense he's jerky. "I hate his guts, but I can't leave him for dead like some armadillo run over on the highway. If he comes to, I gotta warn you… I'm not sure I ever met a bigger asshole than my daddy, keep your head down. He'll prolly say some stupid stuff, maybe get a little wild, but ignore him. All right?" He waits a second while I chew on my lip. "Nes?"

"Should we call Brookes maybe?"

"He's twenty minutes out. Ain't his daddy."

"Lee? Malachi?"

"Lee'd beat the crap outta him. He'd beat the crap outta Malachi."

"And you?" Panic flares up in me.

"I've taken enough licks to be able to stand 'em, but I don't have a taste to fight. 'Specially not my old man. I'll jest check for a pulse."

"Maybe this is a bad idea." I look into his eyes, the warmest shade of blue. "Tell me the truth. Is it?"

"Hell yeah. Anytime I see my father, it's a bad idea. Might as well get all the family craziness done in one day though, right?" He tears off his hat again and runs his fingers through his hair. In the light of the setting sun, it looks almost pink. "Look, whatever goes down, promise me you will *not* call the cops."

The cops? I swallow hard, remembering the way Officer Hickox eyed me that night, like I was guilty until proven innocent. I nod.

"I'll be back before you know it." He grabs the papers his grandmother gave him and slides out of the truck.

He edges up to his father's body and taps an arm with his boot, squatting close. He says something, then grasps a shoulder and shakes hard. When his father flops back down, Doyle heads to the side of the trailer and comes back with a battered bucket. He sloshes water over his father's face and jumps when the lifeless body reanimates, making furious dirt angels with his flailing arms.

Doyle's boot catches on something and he scurries to keep on his feet as his father rolls to his knees and stands, sways, then lumbers toward him. I can't plug up my scream. Doyle sprints toward the truck, his father on his heels, and I fumble to open the passenger door for him.

I've been angry at my parents before. Disgusted by them. Nervous they'll be disappointed with or pissed as hell at me. But I've never experienced anything like the kind of terror that's plain on Doyle's face as this man—who looks like an older, beat-to-hell version of Doyle—storms toward the truck in a blind rage.

Doyle races to my side and, from the outside, slams shut the passenger door I just opened, then yells for me to lock it, which I do seconds before his father tugs it hard. When he realizes it's locked, he smashes his palms against the glass, and I scramble back and slam the lock on the driver's side too.

I stare at his father's bleary eyes and bared teeth through the window, feeling like he's some zombie in an apocalypse movie, and I'm an expendable character—a sexy black girl? Strikes one *and* two. There's no script where I survive this situation.

"Keep the truck locked!" Doyle yells as his father spins around to face him. "Don't unlock it, no matter what!"

Like a true coward, I sit up on my knees and watch in horror, face pressed to the window. My phone is gripped tight in my hand. I know he said not to call 911, but maybe I should.

I'm not sure what's more terrifying…

The two men circle each other, Doyle quick and tense, his father loose and aggressive. I crack the window and scream, "Doyle! Please! Get in!"

"It's okay, Nes!" Doyle raises one palm toward the truck, one toward his father, like a wild animal trainer attempting to keep a rogue predator at bay.

"What the hell you crawlin' here for, boy? You need your old man for somethin'?" Doyle's father speaks in slurred shouts. He runs a hand over his hair, exactly like the movement I've seen Doyle make a thousand times.

Doyle mirrors his father, maybe without even realizing he's doing it. "I don't need nothin' from you." His drawl comes on so strong now, I barely catch what he says. "Now I'm here though, might as well try and get done whatcha refuse to. Gramma wanted me to come by and drop this paperwork off, 'cause you don't bother comin' 'round to sign nothing when she begs. Got the accountant houndin' her 'bout Pawpaw's estate. She jest wants to settle and put things to rest. Give her some peace and sign."

"Settle, is it, now? More like tryin' to cheat me out of what's rightfully mine, what Pawpaw wanted me to have more 'an the others who won't 'preciate it none! Them brothers of mine got her ear and twisted things against me, I bet my life on it. Why the hell don't she tell me herself?" He throws his arms wide. His shirt is filthy with crusted food dribbled down the front, and there are rings of sweat radiating from the armpits. There's no way I should be able to smell him from this distance, but I gag on the acrid stink of days-old body odor.

"No one picks up at your number, 'cept a lady once in a

while, and she claims she don't know you." Doyle kicks at the gravel in the driveway. "So Gramma sent me to drop off these papers. Don't think she expected you to be around."

Damn Doyle's naïveté. After the "boo hoo family" speech his grandmother made, I have my doubts about what she expected would happen. I wonder if this is the heartwarming family reunion she had in mind.

"Fine mama I got, don't even come see me herself." His father paces like a caged animal. "Sends you like some messenger boy."

Doyle holds out the roll of paper. "She's had a couple bad spells."

His father squares up. "Bad spells?"

"Doctor's having a hard time regulatin' her blood pressure, I guess." Doyle shakes the papers, but his father ignores them.

"No one saw fit to tell me? I'm her *son*!" His taunting voice switches gears, hot with rage now.

"Yeah, well, you coulda stopped by and seen her yourse—"

Doyle's sentence is cut short by a hard backhand from his father. His knuckles smash against Doyle's mouth, and my heart slams into my ribs before I even notice the blood gushing everywhere. I yank at the door handle frantically, then remember it's locked.

It takes me a few seconds too long to fumble the door open. Doyle's already stumbled to the truck and thrown his weight against it, slamming it shut before I can get out. I can see the spreading blood begin to stain his five o'clock shadow through the window.

"Don't," he mouths as his father's hand closes around his shoulder.

His dad's fists are huge boney weapons, and he lands punch after punch around Doyle's head and on the curve of his rib

297

cage. I beat on the window and scream with primal fear. The noises coming from my throat scare the hell out of me.

I need to stop panicking and *think*.

I'm ashamed of how scared I am to get out of the truck. I don't even know what I imagine I can do, short of calling the police like Doyle asked me not to, but I have to do something, *anything*, because I know in my marrow that Doyle's father isn't going to stop until he beats the life out of his son.

I crawl frantically to the driver's side, turn the key to start the ignition, and tumble out the driver's-side door. When I come around the back, Doyle has rolled to the side to avoid any more punches, and he staggers to his feet, holding up both fists.

"Get back!" Doyle yells when he sees me, his eyes wild with terror. "You'll jest get in the way!"

His father sways in a woozy circle, blinking at Doyle over and over, like he's only just realized it's his son in front of him, beaten to a pulp by his own hands. Blood pours out Doyle's nose and mouth, and he's hunched over like he's protecting his ribs. Doyle's hurt, and I take back every joke I've ever made about my bad nursing skills.

I've never wanted anything the way I want to help him right now. But I've never been exposed to this kind of raw violence close-up, and it shreds me into pieces, leaving me so shaky, I clutch the tire for balance.

Doyle squares his shoulders through a shudder of pain. "I never hit you back before this." He speaks to his father in a clear, quiet voice stripped of any fear. "Granddaddy says one hit to the head'll likely kill you."

"Your granddaddy always talks like he knows every goddamn thing." His father rubs his jaw, his face emptied of all prior viciousness. His shoulders fold forward over his chest like he's a puppet with loose strings, and he sags to the dust like he couldn't hold himself up if his life depended on it. I pray this means it's over, that Doyle's going to climb in and drive far away from this madman.

"Fair 'nough. Imma let you test his theory. I shouldn't never've gone off on you like that, son." He holds his arms out on either side of his body, like he's about to be nailed to a cross. "I'll give you one. Right to the jaw. C'mon, now. Don't hold back."

Doyle pulls the hem of his shirt up and wipes away some of the blood that's clotting on his chin. "I don't need you to give me one. This ain't an exchange. I took what you gave me because I *can* take it."

"What're you tryin' to say, boy? You don't think I can take a punch from my own son?" His father's rusty laugh rattles out from behind his broken teeth. "Come at me, little man. I taught you how to put 'em up. Remember back that far?"

"I remember you givin' me my first black eye the day after my eighth birthday." Doyle reaches for the papers, dusty and spotted with a spray of his own blood. "Sign these. Now."

"Don't make a fuck of difference anyhow." His father snatches the papers and scrawls his signature across the bottom. "They're thieves and liars, the whole lot of 'em. You and Malachi and Lee think they walk on water. Guess what? They're a bunch of robbin' backstabbers."

He tosses the papers back so Doyle has to bend down to pick them up. I finally get over my cowardice and rush over, throwing a hand out to stop Doyle from causing himself any more pain. I collect the sheets and wonder if that illegible scribble will count as a signature.

Doyle's father's gaze bores into me as I scuttle in the dirt. "You're bein' brainwashed by every last one of 'em. You oughta wake up and see the truth. Hey, you look at me when I'm talkin' to you, son!"

I try to steady my knocking knees as I stand. I want to leave, *now*, but Doyle glares at his father, hackles raised, not about to back down.

"Take a crack." His father points to his chin and eyes Doyle's fist, balled tight at his thigh. "I know you wanna. It'll clear the slate."

"Nothing's ever gonna clear your slate, far as I'm concerned." Doyle spits blood at his father's tattered boots. "You ain't worth it. Ain't worth my time, ain't worth my energy."

The hate wells up in his father, narrowing his eyes—a paler blue than Doyle's—into slits of granite. "You think yer somethin' else, don't ya? I don't know how you come by that particular conclusion." He slides his eyes up and down my body in a slow drag. "Can't even getcha a white girl? You resorting to datin' a n—"

My knees give out. I collapse into the truck, the back of my thighs singed against the hot chrome bumper. But I won't step away from the burn. I can't move any closer to the hate he spews.

That *word*. That ugly welt of a word.

When Jasper first had it hurled at him, we sat down as a family and talked about it. Dad had his story, Jasper had one too…and I hoped hearing that word was a big, terrible *if* that would never come. I should have listened to my father, who was telling us what to do *when* someone said it to us; to stand tall; to not let them see how it hurt; to talk about it with our parents, not let it boil and fester until it poisoned us with the power of its hate.

My father heard it directed at him the first time at a candy store when he was six and visiting a relative in Sosúa in DR, ten years before he moved to the United States. He swiped a peppermint from a big barrel, and the shopkeeper grabbed him hard around the wrist. My father remembered the man's face contorting with rage—like Doyle's father's. "I don't need little thieves emptying my shelves! Come back and I'll have the authorities haul your ass away, n—" My father had panic attacks in every store he went in until he was a teenager. He still hates candy stores.

My brother's first time was in the locker room of his tony middle school, which was ninety percent white. One of the eighth graders was benched for a game while Jasper, a lowly seventh grader, played and scored. "That should have been you," the benched kid's best friend said in the deserted locker room just as my brother went back in to grab his cleats. "Jasper only got to play because he's a n—" Jasper brushed it off as dumb kids playing tough, trying out some swagger—like swearing for the first time. He changed middle schools the next year though.

So here's my first time, out of the mouth of the father of the guy I'm falling hard for. I think I would have preferred a physical punch.

I cover my ears with my forearms, like that can erase it. I shrink down, crumple into something cheap and small, and at the same time, I'm possessed by a howling fury that rises in my soul even as my body fails to keep me upright. This pathetic, deranged drunk will not make me feel worthless with a single knife blade of a word.

"What the *fuck* did you say?" Doyle's voice splinters with fury.

"Get used to hearin' it. In this town, people ain't gonna look the other way if a Rahn dates a—" He doesn't say it this time, because Doyle's already hurled himself at his father, slamming his fist into the older man's teeth.

"Doyle!" I scream.

I propel myself forward, grab him by the back of his T-shirt, and yank him toward me with so much force, we both sprawl back into the dirt. My ankle twists at a funny angle, and the strap on one of my flip-flops snaps.

I put both hands on Doyle's neck, turn his face toward mine, cup his jaw. I try to say the words without letting my voice crack into a thousand shards. "You were right. He's not worth it. Let's go. Please? Take me away from here."

His father moans, dabbing with dirty fingers at the blood that trickles from the side of his mouth. I tug on Doyle's elbow. He stares at me in a daze for a few agonizing beats, then snaps back to life. "Get in the truck, Nes. We're getting the hell outta here."

TWENTY-ONE

"**A**re you okay? Did'ya hurt your ankle?"

"Don't worry about my ankle. Are *you* okay?"

Instead of answering me, he reaches in the back and grabs a pair of boots. "Malachi's. They should fit you. And he'd want you to have 'em, after the way you stood up for him with my granddaddy. Rahns are good at knockin' each other down, so a little loyalty goes a long way with us."

I kick my tattered flip-flops off my feet, which I stick in the too-big boots. I'm having a hard time wrapping my head around how we went from prom talk and peach cobbler to… this. I think about how we discussed Grimm fairy tales earlier, and I realize I'm living a real-life version of one, with the violence and ugliness snaked tight around the romance and beauty.

Doyle drives silently, blood and tears dripping down his face. We switch onto the main road, then amble down back roads I didn't know existed. When we finally rumble to a stop, it's in a deserted field overgrown with grasses and low-branched, shadowy trees. Doyle leans forward till his head's pressed to the steering wheel, and he sobs so hard, I can hardly hear the insane buzz of the bugs that never seems to die down.

I hold my hand out to touch him, but pull back, unsure if he needs space more than he needs comfort. Anyway, I'm not confident I even know how to comfort him, or how to process the domestic violence I just witnessed.

"I can drive you back to your grandparents'," I offer, because I want to make up now for not helping enough when he needed me, when his father was using him as punching bag.

"I'm such a *fuckup*."

I think that's what he's said. I can barely understand him, and it gets harder with every second that trips by. I slide out of the passenger seat and run around to his side of the truck fast, like I'm afraid he'll take off before I get there. I manage to swing open the door, and he's hunched over the steering wheel, blood crusted around his lips, bruises already purpling his arms.

I've never felt hate so smooth and sure, like the edge of an ax fresh from being sharpened, the metal still hot to the touch. I want to *murder* Doyle's father. Screw that he's incapacitated, sad, uneducated, addicted—a whole string of sorry excuses that will never make me forgive what he did to Doyle.

"Look at me." He won't, so I put my hands on his cheeks, not sure if I should press hard to get him to look my way or handle him gently so that I don't do more damage to his broken, bruised skin. His face turns in my direction, but it's a blank mask, like he doesn't hear a thing, doesn't see a thing. "*He's* the fuckup, Doyle. Not you. Never you."

"I shoulda beat the shit out of him for sayin' that 'bout you. I shoulda kept punchin' and never stopped. I can take what he throws my way, but he's out of his damn mind if he thinks he can get away with talkin' to you like that. I'm so sorry, Nes. You have no idea how ashamed I feel—"

And that's when I stand on my toes and tug down on his neck.

Because I'm about to make our first kiss happen.

In the middle of all this craziness, all this pain, this kiss is a chance for a singular glimmer of good.

I wonder what the hell I've been waiting for.

Suddenly life feels more urgent, less like some game we can take our time playing.

Half an hour ago, Doyle was whole and fine. Now he's broken and sobbing. There isn't a thing I can do to reclaim what was lost. But I can be brave enough to give us what we both want in this moment.

I know what's in his heart because it's the same thing roaring through mine—it's love. And that love makes us want to protect each other, whether or not we can.

I know the honest truth is we can't, not always.

But we *can* be there for each other when we get knocked down by forces completely out of our control. Right now, in the stillness of this dark night, we're far away from anything that can hurt us. Safe.

I lick my lips, then I lick his, salty with blood or tears or both. He turns to the side, plants his boots on the running board, and leans down so that he can put his hands behind my neck, down my shoulders, and pull me against his body. I think he might still be bleeding, so I lean back and lay hands on him to check. He turns his head to the side, against the seat rest.

"I'm embarrassing myself, right? 'Course you don't wanna make out with me. I guess sobbing like a damn baby ain't a turn-on."

I climb onto the running board, my feet set wide on either side of his, yank the sleeve of my hoodie over my hand, and set to work mopping his face with quick, light swipes.

"You'll ruin your sweatshirt. Stop. Nes, *stop*." He tugs on my sleeve, but I pull it back and ignore him.

"It's okay. It's black. The blood won't show."

"I can't fuckin' *believe* what he said to you. I can't believe what I let 'im say—" The last word catches on a sucked-in breath.

I have no patience for the way he's blaming himself for things that were totally out of his control. Plus I'm ready to kiss him some more. To shut up the noise in both our heads. Life rolls by in a tangled, crazy tumbleweed of emotions, and I want to press Pause on the pain and focus on the pleasure right now. I want something I can control. *We* can control.

I can control kissing him. He can kiss me back. We can own this moment.

"I've never wanted anyone more than I want you right now."

He snorts and turns his face. "I never wanted to be some rebound guy. But I never figured my alternative was gonna be a pity make-out session."

He's primed to say more, but I don't give him the chance. I cover his mouth with mine and kiss him softly, brushing my lips over his and breathing deep to catch the familiar smell of his skin under the metallic tang of blood. His hands tighten on my hips and inch me closer. When he groans softly in the back of his throat, the vibration rolls through my body.

God, it's so good. The taste of him, the way his arms wind around me like he's claiming me as his. Like he wants to protect me. I love how his mouth is quick and hot, but slow and savoring all at once. This? This is a kiss worth waiting for.

"Does it hurt?" I close my eyes and murmur the question before I pull away.

"Nah. Feels freakin' amazin'. Don't stop, Nes, please."

His mouth claims my waiting lips, and his kisses come harder and faster. My breath catches as something low in my gut knots tight and I go slick between my legs. I slide my tongue out delicately, lick his sore lips, aware that he's taken a beating in a place that's already so sensitive.

"Are you sure this is okay?" I whisper.

"Okay?" The slow grin he dry runs is only, at best, a shadow of his usual smile. "How come you like me so much when I'm in pain? First you're hugging up on me after the dentist, now you can't keep your hands off me after my daddy—"

"Stop." I brush his hair back with clumsy fingers. "You don't have to make it a joke, okay? It's not a joke."

The light he worked so hard to stoke extinguishes. "Jokin' 'bout it's the only way it don't become a tragedy."

"I don't want you to feel like you have to brush it off. Or pretend it never happened."

"No worries 'bout that." Where there were flames in his eyes, there's only charred debris and acrid smoke. "What you jest witnessed—or some ugly version of it—runs in the back of my mind every day of my life. I make sure it does, so there ain't no chance I'll forget what's in my blood. The day I forget is the day I risk lettin' that become my future."

"That could never happen."

"My daddy wasn't always a shamble of a man. He had good and bad in 'im, same as me, but his bad strangled out everythin' else. I hope I'm stronger 'an that, but I ain't taking chances. But I don't wanna talk about him. What I want is to kiss you again," he says, his voice gravelly and raw. "And again. And then I wanna do a whole lot more than kiss you, Nes."

"What if I hurt you?"

"Oh, no worries. I ain't a virgin." He waggles his eyebrows when I sigh.

My fingers execute a gentle exploration over his ribs and up along his shoulders. "This? Does this hurt?"

"Are you giving me a medical exam or trying to get into my pants?" he jokes, even though I see him wince through the laugh.

"A little of both," I admit. "Do you need to go to the doctor?"

"Hell no." He fits those big hands on my waist and makes me feel petite, wanted, sweet. Things I am only irregularly, and most often with Doyle. "No doctor will see me without needin' to know what happened, and this is a tiny town. Before you know it, I'll have DFCS knocking at my door, all ready to investigate and make my gramma's ulcers worse. I know you think I'm off my damn rocker, but my dad can't wind up in jail. He's got a big mouth and nothing to back it up with. I might hate his guts, but he's still my daddy. I can't live with him getting beat to death in prison. Plus if he lays off the bottle for any more than two days, he gets the shakes so bad he cracked a crown once."

He nuzzles his face against my collarbone, and I press his cap off his head and run my fingers through his hair, loving his low moan in response to my touch.

"Did he try to stop before?"

"Really? We're gonna talk about my old man's alcoholism right now?" He wraps an arm around me too fast and tight, and sucks breath through his teeth in a sharp snatch. I'm seriously worried he broke a rib. Or four. "He only ever tried to stop whenever his disability check got delayed and he ran outta shit to drink. And by 'shit to drink,' I mean he ran outta mouthwash, rubbing alcohol, all the cough syrup... He even drank some of his own aftershave. For days, anytime the bastard coughed, it smelled like Old Spice. Still makes my skin crawl to this day if I catch a whiff."

We both make rusty noises that are getting closer to actual laughter.

"That's good, because Old Spice freaks me out too," I admit. "I had a creepy science teacher who wore it in middle school, and he used to rub up against the lab tables while he asked the girls to recite rows from the periodic table. Then he'd lean close and sniff our hair." The memory of the panic Mr. Ling inspired during my tween years loosens a hysterical laugh from my throat.

"Not funny." He kisses my neck so softly, and I'm not sure whether or not I feel the tip of his tongue. "That pervert shoulda been run outta town. You gettin' molested by him ain't a joke."

"None of this is." I wrap my arms around his neck and hope he's okay enough to let me hold him tightly for a moment. If he's not, he doesn't buckle under my touch.

The wide-open, star-speckled jigsaw pieces of sky and land brighten behind his silhouette. Maybe I'm imagining it, but I swear I can smell ocean salt mixed with larger amounts of gardenia. The trill of cicadas cloaks us in humming, wishful peace. The world's never been more beautiful than it is tonight in his arms.

"What the hell are we gonna do?" He cuddles closer to me, like he's trying to ball up and fit in my arms.

"About what?" I twirl small pieces of his hair around my fingers and lift, looking at the stars through the strands.

"You and me. And them." His chin tilts up, and I settle my hands on his cheeks, running my thumbs very softly over the angle of his cheekbones.

"Us? Them?" Then I repeat the old refrain that's more habit than truth. "Doyle, you know I'm leaving."

It's probably the most hateful thing I could've said to him of all people, right now of all times. My regret is instant.

He coughs, and presses a hand to his side as he grimaces. "Lemme getcha back home." He drags his legs forward in the seat.

"Doyle, I didn't mean—"

"Get in the truck." The cutoff is the icy slap to the face I deserve. Actually, I deserve way worse. He starts to close the door before I have a chance to jump off the running board. I land with a thud in the boots that belong to his brother.

"I don't mean to say I don't care about you or that I—"

"Stop." It's a dull whisper. His violet eyes, ringed in a crueler purple, study the torn flesh of his knuckles on the steering wheel. "You got good instincts. That's what kept you from goin' back to your ex. Use 'em. Trust 'em. Stay away from me and all my chaos."

"C'mon, stop, Doyle. I don't want that." The window is rolled down, but there's the metal of the door between us and a wall Doyle's erected for his own protection. I can't blame him... "I want you."

"And my ill-bred, racist, ignorant kin?" A mean chuckle skids out of his mouth. "I ain't about to put you through any more trials by fire. Every single problem you knocked up against since you came here can be traced back to me somehow. Think on it for a second. Every single one. I'm sure as hell not gonna stand by while that keeps happenin'."

"So this is it?" I demand.

His shoulders rise up, then fold with the collapse of his sigh. "Jest get in the truck."

"No." I punt a clump of dirt and grass so hard, my boot half flies off. "You know what? This? *Us?* Whatever the hell it is we're doing...it isn't remotely a big deal in some places.

If you and I met in Brooklyn, no one would bat an eyelash if we showed up anywhere together."

He's silent for a few long beats. "In this fantasy of yours, is my daddy some fancy professor too? And my mama never hightailed it outta my life? You forget if you pick me up and drop me in Brooklyn, I'm the dumb hick you dragged outta some backwater hellhole. I stick out just like you do, but I don't get to go back to better when I've had enough."

He should be furious, but his words drag and plod like bootsteps in the heavy mud.

"No one would think that way about you." I wring my hands because this night is like a paper town catching fire, more houses and roads and bridges exploding into flames around me every nanosecond. "Even if you didn't fit in, you'd never be abused."

"So there'd be nothing for me to fight?" He turns his eyes my way accusingly. "Nothing left to stand up for?"

"Don't." I jerk my head from side to side. "Don't do that whole noble martyr thing." The mosquitoes have set up a blood-bar feast on my legs, and I slap at them with all the force of my frustration.

"Things need to change *here*, *now*. I don't feel like runnin'. I feel like fightin'." His fierce look is a dare I can hardly see around the salty burn of my tears.

"*Coño!* That's easy to say when you don't have to watch your back every second because of the color of your skin!" I snarl. I whirl away as he reaches out to grab my arm. "No! I've stood by and fought a dozen tiny battles every damn day because I don't fit anyone's idea of who I should be. I've never, *ever* had to walk around afraid I'd be harassed because of the color of my skin before! What do I do with that, Doyle?"

"Nes." Doyle's voice pleads, and that tugs at my heart. But the second he swings the truck door open, I bolt.

Usually I can't outrun Doyle to save my life, but he just got his ass handed to him, so he's limping along way slower than usual. He yells my name every few steps but it's barely recognizable because of how hard he's panting.

I have no idea where I'm going or how to get home from here. Every step takes me farther away from the truck and my only sure way out of this unfamiliar wild. Plus I'm scared Doyle's lungs are filling with blood or something. I don't want him to hurt any more than he already does.

I've never wanted to cause him any pain, even though I know I haven't been able to avoid doing exactly that.

So I stop, but he has too much momentum and accidentally tackles me. The thick grass cushions our fall. Doyle wraps his arms around my body, kisses my neck and ears, my hair, and my face like crazy. For one claustrophobic second I struggle to push him away with my hands and twist my body out of his embrace.

But then he blurts out words that shock me silent.

"I love you. Nes, I love you more than I ever thought I could love anyone. And I'll run as far and fast as you need me to, to keep you safe. You hear me? *I love you.*"

The hoarse rasp of his words hangs in the air between us. I go still. We're pressed so close, the thump of his heart against my ribs is as strong as the pounding of my heart inside my chest. Our hearts answer each other, beat for beat, without fail—like my heart knows better than my brain that love always answers love.

"No. Please, no." When I didn't answer immediately, he pushed up and away with his arms, but I tug him back down on me. His weight helps ground the wild feeling that whips through me so fast, I swear it could carry me away. "Don't let me go."

He collects me to him with a rough pull and buries his face against my neck. "Dammit, I'm sorry. I'm outta my mind tonight."

My fingers waterfall over his face, his neck, his shoulders. I rain kisses all over him, only slowing down when he flinches because my passion is a little rough. I try to slow down so I don't hurt him, but it's hard. I'm tired of being scared, being cautious. Wasting time. I want to live, and I've never felt more alive than I do in Doyle Rahn's arms.

"I...love you, Doyle. I love you."

I sink under the weight of those words. Before I drown, I kiss Doyle again, hard and desperate, like he's my lifesaver. That kiss drags me up from the sucking depths of my uncertainty.

When I kiss him, I can breathe again.

I've said those words to so few people—to my family, to Ollie, to Lincoln when I thought he loved me back. But I've never meant them the way I do right now.

I feel like I can't press close enough to Doyle, even though there's no space left between us. We're rolling in a field full of scratchy grasses and nipping bugs, but that doesn't stop us from lying back and kissing hard and hot, as long and as much as we can. He licks along the edge of my jaw, around the whorl of my ear, back against the seam of my lips.

I thrust my hands up under his shirt and run my fingers up over the long, sweet length of his back and down into his waistband, where his boxer briefs hug tight to his hips.

"Dammit." He gathers me up and brushes my back and hair off with quick, strong sweeps of his hands. "We're goin' at it on an anthill."

"I hate these ants," I grumble, slapping at my legs and ass. "Come to the truck with me?"

His thumb bumps along my knuckles, and I can't stop thinking about the box of condoms he keeps in his glove compartment, crammed in with the hot sauce packets. I'm still thinking about that black box when he opens the door for me, stopping on the running board to fold me back in his arms and kiss me so hard, he opens his cut lip. He flips the passenger seat forward, and I crawl into the back, lying down on the narrow bench seat with my breath held.

He climbs back and slams the door shut. The cab goes quiet, and the only light comes from the sliver of moon shining through the window. He tries to settle next to me, but there isn't enough room, even if we both tilt sideways on one hip.

I find his hips and pull him on top of my body, flipping under him as I do. "It's okay," I assure him.

"I'm gonna crush you." He's holding himself rigid a few inches above me along the entire stretch of his body, wincing in pain.

I press my hands over his shoulders and down along the dip of his spine. I can see his eyes widen when I grab lower and squeeze twice. He laughs, and I lure him down, so our hips nest. "I like how you feel against me."

"You sure now, Nes?" He whispers it, and I whisper back a yes that barely breaks from my mouth before we're kissing again, our mouths everywhere and not enough places at the same time.

We tug up at fabric, sometimes too distracted by the kissing to get it all the way off. Doyle tries to be careful because he always is with me; I try to be careful because he's bruised and barely held together right now. When he looks at me, I wish everyone could see me the way he does because it's clear he's looking at the best version of me there is.

We almost fall off the backseat more than a few times, and we laugh every time we have to rearrange our awkward limbs. It sucks that I make him wince and groan with pain twice as much as I make him moan with pleasure, but every time I ask if he wants to stop, he rolls his eyes and repeats one adamant word: *no*. When I'm so crazy-ready my head spins and I can't wait anymore, he reaches up front and pops the glove compartment open, fishes past the hot sauce, and takes out a condom.

"You sure?" he repeats, and I repeat my yes, grabbing him to me greedily to prove that I mean it.

And then, in the safe, quiet back of his truck, with a dizzying curve of stars shining through the windows, Doyle Rahn and I tumble over every line we ever drew in the clumsiest, most beautiful way possible. And when it's done, we just lie there, grabbing on to each other tight, happy together in this perfect moment we stole from under fate's nose and made our own.

TWENTY-TWO

I need a witness to the love that wants to geyser past the confines of my ribs, so I dial Ollie. The phone rings and rings. Ollie's bassoon solo plays over my speakers.

It should be a fairly uncool instrument—in the symphony *Peter and the Wolf*, the bassoon represents Peter's exasperated, scolding grandpa—but it becomes something else entirely when Ollie plays. She plays on the edge of a chasm, unafraid to throw preconceived ideas about the beauty of sound out the window. My best friend is utterly fearless with her music.

That's the way she is as a friend too. It was Ollie who gave me hope that my heart would trust again after Lincoln's betrayal. I'm ludicrously glad I trusted her now.

"Nes!" My ears are so consumed by her haunting music, I startle at the sound of her voice. "You're calling to tell me you've fallen madly in love with your new Southern-belle best friend, probably named Peaches or Feather, who has the cutest drawl and asked you to be part of the Ya-Ya Sisterhood and feeds you pralines—what *are* those anyway?—because your actual bestie is a monster who doesn't return your calls, aren't you?" She skids to a stop, half excited, half panicked.

"Blasphemy. You're never getting rid of me, bestie. You *should* be ignoring my calls. I know this year has been a beast for you. But your solo… Olls, I'm holding up my arm and all the little hairs are sticking straight up. This is other level. This is *amazing*."

"Thank you," she whispers. "I have a confession."

"Confess away."

"It's not just hours of practice."

"Really? Spill."

"There's a muse. Nes, I think…I think I'm in love."

It's like after sludging through every kind of hell—parental, romantic, scholastic—life just decided to lift its magic wand and *bibbidy bobbidy boo* everything in my world. The pumpkins and mice and old rags have been transformed into carriages and horses and glittery dresses complete with coordinating glass slippers, all of it illuminated by showers of sparkling light.

"Tell me." I want to start at the *once upon a time* of Ollie's fairy tale and listen all the way to the "and we all lived happily ever after" part.

But Ollie's tale has a shocking twist—it wasn't either chair at either school or pretzel guy or skateboard guy or any combination of the guys Ollie has been flirting with all semester.

The prince charming of Ollie's story is… Thao.

"*Thao* Thao?" I can't wrap my head around the idea of Thao and Ollie…together.

"I know," she moans. "I can't stand him. Or I thought I couldn't. What kind of idiot falls for a guy who tortured her through her entire childhood? At first I thought it was a demented case of Stockholm syndrome."

"He did put you through distressing amounts of torture. He pulled out *a lot* of chairs just before you sat…" I point out.

Like, blooper-reel levels. But I am not laughing because I'm a *real* friend.

Who is choking on silent laughter.

"And chopped off my left braid when I was six so my mother had to cut my hair into that hideous bowl cut. He held me down and made me eat a worm when I was eight. Hid that scary Vietnamese mask in my closet when I was ten. I didn't sleep for two months! Last time I checked, the only thing he was good at was farting and uploading YouTube videos of his friends falling off railings on their bikes."

Hmm. Okay, not exactly the chirping birds/harmonious love-duet, fairy-tale beginning I had in mind.

"I remember that! Whatever happened to that one kid, the one with the spiky helmet—"

"Over thirty stitches and two fake teeth," she finishes before I can remind her of the gory details.

"So… You didn't just develop a love of flatulence and masochism since I've been gone, *right*?" I only relax when she laughs.

"I was so wrapped up in school and rehearsals I hardly noticed he left last year, apparently just after fall break. It winds up he got in big trouble at his school because of the bike-stunt stuff. He destroyed some property, wound up pretty badly hurt. His family kept it under wraps—you know the whole 'you shamed the family name' bit my people seem to love so much. But he got shipped off to Vietnam to train with his uncle who does Vovinam, which is like this old martial arts stuff that teaches discipline or whatever. Anyway, Thao came back." She sighs, a happy sigh that makes me picture her resting her chin on her hand.

"And?" I prompt.

I hear the springs creak as she falls on the bed in the kind of Victorian-era swoon she uses to add heightened drama to her stories. "My, oh my, the boy became a *man*, Nes! Like, in every way. The way he looks, the way he talks, what he's passionate about, who he cares about—spoiler alert, it's me. He cares about *me*, and I swear I can't stop tying little heart-shaped knots around everyone's wrists like it's Valentine's Day every day, Nes. It's like my brain has been replaced with confetti, and *I like it*, dammit!"

I can't fully wrap my gray matter around this shocking news. "I believe you, because you never lie. But, Olls, this is blowing my mind. Geeky little Thao? Spaghetti arms? Pimples? Buckteeth?"

"He left an ugly duckling and came back a swan," she sighs, the drama oozing out of her words.

I'm still stunned, but I'm happy, of course. I love that my best buddy found unexpected love, especially with this dark horse. Who doesn't love an underdog? And I'm completely curious to know what Thao looks like and acts like… To be honest, I always harbored a sneaking suspicion that he had a thing for Ollie and the only way he could think to get her attention was by doing what he did best. Which, unfortunately, happened to be farting and playing mean practical jokes.

"So Thao. Wow." I clear my throat. "In other love-related news—"

"Agnes Penelope Murphy-Pujols!" Ollie gasps. "Did you and Doyle…?"

And it pours out, like a dam burst, like a deluge. Every detail. First every incredibly beautiful piece, and then, when she's softened from it, all the rotten ugly bits. There's physical distance between us we can't bridge right now, but I can still feel every ounce of happiness and disgust and outrage and pure love vibrating across the miles and fluttering right against my heart.

"What are you going to *do*?" she demands.

"I guess just make out a ton?" Evidence of how twitterpated we are: we both roll, laughing over that stupid joke.

"So you're like an item? Boyfriend and girlfriend? Or courting? Is that what they say down there?"

"Um…" I clear my throat. "I'm not sure."

"About exactly what you two are to each other, or Southern slang for dating?"

"Both."

"And about prom?"

"We're supposed to meet with the principal this morning. I'm not totally convinced this is such a good idea. Doyle wants me to state our case for having an inclusive prom, but Armstrong hates my guts, and I just feel like…" I peter off, not wanting to admit that I feel like quitting before we even get started.

"It's funny, because based on the tone of your voice, I would assume you're not seriously considering melding the two most important things in the world—*romantic love and social justice.*" Ollie's voice pitches up like it does when she's about to drag out her soapbox.

"Ollie, I have *stress*," I whine.

Instead of pointing out how she's maintaining an unreal GPA while she chairs a dozen extracurricular activities, becomes a musical prodigy, and turns a prank war with the pesky boy next door into true love, Ollie levels me with a long, judgmental silence.

"Ollie," I whine.

"Stop."

She centers the soapbox.

"But—"

"Zip it!"

She puts one foot up on it.

"I don't wanna—"

And *here* she goes…

"I'm not going to mince words just because you're my best friend and soul mate. Your reluctance to get involved is an embarrassment to the SPARK club. I'm not exaggerating when I say you are, without a doubt, letting down every past, current, *and* future member of the Crown Heights chapter of Feminists Now. And no one from the Random Acts of Kindness Club is going to give you more than, like, one *really quick* hug before they turn their backs on you until you remove your head from your sphincter! Moving to another state does not mean you abandon your good works, Ms. Murphy-Pujols. Get out there and *organize!*" My bestie's rallying cry prods me right where she knows it hurts most—in my guilt vortex. "Don't let us down."

"Okay, okay." The familiar roar of Doyle's truck sends me scrambling for my backpack. "I actually just heard Doyle pull in. I promise, I will not be a blemish on the face of social justice."

A tiny sigh whooshes out as Ollie momentarily retires from her post as head life coach and goes back to being my best friend. "I don't even know him! How do I not know the guy you love, Nes? How is this our real life? Our senior year?"

"You're seriously asking me? You're the one who fell in love with your nerdy arch nemesis. I feel like we're living in some crazy alternate reality." We both laugh hard, partly to cover up how much it really does hurt. "I love talking to you, but I miss *you.*"

"I miss you. Tell Doyle he has to come to Brooklyn this

summer. Tell me what happens, with prom planning and everything. And I'll send you a picture of Thao and me?" she offers shyly.

"You better if you know what's good for you," I threaten. "I'm litera—I'm *metaphorically* dying to see the transformation your beautiful swan made."

"Oh, Nes." Her laugh and choke cyclone together and blur into a wet sob. "I miss you so hard it's *literally* breaking my heart."

"You hate when people misuse *literally*," I scold. "That said, I will literally come mend your heart with my own two hands. Soon, lovey. So soon."

"Love ya."

"Love ya."

I run out, still giddy over the fact that when I get in Doyle's truck now, we kiss. When we pull back sooner than either of us really wants to, my phone buzzes. I open the image Ollie texted me and gasp.

Doyle glances over, worry lining his face. "Looks like you've seen a ghost."

I stare at the image of my gorgeous best friend and her… really hot boyfriend who looks like *maybe* he could be Thao's super buff, clear-skinned, straight-teethed second cousin. Twice removed.

"Just marveling at the wonders of modern orthodontia combined with some muscle mass. Holy Thao."

I love the way he grins, like he gets there's a joke he's not privy to, but he's more than happy to wait until I'm ready to tell him.

It's one of the many (many) reasons I'm intensely in love with Doyle Rahn. And I try to shield myself inside the confines of that beautiful, perfect bubble of love as we pull up at Ebenezer High.

"So how are you feeling?" I ask. Yes, it's partially stalling because I don't want to go in, but I do want to know.

"Better than the time I fell off the roof of my granddaddy's barn. Lee says my bones're made of the same stuff Wolverine's are." When he tries to smile, his lip almost cracks open at the scabbing split.

"Adamantium."

"That's it. I got adamantium bones."

"You're bleeding." He leans back as I dab the blood away with a tissue from the pack in my bag, but his features go hard at my next question. "What did your grandparents say?"

"They weren't happy, but we all know my daddy's got a nasty streak." He shrugs the shoulders I know are black-and-blue from the man who's supposed to love and protect him.

The tissue is crimson in the center from the blood I had to wipe off his face. "The fact that your father has a history of being an abusive bastard doesn't give him a free pass to kick your ass whenever he feels like it."

"I guess I need to learn my lesson and keep outta his way," Doyle says in a voice as close to a snap as I've ever heard him come when he's talked to me.

"How the hell am *I* the one you're pissed at? You wouldn't even have been at his place if your grandma hadn't guilted you, but you're not mad at her."

"You don't know that." His words lash out fast. "It's family stuff, and we got it handled. I'm not on your back 'bout you and your mama, how you give her hell for making some mistakes—"

"I don't give her hell." My protest is weak at best.

"You ain't exactly nice to her. Nobody's perfect. I never got a chance to tell my mama I forgave her for screwin' up,

'cause mine never bothered to stick around like yours did."
He blows out a long breath.

I choose my words carefully. "You have a big heart. You forgive people who, I'm sorry, don't deserve it."

"Mebbe I do forgive too easy when it comes to other people."
He takes my hand. "But I don't forgive myself. Not for exposin'
you to my daddy and his hate. I accept my lot, but I never meant
to pull you in."

"You have it all wrong." I rub my thumb over his battered
knuckles. "You and me? We face the hard stuff together. You
don't have to protect me, because we protect each other."

He tugs my hand up and kisses it. "I don't need you to do
that."

"But I *want* to."

"But I don't want you to." He's dead serious, and the bottom drops out of my stomach.

"That's not how I want us to—"

"Can we talk about this later?" he begs.

I think about how Ollie sometimes pushes me to *feel* things
I'm not ready to feel, which always annoyed me. Now I know
how sick with worry she must've been for me.

"Okay. I guess we should go meet with Armstrong." I'm
not great at faking smiles, but I do my best as we get out of
the truck and Doyle marches to the principal's office as I drag
my feet.

I speed up a little when we get to the door, but he races
to beat me to it. "You ready?" He backs into the glass door,
pushing it open with his battered shoulders, and holds out one
arm in a chivalrous gesture.

I get chivalry, but he needs help now. *Why won't he accept
help from me?*

"Ready as I'll ever be." My stomach is knotted tight, but I fake a confident smile, and it tricks him. "Let's do this."

We walk in lockstep to Armstrong's office, shoulder to shoulder. When we take a seat, I attempt to keep a distance between our chairs, because this isn't some love-in. This is a civil-liberties-violation meeting, and "we need to take this seriously if we want to be taken seriously," as Ollie would preach.

I inch over to one side and, as if on cue, he hooks one muddy boot around the leg of my chair and drags it across the ugly industrial carpet. I toss him a glower that's supposed to level him, but Doyle's charms pummel my defenses. Resistance is futile. I hook my pinkie through his, a stopgap that should tide him over, at least until Armstrong breezes in.

"Mr. Rahn, Ms. Murphy-Pujols." Armstrong's drawl trickles out with an extra dose of annoyance.

I'm thinking these uncharitable thoughts when he glances up and stares at Doyle with a mix of shock and sadness on his craggy features.

"Doyle." Armstrong strides forward and crouches, hands on his knees, eyes squinted as they rake over Doyle's battered face. It's amazing how quickly I stopped registering the sickening extent of Doyle's injuries. "Was it Boyd? You can tell me, son."

I breathe a secret sigh of relief. If Doyle can't accept help from me, maybe he can from a respected adult member of the community. Maybe he just needs someone more capable of handling things than I am.

I thought my feelings for Armstrong were set in stone, but I realize I'd sing his praises from the rooftops if he was the one who helped Doyle.

Doyle trains his eyes on his boot. I had pulled my pinkie back when Armstrong made his entrance, but Doyle's hand flounders frantically for mine, and his face doesn't relax until our hands are pressed palm to palm, fingers wedded so tight, I grit my teeth.

"No, not my old man, sir. Just an argument with some guys my cousin had words with, got outta hand. Stupid."

I'm about to tell Principal Armstrong that that is *not* what happened, but Doyle tugs on my hand and shakes his head subtly. We have an argument right there that consists entirely of widened eyes and pinched lips, hand squeezes and head shakes. I back down only because I don't have enough faith in Armstrong to lose Doyle's trust on the chance he can help.

"That's the full story?" Armstrong raises a disbelieving eyebrow.

"Yes, sir. My grandparents already gave me an earful. I won't let myself get into a situation like that again."

Doyle swallows hard, and Armstrong swivels his head my way. His entire face suddenly tightens, as if he's solved this puzzle—and it seems he's read between the lines of what we're not saying and decided that *I'm* the reason for Doyle's pain. Armstrong thinks he's connecting the dots, and the picture they make is of an upstanding young white man getting his face beat to a pulp because his smart-ass, Yankee girlfriend is black.

It's the sickest kind of irony. I'm the only one who seems to really want to help Doyle, and I'm the one being blamed for his pain.

My eyes prick with tears that I refuse to shed in this dismal little office. Compressing my sadness mutates it into rage. I want to scream in his arrogant face, tell him that I actually care about Doyle, and it's not my fault any of this has happened to him.

I'm sorely tempted to drag Doyle out of here by his bruised hand and *run*. Screw fighting the "good fight." Time to do as Mama Patria advises when there's no way out of an argument: *pa'lante*. Move on.

"Ah. I see." Armstrong backs away from Doyle, who slouches against the plastic chair and loosens the iron grip he had on my fingers. I pull my hands into my lap, shaking with anger at Doyle for not clearing things up, for letting me take the fall so he doesn't have to come clean about what his father did to him. "Did you bring any of this up with law enforcement?" Armstrong presses, looking down his bony nose at us.

Of course not. What's the use calling the cops when they don't do anything anyway?

I know I'm lumping all law enforcement into one ugly pile based on what I experienced with a single officer, but I'm not feeling especially charitable right now.

"No, sir, and I don't plan to. Neither do they. What's done is done, and everything's settled, sir." Doyle's voice yanks tight, like a string wound around the tip of a finger, cutting off all the blood. He reaches for my hand again, and I know he's reliving the whole scene in his mind. Angry as I am about his lies, I want to help him. I meant it when I said it. Right now, that means holding his hand when I want to give in to my own anger. "But we—Agnes and me—we came in here to talk about something else entirely."

Armstrong volleys a tired look from me to Doyle. "I wish we could talk more about *this* topic, Doyle. I don't like what I'm seeing. You getting into fights? That's not like you."

Doyle lifts his eyes and collects every ounce of bruised Southern pride before he makes our case. "You're right, sir. I don't fight much. But that's exactly why we're here today. There's something I've got going on that's worth fighting for." Doyle looks over my way and smiles through the cuts and bruises. It's painfully beautiful, beautifully painful. And it melts away my anger. I know better than anyone how easy it is to accidentally hurt the people you love when you're blinded by your own pain. "Me and Agnes plan on going to prom together."

It's that simple. What we want can be summed up in a single sentence, yet it's so complicated, it sends Armstrong into a blank-eyed, pursed-lipped daze. When the answer crosses his mind, it's like a spotlight shifted off his face and dimmed all the tension of Doyle's blinding declaration.

"Doyle, you know Ebenezer High doesn't hold a school-sanctioned prom. There's nothing I can say about it because it's simply out of my jurisdiction, son."

I have never seen a man so happy to pass the buck in my life.

"But Agnes and I can't go together to either one of the proms put on by the parents for Ebenezer. You know that, sir." Doyle stops short of saying *because we're not the same skin color, even though this is America and it's the twenty-first century, and this should be making people want to riot, but instead it makes them want to shush anyone who mentions it.*

Like it's too ugly to tack on the reason why.

I want to abort this doomed mission and flee this office, because Armstrong clearly doesn't give a single solitary damn and sees no reason to change his stance.

"You know what I *can* do?" Armstrong wags his finger like he's really embracing this whole dilemma on our behalf. I can smell the stink of bullshit wafting from him before it even drops. "I can give you the numbers for Cassidy Mingledorff and Judy Powell. They're the mothers who run our proms. Let's see if they can give you some kind of solution."

He holds out a Post-it note with the names and numbers scrawled across them, like we don't realize he's writing his own get-out-of-jail-free card.

Doyle moves to take the paper, but I shake my head and hold out a hand to interrupt the transfer.

"We're giving these two women the power to tell us yes or no about attending our own prom. This is *our* school. *Our* prom. Any person who attends Ebenezer High should get a bid to *our* school's one prom."

I realize too late that my impassioned plea was utterly devoid of *sir*s, so I'm sure all he heard was the absolute insubordination that's becoming my MO in Armstrong's book.

"Ms. Murphy-Pujols, you are aware that prom is a luxury, *not* a necessity?" He holds the paper scissored between his index and second fingers and rocks it back and forth. "Proms require organizing and funding that some of our lovely community ladies have taken upon themselves to deal with and that our school is ill-equipped for, especially with the end of the school year fast approaching. The school's budget has already been presented and approved by the board for the year. Now, I won't say that I agree with every detail of how each prom is run, but I do know that these women are falling back on decades of Ebenezer tradition as well as the wishes of the student body and the community when they pull this all together."

I'm about to ask hard-boiled investigative questions: *The wishes of which students, exactly? Has an alternative prom ever been offered? Why don't the other schools offer this privatized prom abomination? Why hasn't the ACLU ever come down on you jerks and called you out for being the racist freaks you are?*

Okay, maybe less investigative and more incendiary, but I've never felt my entire body catch flame with such righteous anger. Before I devolve into mad-dog territory, Doyle stands and takes the paper, creased by Armstrong's impatient fingers. I'm about to rally, but I stop short. Doyle knows from painful firsthand experience when he's been beaten, and I know better than to try to fight when Doyle's face says *retreat*.

Armstrong offers an insincere *have a nice day* to our retreating backs, but the words are just a little feather in his authority cap. A bloated filler for all my clearly forgotten *yes, sir*s.

There are a ton of complicated, sticky, *emotional* things to talk about, and, at this moment, I just can't do it. I'm thoroughly beaten down, and I want to rest and refuel.

"Lunch will be over soon. Wanna eat?" I bump Doyle's shoulder, but his head shake is so defeated, it scares me. Doyle is possibly the most optimistic person I know. I expected him to rebound with a plan B by now. "Well, I'm hungry. If you want to waste away…" I lope off toward the cafeteria, but he calls my bluff and doesn't follow. "No food for you?"

"Not hungry." He flips the paper Armstrong handed him around his fingers like it's a tiny, flat baton. "I don't want to feed this mess of a body. It's one of those days I don't feel hungry to even be here, y'know?"

I'd call him on his melodrama, but his words howl from somewhere ugly and scary. I still joke, because I refuse to stop screaming my nonsense in the face of the darkness that works to swallow him whole.

"Very Kafka of you, but don't starve yourself on me now, *cucaracha*. If these biddies won't help us throw the prom we want, I'm going to need to do all kinds of balloon blowing up and streamer hanging. I can't do it without you."

His smile is minimalist. "Maybe I can handle, like, an ice-cream sandwich?"

I link a finger through his belt loop and tug his skinny hips my way. So much has changed between us in a few short days. And I just want to eat some ice cream with the guy I love. "That's more like it. This ice-cream weakness of yours? I think revealing it to me was a big mistake."

"That so?" His boots clomp a step closer, then two, until his feet and mine alternate in a pattern of big and small soles. "Why not? Can't you be trusted?"

"Never. At least not where you're concerned."

Our faces are close enough now that we might break my "no PDA" rule and kiss, right here in front of the cafeteria. But after our visit with Armstrong, everything we do in school—in front of the people who seem to think we need to ask permission just to be together—feels like some kind of activism.

Nothing is unsexier than PDA for the sake of activism.

I dodge ahead of him and buy a crap ton of food neither of us is that hungry for.

"So." Doyle lets the word hang in the air as he collects all our half-eaten garbage and tosses the last melted bits of ice-cream sandwich into his mouth when the bell rings. "What do ya think we should do?"

"I do *not* think I'm the one you should ask about how to organize some huge party on our own, if that's the route you're going with this. I mean, I'm more than okay helping out, but I'm a social misfit. And a Yankee. And a smart-ass."

"Really. Well, I think you could do more than organize it—I think you could be the prom queen." He folds his arm around my shoulder.

I'm worried about the stiff way he walks, like he's trying not to jostle his ribs. "That's probably the most ridiculous thing you've ever said to me, and you've said some really crazy crap. Doyle, admit it—I wouldn't even be the prom queen of an alternative prom."

He stops short, creating a minor traffic jam in the middle of the hall, grabs my face, and slaps a kiss on my lips.

"Brains, girl! You got so many, they solve problems even when you ain't tryin'!" His grin buzzes through me before I'm sure why I'm excited.

"What did I say?" We're almost to my classroom, and he's already scanning the halls. He pats me on the shoulder like I'm a sidekick tucked behind his superhero cape and yells, "Khabria Scott! Where you at, girl?"

"Khabria?" I ask, but Doyle doesn't hear me or stop to explain before he bolts down the hall like a man on fire.

TWENTY-THREE

There's no sign of him until after dinner, when I hear a faint scratch at my bedroom window.

"Doyle." I press my palms flat against the pane and push up, my sweaty hands leaving streaks on the glass. "What are you doing here? I just called you."

"I looked for you after ninth." He tumbles in over the sash. "I rang the bell like a proper suitor come callin', but I think your doorbell's broken. Want me to fix it?"

"'Suitor come callin',' huh? I'll have to tell Ollie that one. Uh, yeah, if you know how to fix doorbells, that'd be cool. Thanks."

His gray T-shirt is rumpled, and his hair sticks out a little too long from under both sides of his navy Yankees cap, the one we keep stealing back and forth. When we were just friends, I could look at him and admire what I liked, but there was no experience driving me to press things further.

Now that we've gunned it right over the friend line, I can't stop the itchiness I feel when he's close and we're alone. It's intensified by my PDA hatred, which forces me to keep a Puritan lid on it anytime anyone else is around. So I'm pretty pent up. It feels out of control, and I'm not sure I like it at all. But that doesn't stop me from tugging on the front of the soft gray fabric of his shirt and pulling until he falls back on my mattress with me. He winces a little and holds his side, but flips me back fast, like he's proving to me just how fine he is.

He buries his head in the place where my shoulder meets my neck and breathes deep. "Mmm, you smell like a coconut."

"It's my conditioner." I stroke his hair, which is rough at the ends like it's been burnt by the sun. "You okay?"

"I heal quick." He flashes that assurance too fast, then bull-dozes onto a new subject. "And I talked to Khabria. So…she wants to talk to you."

"Right. What about exactly? You ran off before you ex-plained." I want to know. I do.

But what I *really* want is to run my hands over Doyle's body, momentarily broken, but strong. I want to be with him the way we were the other night, the two of us against the world. While I'm wrapped safe in his arms, I want to forget all the complicated and incredibly screwed-up situations we deal with on a daily basis. Maybe that's a dangerous perspective to take regarding our relationship, but I'm as addicted as any junkie to this total, beautiful release I feel with Doyle.

It's scary, but I can't get enough of it. Of *him*. I lean back on my elbows, push him away with my foot and sit up cross-legged, resting my hands on my thighs so that I'm not tempted to touch him.

"Because Khabria is like Glinda the Good Witch to Ansley's Wicked Witch of the West," Doyle explains, apparently oblivi-ous to the fact that I'm barely containing myself around him.

I dig my nails into my shins and keep a calm face. "Right. I mean, I don't know her superwell, but she's always been re-ally cool to me."

"Yeah." He creeps closer. I scuttle back and hug Mr. Kitten-face, using my old teddy as a barrier between us—a reminder of a time when I wasn't a total sex-crazed pervert. What's even happening to me? I was never like this with Lincoln. He was the one who seemed to have this intense need for me—the same overpowering need I'm now possessed by whenever I get Doyle alone. I always thought of that kind of desire as seriously alpha, as total strength—but the truth is, I've never felt more vulnerable.

"You okay?" Doyle asks.

I'm not being subtle, because subtlety is an impossibility for me. "It's just... I feel... The other night... It was so good, so amazing, and I..." Usually I have too many words, but I'm at a total loss.

He clears his throat and rubs his hands down his thighs. "When, uh, that happens... When I fight, I don't know... I go to a weird place. I know things got rushed. I didn't want it to happen that way. I know we did...we did things you probably regret."

Everything grinds to a halt. I get that his pride and pain and the lies he feels like he needs to keep for his family got crushed together the other night, and maybe his feelings for me got mixed in, but *what*? Anger and panic kickbox in my stomach, and I'm too thrown off guard to referee. I toss Mr. Kittenface aside and sit up.

"Do *you* regret them?"

Doyle hangs his head. "That wasn't the way it should've been. Not with all that chaos and craziness. That's not what I wanted for us."

"What?" My voice is hoarse.

His almost-lavender eyes are fixed on my comforter, his face so beautifully sad, the sight of it inspires a fist-sized lump

335

in my throat. "That was jest me losing it. Same way my dad does with booze and his fists. Sometimes I lose self-control, and it hits me that I'm following in Boyd Rahn's footsteps no matter how hard I try to do better. Guess you can't escape your blood."

My voice comes out edged with something dangerous Doyle would be an idiot to ignore. "Are you saying you screwed me in some crazy moment when you had no self-control? That you said you loved me, but… What?"

"I *do* love you. That's exactly what this is about. You think that's what the girl I love deserves? 'Specially our first time?" He slides the Yankees cap off his head and crushes the fabric in his fist. "Before, with other girls, I was always enough how I am, and they kinda fell all over me." The smile he attempts fails. "With you, I gotta be on my A game all the time. And I messed up. I know there ain't really any such thing as a do-over in life, but maybe you and me could try this once?"

"A game?" The words crack out with the full force of my fury and disgust. "I don't want to see your *game*, Doyle. I want us to be honest. I want you to accept the fact that you need help, sometimes from *me*, the person who loves you. Showing me your A game is *lying*."

"A lie's not so bad if you're doin' it to protect the people you love," he says.

"That's a total load of crap!" I yell. "I get you love your family, and that's truly noble and all, but their lies and secrets are tearing you up, in every way. Look!" I point across the room, where his bruised reflection stares back at us from my mirror. Doyle lowers his eyes.

"I don't wanna look. I can't. I need to forget."

"What the hell are you talking about?" I stand on my mattress, towering over him so I don't feel so out of control. He stands too, I guess to even the playing field, and tries to hold my hands, but I yank them away.

"I know it sounds messed up. It *is* messed up." He rubs a hand over the back of his neck, his go-to nervous tic. "It ain't gonna get clearer the more we talk. Easiest if we jest forget it happened. Get it right next time. Can't we do that?"

"*Forget* it? It's all I've been thinking about. *You're* all I've been thinking about." I swallow hard, but the next words croak out from somewhere dark. "I *never* want to forget what happened between us."

"I'm sorry." The way he keeps hanging his head like he's *ashamed*—of what we did? Of being with me?—stirs my fury. "I knew I should have never brought you around that drunk asshole. You got no idea how sorry I am for all this. I can give you time if you need time. I know you ain't used to seeing things like that. I guess it's easier for me to jest put it outta my head because, in my screwed-up world, that's what I gotta do to keep goin'. I've had years of practice though."

He lifts his chin, and when our eyes meet, I know I'm not imagining our connection. It's an undeniable something in me, in him, in the air between us.

How can he be so completely mine and so out of my reach at the same time? It's like we're soul mates who speak different languages.

The need to make him understand is so intense, it scorches through me.

"I get that it sucks to rehash everything that went down between you and your father. Honestly, I get that. But what happened after, with us? I can't forget that. I won't. And I have no idea why you'd want to." The air between us goes thick and silent.

When he finally says the next words, they're slurred with emotion. "I guess I really don't get it."

"I loved being with you. *Exactly like we were.* I don't want a do-over, Doyle. If we're going to be brave enough to be together, we have to face all of it—the good, the ugly, *all of it*, head-on. I can't stop thinking about it, and I don't want to. In fact, I refuse to."

His eyebrows crush low and his mouth twists into a scowl. "But I'm askin' you to stop thinking about it. Fact of the matter is, I need ya to. I'm asking you to do it for me. Because that guy you saw cryin' his heart out, beat to a pulp? That ain't me. That guy's nothin' but a weak goddamn mess. He ain't me."

"Really? Well, who are you, exactly, Doyle? Are you the guy who's always smiling? The guy every girl crushes on and every teacher lets get away with murder because you're so charming? The good friend, the good worker, the good boyfriend?" My voice rises with the swell of feelings rolling through me. I'm more than a little off-kilter after every crazy thing that I've seen and put up with in the last few months.

"Yeah, all that. All that, Nes, and better. Or at least I'm *tryin'* to do better. I'm tryin' because it's what I demand from myself. And it's what you deserve outta me." He throws his hand up, surrender-style when I won't agree with him. "Why don't it make sense that to you I don't wanna be the guy who never amounted to nothing 'cause his daddy's the town drunk, and he followed that same path? There's plenty of guys like that in this town, and I can't stomach the sight of 'em. The truth is, I don't want you to love that guy. You're better than that."

"Don't you dare try to tell me there's any part of you that isn't good enough for me. You can't just slice out the pieces of yourself you don't like." I lean close to him, my hands planted on his wide, steady shoulders, my fingers curled around the strong muscle and bruised skin. "You can't pick and choose which parts of yourself you want to show. Not to the people closest to you. Not to the ones who love you."

He reaches up and closes his fingers tight around my wrists, his eyes wild. "That's the thing. I want for you to see the best in me, nothing less. I *hate* that you saw me the way you did."

I inch closer to him, keeping my voice low and gentle, like I'm talking to a wild animal that's spooked. "That's the way it goes when you really care about someone. Fair's fair, Doyle. I feel like the *only* way you ever see me is at my worst. You don't know what I was like back in Brooklyn. I wasn't this loner rebel. I was a cool girl, smart, fun. I was popular. I know this is hard to imagine, but my teachers and classmates actually *liked* me. I was nice. God, I used to *hate* that word. *Nice.*"

"I like you jest fine the way you are right here, right now." He strokes his hands up my arms and pulls his fingers back down, leaving a trail of goose bumps on my skin. "You're a helluva lot more than *nice*, Nes. You're brave. Strong. Smart. And you've got the best heart of anyone I've ever known. Knowing you makes me wanna be a better man. Makes me wanna prove to you I'm not that guy you saw lose it. Why can't you see that?"

"The way I saw you the other day was *honest*, Doyle. It wasn't the phony face you put on whenever you want people to think everything is okay. I hate what your dad did. I can barely sleep because every time I close my eyes, I see him beating you."

"Don't remind me," Doyle mutters, dropping his hands.

I try to grab his hands again, but he won't let me. "But I'm glad I saw it too," I confess. "Because I was just as tricked as everyone else. I bought it, Doyle. You're really, really good at pretending everything's okay. As close as I thought we were, I had no idea what you were dealing with."

"I wish it was still that way. I wish you never saw that guy I was the other night." His words burrow out from somewhere dark and bitter.

"You think that guy is weak? Screwed up?" I whisper, tears chasing hot and quick down my cheeks. My nose runs, and I wipe it on my wrist like a little kid. "I'm *in love* with that guy, Doyle. That's the truth."

"Holy hell, Nes, please don't say that," he begs, his voice cracking.

"No, I *will* say it. I'm sick of not saying what I feel. I'm sick of hiding the truth. I've *never* felt as close to anyone as I felt the other night with you. Explain that," I dare him, my body quaking with frustration because I can see he's working hard to ignore my arguments and reject the love that feels so fragile already.

"Adrenaline," he bites out. "Drama. Fear. Dammit, Nes! I thought you, of all people, wouldn't be into all that."

"'Into all that'?" I repeat slowly. "What does that mean exactly? You think I get off on the fact that I watched your father beat the crap out of you?"

"It doesn't make a whole lotta sense, but what the hell else am I s'posed to think?" he demands, his words pure ice.

"There're a lot of lies between most people. But you and me? We're stronger than that. I've been lying and lied to for so long. I'm glad we were forced to be honest the other night."

"Honest?" His laugh snarls somewhere behind his gritted teeth. "Guess that's one word for it. Look…" He takes a deep breath and combs his fingers through his hair, neatening it up this time. He won't face me. "I can't… It's not gonna… Look, mebbe I shouldn't have come 'round at all. I'll see myself out."

"Doyle! Wait!" He stops when I call his name. So my voice still has some power over him. But not that much. Not enough that I can use it to bring him back to me right now. "I… I'll see you around?"

It's weak. It's nothing near what I want to say, but I'm afraid to take the fight any further. I think I've already pushed too much, and I don't even dare think too hard about what the consequences might be.

Doyle Rahn stands, tall and hurting and almost mine, but not quite, in the middle of my room. There are a thousand things we both should say now, right now, before it's too late.

"Sure."

He climbs back out the sill, and, when I hear his boots hit the ground, I crush my fist into my mouth and fight back the sobs.

TWENTY-FOUR

My life, already spiraling out of control, is officially a certified nest of insanity now that I've screwed everything up with Doyle.

Ollie assures me it's going to be okay. That we're going to figure it out. That boys are complicated. I know she wants to swing her arms out *Sound of Music*–style and scream with giddy joy about how alive all her hills are with sweet love music, but she isn't the kind of person who'd do that when her best friend is in a permanent funk.

"Talking to my best friend makes me happy," I tell her when she wants to see me happy again. "Happy isn't a 24/7 pity party you force your bestie to chaperone. I demand you tell me about the bike ride to the bridge."

She makes a noise in the back of her throat, like she's trying to strangle the words back but just *can't*. I'm glad when they explode out in this narrative glitter typhoon.

"It's been killing me not to tell you! It was incredibly romantic, and he made me ride on the handlebars, like I was a freaking baguette in a basket and not a full human who weighs a very decent amount! And his legs and arms are *pure muscle—*

which I know makes me completely shallow for even notic-
ing, but does it count if I love those muscles more because I
respect the work he put into disciplining himself, which, in
turn, made that muscle? No? Okay, it's all right, because I'm
a girl in love, and he's a boy who took me to a bridge on the
handlebars of his bike and he brought a lock, like lovers do in
Paris—except now the authorities are putting up guards because they apparently hate love in the City of Lights—and we
wrote our initials on it and locked it and then he kissed me
until I was *literally* seeing stars. Romance is killing my grasp
on the laws of grammar, and I don't care! I'm happy being a
linguistic outlaw in the name of love." She finishes her crazy
rush of a story with that final, ludicrous declaration, then follows it with, "I'm sorry. This has to be the last thing you want
to listen to."

"Are you kidding me? I'm secondhand swooning! I mean,
it's weird because Thao is still a weasley freshman in my mind,
but your story gives me hope, Olls. That love isn't dead. No
matter what the French authorities want to pretend."

Her laugh is the puppeteer pulling the strings on my smile.

"It's alive, and its heart is beating. Hard. Doyle Rahn is
going to call you. I promise. I never lie."

That's true.

Ollie never lies.

But Doyle doesn't call. I start a thousand texts and delete
every one before I hit Send.

He still waits for me at my locker, but the silence when we
walk down the halls is so uncomfortable, I start to dodge him.

He jogs down the hall to help me with a box of books Ma'am
Lovett asked me and Alonzo to grab from the book room.

"Here, let me." He reaches out, but I turn away and watch
his eye twitch.

"Thanks. I've got them."

Like he can't hear me, he tries again.

"Doyle, I *said* I have it," I snap. "I don't need your help."

He grabs the box and tugs. I yank back. Alonzo comes up behind the two of us. "Here, give me." He takes the box from our hands and hands it to Doyle, who gives him a nod before he stalks into class with his arms full.

"What kind of macho crap was that?" I demand. "Look, he's hurt, Lonzo. He doesn't need to be carrying those books."

"They ain't that heavy." Lonzo balances his box on one forearm like he's proving his point.

"If they aren't that heavy, why couldn't I carry them?" I cross my arms tight over my chest.

"Because you were tryin' to keep him from getting hurt." Lonzo glances into the classroom, where Doyle is slumped in his seat.

"That makes *no* sense," I huff.

"Doyle Rahn'll take a beating over pity any day." He shrugs. "You gotta accept that's who he is."

"So I should ignore his bruises as long as his pride's intact?" I sneer.

"Nah." Lonzo hands me a few books from his box as a crappy consolation prize. "Some people're hard in the head. They think acceptin' help is a sign of weakness. But you're smart. Mebbe you can make him see that kinda thinkin' is his daddy's way, not his."

Alonzo's words rattle around in my head nonstop. I know he's right. All except the part about me being smart enough to get through to Doyle.

I try, a few times, to approach Doyle about it, but the feelings between us are too charged. Drawing close to him is like holding my finger out to someone's fuzzy sweater after

I scuffed my socks on the carpet—just waiting for a shock. I only admit how much I miss him in my tortured dreams every night.

In English, Ansley makes an unoriginal joke that's kind of funny. Doyle's laugh feels like betrayal. She's at his locker. Her Jeep is parked next to his truck. The school paper runs a story on the Rose Queen candidates. I see Doyle behind Ansley in a candid shot and can't decide if it's a coincidence or something more.

As pukey as seeing them together makes me feel, the pain of losing his friendship is a thousand times sharper than any jealousy could ever be.

We make clumsy attempts to fix things between us. He buys me ice-cream sandwiches I eat, even though they taste like the memory of our better days. I leave a pamphlet for Al-Anon, the group that's for families of alcoholics, in his locker. He doesn't say anything about it, but a week later he asks me to read his personal essay for college applications.

"You don't gotta, if you're busy—"

"No, I'm not," I say too fast. "I'm happy to read it."

"I jest don't wanna come off like some backwoods idiot. Try not to laugh too hard. I did the best I could."

He hands me the square of folded paper, and I realize it's a huge step for Doyle, to let me see a part of him he doesn't think is good enough. I think about what Lonzo said to me about Doyle as I take the paper.

"I'd never laugh at you, Doyle. This is the least I can do to thank you."

His eyes sparkle like they're sprinkled with purple glitter. "Thank me?"

"If it wasn't for you, I would've run away from this place screaming before I made it through the first week." I wait with my breath held for his grin, my exhale timed with the uptick of his lips.

"I hope you don't hate me for convincin' you to stick around," he says, his words burred. We lock eyes.

"I have no regrets."

That's the truth.

Later that night, I sit on my bed and bawl my eyes out, Doyle's heart, in essay form, smoothed on my lap. The sentences about his tortured childhood are blunt and honest, and I realize he's still making peace with the love he feels for people he was never able to trust, people who made him feel like he had to tackle life on his own. The essay's hopeful conclusion hints at a friend who won't give up on him, and a group he's joined that makes him feel less alone.

I want so badly to be the hero he paints me as at the end of his essay, but all I do is correct the mistakes with a green pen and hand the creased paper back to him with the biggest understatement I've ever uttered. "It's good, Doyle. *Really* good."

"Thank you, Nes." There's a moment where I think we'll bridge this weird gap, where I'll say all the right things and we'll navigate through this. But I keep my mouth clamped shut, and he turns on his heel and leaves me contemplating my own cowardice. Just like that, we're back to square one.

Our awkward bachata goes on for one long week that slides into two.

Space, space, space. Maybe that's what we need.

I doodle wild exploding hearts and sprawling stars all over my computer science binder, barely listening to my teacher drone about HTML tags. I can give Doyle all the physical space he wants, but my mental space is full of him and me, us together, and—at the darkest edges—the two of us on our own.

Which is probably exactly the way it needs to be.

I start typing when everyone else types, but my code is all screwed up and the text is running up and down the page like I've lit some kind of coding fire. I sit back and watch my program implode. So many crappy life metaphors right on the screen in front of me.

Maybe Doyle's had a skewed perspective on our relationship because I've needed him to be some kind of ambassador for me as I navigate an alien place he knows so well. But he can't honestly expect me to accept his help and then never help him back.

If he loves me like he claims he does, wouldn't he *want* to let me in? Let me be a shoulder to lean on when he's cut low, when he's limping and aching?

Maybe I'm rabid for there to be this truth between us because I turned my back on truth when Lincoln's life was spiraling out of control. I covered for him, lived in his fantasy world, hoping that if I faked it well enough, the bad parts of our relationship would disappear.

I'm still thinking about it three periods later, when I'm parked on top of the bleachers, surveying the big, noisy gym below me. The entire place went nuts as soon as the coaches made the announcement about some sport sign-up, so it's outright pandemonium on the floor, which gives me a chance to avoid soccer drills in ninety-percent humidity. Sweet.

There's a light vibration on the bleachers, and when I glance over, someone leaps up like a deer and takes a seat in front of me.

"Nes?" Khabria asks cautiously.

"Hey, Khabria." I was prepared to hide out alone this period, but my social hermitage has been pretty intense since my

fallout with Doyle, and I'm pretty happy for any interaction…
"What's up?"

"I wanted to talk to you." Her voice is crisp. I'm dying to ask her what kind of lipstick she uses. It looks like it's not even a mere cosmetic. It looks like it's red velvet. Most of the time my attempts at lipstick make me feel like a clown with wax lips. "About all this bullshit."

"Uh… This bullshit?" I stammer, following the jut of her thumb. One of the huge glittery posters for Rose Queen is behind us, and I realize the gorgeous, laughing girl with the glittery crown who looks like one of the Supremes is, in fact, the girl with the scowl sitting in front of me. "Oh yeah! Doyle and I saw your poster a few weeks back. Cool. I hope you beat Ansley."

"Not sure if that's even possible." Khabria scrunches up her nose. "Maybe I shouldn't have rocked the boat. My girls were sure I'd win Rose Princess, no problem. I decided to drop out of the princess race, which was bad enough. But going up against Ansley and her crew? May not be my smartest move yet."

I'm not well versed enough in Ebenezer tradition to know what the difference between Rose Queen and Rose Princess is—Doyle declined to answer back when I asked him, but I figure I'll ask Khabria. Who looks royally pissed about the whole thing.

Okay. Maybe I'll ask her once I work up the courage.

"Guess I don't have much choice now either way." She smooths the navy skirt of her cheer uniform and tucks one of the thousands of silky braids twisted around her head back into her intricate bun. "Why not shake up all these stupid traditions? I don't know if you want to help, but Doyle said we should talk."

Doyle! I look around, like Khabria might summon him just by saying his name.

Of course, he's doesn't appear, and I do my best to club back my disappointment.

"Sure. I mean, I'm happy to help. Just…" I twist my hands and shake my head. "I'm a little confused. What exactly do you want me to help with?"

"Prom." She lets the word pop out of her mouth, and the twitch of her lips signals a mix of excitement and revulsion.

"Oh." I glance back at the poster, wondering what exactly Doyle talked to her about. He never got around to telling me before he broke my heart. "I don't think I'm even going to prom."

Her eyes remind me of toffee, but with a hint of danger— like toffee that's been broken into sharp shards. She flicks them over me like she's deciding if she should push me off the bleachers or just get up and leave without bothering.

"Why not?" Her eyebrows rise to danger-zone levels.

Crap.

"Doyle told me about the whole two-prom thing—"

"Right." Her eyes narrow.

"I mean, I can't go to a prom where I can't…" *Where I can't dance with the guy I love because of the color of my skin.* "Go with all my friends," I finish lamely.

"You think I'm going to some racist prom?" Her voice warns me to tread carefully.

"I get you want to have an amazing prom," I rush, then skid to a stop, not sure where I'm going with this train of thought. Khabria has me nervous.

"*Everyone* wants to have an amazing prom." She says it like it's the opening line of an acceptance speech. "And one that's not racist. With one Rose *Queen* and one Rose *King* who the *entire* student body picks."

I seize my chance to redirect the conversation by asking for some clarification.

"Is the Rose Queen like the Prom Queen?" I ask, and she stares like she's trying to gauge if I'm pulling her leg. "Cut me some slack, okay? I never know anything unless someone takes pity on me and explains."

"I getcha, girl." She leans back on her hands and kicks her feet out, getting comfortable like we're old amigas. "Rose Queen is the *official* queen of the *unofficial* prom, since, y'know, Ebenezer High is home to one of the most spineless administrations in the States and they don't recognize any *official* prom." She lifts her hands and makes graceful air quotes around the word. "Problem is, the Rose Queen can be the queen of only *one* prom."

"Ah, right. So, I guess you could have a Rose Queen go to either…" I'm about to say *the white prom or the black prom*, but I swallow those words and start fresh. "You can have a Rose Queen go to one prom and a Rose King go to another? Hypothetically."

"Well." She raises one finger and shakes her head. Her gold earrings pick up the dusty sunlight struggling through the windows and shimmer. "Thing is, black kids are s'posed to run for Rose *Prince* and *Princess*. Only. The other crowns are *reserved for other students.*"

There's been a lot of weird racist crap since I got here, so, seriously, this should neither surprise nor upset me, but I am *floored*.

"You've got to be *joking*," I whisper, too stunned to even scream in the face of this lunacy.

Khabria shakes her head and pops her mouth around her

defiant, "*Nope*. Now, it's not a *rule*. It's a *tradition*," she explains, pulling her voice up prim and proper and dropping a big dollop of sweet-as-cream Southern charm on top. "So, what I did? Running for Queen?" She points at her regal image on the poster board, and I can't imagine her as anything *but* a queen. "It's not breaking any rules." She arches her dark eyebrows. "But it's breaking *every* tradition."

My palms are slick with sweat because, after so much time talking, this is someone actually *doing something*. This is action, and, even though I'm not sure I'm brave enough to help, I definitely want to know all about it.

"So what happens? With the Rose Queen vote? I mean, what will happen?" I'm thrilled by the quiet anarchy Khabria is poised to unleash on Ebenezer's whole quivering Jenga tower of racist traditions.

"How would I know that?" She lowers her eyebrows. "I don't plan on stuffing the ballot boxes. I'd say the administration will do what it needs to to keep things from blowing up, except there's this whole protocol for voting, and you need to have two witnesses when the ballots are counted. One is always black, one is always white." She snorts. "Not a *rule*, of course. Just a…"

"Tradition," we say at the same time.

"That's badass, what you did," I say as she shakes her head. "Yes, yes it is. It's beating them at their own game. It's subtle, and it's brilliant."

"My friends aren't on speaking terms with me." She nods down to the tables in the center of the gym, where dozens of noisy students jostle around. The navy-skirted cheerleading squad seems to be at the center.

Except for Khabria, who's hanging with me, the school outcast.

"*Some* of your friends aren't," I correct, offering her an uncertain smile. I'd like to think she and I could consider each other at least friendly acquaintances, but I don't know how Khabria feels about that.

She smiles sadly. "I know it. And thank you. My girls think I'm being uppity, like I'm saying our prom isn't good enough the way it's always been. The white girls are just pissed because Ansley Strickland allowed some of her minions to 'run' against her this year, even though she knows she'll win. She thinks if I get the entire *African vote*, I'll win because the white votes might get divided between her girls."

"Did she *say* that?" I ask, my voice hushed in horror.

"No one comes out and *says* anything, sweetie," Khabria mutters. "No one has to. What has always been will always be, and anyone who mucks with that is enemy number one. That's the way things work here."

"Except it doesn't. Work," I add when she frowns at me. I shrug. "Well, it doesn't."

"Don't I know it." She rearranges the pleats of her cheerleading skirt. "Don't think this is all just to make a statement. I've got my own shallow reasons for doing what I'm doing." She crosses one slim leg over the other and kicks her bright white shoe out. "You don't have the market on interracial dating cornered in this school."

"Oh! Doyle? The thing is… I'm not… We're not exactly…"

"Zip it." She shuts me down with a wave of her hand. "It's like you two are in your own love bubble. It's a li'l nauseating." She wrinkles her nose, then winks at me. "But I'm happy for Doyle. Lord, that boy could pick some fool girls to date. He finally made a smart choice."

It's incredible how bubbly and light one compliment from Khabria makes me feel. Now I get why peasants scrape and bow before royalty—it's an overwhelming feeling when you're in the presence of someone regal.

"Thanks?"

"Thank *you*," she says. "I'm sure you two fell into it without 'seeing color' or whatever, but you opened Doyle's eyes to something this school's needed to shake up for a while. The boy's a romantic, and I know he wants to get his tux on and take you to prom. But he's got the same issue I've got." She gives me a smile so soft, I know her next words will be bruising. "His date ain't black *or* white."

I rub my hands over my thighs and feel like my skin has been peeled back and examined a million times by too many eyeballs since I got here. People look at me and see black skin—skin I love, skin I'm proud of—but they think they know my whole story after a single glance.

It must be easy for Khabria. She is who she is, and she has this whole don't-cross-me vibe that dares anyone to even try to mess with her. I'd make some shady deals with the devil to be that comfortable in my own skin at this point in my life.

"Right. I know some people guess that I'm biracial," I begin. She's curiously quiet, which opens the floodgates her straight talk would have otherwise slammed shut. "I'm black, but I'm not African American. My father is from the Dominican Republic. And it might be hard to tell if you don't know, but my mother's family emigrated here from Cork, Ireland, two generations back. My old school was this hippie-dippie Quaker school, which was a big draw for dignitaries for whatever reason. Like, I went to school with two daughters of a sheikh and a guy who was twelfth in line to be the king of Norway. Everyone knew me, and no one saw me as anything other than my own boring self. I guess I wasn't ready for... all of this."

I wave my hands around at…the air in the gym? The school itself? Georgia? The kind of nagging racism that never, ever lets me think about anything without analyzing this one narrow aspect of myself?

I don't know what I mean, and now that I opened my gaping mouth so I could puke my cultural/racial backstory out, I close it fast and tight so I don't sob like an infant in front of Khabria. Despite my best efforts, I wind up choking out an ugly sound and blinking fast while Khabria stiffens next to me.

Fantastic.

"Sorry. I just… I don't know what's wrong with me lately."

"It's complicated." Khabria pointedly stares to the side, giving me some privacy so I can to get my panic under control. "You know, I'm not *just* African American. My granddaddy fought in Vietnam, and that's where he met my grandma. She's the one who stayed with me while my mom went back to get her nursing degree, so I speak Vietnamese and all that. But I hardly look like her. I take after my mama's mama."

"My best friend is Vietnamese," I tell Khabria. "I'm visiting her family in Vietnam with her this summer."

"Yeah?" Khabria looks excited. "That's cool. I'd love to go sometime. Ba Ngoai told me about the village where she grew up, but she was nervous to go back after so many years away." She blows out a shaky breath. "Some days I want to tell people exactly who I am and where I come from, let them know they don't know me just by looking at me the way they think they do. Other days I want everyone to mind their own goddamn business. Actually that's most days."

Oh. There are so many layers to the prejudices and stereotypes swirling around, I guess we've all been guilty of thinking we know people when that's not the case. Maybe that's not such a depressing thing. If we're all messing up, we're all going to have to try to do better and fast. That's a solid, clean-slate starting point.

"I've been blowing this whole prom thing off," I admit. "I didn't feel like dealing with it. So… I suck."

"Nah, you're fine. My ex-boyfriend, Calvin, is running for Rose Prince. That was part of the reason I wasn't about to run for Rose Princess. See? Shallow." She tugs on my arm and points to the door, where the baseball team is jogging out in their navy-and-white uniforms. She nods to the back of the line. "See the Chinese guy with the big ole shoulders?"

A tall, muscled guy with a shiny black undercut and goofy smile catches sight of Khabria and waves so hard, I'm scared he's going to dislocate his shoulder.

She waves back with the tips of her fingers and puts a hand over her mouth to cover up a gorgeous laugh. "Bo Han. His family owns China Delight, that place across from Walmart. You know it?"

"My mother and I would have starved to death if it wasn't for the delicious takeout from China Delight. I love that place." My stomach rumbles just thinking about their Happy Family combo platter.

"Cool. Remind me, and I'll hook you up with some coupons. Bo asked me out right after I broke things off with Calvin, and…" She whips out this huge shrug/giggle combination that instantly transforms her into a whole different version of herself. Even more beautiful, which I didn't think was possible. "I think I love this boy and, *trust me*, I don't fall in love easily."

I nod and I trust her. Khabria strikes me as someone who's all or nothing about the important stuff.

"But he's not white. And he's not black. So…" She narrows her eyes so they're sharp with determination. The next words lash out like a fierce vow. "We need to get ourselves a new prom." She peeks at me from under her eyelashes with a sheep-ish smile. "See? Not noble at all. I'm just a sap who wants to dance with her man."

I look at Bo Han, so busy grinning like a fool at Khabria, he doesn't hear the coach call his name three times. He's still grinning like a fool when his teammates shove him where he needs to go. I'm in the presence of pure, beautiful, stupid love.

I turn to Khabria, and it's like love itself has given this mission its blessing. There's no possible way we can screw this up.

"You're just a girl who wants to dance with her man? Well, Richard and Mildred Loving were just two people who wanted a wedding certificate. Let's do this."

TWENTY-FIVE

"I need to talk to you about the prom." I'm leaning against Doyle's locker, feeling a combination of guilt and regret over the sad fact that it was always him staking out my locker before.

That ship has sailed. I thought Doyle was the most easygoing person I'd ever met, but I've seen a whole new side of him since we fought about That Night. Boy can bottle up his feelings like nobody's business and, coming from me, that's saying a lot.

A familiar fire crackles in his eyes when he looks down at me. "Yeah?" He stuffs his books into the top compartment of his locker and a grin slides over his lips. "So are you gonna ask me—" He stops short, and his cocky smile turns panicked.

I realize he was probably about to say *so are you gonna ask me to prom?* Then flex his biceps and brag about how he can "cut a rug" or whatever weird Southern saying he'd whip out on the fly. But he hit the brakes on that joke because (a) our school prom is a racist joke and (b) we lost that fun, easy back-and-forth that I took for granted, and we can't seem to get it back.

Reason A should have me furious and upset, but, to be honest, it's reason B that's breaking my heart. How can it be so hard to reach someone I love so much?

"You know, actually I'm gonna be late for ag class." The skin on his cheekbones flames bright red. "Mebbe I can catch you at lunch...?"

"It'll take two minutes." On impulse bred of stupid habit, I grab his hand.

He pauses. It's like I can feel the hairline crack, and it gives me hope.

"All right." He draws closer, and all of him—the lavender eyes, the sweet grin, the golden stubble my hands are itching to rub against—makes me a little woozy. It's impossible not to take inventory of how his bruises have gone from purple and blue to sickly yellow and green. It brings up memories I'd much rather bury, the way he asked me to. The way I fought against.

Why do I always fight what's easier?

I try to focus on what I need to do instead of how screwed up things between Doyle and me have gotten.

"I talked to Khabria. And she's in." I wanted it to come out badass, like we're members of this supercool club of defiance, but Doyle plays dumb and ruins the effect.

"In for what now?" he asks cautiously, but the flicker in his eyes dances brighter.

"The alternaprom." My smile overstretches my mouth painfully.

He frowns. "Oh. *That*."

"What do you mean 'Oh. That'?" I demand.

He sighs. "It's just...putting on an alternaprom's gonna be a lotta work. We'd have to plan and organize and fund-raise—"

Every molecule in my body goes Irish, and my temper blazes with the fury of a thousand drunken redheads. I cannot *believe* that, after the way he pushed for us to march in to see Armstrong, he's willing to just give up because it's "gonna be a lotta work."

I slam his locker shut, barely missing his fingers.

"You know what? Screw off, Doyle! You should just go to the racist prom with Ansley, Queen of the Friggin' Roses, and you can be her puppet king, ruling this hick county by her side, and it'll all be goddamn amazing!"

I spin on my heel and stomp away, not even caring that Doyle doesn't follow. At least I'm pretty sure I don't care, until my heart flutters at the thump of his boots.

"Hey! Hey, hey, Nes. Wait." Doyle grabs me by the elbow, and I shake him off.

"Go to ag class or whatever you have to do," I say over my shoulder, warming to the feel of the ball bouncing back into my court.

"Nes!" I stop and wait. "I don't wanna do this thing if…if we don't wind up goin' to prom together."

I turn slowly and clear my throat, because I'm a little choked up all of a sudden. "Huh."

"Huh?" He raises an eyebrow at me.

I blink back tears of relief. "I wondered what force would be strong enough to topple that massive ego. I guess I'm just surprised it wound up being prom. I mean, if you're too chicken to do this unless you know I'll take pity on you and be your date—"

The sparkle in his smile radiates like sunshine off the morning dew. "You callin' me chicken?"

"If the *bok* fits…" I flap my elbows at my side and cluck slowly. *"Bok, bok, bok."*

"All right, all right," he laughs. "Cut it. I guess I can be a little late. What did Khabria say?"

"That she's just a girl who wants to dance. With her guy, Bo Han, who's stuck in the middle just like I am. It's messed up that she and Bo can't go to prom together."

"Maybe they can." He reaches out, and his fingers curl around mine. I let him, because I'm allowed a weak moment. He leads me into an empty room just as the bell rings. It's dark and so quiet, I can hear the sound of our breathing, his exhales staggered against my inhales. He kicks the door shut and keeps his hands on me. "You'll get in trouble for skipping."

"I'm tired of following the rules." This dim, unfamiliar classroom feels neutral, so I make a quick decision to tell him every single thing I've kept bottled up since he jumped out of my bedroom window, I put it out there in such a rush, I almost pass out from not taking a second to breathe. "I meant what I said that day in my room, but I never meant to hurt you—at all—and if that's the way you took it, *I'm sorry*, but someone needs to tell you that you're allowed to be something other than the white knight who rides in on your steed and saves the day for everyone." I swallow the huge breath I'm trying to suck in and hiccup out, "And I miss you, okay? I l-lo—really care about you, Doyle."

Damn my wimpy heart.

The seconds stretch into an awkward infinity of regret while I wait for him to answer.

"I know it," he whispers, his eyes hooded, his hands running up and down my arms in a slow massage that's the polar opposite of my jangly, breathless confession. "You got no idea how bad I've been missin' you, Nes. And much as it pains me to admit it, you've been right all along. I got one of them hero complexes, and I didn't like you pointing that out, I guess. I don't like anyone seein' me fall. 'Specially you."

"That's what it means to l—" *Love* is balancing on the tip

of my tongue, and I'd mean it with my whole heart if I let it tumble out. But that word is still stuck deep in the bowels of That Night, twisted in a strange combination of beautiful and horrible. "That's what it means when you care about someone. You stick by them through the good *and* the bad. Especially the bad."

"I always feel like, if I'm not doing it all jest right, I'm lettin' down the people I love." He wraps an arm around my waist not so much to be romantic, but like he's anchoring himself.

Like he's leaning on me, finally.

"Have a little faith in me."

"Okay. But it's not easy for me. I want to, I really do." He dips his face close to mine.

I want to kiss him so badly, my lips tremble like they'll fall off my face. But I can trace a direct line from all our troubles back to the night we got physical. We've just patched things up, and I'm not about to sledgehammer it apart again for one quick kiss.

I position my palm flat on his chest and push back. "So let's not make this any harder." I stick my hand out to shake, and the gesture puts more distance than I'd like between the two of us. "Friends?"

He stares at my hand, regret sharp on his features. But then, typical Doyle, he shakes it off, cups his hand over his mouth, and hocks a loogie.

This time I don't hesitate before I spit.

"Friends," he declares as our loogied palms slide against each other.

The line we just drew in the sand is wavy at best. He wouldn't stop me if I pushed for more. I *could* tug him closer, press my lips to his, run my hands all over his—

"Right. So how are we gonna plan this alternaprom?" I ask

in a rush, yanking my hand away so I can wipe it on the leg of my jeans. I need immediate distraction.

"You wanna brainstorm?" The best imitation of his old smile stretches across his face. He grabs an easel.

"Pull it over here. Let's start by making a list of people who'd actually *want* to break some precious Ebenezer traditions and raise some hell."

I uncap a marker from my backpack and get ready to detail the lists and plans that will help us take down some decades-long racist traditions. In the meantime, I just have to avoid kissing Doyle Rahn…at all costs.

Should be a piece of cake. I'll just have to figure out a way to will myself into a constant lobotomized state.

TWENTY-SIX

I dreamed of a senior spring break full of beach days with Ollie, but she's holed up practicing for her spring concert. Doyle is working extra hours at his family's business while Brookes is on a mission trip with his church group.

I wind up spending hours with only my mom for company, floating in the pool, trying to fill time until Doyle comes over to help plan for alternaprom.

"I cannot believe how muggy it is." Mom fans herself with a copy of the *The New Yorker* as she walks out onto the patio smack in the middle of spring break week. "I got the mail."

"Mmm-hmm." I let my fingers drift in the water and try to will myself to unstick my sweaty skin from the float so I can get in the pool and cool off.

"You got mail," she singsongs.

I perk up. "Yeah?"

"It's postmarked New York," she says, her smile wide. "New York University."

"Oh my God!" I screech, falling off the float and into the cool water. I come up choking and sputtering like a little kid and claw my way onto the deck. "Is it…? Is the letter big or small?"

"Open it and see!" Mom is trying to build the excitement, but she knows exactly what a college rejection letter looks like, and if she thought I got one from NYU, there's no way she'd be smiling like she is.

I tear the envelope open, my fingers shaking, and scan the words.

We're happy to inform you… It's our pleasure… Congratulations!

I jump up and down on the patio bricks and scream, "I'm in! I'm in!"

I do a victory lap around the yard, stopping to run my fingers over the strong, green leaves that have pushed through all over Doyle's tree. I feel like the tree and I are going places—me to a future focused on a top-notch liberal arts college degree, the tree to a future full of photosynthesis and vegetative will to thrive.

Mom laughs and hugs me tight when I race over to her. "I'm so proud, honey. Call your father right now."

"I'll try him later, but I have to call Ollie right now!"

"Aggie…" I can tell my mom doesn't want to spoil the excitement of this moment. "Your dad deserves to hear the news directly from you."

"And I will tell him. I promise! Just… I have to call Ollie really, really quickly." Before my mother can protest, I race to my room, lock the door, and allow myself the giddy freedom of yelling and screaming with Ollie over my freaking awesome, fantastic, amazing news.

I mean for it to be only a minute.

Two hours of excited college talk later, she sighs, "So I'll be at Oberlin, you'll be at NYU, and we'll just keep on keeping on with this whole long-distance thing."

"It's not so bad, right?" I ask, my voice hitching. "We'll spend breaks together." I hope. If Ollie is this tied up in her music now, what will it be like when it's her major?

"Absolutely. I need to work on my music/life balance. You know it's bad when even my crazy-strict father is telling me to loosen up and have some fun."

"Whoa! Have I mentioned how I cannot wait for summer? I miss you so much, Ollie." My throat squeezes shut.

"I miss you, too. And I'm so proud! Go, call Doyle. I know you want to."

I do. But Doyle can't answer when he's on the job. He can check texts, and I figure that's an easier way to let him know. He hasn't given me any updates on colleges, and I'm afraid to ask... What if the answer is radio silence from all of them? I figure when Doyle has something to tell me, he'll tell me.

I get back an explosion of congratulatory emojis, with promises to meet me for a cheesy-grits breakfast to celebrate in the morning, since he'll be out late in the fields tonight.

I try to call my father, but by now, it's dinnertime in Paris. Dad has a strict "no phones at the table" rule. I leave him a voice mail with the news, relieved I didn't have to listen to him tell me there's still time to appeal to admissions boards and get into an Ivy.

Other than that one gleaming day of excitement, the rest of spring break is spent idling. I feel like I dived off a cliff into deep water. I keep swimming toward the surface, breath held, but I never seem to break through. And then my "vacation" is over, and I head back to Ebenezer for the final two-month wind down before graduation and the beginning of the rest of my life.

But first I have to make things right where I am now.

★ ★ ★

Newton wasn't kidding about those laws of motion. Once Doyle and I set a few things rolling, they stay in continuous, crazy motion that tentacles out and creates more motion.

Holy crap. *A ton more motion.*

School had been creeping toward its inevitable end as winter crept into the unceasing torrential downpour of early spring and then the dull mugginess of full spring.

But it rapidly became less about papers and tests and more about the tradition we're doing our best to chip away at. The support we wind up rallying is way more complicated than Doyle and I ever expected—and it reveals all the multifaceted ways our peers can be total and absolute morons.

"A'right, I got a list of three dozen yes people, thirty-eight maybes, and seven hard nos." Doyle drops his lunch tray next to mine and takes out the binder he's been stuffing full of prom information.

"Good, right?" I toss a grape his way, and he opens his mouth and darts his head to the side, crushing it with his teeth and throwing me a grin.

Dark circles ring the skin under his eyes. Doyle's been picking up extra hours for his family's business because Lee's R & R is almost up and his brother's busy preparing for another deployment. On top of that, he was only passing calculus by the skin of his teeth when the semester started, so I've tutored him late into the night before a big quiz a few times now, but it seems like his mind is somewhere else when we're supposed to be focusing on delta limits.

This semester has been defined by change, so I shouldn't be shocked that things with Doyle have turned a weird corner. We lost some of that light breeziness, the easiness that made me fall for him so hard and fast—and I honestly don't know if it's ever coming back. But I guess that's what happens when you finally see someone's darkness after basking in nothing but their light. It's chilly in the shadows.

I pulled back Doyle's mask and saw the face he was desperate to keep hidden. I may be the one person on earth who knows him best, and the one person he's most skittish around now.

I try not to think about it as losing anything, but I know I got a bum trade. The sweet is gone, but we didn't gain the deep, so we're stuck in limbo. As the days flip into weeks, I'm haunted by the fact that the clock is ticking and we're wasting the stupidly short amount of time we have left.

"I guess. Every no was a crazy long shot anyway. Not ever sure why I bothered askin' any of 'em. Critter's only a maybe 'cause his new girl dumped him. He's holdin' out hope she'll take him back, and she has stake in the whole Rose Queen business. But I doubt she will after all the nonsense that half-wit put that poor girl through." He squints at the list.

"What about the other maybes?" I trail my finger down the names. "Is there something holding them back? Maybe we can organize a meeting and, you know, address concerns or whatever."

Doyle raises his light eyebrows. "Right. Well, Donnie Ryan's a maybe 'cause he was dating Danielle Simmons, who's a senior too—he's black, she's white. But then he started goin' with her sister, who's a sophomore, and he wasn't sure what grades were gonna be allowed."

"Donnie sounds like a douche bag."

"Yeah, he's a dog fer sure. But we ain't in a position to be real picky."

"You're right about that. What grades *are* going to be allowed?" I ask.

"Regular prom—well, regular *white* prom—invites all seniors, and it doesn't matter what grade their dates are in, as long as they buy bids. But we may have to extend ours to the junior class if we want a decent showing, which the black prom usually does 'cause of numbers. Our senior class is 'bout seventy percent white, thirty black. Roughly."

My stomach acids start to churn. I've never been to a prom, let alone tried to plan one, let alone tried to buck hundreds of years of antiquated, racist traditions in a new school by hosting an independent alternaprom.

"What are the other maybes worried about?"

"Decorations, theme, food, music, location—people want specifics. They wanna know if there'll be some kinda pushback from the administration. They wanna know who else is comin' *definitely*, how big it's gonna be, if it's gonna be the same day as the other proms. They wanna know what bids'll cost, they're asking about DJs and bands, photographers, how long it will be." Doyle drops his head in his hands. "Holy hell."

I have that specific pukey feeling that always slams over me when I realize I bit off more than I can chew.

"We need someone who's planned big events before," I muse, because thinking out loud hushes the panic. "Someone artistic. With passion. Someone like… Holy crap! I know who to ask! I'll be back." I throw my bag on my shoulders and dash out of the room, ducking the monitors and sneaking to the outside lounge.

Technically any senior can sign out of lunch or study hall to hang here, but it's a million degrees and so muggy, my shirt is already sticking to me, so I've got the place to myself. Which is perfect because I need to talk to my bestie in private. I gnaw on my lip as I wait for FaceTime to connect.

"Olls?" I whisper, even though there's no one to hear us.

Gah, her face! That beautiful, sweet face makes everything feel like it's going to be just fine.

"Nes!" She glances over her shoulder and grins. "My lips are so chapped from bassoon practice. I wish they were chapped from a serious make-out session, but Thao had some Vovinam tournament in Virginia. And on the subject of making out... What's up with Doyle?"

"Complications," I mutter. "We're working on the alterna-prom though." Best to switch gears before Ollie and I embark on another hours-long marathon dissecting my sticky relationship with Doyle Rahn.

"How's it going? Do you have a theme? Do you know where you'll hold it? Did you book your caterer? When is it again?" She flips the phone closer so her face fills the whole screen and my entire heart.

"I was all 'eff the man' and 'let's rebel' and now I just wanna curl up and die, because I. Can't. Do. This."

"Sweetie, this is why you were always cotreasurer with me," Ollie singsongs. "Tell me everything."

It's an embarrassingly short tale, but Ollie isn't phased.

"Right. Okay. What we need is to crowd-source the funds so you can solidify some plans. Call your dad and reach out to your mother to see about donors through the organizations they work with in their colleges. Go through your definite yes list and find out who can get you what and how quickly. I'm at my laptop now—your donation and information page will be live in a few hours. Then we open a forum for discussion."

She's like the badass CEO of my alternaprom. "You don't have to do this. I know you're under crazy amounts of pressure right now."

"One, you are my best friend in the world. Two, this is, like, a civic duty. Helping to desegregate one of the last segregated proms in the country? It's my obligation as *an American*. Oh! I should talk to Ms. Barcella. I bet she'll drop her Greenpeace lecture next week to showcase this… Where was I? Three, yes, this year has been kind of ulcer inducing, but I'm trying so hard to not stress, and what better way to ignore my senior showcase piece than with some focused procrastination? Okay, I have a banner space, but what's the theme?"

Ollie waits patiently while I try to get my head to stop spinning because I've just fallen in love with my best friend all over again.

"Um…"

"Oh, Nes," she sighs. "I love you so much. But, seriously, what would you do without me?"

"I don't even want to imagine an existence where you're not around."

"You're dreamy when you get all Gothic-lady romantic with me. Okay, you know what you have to do. *Theme*. Make it epic. No pressure. I believe in you."

"Right." I try to let that—her belief in me—radiate through my body and give me strength.

"And, Nes?"

"Yeah?"

She presses her lips together, and I break into cold-sweat mode. This is going to be hard to hear, because best friends throw hardballs no one else will, then cheer you on until you get the guts to take a swing.

"There are only a few months—weeks really—left. He's a really good guy. Whatever you two decide to do or be, don't waste this time, okay? Love you, gotta go, planning to get it done."

I'm left taking the long walk back to Doyle with Ollie's words ricocheting in my brain.

He glances up from across the classroom and the second his eyes find my face, he smiles. As usual, Ollie's right. No matter how weird things feel right now, Doyle Rahn is pretty freaking amazing.

We don't have a second to waste.

TWENTY-SEVEN

"So, you callin' your pops?" Doyle lounges against the door of my car in the school parking lot.

"Why are you bugging me about it?" I grumble, tossing my backpack into the backseat.

"I overheard your mama tellin' you to call him again when I was helpin' with the dishes yesterday." I'm still psyched about the fact that Doyle's regularly back to eating dinner at my place. "Ain't you at all curious why your mama wants you to call him so bad?" Doyle shrugs. "Jest, if I had a mama as sweet as yours—"

"Stop. Just because my mom cooks for you and lets you swim in our pool doesn't mean you know the ins and outs of our entire relationship."

I don't say much more because there's another, sadder component to Doyle's soft spot for my mother. He looked his mom up on social media recently and found out she'd gone to work in an Alaskan cannery and, I guess, attempted to nab a local crab fisherman. "A guy who brings home a big pot o' money and is only around a couple months a year? I guarantee my mama decided that was the best deal she'd heard of," he told me with practiced indifference when we took a break from converting complex numbers from polar to rectangular during a long study session.

When he noticed me eyeing him with concern, he said, "Don't get all worried 'bout me. I'll talk to my Al-Anon crew about the whole thing. Who'd a thought I'd *like* going to meetings and talkin' 'bout my feelings? I'm even signed up to bring biscuits next Tuesday night. And I'm draggin' Malachi along. That kid needs to deal with his feelings big-time."

The downside to helping Doyle get a hold on his problems is that he now wants to help fix all of mine. Between him and Ollie, I'm going to wind up incredibly emotionally stable… or I'm going to run away and become a hermit so I can have two seconds alone with my cold heart.

"All you gotta do is call," he urges.

"I've texted him. Yesterday. Look." I flip my phone screen to him as evidence, and Doyle's eyes go wide.

"Why's that lady got a sword through her neck?"

"Oh right." I forgot the text before my promise to "call soon" is one of the classical art memes dad loves to send me. He's even used a few laughing face emojis recently. We're making a lot of texting progress. "It's a famous medieval painting of Saint Justina of Padua. She had her eyes gouged out and then she was beheaded, so they paint her with a sword through her neck."

"I'm not real big into art, but…you guys *like* that paintin'?" He squirms away, like he's afraid he's befriended some kind of insane sociopath.

"No! I mean, we appreciate the art and history and all that… but it's a meme. See how calm Saint Justina looks, even though she has a *sword in her neck*. See the text bubbles…the Mother Superior is all, 'Are you okay?' and Saint Justina is like, 'I'm fine.'" Explaining it makes me crack up all over again, but Doyle looks horrified. "Well, my dad and I think it's a riot. Maybe we just have a weird sense of humor?"

"Maybe y'all need to stop laughing 'bout decapitated ladies in art and you need to *call your dad*. Memes ain't gonna help you have any kind of real conversation."

I fiddle with my phone and sigh. "I'm pretty sure he wants to talk me out of going to NYU this fall, and I really, really don't want to have that conversation with him. So I'm just going to send him this meme. I think it's early Renaissance? See this guy has an arrow sticking out of his eye and the guy with the feather in his hat is all, 'I'm sorry. You're fine! Don't tell Mom!'" I show Doyle, and this time he laughs.

"Now *that's* funny. I gotta send that one to my idiot brothers." Then he frowns. "Call your dad."

It's useless to argue with Doyle, who thinks I'm a total brat for not being overjoyed that I have two parents who *want* a relationship with me. He's right. His family situation has given me a ton of needed perspective.

I've made progress. Mom and I had a *One Hundred Thousand Beats* marathon and gorged ourselves on guacamole and frozen margaritas—virgin for me—with sugar on the rims. Just like the whole Doyle debacle, things with my mother aren't the same. But, unlike with Doyle, our relationship is getting *better* now that I built an avocado-and-medical-drama bridge between us.

"The truth?"

"I wouldn't expect anythin' else from ya." He meets my eyes for a few seconds.

"I'm scared this call isn't about NYU. Everyone keeps telling me there's no problem, but there's something, and...maybe I don't want to know. I know this is stupid, but I thought my parents were getting back together. Then, like, a week later, my mom got caught fooling around with a married guy in her department."

Doyle's eyes widen. "That was all back when you guys hightailed?"

"Yup. Funny how one bondage snap texted to the wrong number can change the course of your life, right?" I'm trying to joke, but it still weirds me out.

Doyle's face is on fire. I don't think he'd be able to make eye contact with me for a million dollars. "Jest… Not that I know about your mama's, um, personal business…but it seems kinda outta character for her."

"Well, she doesn't *just* cook dinner and swim," I tease.

"Not that she doesn't…you know—" Doyle curses under his breath in frustration. "I mean, wasn't it with a married guy?"

"Yep."

"Jest seems like there must've been somethin' else goin' on. Mebbe it was revenge or something."

"Holy crap." I was so busy being ragey at my mother, I never thought about that very obvious potential angle. "Hey, I have to go call someone."

Doyle taps the roof of my car as I get in. "Keep me posted."

"Okay." I pause, wanting to relay to him how much it means to have him back in my life as a friend, even if we're not together. But it's too much, so I opt for a simple thank-you.

"Anytime." His smile gives me courage.

I'm glad Mom is out when I get home—the ladies from the Italian department have a bowling league, which seems kind of bizarre, but who am I to judge? Mom's trying to bowl a three hundred, so I can make this call in private.

"Bonjour, Papa," I say when he picks up.

"Agnes! ¿Cómo estás, mi hija?" No matter how many of these

temporary and permanent separations we endure, hearing his voice on the phone when he's so far away makes me sad.

Sometimes it's easier to not think too hard about how much I miss Jasper and Dad. To just let them be and know they're happy there and Mom and I are plugging along here. What makes that even sadder is the fact that my very happiest memories are the ones where we were all together, no matter how chaotic it was.

"Bien, papá. ¿Podemos hablar?" I pause, and he waits. My father is incredibly patient. Sometimes that drives my mom nuts. She says she just wants him to flip out or rush or get aggravated like she does. It isn't his style. *"Lo siento, no llame…* I… I'm sorry I haven't called in a while." I switch to English because I don't know if I can translate everything I need to say accurately enough in Spanish.

"Don't apologize." His English has this slight accent that sounds a little Dominican and maybe French, I guess. Mom rolls her eyes about it, but I've heard her tell her friends he has the best phone voice of any man on Earth. "Senior year is so vital for the rest of your academic career. The last thing I expect is for you to call your father when I'm sure you're studying like mad."

Right. Studying.

"I called because…first of all, I have a social activism project." Yes, I am avoiding the personal in favor of the political.

I can practically hear him sit up a little taller, his interest piqued. "What is it?"

"Before I tell you, I don't want Mom to know yet. I don't need her worried."

"I can't promise that, but I promise I'll use my discretion."

"I'm attending a school without an official prom. The independent proms they hold are segregated." I think Jasper learned the art of sighing from our father.

"A segregated prom? If I'd never been to the Deep South, I'd think you were joking. I told your mother another position in the city would have suited you two better."

"I think she wanted out of the city. Plus it's expensive to live there, Dad."

"I'm making more than enough off my publishing royalties."

As brilliant as my father is, he has a hard time wrapping his head around the fact it's not easy for Mom to hear him humble-brag about his success when she gave up her career so that he could have it.

"Anyway, here we are, and now my friends and I are raising funds for this alternative prom and we're trying to get the word out—"

I can practically see the Harvard crest dancing in my father's eyes. "Let me know where to wire money. And I'll make sure the right media outlets hear about this." His pen scratches furiously as he takes notes, and I figure I'd better find a way to tell Mom before she reads about it in a column one of Dad's colleagues wrote for *NPR*.

"Ollie is helping with all that," I tell him.

"Wonderful. Her parents have strong connections. This will be an absolute boon to your portfolio. Agnes, this is the kind of story the Ivies salivate over. I know you think you want to go to NYU, and that's a solid school, but all top universities are open to reexamining a candidate on a special case-by-case basis. I certainly think spearheading such a radical social movement will give you a fantastic edge for reconsideration. The academic world will be your oyster. Maybe this move to such a rustic area wasn't a total loss."

I'm not going to tell Dad there's no need to reexamine anything, because I'm going to NYU. I'm happy about my decision. Dad will have to get used to the idea.

"Dad—"

"Hold on for one second, Agnes." My dad puts his hand over the speaker to muffle his voice, and his French is too fast for me to untangle even if I could hear clearly. What I can make out is his tone, which is light and flirty.

A woman answers back. The voice sounds…young.

It's 1:00 a.m. in France right now.

"Dad?"

"Sorry, honey. That was just Celeste, my…intern."

I flip open my laptop and Google her first name and my father's university. She's there in a dozen press photos, beautiful with sly eyes. She's maybe in her twenties, grew up in Haiti, and got a scholarship in my father's department this past fall.

"Your intern?"

This time his pause isn't patient. It's cautious.

"Did your mother tell you about us?" He drops his voice, and I wonder if it's because *Celeste* is listening.

"Mom said you had something to tell me." Dad doesn't seem to know how to fill the expectant silence.

"You know the divorce was finalized months ago." Pause. "I met someone." Pause. "It was early this fall, before you came for the holidays. Your mother and I… It's complicated." Pause. "I married the woman—Celeste is her name—in September…"

"Celeste, your intern, is Celeste, your *wife*?" Shock incinerates all rational thoughts.

"At first it was purely a marriage of convenience, no romantic feelings involved. I wasn't going to mention it to any of you because we planned to end it quietly as soon as Celeste was able to achieve tenure. She'd like to accept a prestigious job in the United States—"

"You're moving back?" I pace my room like mad, trip over a flip-flop, and crash one shoulder into the wall. "Does Mom know? Did she know when we were in Paris?"

"Possibly. It's complicated, Agnes." Pause. Pause. Pause. "I should have been clearer about Celeste with your mother earlier. I should have let everyone know as soon as emotions started to build between us. I know your mother and I had talks about reconciling, and I should have been honest... I know the extent of my feelings for Celeste came as a surprise. For everyone."

"Yeah, Dad, an unexpected fact is the literal definition of *surprise*. How could you have expected anything else?"

Pause.

He stumbles through explanations and rationalizations, and I'm struck dumb with guilt. All this time, I blamed Mom. Not that I was totally out of line. She *did* sleep with a married man. She *did* use technology like a bonehead. But...

She was hurt. Her heart was aching like mine after I found out about Lincoln. She could have ratted my father out. She didn't have to put up with my accusations and snark. Why? What possible reason did she have not to tell me? Why didn't Jasper?

I guess they wanted it to be between me and Dad. And now that I've finally made the call, I feel...empty. Sad. Let down. And a little more grown-up.

The adults in my life aren't the all-knowing problem solvers they were when I was a little girl. When I was a kid, I felt like becoming an adult would be synonymous with figuring things out, but I realize things are only going to get more complicated from here on out. It makes me glad I've had such wacky stuff to deal with my senior year: at least I'll be a little more prepared for whatever life throws me down the road.

I end my call with my father as quickly and painlessly as I can, reverting back to Spanish for the *I love you*s and *goodbye*s, because I want to hold on to some special connection with him, just a few words exchanged in the language he taught me first, I spend the next few hours thinking.

When Mom comes home later that night, I'm waiting in the kitchen with a sleeve of Thin Mints. My nerves forced me to devour the first sleeve alone as I tumbled my parental dilemma in my head.

"Girl Scout cookies?" She bites into a chocolate disk and moans. "Where did you get these?"

"One of Doyle's cousins's daughters is a Scout, so he used his connections to hook me up when I mentioned we're total addicts. So, how was bowling?"

"Your mama bowled a turkey!" Mom holds her arms over her head, snaps her fingers, and whoops, cookie crumbs on her bottom lip.

"I assume that's a good thing?"

"It just means I might leave the department chair and take up pro bowling."

My heart is an overfilled water balloon still attached to a running hose.

"Mom? I...I called Dad."

She drops her arms and her smile. "You did?"

I hand her another cookie and nibble on my own. "Why didn't you just tell me?"

"I know at Thanksgiving you thought things were going a different way..."

"But they weren't. So why not let me know?"

She leans her elbows on the counter and sighs. Unlike my

father's and Jasper's, Mom's sighs are almost musical. "At first I was furious. Your father tried to tell me, but I was blinded by having us all together again. I'd been really lonely. But I knew something was off. After?" She goes to the fridge and gets out the carton of milk, grabs two tumblers, and fills them up. "I messed up, honey. And I'm an adult. I knew you were mad at me, and I knew you weren't sure where you wanted to stay. I didn't want you to feel like you couldn't go to your father. He and I agreed to keep his marriage quiet if you decided to finish your school year in France."

"But I didn't," I point out, slurping a sip of icy milk.

"No, you didn't. But you were settling in so nicely. And we were...well, we weren't getting along that well, but I knew we'd find our way no matter what. I wanted you to forgive me on your own, not because you felt bad for your jilted old hag of a mother."

I put down the milk and the cookie and stalk around the counter. I wrap my arms around my beautiful, crazy, flawed mother.

"Aggie?"

"Shh. If you call yourself a hag again, I'll never, ever share my Thin Mints with you."

In the kitchen where I danced with Doyle, I hold my Mom tight. I pause and feel a peace that's filled with crags and bumps and fracture lines—and I recognize it for exactly what it is.

Love.

TWENTY-EIGHT

I twist my hands together as Doyle swings my front door open over and over again, inviting more people into my already-crowded living room. The space felt pretty big before it was full of our belligerent, infuriating classmates.

Black, white, and every color in between, they perch on my mother's couch, the hearth, the floor, and the coffee table and scowl like the entitled jerks they are.

Mom rushes in and out with bright veggie trays and bowls of chips—the good ones we have to drive to a special grocery store forty minutes away to get. I bet everyone is wondering whether or not she's my biological mother, and then if they've decided that yes she is, indeed, the woman who birthed me, how such a wide-eyed, shiny-haired stunner gave birth to a surly toad like me.

"Mom, stop," I hiss, leading her back to the kitchen. "They're assholes. You don't need to feed them."

"Agnes, good Lord, your *mouth*!" She glances into the crowded living room as a few more people file in. Khabria and Bo smile, mingle, try to keep the grumbles down to a dull roar. "Not a single one of those kids failed to say thank-you."

"Ugh, manners are like their religion down here. They're preprogrammed like little Southern droids. Don't be fooled."

"They also called me ma'am. How adorable is that? I think they seem lovely."

"Lovely assholes," I mutter as I mentally tally the list of complaints Doyle and I have already fielded for this currently nonexistent alternaprom.

Any ridiculous crap a person could imagine has been the topic of debate in the hallways, in every class, through texts, and in the comments section of the beautiful website Ollie put up for us. They're every-freaking-where and they're like rabid mad dogs who are positive we're dying to give our undivided attention to their endless petty complaints. Their lists of demands and opinions literally never stop, with topics including, but not limited to, the theme song, the colors, the invitations, the playlists, the length, the date, the food, the photographer, and the election of a prom court.

And it's not like some friendly town-hall type thing. It's drenched in threats and foot stomping and the lowest-common-denominator, YouTube-comments-section ugliness.

Assholes.

It was Khabria and Doyle's screwball master plan to gather all the miscreants together in person so we can resolve all these differences and sing "Kumbaya." Or let them riot and boil us in oil.

Mom knows this is a gathering for an alternaprom. Before our mother-daughter fallout, she would have weaseled every detail out of me, but she's handling this era of renewed peace with kid gloves, so she doesn't realize we're organizing this alternaprom because of racial segregation. I'm sure she thinks we're going to dress as zombies or maybe wear sweats—something ironic and harmless. I don't want to admit how scared I am for her to find out the ugly truth.

It's basic logic that if I didn't want her to find out, I should have reconsidered hosting the planning committee at my house, but I doubt anyone's going to talk about the most important reason we're doing this—after all, why discuss unity and equality when we can bitch about centerpieces and mylar versus latex balloons? I'm actually relieved when I overhear two girls fighting so fiercely over tablecloth colors. My living room might turn into an MMA arena at any second. Keep it shallow, Ebenezer High.

"Hey, y'all, let's get things started." Doyle's voice booms around the room. Everyone snatches up the last wilted celery sticks and the oily remnants of chips from the bottom of the bowl. Pack of locusts. "We've gotten a lot of messages from e'rybody 'bout what you'd like to see happen at this prom and all that. Nes's friend's been cool 'bout setting up a website so it's all pretty organized—"

"What do you think is organized exactly?" snaps a girl in the front. She pats her hair and snaps her gum. "We don't have no date, no time, no place, no nothing. So what's all been organized is my question?"

All around this loudmouth are other loudmouths nodding and uh-huhing and calling out their own asinine complaints until Doyle stumbles back, overwhelmed by the whine fest.

I mutter things so evil, I may be advance purchasing a one-way ticket to hell.

In the face of my passive aggression and Doyle's lack of authority, Khabria takes the leadership reins.

She harnesses her cheerleader voice. "All right now, that is *enough!*" The room goes silent and she paces. "Thing is, we've never done this before. We're learning as we go. This ain't some easy thing, y'all. This needs to be done *right*. Everybody's sitting here crying, 'we don't have this, we don't have that,' and that's a big load of bull. Truth of the matter is, Nes's friend—a girl who doesn't know any one of us from Adam—is doing all kinds of amazing things for us."

I was supposed to do the slide-show portion of this whole debacle, but Khabria plows ahead, and I'd be an idiot to jump in front of her magnificent freight train of power. She grabs the remote and brings up the webpage on Mom's big-screen TV. Under the obvious public site is a password-protected administrative area, and Khabria clicks on the page that shows the donation statistics.

The room goes *blissfully* silent.

"Uh, where did all that money come from?" demands Alonzo, finally breaking the silence.

It's rumored he's neck and neck with Khabria's ex for the title of Rose Prince, so he's only a maybe, but he's got more opinions than anyone else so far.

I clear my throat. "We've had really generous donations from different universities, social interest groups, and fundraiser pages. My father has a connection at a big online news site. They ran a feature on us, and it's picked up a lot of traffic."

I turn to the screen, and Khabria already has the article up. There's a picture of her, me, and Doyle sitting in the Ebenezer courtyard, looking thoughtful and busy. What we're actually doing is trying not to get bit by fire ants and looking at Khabria's Spanish folder while Bo puts his finger over the flash *three separate times*.

Bo is very handsome. Which is a good thing for him, because—as my classmates love to say—*bless his heart*, that boy is as dumb as a box of rocks.

All around the room phones whip out and there's a few

seconds of silent sustained reading before someone howls, "Y'all, we're famous!"

It's funny how a surprise trust fund can change things. The room loses its viper's hiss and converts to docile, sheep-like democracy. Khabria whips out a glitter-festooned ballot box and photocopied voting ballots.

I silently vow to *never* lose my connection to this girl because there isn't a doubt in my mind: she's going run the whole damn world one day.

Doyle flips up screens with options Ollie helped us price out. We don't need this prom to become some *Rich Kids Gone Wild* scenario, so Doyle, Khabria, and I agreed on a fair budget, and extra funds will go toward next year's alternaprom.

Alonzo sits up as the ballots for caterers are being cast and holds his phone over his head. "Yo, we're trending on CNN!"

Doyle tugs me closer than he has in too long. "Better than I expected for sure," he says in this sweet, held-back way of speaking he never used with me before.

"Thank God you charmed Khabria to our side. She's like a cheerleader Machiavelli. Seriously, if we wind up in an apocalypse, I wanna be on her team." I chew on my lip as I watch the revelers. "It's good, right?"

"Of course it's good." He grins. "Seriously, I kinda thought it would be—"

Doyle never gets to finish his sentence. The scream of tires on the road outside my house sends a few kids running to the door, and when I see what they're looking at, my knees buckle.

I would have hit the floor hard if Doyle hadn't caught me under the arms, then curled me into his chest, trying to shield me from the hellish glow in my front yard. But it's too big, too bright to block out. Anyway, he can't stop my nostrils from filling with the sharp smell of gasoline that burns all the way down my throat. He can't block the steady heat of the flames, licking at my skin with the threat of third-degree burns. He can cover my ears to mask the crackle, but I've breathed the danger into my lungs, my body, and it's branded me in a way I'll never be able to escape.

The girl who complained first tonight lets out a choked sob. Alonzo unleashes a long line of threats and curses. Khabria is stone-faced, shocked, seeped of power. When I see how at a loss she is, it scares the crap out of me. Bo puts his arms around her, and she doesn't push him away, but she doesn't lean into his embrace either. She's a statue made of solid, cold stone.

It's hushed in the crowded foyer when my mother walks out with a tray of cookies. I breathe deep the hot vanilla smell— not quite homemade, because Mom is a dodgy baker, but freshly baked—and contemplate how damn weird it is, the mix of Toll House and gas, comfort and marrow-deep fear.

"Is the meeting over? These just came out of the—oh my God, what the hell is *that*?" my mother screams.

The cookie plate drops to the floor and shatters the quiet. Two girls rush to help clean it up as my mother darts onto the lawn, Doyle and me at her heels, the cacophony of so much pissed-off confusion at our backs.

Mom puts her hand up to her mouth and stares.

"It never looked this scary in my history books," I whisper, staring at the towering cross upright on our lawn, the orange-and-red flames licking into the pale purple evening sky.

Mom's face crumples with pure, gut-deep pain, illuminated by the light of the fiery cross in our yard.

She clutches a hand at her throat before she turns to me, her eyes wide. "Jesus, Aggie, what the hell did I do? Where did I bring us? Are you being bullied? Harassed? I'm calling the cops, *now*. We will fix this, sweetie. I swear—"

"This ain't about Agnes, ma'am," Doyle says, and, in the midst of this madness, I reflect on how much I love the way my weird, old-fashioned name sounds when he says it. "Not directly. It's about all of us, here, doing this our way. Throwing all their traditions in their face."

"The alternative prom?" Mom's expression is bewildered, and my guilt is a thousand times heavier than my anger ever was.

"It's not, like, an ironic prom," I attempt to explain.

Mom waits, her eyes wild with the reflection of the crackling flames.

When I don't explain further, Doyle jumps in. "We're doin' this because Ebenezer holds segregated proms."

"I'm sorry." Her words drag out slowly. "*What* did you say?"

"It's been tradition—shitty tradition, pardon my French, ma'am—to hold a prom for black folks and one for whites at Ebenezer. Me and Nes and a couple others decided it was bull…crap, so we started to rally for some change, and—" He gestures to the flaming cross licking and crackling in our yard. "It must not've sat well with some folks."

His arm draws me hard to his side, and I accept the embrace happily. I want to be close to someone who has grown up in this crazy culture and can forge a sure path out of the danger.

My mother is breathing heavily, one hand pressed to her stomach, the other pulled back to curve around her body, empty. I don't want to leave the safe haven of Doyle's arms, but I go to my mother and fill the space left open by her confusion and terror, hoping our double fear will somehow cancel itself out.

Doyle stalks away with purpose, and drags back the hose he first used to water that stupid stick of a tree the day I met him. He turns it on full blast and douses the fiery cross, like he's the prince who breaks the spell. We all blink and come out of our shock once the orange-flamed cross is reduced to a charred, smoldering relic. A few other guys race over and, even though it must still be hot, they shove, grunting as it collapses like a felled giant in my front yard.

"How do we get rid of it?" one of the guys asks, wiping soot on the legs of his jeans.

"I say we bring it back where it came from." Alonzo turns to the crowd of kids huddled on my front steps, speaking like one of those charismatic cult "prophets."

"They think they can come here and intimidate us?"

"No!" comes the resounding yell.

"They think they can scare us with ass-backward KKK tricks?"

More voices join in, louder and more insistent.

"No!"

"We need to show them what we're capable of!"

The verve in the air goes from meek to menacing, and though I hated feeling that buckling fear, I hate this blind fury even more. Mom's fingers bite into my arm, and Doyle rustles at my side, but it's Khabria who walks straight over to Alonzo and stares him dead in the eye.

"What we're *capable of*?" Her confident, measured voice leaves no doubt in my mind she is a descendant of royalty. "I feel like you might be talkin' *violence*, Alonzo. I really hope I'm wrong 'bout that."

"So they come burn a cross in the front yard and we ignore it? We s'posed to ignore it if one of us gets dragged behind some pickup or lynched too?"

The murmurs behind Alonzo get louder.

"They did this 'cause they're cowards." Khabria crosses her strong arms over her chest, her feet spread wide, in a true warrior stance. "They want us to go wild. They want us to get in our trucks and go cruisin', out for blood, and prove exactly why this county has insisted we *need* a segregated prom. I, for one, ain't taking their coward-ass bait. I'm gonna go back in and vote on streamers and songs and all that normal prom crap." She turns her back to the crowd and takes three steps toward the house.

"So you're gonna let them win?" Alonzo sneers, throwing his arms wide.

"Naw." She spins so she's looking right at him. "*I'm* gonna win. I'm not gonna let them control how I act and what I do. When I dance the first dance with the guy I love at *our* prom—*then* I win. We *all* win."

Khabria marches back in with a pretty decent rally behind her, but not everyone heads her way.

"We can't let this turn into eye-for-an-eye payback, or it'll never stop." Doyle pitches his voice low against the whoops and hollers of the group gathering in a clump around the settling ash in my yard.

"You can turn the other cheek if that's your thing, Doyle," Alonzo says, his mouth stretched tight. "My granny talks about how her daddy came out to a burnin' cross in their yard the first time he tried to set up his own business back in the day. They didn't have no choice but to lie down and take it. But it's a different world now."

"This is cowardly crap, man. Prankin'," Doyle argues, but Alonzo cuts him off, squaring off with him.

"A *prank*, Doyle? Be serious, man. Don't pretend this is someone eggin' the house or throwin' some toilet paper up in the trees. This is a *message*, loud and clear, that we—we *black folk*—better step down and get back in our place. I'm not about to retreat. Back off, man. This ain't your fight anyway."

Doyle rips off his hat and rakes his hands through his hair until it sticks up in a dozen light spikes as we watch Alonzo and the group he's rallied head to their cars, pull out, and speed off into the night to search out whoever started this war.

"Doyle? I don't want you getting caught up in all this. If you kids want to throw a prom, my house is open. You can invite whomever you want. But maybe, *officially*, you should back off." My mother glances at me, the fear in her eyes burning brighter than that flaming cross. "Baby, I know how hard you've been working, but—"

I shake my head and step back, away from her and her total lack of understanding about the crazy circumstances I went through to finally arrive here, and why this is happening no matter what. "We can't back down now. I don't want things to get out of control, but I can't—we can't—let things stand the way they are."

"Sweetheart, I admire what you want to do." Mom's voice and eyes and shoulders all sag with exhaustion. "But this is getting dangerous. It's not up to you to change the world."

Tears prick behind my eyes, but I hold them back. "If I don't change it, then the people who lit that cross in our front yard get to call the shots. You have no idea, Mom. *No idea* how crazy and…idiotic this is. They get to keep things the way they've always been because no one wants to stand up to them? I can't just lie down and let it happen."

Mom presses her lips together and puts both hands on my shoulders like she wants to root me in our front yard—the front yard that used to be a safe place, a private place. It's scary how quickly and completely your safe haven can be taken away from you for good.

Mom looks a little calmer in the cool moonlight than she did in the face of the mini inferno, but she's still obviously shaken.

"I can find a sub position back home. If Newington can't let you back in, you can always finish remotely. There are solid online programs, and you'll get a legitimate high school diploma, not just a GED." She blinks hard. "I know... I should have handled this better. I should have let you finish in Brooklyn, but I didn't—"

"Mom, it's okay. Honestly."

There's too much to fight for in my life right now; I have no energy left over to fight with my mother, who I know, without a single doubt, loves me. Wants to protect me. Wants what's best for me.

A few months ago, I was too trapped in my own little pity bubble to see all the love being heaped on me. But my perspective has changed. There are things I wish I could unsee, except for the fact that witnessing them helped me realize my place and all I have to be thankful for. Including my mother, who's standing in front of me, asking for my forgiveness. I've waited a long time for this and, now that the moment's here, all I want to do is assure her there's nothing to be sorry about.

"I messed up, Aggie. I didn't realize just how badly until tonight. I can't believe I brought you here. Trust me, I know I can't just apologize for this—"

I take her hand and we both get uncomfortably quiet. "These last few months I've had to come to terms with who I really am. It wasn't always pretty, but I'm glad. I'm not the same girl I was when I came down here, and that's a really good thing."

Mom rubs her free hand up and down her arm. It's not cold by any stretch of the imagination, but I think the Georgia warmth has thinned our blood. We've acclimated to this place in ways we never expected. It's changed us on a molec-

ular level. "I'm all for growing as a person, but this is dangerous. I don't like it, baby."

A few months ago, the next words out of my mouth would
have felt sweet. Now I hate to add to her worry.

"I'm sorry if you don't like it, but I have to do this."

Doyle inches back to the house, giving my mother and me
the space to say what we need to say in private.

"We should have never left Brooklyn." It's a refrain I don't
think she'll give up on for a while after tonight.

"But we did. And there's no way I'm leaving now." I give
her a quick hug, then pull away. "It'll be okay."

Her smile is haggard at best. "That's what I'm supposed to
say to you, baby."

"I know," I whisper. She cups my cheek with one hand,
then nods at the front door.

"I'm going inside to call the police and see about filing a report. And I'm going to make sure I'm the squeakiest wheel in
their station until this gets resolved." She takes a deep breath.
"I guess you have a prom to plan."

"Yeah." I look over my shoulder and grimace. "If these bastards can decide on streamer colors."

"Agnes, *mouth*," Mom says, but it's basically an autoresponse
at this point. She caresses just under my ear with her thumb,
the way she used to when I needed comforting as a kid. "Be
careful, baby. If you need anything, if anything comes up, if
there's any trouble, I'm here. I'm here for you."

"I know that, Mom."

I do know. And I realize that's all I need to know to vault
the worst of what went wrong between us. That doesn't mean
I'll be able to come to her as much as she'd like me to. It's my
fight to see through to the end.

But it's nice to know she's there for me anyway.

TWENTY-NINE

Ebenezer becomes a high school divided.

Someone—we never figured out who—snapped a picture of Doyle, my mother, and me, arms around each other, backs to the camera, staring at the flaming cross in my yard. It got shared a few dozen times on social media and went viral within a couple of hours, and our prom campaign went from incredibly generous to holy-crap old-oil-tycoon-trust-fund levels overnight. No one is sure who's in charge of all the excess funds, and I have a feeling it could cause real problems in this place, where so many people have never had enough.

As if we don't have enough to worry about, reporters are tracking us down, blogs, and news sites are foaming at the mouth over us, and a few colleges have reached out with their glossy, tree-covered catalogs and wink/nod hints about possible scholarships. I'm ignoring it all. It's snowballed into so much more than I was ready for, and I feel like an insect pinned to a display board and sealed behind glass, still alive but just barely. Some of the others seem to bask in the attention. Alonzo is rumored to be in talks with some big prime-time investigative journalist.

When I first got here, the rah-rah Ebenezer school spirit was a little grating, but the recent dissolution of any kind of school pride is kind of terrifying.

"It's like some evil alternate universe version of Ebenezer," I mumble to Doyle as we stride through the halls, which seem bleaker than ever.

"The whole damn place's gone straight crazy." Doyle half raises his hand to wave to a group of guys who intentionally turn their backs on him.

It's like Doyle's natural magnet got flipped, and he's repelling the very people who used to worship him. Doyle Rahn used to be the Daryl Dixon of Ebenezer High—now he's the Merle.

"So what do we do?" I ask, even though what I mean is *what will* you *do*, because I'm used to being on Ebenezer's crap list.

"Keep my head down. Try to remember why exactly I'm the guy they all hate." His smile is a fraction of its normal wattage. "That makes things easier."

The remnant of a smile is enough to rev my engines, but, like electrodes wired to a dead frog, what's making me jump is an illusion of the real thing. What we have now isn't what we had, and I have to accept it, no matter how much it sucks. "Is it still worth it?"

He stops and runs his eyes over me in that kind of possessive way that makes me feel like maybe this isn't just forced electricity. Maybe this is real and undeniable and *love*.

Holy Mary, mother of God, please let it be love. Please.

"Of course it is," he insists in a voice I don't trust for reasons I don't understand. He leans over, and I pucker as his lips brush my cheek.

"See you in English?"

Doyle deserts me while the hope of a real kiss is still perched

on my lips. I look around at the school I thought I was starting to know and feel an eerie sense of displacement.

The lines are drawn in intersecting grids all over Ebenezer
High. It's not just the group of us doing the alternaprom fighting the people who want to white-knuckle what's always been.
Sides get taken and retaken, old friends flip each other off in
the hallway, the Rose Court campaign posters get so regularly
defaced, they're all taken down, and there's this crackle in the
air, like we're suspended in those few sparking seconds it takes
for a fuse to burn down before it explodes a firecracker. All of
us wait with our breaths held for the boom.

"I finished." I've waited for everyone else to file out of class,
Doyle included. He's racing off to double-check his senior
project in the greenhouses behind the courtyard. He gave me
a quick wave on the way out. I try my best to ignore Ansley,
yipping at his heels.

Ma'am Lovett eyes the copy of *Passing* I'm holding out to
her. "And?"

"And it made me wonder if *I* might be passing. And if I
am, what am I passing as?" I pull the paperback close to me
again and flip through the pages idly. "I don't have the same
problems Clare and Irene did. But there are things that are
complicated in my life right now. I'm black in the South, so
people seem to assume that means I'm African American. But
that's not my experience. Yes, I'm black. But I'm Dominican
and Latina and Afro-Caribbean and European American, and
I'm proud of that. Of all of that! I want to celebrate it, I want
people to know that about me. But it feels like the powers that
be just want everyone to keep quiet, fit in their little assigned
boxes, and not speak up about who we are and how we want
to be heard and seen. Like with Clare and Irene, they want us

to stay on one side or the other, to choose and take sides. To not challenge the status quo. So many people are sick of that, myself included. And I have a feeling things are going to get crazier before they calm down."

"This whole prom business is shaking things up, isn't it?" A crease deepens on her forehead. It's the first time I've noticed any kind of glitch in Ma'am Lovett's cool.

"It's a freaking mess," I agree. "People are pissed, and things are escalating fast." I button my lip before I say more about the rumors I've heard, the plans that always seem to be simmering in the lunch line, in the parking lot, online, and everywhere at once.

Maybe I don't want to admit that the swaggering braggarts might actually make good on their threats because that would create a level of terror I'm not prepared to face right now. "I kind of want it to be over with already. I would never back out now, but I want to fast-forward to the end."

"I heard about what happened at your home." Her lips flatten into a line that makes it clear how furious she is.

"Yeah, it was pretty terrifying." When I close my eyes I'm instantly back in that surreal moment. I can still feel the heat of the flames, smell the acrid bite of smoke that seems permanently stuck in my nostrils. "My mom was ready to book me a ticket into JFK that night."

"You didn't want to go back?" Ma'am Lovett asks like she's genuinely interested in the answer.

"Part of me did. Still does," I admit, then I lose my words for a few seconds. "But I'm not who I was when I left anyway. I'd go back, and it wouldn't be the right fit. So I'd lose the memory of what I loved about being there. And I'd lose the chance to find out who I am here." I slide the book over to her. "I'm sick of passing, I guess. Sick of pretending to be someone I'm not. Problem is, I'm not doing that great a job figuring out who this 'new me' is either."

Ma'am Lovett smiles reassuringly. "You're doing just fine. Sometimes stretching yourself hurts, Agnes. But it's always worth the pain. Are you ready for more?"

Between studying for finals, planning this crazy prom, and dealing with the fact that Doyle and I are still on shaky ground, the last thing I need is extra reading from my English teacher.

But I'm always up for a challenge.

"Sure."

She hands me Toni Morrison's *Song of Solomon*, Zora Neale Hurston's *Their Eyes Were Watching God*, and Ralph Ellison's *Invisible Man*.

"Enjoy." She laces that command around the kind of wicked smile that lets me know she's using the cruelest form of irony.

"That one made me stay up every night for the last week trying to think things out till my brain hurt." I nod at the copy of *Passing* on her desk, and she points to the books tucked into the crook of my elbow.

"Get ready for more sleepless nights. Scoot before you're late."

I drop the books into my bag and start down the hall, trying to convince myself I'm not looking for Doyle. I'm still not over the fact that he isn't magically there wherever I am, popping out from a classroom as I'm walking by or rounding a corner just in time to catch me in his arms. I was spoiled by the way he treated me, and I never realized it. Apparently I'm pretty good at brushing off the people who love me most.

He's not at my locker at the end of the day, and he's nowhere near his when I check either. By the time I make it to the parking lot, more than half the cars are long gone, his truck included, and my stomach drops.

Then tightens when I hear screams. Ansley Strickland is hopping up and down in her cheer uniform, white foam all over her hands and arms. My first instinct is to run over to help, but since it's Ansley and there doesn't seem to be any blood or danger to compel me to intercede as a Good Samaritan, I make my way to my own car and lean against the side to watch this spectacle unfold.

A group of her cheer cohorts stampedes to her rescue. They yank all the doors of her Jeep open, and foam spills out everywhere, covering them while they scream and slide around on the asphalt like some kind of twisted Monty Python sketch gone bad.

"Who filled my Jeep with shaving cream?" Ansley shrieks. Her entire group runs around her car, flapping their arms like a flock of headless chickens.

Khabria jogs over to them just as the wailing and hand wringing reaches its peak.

Don't these twits use shaving cream every day in the shower? It's not a burning cross, for God's sake.

That's what I expect Khabria to say (or some version of that at least), but she doesn't. She's not freaking out like the other dimwits, but she seems concerned. When she attempts to help sop up some shaving cream, Ansley turns on her like a rabid dog.

"Don't you *even*, Khabria! I bet you were in on this!"

I move a few steps closer and overhear Khabria explain that she has no idea who did this or why.

"You have no idea? Really? You must think I'm a damn idiot." Ansley brushes shaving cream off her arms and shakes it off her fingertips, flecking foam on the other girls, who don't mutter a single protest. Ansley is like the Red Queen in *Alice in Wonderland*, terrifying her minions.

"Ansley, if I had any idea someone was about to do this, I would've stopped them or let you know. I don't think this is funny at all." Khabria holds up her hands, palms out. Innocent stance.

But Ansley has already decided Khabria is guilty, and she's not even contemplating another possible scenario.

"This Jeep has leather seats. My daddy had seat heaters set in it last winter. If that got screwed up, *your* daddy's getting the bill, I swear to God." She turns to the cowering girls behind her. "Help me clean it out!" she snaps.

Apparently *help me* means *do it for me* in Ansley's world because while the other girls sprint into action collecting paper towels to deal with the foamy mess, Ansley turns back to Khabria.

"No one cares about your pathetic little prom, Khabria. I don't know why y'all gotta attack us because we want to do things according to our traditions." She wrings out her ponytail and fluffs it. "And if this is about the Rose Court thing, I'm sorry if you're mad I'm in the lead. I don't know what to say about that, 'cept when you try to change the way things have always been done, you're gonna rub people the wrong way."

"I have no clue who did this or why, but you need to stop pointing fingers when you have zero facts." Khabria watches the girls detail Ansley's car like…well, like cheerleaders at a carwash. She shifts on her white sneakers, not sure where to go because she has no place. I recognize a comrade in total ostracization.

"Hey, Khabria!" I call out before I think through the ramifications.

A smug smile curls over Ansley's face. She raises her eyebrows high and waves Khabria away with her hand. "Go plan your next *hilarious* prank. But, Khabria?" She waits until she has our undivided attention. "Y'all best watch your backs."

Ansley goes back to hyperventilating about the possibility of the foam discoloring the Jeep's stitching.

"Sorry." I lean on my car's hood and Khabria leans against the bumper.

"For what?"

"For making it look like I was your accomplice."

"Don't worry about that. Ansley loves drama, but even she would need evidence she won't get, since I didn't do it." She asks, shaking her head, "How did everything spiral out of control so fast?"

"No clue." I squint as the cheerleaders back away from the scrubbed-down Jeep, hands clasped, waiting for the inspection to be complete. Ansley gives a loud whoop when the Jeep's engine roars to life with no problems. "Although I heard two girls from my computer science class whispering about finding empty chest freezers in the home ec room the other day." When Khabria gives me a confused look, I nod to the foam slowly melting in the sun. "Frozen shaving cream. My ex did it to his best friend when he graduated. It takes dozens of cans. You break the frozen cream out of the container and..."

"So, you know how to do this?" Khabria's voice hitches right on the edge of accusation.

"Yes." I clear my throat. "It's a really common prank, actually."

"I never heard of it." Khabria's voice is soft. She adjusts her backpack on her shoulders and shrugs. "I gotta go."

"I didn't do it," I confess, sounding like a criminal who's trying to weasel out of trouble.

"I didn't ask." She examines her navy fingernail polish.

"No, but you definitely insinuated. If I did this, I'd fess up.

Trust me, I'd want credit. That had to take tons of prep work to pull off. And I don't think it's such a huge deal. It's a *prank*. And a funny one."

"'Cept *whoever did it* hurt Ansley's pride. She's gonna retaliate, and it may not be so innocent when she does."

"Do you think she did the thing with the cross at my house?" I ask just as she's turning on her heel to leave.

Her shoulders buckle. "I don't know what I think about anyone or anything anymore. I don't know how it went from wantin' to go to some stupid dance with someone I love to everything I care about falling apart." She opens her mouth to say more, then seems to think better of it.

I watch as she marches away, then I get in my car.

But not before I check it carefully, inside and out…for what, I don't know.

THIRTY

To think this started when a bunch of jerks of all races got together to whine about prom colors and themes.

After someone interrupted our pity party with a hate crime, Alonzo and his posse went roaming, but I didn't hear about it resulting in anything more than cruising around and talking crap.

What I told Khabria is true; I *did* overhear Telly and Manda—a couple in my computer science class who had recently come out and wanted to attend the alternaprom—making plans to freeze a ton of something just before a ton of frozen shaving cream wound up in Ansley's Jeep. There wasn't a race issue keeping Telly and Manda from prom, but I asked around and no queer student had ever gone to prom with his or her partner in the history of Ebenezer proms, black or white. Bids to both segregated proms were sold one per couple, and it was an unwritten rule that the couple had to consist of one guy and one girl. Single prom goers had to pay the two-person bid price even if they couldn't find anyone to go with them. We made sure it was clear that alternaprom welcomed any Ebenezer student regardless of race or sexual orientation, and our bids were sold as single tickets.

Ansley drove home in a fury once her Jeep was clean, clearly with thoughts of revenge dancing in her head. She got online and, through the almighty power of social media, whipped up a frenzy she labeled "promoting school pride" with her long-winded "keep Ebenezer great and respect our traditions" posts. The next day Ebenezer looked like a *Dukes of Hazzard* promotional tour gone so, so wrong.

Before I moved to Georgia, I rarely saw a Confederate flag, and every time I see one here, I flinch. It's like a blasé reminder that I'm not welcome or should be on guard or have to watch my back. But, the day after Ansley's Jeep debacle, I had only to walk the halls of Ebenezer for a single hour surrounded by Confederate flag handkerchiefs, belt buckles, T-shirts, and stickers on binders, before I was cured of Confederate-flag flinching for the rest of my life.

Was it because I was forced to face the root of my discomfort or simple desensitization?

"What's going on?" I ask Doyle, hating that one of the few precious minutes I get with him is being bogged down with this particular craziness.

Short the white students who signed up to go to alterna-prom, every other one of my pigment-deprived classmates is decked out like the star of some hokey honky-tonk video. The defiant flag wearers are met with curled lips and sneers from a pretty wide spectrum of the rest of the school population, and the vibe is more tense than ever in the halls of Ebenezer.

Doyle's expression is grim. "More of Ansley's damn nonsense. I'll see if I can talk some sense into her."

"Isn't it against dress code to wear the Confederate flag?" I get it's a long shot, since I've seen kids with Confederate flag paraphernalia before today, but I figure it might be one of those things teachers ignore every now and then. En masse, maybe it's a violation the administration can enforce. Any hopes that this might get handled by semireasonable adults before it causes a riot are dashed by Doyle's wry look. "I mean, it wasn't allowed at my old school," I finish lamely.

"Nes, you know you ain't in Brooklyn anymore."

He hesitates before he leans in to me like he *wants* to kiss me, then backs out after an awkward hug. As he rushes off, I attempt to squash the feeling of intense jealousy that wells up in me. I know he's going to find Ansley to have an argument, but I guess it's the point that he's on a mission to hunt her down while he's simultaneously attempting to avoid me.

Two periods later, as we walk into the cafeteria together, Alonzo fills me in on everything that went down. "Your boy was *pissed off*. He got right up in Princess Ansley's face and let her have it until the art teacher came and told him to get to class." Alonzo puts a hand up to his mouth and laughs, shaking his head. "You should've seen her opening and shutting those big ole pouty lips like some giant blond trout. Even her little friends were laughin' at her. Funny as hell."

I should be happy, I guess, but I'm not. I'm just waiting for what's next. Khabria pointed out that Ansley doesn't deal well with hurt pride, and now Doyle will be in her crosshairs.

I can't help looking over my shoulder obsessively for the next few days. Doyle's busy with his ag project and getting the word out about the winning song/theme for alternaprom— "Stand by Me," chosen by Doyle himself and sung to me soulfully in his truck one day after school. When I hesitated, he put it on repeat until he had me singing along and agreeing it was crazy brilliant.

Who can argue with Ben E. King?

And *I* can't argue with Doyle Rahn, especially not when he's on fire.

Doyle says I'm going to need to lock myself in a panic room if I don't calm down and stop assuming some kind of crazy backlash is coming after his confrontation with Ansley.

But I can't help waiting for the other shoe to drop.

THIRTY-ONE

It's the end of another long, tense, hot-as-hell school day. Khabria's little brother, Khalil, is hoping we'll let sophomores attend the alternaprom so that he can impress his new girlfriend, who's on the cheer team. We're working on the bids in an empty classroom, and, mostly to get Khalil to stop whining, Doyle tosses him the keys and sends him to grab the binder that's on the seat of his truck.

"I guess I'm missing my Future Farmers guest speaker," Doyle whispers as he glances at the time on his phone. "But if I had to hear that kid mope about prom for another second, I was gonna lose it."

"You're missing a Future Farmers meeting?" I feign shock. "But what if the speaker is addressing cotton fleahoppers?"

"Impossible." Doyle grins. "I'm giving that talk at the next meeting. This'll be the first meeting I've missed since freshman year. I hope this prom is worth it." He winks at me, and my heart truffle shuffles shamelessly.

A minute later, frantic screams send chills rushing up and down my neck. We all go still and stare at each other before everyone jumps up and rushes to the door.

"Khalil!" Khabria screams as Alonzo runs into the class-room, Khalil in his arms.

"I called 911! Ambulance is on its way! We need cold water, ice, *now*!"

"This way!" Doyle knocks over a chair as he rushes to the cafeteria.

"Go, go with them," I urge Khabria, who's doing that heart-breaking, openmouthed silent scream, hand clamped over her face. "I'll wait for the ambulance."

I check the nurse's office, but she left for the day. I pace just inside the front until the ambulance pulls up with a screech. I push through the doors and jog outside, waving my arms over my head like a castaway trying to get spotted by a ship.

"Here! He's in here!" I run, they follow, and we all burst into the cafeteria together.

Khabria has her arms around her brother. She's rocking him back and forth and running her hand over his head. Doyle holds a huge stainless-steel mixing bowl Alonzo dumps cup-fuls of ice into.

"It's okay, little man. You're gonna be fine," Alonzo soothes.

"What happened here?" the tiny female EMT asks, immedi-ately moving in to check Khalil's heart rate and blood pressure.

Khalil is crying so hard, his face is coated in tears and snot. "I—I—I went to the parking lot. I opened the truck door and the handle...the handle was burnin' up!"

"It *was* pretty hot today," the EMT says, nodding to her partner, a quiet, nervous-looking guy. Gently, he lifts Khalil's hand from the water, and I'm not the only one who gasps.

"This is third degree," he says, his voice hardening. "This wasn't just the sun. In fact, I can't imagine this happening by accident."

The woman EMT gives her partner a death stare and shakes

her head quickly, then asks if anyone put any ointment or cream of any kind on Khalil's hand. I look over at Doyle, who's already backing away, his eyes wide, his face pale.

Alonzo has his arm around Khabria, and the EMTs are doing a solid job reassuring Khalil that he's going to be fine. I follow Doyle.

"Hey." I grab him by the elbow. His entire body is shaking.

"There's dozens of people who know I never skip a Future Famers meeting. If it wasn't an accident, then Khalil is hurt 'cause someone was goin' after me. I plan to find out who that is." He turns and runs, his boots thudding on the linoleum.

I follow him to the parking lot where people are milling around, some with phones out, a few cheerleaders huddled and crying wetly.

"Get the hell away from my truck," Doyle snarls, pushing past shocked classmates.

He reaches a hand out, then hesitates. He brushes his fingertips over the metal door handle and snatches them back. He turns to glare at the group assembled, and the ferocious expression on his face sends more than a few people stumbling back. "Who did this?"

No one answers. There's a lot of murmuring, a lot of shuffling feet.

"You damn cowards! *Who did this?*" Doyle bellows. "Khalil Scott is sitting in the cafeteria nursin' some third-degree burns that were meant for me. So come on out, whoever did it! Come and let's fight it out, here and now. 'Cause this shit ends today!"

"Look, Doyle, no one saw nothin', I swear. We all been out here since Lonzo brought the kid in, e'rybody's been askin' the same thing you are. Nobody's happy 'bout what happened." Critter tries to move closer to Doyle, but Doyle shoots daggers pointedly at the Confederate flag bandanna hanging out of Critter's front pocket.

I'm pretty sure Critter had that same bandanna tied around his biceps the day we went mudding, but everything's been twisted a thousand different ways since that laid-back day of fun. Doyle snaps his arms out, daring anyone to come near.

"Well, *somebody* heated that door handle up, likely with a blowtorch, so I don't believe for a second *none* of y'all knows nothing about it. This wasn't no accident. Now some kid got hurt over something that's got nothing to do with him. I want this ended before another innocent kid pays the price."

Doyle glares in turn at each of his classmates, but no one meets his eyes or comes forward with any information. Not that they would after the way he cut Critter down.

A squad car bumps along the gravel drive that leads to the parking lot, and my heart dives into my stomach. I close my eyes and ball my hands in Doyle's T-shirt, shrinking behind him as panic sets in. He puts an arm around me and drags me to his side protectively. I turn my head into his chest and take deep, steady breaths. My body sags with relief when the door opens and it's not Officer Hickox.

"Afternoon, y'all. I'm Officer Tomlin. Station got a report there was an accident here. I'm gonna need y'all to stay put while we get your information. Don't be nervous now. Just tell us whatever it is you might've seen, no matter how insignificant you might think it is. You never know what might help. Officer Washington will be helping me get down the information today."

He waves his hand at his squad car, and a young, seriously good-looking guy gets out and walks over without making eye contact. There's an explosion of frantic whispers, and when I look to Doyle to explain, he leans down and says,

"He's Lonzo's cousin. Went here a few years back. Heard he joined the air force, but I guess he's on the police force now. Prolly partied with the brothers and sisters of half the kids here back in the day. He had a pretty wild rep."

The two of them make the rounds, and when Officer Tomlin gets to me, I offer up a wobbly, nervous smile. I wonder if it was on purpose that two black officers were sent out. How many of the force are minority? How many are women?

When did I start thinking about things like the racial and gender breakdown of a local police force?

I guess when it started mattering to me personally.

"Your name, darlin'?" he asks.

I ignore that he called me *darlin'*. It was a nice, fatherly kind of thing anyway, not at all pervy. "Agnes Murphy-Pujols."

He pauses, pen hovering over his pad. "You're the young lady organizing the desegregated prom?"

"One of them, sir," I say, proud I remembered my *sir*.

"Good work you're doing. The force took up a collection to donate to your fund. I hope you kids have fun." He smiles, and, stupidly, I'm choked with tears.

"Thank you," I croak out, and I have to roll my eyes to stop myself from bawling on his shoulder. To stop myself from sobbing in front of the kind officer, I picture him passing around a hat to collect funds for our alternaprom, and Hickox having to dig into his cowardly pockets to pull his donation out.

Imagining the way he must have squirmed helps still my quivering emotions.

The rest of the interview involves me telling the few things I know about what happened to Khalil. I'm not sure if I should, but I tell him about Ansley's car, the Confederate flag bonanza, and Doyle's talking to her (downplaying exactly *how* it was rumored he conducted the conversation). By the time I'm finishing up, Principal Armstrong is making his way to the lot.

He looks beyond tired. He looks haggard.

"How's the Scott boy, Principal?" Officer Tomlin asks.

"He's badly burned, but he's getting the best care there is, Officer Tomlin. The doctor assured us he'll make a full recovery." He eyes me and seems to buckle under an extra dose of weariness. "When you're through, maybe we could take this to my office?"

"I can come with you now." Officer Tomlin gives me a parting smile. "Thank you for all your help, Agnes."

I feel another tiny burst of satisfaction when Principal Armstrong's mouth twists, but it's extinguished too fast to elevate my deflated feelings. Doyle is leaning against his truck, hands stuffed in his pockets, kicking gravel.

I stand next to him and duck low to catch a glimpse of his glower. "You okay?"

The way he shakes his head, it's like the weight of this entire disaster is pinned on his shoulders. "Did you see the burns on his hand?"

"Yeah," I whisper. "I did."

He slides his hands out of his pockets and holds them open, palms up, staring at his calloused, unburned skin. "It was supposed to be me."

"It's not your fault." I press my hands, palm to palm, against his.

"I'm the one got up in Ansley's face." He threads his fingers through mine, then lets out this heavy sigh like he's been waiting for this, like he can breathe now that we're touching each other this way again.

"You think this was Ansley?" I'm tight-roping between the thrill of our closeness and the fear of having it snatched away.

"Not exactly like I can picture her with a blowtorch, but, yeah, if I had to make a bet, I'd say it traces back to her. Most likely she asked someone to do it. Or paid 'em to." He tugs me closer, tucks my head under his chin and blows out a breath that tickles my ear. "Problem is, when's it gonna stop?"

I wrap my arms around his waist. He was always thin, but now I can feel the bones of his hips and ribs. "We could call off the alternaprom."

He makes a gruff sound deep in his throat. "We can't. It's the one good thing I've ever done. It's something we need to do, no matter what anyone else says."

"I don't know if we can clean up a couple of centuries of residual craziness in the last few weeks before graduation." I tilt my head back and look up at him. "Maybe we just keep our heads down until this is all done with."

Finally, like the first sunny day of spring after a polar-vortex winter, Doyle Rahn cracks the widest, warmest smile I've ever seen. "Agnes Murphy-Pujols thinks we should keep our heads down." He tilts his face to the sky and stays that way for a few long seconds.

"What?" I ask, looking up and failing to see what he's staring at.

"Aw, I was waiting for the bolt of lightning to come crack us on the head or somethin'. Never thought I'd hear those words outta your mouth." He laughs as I deliver a few light jabs to his bony ribs.

"I can change," I mutter as he bats away my hands.

He abandons the smile and goes serious. "Don't."

"Change?" The word barely squeaks out.

"Never." He drops those lilac eyes like he's ashamed. "Even if some asshole tells you to. Don't listen to 'im."

"I won't then." I attempt a laugh, but it gets tangled, and he winds up making the same confused sound.

Somewhere, in the midst of that uncertainty, a chunk of tension melts away. I decide to seize the moment.

"I may be perfect the way I am, but you need some work." I pop a hip to the side and cross my arms, studying beautiful, complicated Doyle Rahn.

"Is that right?" He strokes his chin, *thinking.* "You got somethin' specific in mind?"

"I think you need to go on a date."

Those blond eyebrows shoot up into his hairline. "We're in the middle of the second War of Northern Aggression, and you wanna go muddin'?"

"What's going on here isn't something either one of us can fix. And I have no intention of going *muddin'*, Doyle. I'm asking you on an honest to God, dress-up-nice, go-out-somewhere-with-cloth-napkins-and-low-lighting *date.* Would you like to go out with me Friday night?"

"I work this Friday," he says, staring at me with a look I interpret as slightly mesmerized and totally confused.

"Saturday night then." I was so sure he'd jump on the invite, I'm a little nervous now.

"Do you want me to wear a white suit and bring my corncob pipe?" I calm down a little at how cartoonishly huge his eyes are.

So huge they might explode into animated beating hearts at any second. It's a good sign, I think.

"Save it for the prom. Casual nice."

"Like khakis?" He frowns.

"Less Future Farmers of America conference, more night in Savannah with your hot—" I'm about to say *girlfriend*, but I'm not. Am I? Whether or not I am or will be, it's not something I'm wasting time figuring out now. "—date. Your hot date."

He nods like a fool. "She sure is." Then he grabs me by the wrist and inches me to him until we're as close as we can get.

For one blink of his golden lashes, I'm sure he'll pull back the way he has been these past weeks, but he leans in and kisses me, soft and sweet on the lips like he means it this time, and my blood crackles like it's been lit on fire. When he pulls back to speak, it's in the intimate space between our pressed-together foreheads.

"I never thought I'd be lucky enough to have a girl like you ask me on a date."

"What does that even mean?" Stars spin inside my cranium. "'A girl like me'?"

He stops short and kisses me again, not stopping until he wrangles a moan from me. "Good point. There ain't no other girl like you. Thank the Lord."

I'm pretty sure it's a compliment, so I take it and another kiss—still sweeter than I really want, but deeper and hotter than the last one—before I watch him pause, grip the now-cooled door handle, and drive a little too fast out of the parking lot of mayhem, honking and waving like a fool as he goes.

THIRTY-TWO

"**O**h my God. Was he badly hurt? Will he be okay?" Ollie's voice is a huge comfort, as always. These last months have helped me realize how important the people I love are to me.

Tonight I multitask, filling her in on every crazy thing that's gone down recently as I put on my makeup and try to decide what I'm going to wear on my date with Doyle. Getting ready for a date is stressful, but wholly unlike what I've gone through lately at school. It's the good kind of stress.

Mostly.

Now that the floodgates in my brain have opened and Ma'am Lovett has pumped me full of mind-altering fiction and we might be on the brink of martial law at Ebenezer High—where fury seems to be constantly bubbling just under the surface of every interaction—I can't look at *anything* the same way I did before.

Tiny things dig at me, like the fact that none of the upscale drugstores my mom loves in Savannah carry the kind of makeup that works for my skin tone. On a totally ordinary shopping trip, I find myself wondering why the black beauty products are all clumped in one specific section, like no one white or Asian might want a do-rag or olive oil–based conditioner. Or maybe they're being hidden—or maybe there's no way they could be placed next to all the "normal" hair-care products? I don't know what the real answer is, but the ones I come up with make me sick to my stomach.

I start to notice the people who see me as a smart-mouthed black girl instead of a nice, upstanding young lady. There are the clerks who eye me warily when I run my fingers over racks of expensive jeans they assume I can't afford and might steal. Or the guys who check me out but look undecided—black guys, white guys, and every color in between—like they're not sure if they're supposed to like what they see. I always walk away with my chin up, but it isn't always easy.

For every person who excludes me or acts like I don't fit, there's someone reaching out to claim me as a member of their tribe. I'm not sure if I fit or don't fit, who I belong with, if I'm passing, or what exactly I could be passing *as*…if that's what's going on in the first place.

My brain hurts. I need a night of pure, mindless fun to clear it and hit the reset button.

"Khalil was hurt pretty badly, but Khabria said he should be able to play basketball in the winter. Which is good, because he's really bummed he won't be healed in time for football training camp this summer." My hands shake a little as I mix two foundations together in my palm, trying to get the perfect match for my freckled, dark-but-not-that-dark, light-but-not-that-light skin. "There was more crap. Sugar in gas tanks. Lug nuts that got loosened. Lockers broken into, bleach poured on uniforms, laxatives in water bottles. Bad, bad crap."

Ollie gasps, pulling the phone too close to her face, and it's disarming the way she seems so close. Even though I know, sadly, she's *not*. "Why didn't you call?"

"Because you had to practice for the senior showcase. Thao just got back from his tournament—tell him I said congratulations on placing third by the way! You already spent a ton of time on the website for the alternaprom—have I thanked you for that lately?"

Her grin is shy and completely pleased. "Only a million times in the last week. I told you, no sweat."

"Lots of sweat," I counter. "Buckets of it, and you could have been using that sweat practicing. The good news is, I get out of this hellhole in May, so I'll be there for senior recitals."

I watch Ollie's eyes widen. "Wha...? Are you serious?" She pops up on her knees and bounces on her bed, excited as a puppy.

I miss her excitement! I miss all the uncomplicated, constant fun we had. I miss her unwavering loyalty and the way she understood—with a single look—me, the *real* me, the me I wish everyone else could step back and see. I miss my best friend so badly, I ache.

"Yep. Graduation is earlier here, thank God." She purses her lips at me, and I suck my cheeks in and brush blush on the apples with slow sweeps. I avoid her eyes and, ultimately, her scary judgment. "What? Why the disapproving look?"

"Not disapproving. Just... I know it's been, like, a big, crazy ball of stress for you lately. I mean, did that lady from CNN finally stop calling?"

"I passed her info on to Khabria. She's a way better public speaker than I am." I whip out my mascara wand because my lashes need some serious help, but, also, I don't want to see *that look* on Ollie's face. The one that means she's disappointed in me.

"It's gotta be so much." Her voice oozes pure sympathy, not judgment.

I stop coating my eyelashes and look at her perfect face on the screen, ashamed I doubted the most loyal person I've ever known.

Attempted truth time. This is never easy, but Ollie makes it possible. "I guess I wanted to come here and disappear, you know? After everything that was going on in my life, getting out of Brooklyn and coming to Nowhere, Georgia, felt like the way to go if that's what I wanted. Funny how that turned out," I grumble.

"No kidding. It's like you have social-justice, newshound paparazzi following you around wherever you go now. So awful and weird." I watch her play with the corner of her paisley quilt, avoiding asking whatever question is eating her alive.

I carefully coat the lashes on my other eye. "Ask."

"What?"

"Whatever it is you want to ask. We don't need to play these games, babydoll." I flutter my lashes at her and she laughs.

"You know what I'm going to ask about. Or, better yet *who…*"

"Why do you think I'm getting all dressed up?" I tease.

"Oh my God, a date?" Her voice could possibly shatter glass, and I resist the urge to cover my ears. "With Doyle? Do you know where he's taking you? Oh my God, I need to breathe."

I fall back on the bed, my toes curling with giddiness. "Breathe, Olls. Your brain needs the oxygen. Of course I know where we're going. *I'm* the one taking *him* on the date. All of your romantic Thao stories inspired me. I mean, I'm not going to put Doyle on the handlebars of my bike or anything…"

"Holy crap, you have no idea the price I'd pay to see that!" She screams with laughter imagining it, and her laugh makes me smile through my nerves.

I put a hand up to touch my hair, tamed into soft waves

that fall down past my shoulders. I might pin it up just because Doyle's mentioned how much he likes my tattoo.

My heart stutters. Romance is dangerous.

"I'm super proud of you for asking him!" Ollie sounds shocked with a side screech of impressed. "That was bold."

"Necessary," I correct before I come off sounding more impressive than I am. "Things have been strange with him and me. With all this other stuff going on, I guess we've kind of grown apart."

I don't have to finish my thought, because Ollie gets it. "Not good. Especially when you don't have much time left. I'm sorry."

"Don't be. When I leave here I get to come home to you."

I don't expect *leave here* to twist my heart. I don't expect *home* to have such a murky meaning.

"Will your mother come visit this summer? Are you guys planning to do your family vacation in Santo Domingo?" Ollie's happiness is renewed by all this good news. Exciting news.

News I don't want to think about right now.

"I'm not sure what she has planned. I'll go when you and I get back from Vietnam, but I don't know about Mom. I mean, is my father going to invite Celeste?"

Ollie sighs. "Yikes. That would be so weird. Would that be weird for you?"

"Yeah, it would be. But my grandmother is facing her fear of flying to go for the first time in years, so I definitely want to be there, no matter who Dad decides to bring along." I hear the roar of a truck in the driveway. "Crap, that's Doyle! I'll call you later. Text you sooner!" I smack a kiss on the screen before we sign off.

Doyle knocks while I tear my old tank over my head and

kick off my tiny cotton shorts. As my mother greets him, I whimper and reach for one outfit, then another.

"Damn, damn, damn…"

I know this decision isn't as important as I'm making it, but I'm tired of thinking about inequity and injustice and the tiny wars we wage with the people we just don't understand. I want to worry about whether I should wear the demure purple flowered one-piece that's gorgeous but hard to pee in or the scandalously tight black skirt and white top that has a high collar but shows off a slice of skin right at my midriff.

"Doyle, don't you look handsome. Are those cowboy boots? Very rugged," Mom says.

Cowboy boots? Well, well, well, Doyle Rahn's bringing his A game tonight.

Decision made, game on.

I slip into the black skirt, pull on the white top, slide my feet into dangerously tall red heels, and apply lipstick that matches. When I stride into the hall, Doyle stops midsentence.

"You were saying something incredibly boring about irrigation?" I prompt in my best vixen voice.

I think he tries to smile, but it's like he's had a stroke. One side of his mouth jerks up, but he seems to forget what he wants the other side to do.

"My granddaddy'd say you look prettier than a speckled pup," he finally manages.

"In the South, telling a girl she looks like a dog is a compliment? How the hell did you guys get a reputation for being gentlemen?" I ask.

"I think it's kind of sweet," Mom ventures, then looks me over with an indulgent smile. She's not big on midriff baring, but she tries to give me space when it comes to fashion. "You look ready to dance the night away."

I eye Doyle from under the safety of my lashes. He's looking edible in his dark, stiff blue jeans and crisp white button-down. "Do you feel like dancing tonight?"

"Do one-legged ducks swim in circles?"

My mom chokes on a laugh, and I roll my eyes.

"Okay, let me get a picture before you go, then I have to run. I'm meeting the girls for some Bunco. Make sure you text me when you get home, sweetie." She herds us toward the fireplace, and I realize this is the first time in months she hasn't hesitated and double-checked before she asked me to do something so basic and *momish*.

I am so done with angst. It's nice to officially have my mom back.

"You don't need to rush home. Last time you left when you were on a winning streak," I tell her.

She rearranges us so she can snap a few thousand pictures. "Deidre did say I could crash in her guest room if it got too late. And Lori is making that sangria we all love…"

"Mom, it's the twenty-first century. We have these devices called phones. Stay out and have fun, I'll text you to let you know I'm home safe."

"You're sure?" she lowers the camera.

"In a few months I'll be living in a dorm full-time, Mom," I say, my tone both joking and gentle.

She presses her lips tight. "You're right. Okay. A few more shots, and then you kids go have fun, and I'll go win that Bunco pot if it takes me till dawn to do it."

"I believe in you and your mad Bunco skills, Mom."

Doyle slides an arm around me, his hand warm on the bare skin between my top and skirt. It makes my nipples go tight, half with memory, half with anticipation. We smile for a dozen pictures before I whisper, "We need to leave *now*, before she wants video."

"Right. You and me on video would be a real bad thing."

"Are you trying to get me all riled up?"

"Do frogs have watertight butt holes?" His smile is so huge, it's ludicrous.

"Are you going to impress me with these charming Southern sayings all night?"

"Does Dolly Parton sleep on her back?"

"Jesus, Doyle!" I'm laughing as I lead him to my car.

Which brings us to an impasse, since he's headed to his truck. "Where are you going?" I point to my car. "This is my date. We're taking my car."

"I love that you got all Yankee ballsy and asked me out, but I can't ride in that hamster wheel." He levels a look riddled with disgust at my ride.

I crook my finger. "My date. My rules. My car."

"You know I'm an easy guy. But I gotta have a line in the sand and… This. Is. It." He stands with his feet spread wide, and—though I admire how surprisingly sexy those cowboy boots are when I take in his stance—I'm not about to let Doyle Rahn boss me around.

"Cool. Well, I look hot, I have reservations for two… If not you, I'm sure I'll find someone willing to go on this date with me."

He's jogging over by the time I tug down on my skirt and slide into the driver's seat.

"Damn, girl, you're cold as ice." He manages to grab my door at the last second and shut it securely. He hurries to his side and buckles up, grinning like the fool he truly is. The fool I'm totally in love with. "It's hot, watching you drive."

"It's not hot, listening to you be a caveman." I let him see the full 360-degree roll of my eyes.

"You're pretty when you're a little fired up."

"You're handsome when you're quiet." I swat his hand away when he reaches toward the radio knobs. "Forget it. Then think about it for a second and forget it again. Life's been depressing enough without the mournful wail of country music."

"What do *you* wanna listen to?" Doyle turns in the seat so he's looking right at me.

Usually the person who's not driving becomes the default fidgeter in the car, but Doyle's sitting in the passenger seat, chill as can be, while I thump my fingers on the steering wheel, readjust my skirt, and tap the toe of my left foot on the floorboard like I'm a six-year-old who drank an espresso. I *love* driving. Living in Brooklyn, I rarely got to drive, and these last few months have made me realize how much I enjoy it.

"Something loud. Something we can sing along to. Something angry." I fish around for my iPod and toss it to him with the cord that connects it to the stereo. "I've got tons of playlists."

"Juan Luis Guerra, Daddy Yankee, Shakira, Cuco Valoy..." He's already scrolling through. "This mix is called 'STFU and Riot.'" He raises his eyebrows.

"It's gone platinum on 8-tracks," I brag, singing along too loud to Siouxsie and the Banshees's "Hong Kong Garden" when he pushes Play. "I remember dancing around to this with my mom while she mopped."

Doyle's eyeing the iPod warily. "You and your mama cleaned up to this noise?"

My laugh loosens something that's been tied down too tight. "Stop looking so shocked. This mix starts out pretty tame. Wait till we get to Pussy Riot."

We're flying along the highway now, and we both roll our windows down and let the warm air rush in. Doyle is one of those people who catches on to lyrics incredibly fast, so we're both singing along loud and strong to early Debbie Harry, Bikini Kill, L7—all the great punk my mother introduced me to and some stuff Ollie and I found on our own.

"So your mama—the lady who listens to Harry Connick Jr. while she cooks—really likes…" He grabs my iPod and flicks the screen on, reading the artist of the next song (which is freaking awesome, not that he'd acknowledge it). "The Cramps?"

"Who can resist punk-tinged rockabilly?" I pat his knee. "There, there. We're almost to the restaurant, and I'm pretty sure they won't be playing punk."

"Pretty sure?" He sticks a finger in his ear like he's trying to clean out the noise.

"I try to keep myself open to the possibility of pleasant surprises." We pull up to what looks like a strip mall. I notice Doyle eyeing the Outback Steakhouse across the street as I turn off the ignition. "We're not going to Outback."

"I love me some bloomin' onion," Doyle mourns.

"Well, you can take some other girl to get one when I leave," I snap, and we both still.

"Why do you keep doin' that?" he asks, his voice low.

Traffic buzzes past in jolting, frenetic starts and stops that I watch in the rearview mirror. My voice sounds thicker than I expect when I answer with words that are simple and not enough. "I'm sorry."

"Don't apologize. Tell me why," he coaxes.

I grip the steering wheel too hard, pressing my arms straight and tensing back into the seat. "Dammit, Doyle! I don't *know.*"

"You do too," he baits.

"We're going to be late for our reservation."

"Screw the reservation, Nes. I want you to tell me why you use the fact that you're leavin' to slice at me like that. It's dirty fightin', and I expect better from you."

"Really?" If it comes out a little sneered, so be it. "Dirty fighting like, oh, I don't know…maybe *screwing me* then telling me it was the biggest mistake you made and we should forget it? You've been so damn busy running around, doing your ag class and prom crap and who knows what the hell else, you made it totally clear what's important to you. So don't start accusing me, Doyle. Don't you *dare* point the finger at *me* when you're just as big a coward as I am!"

I throw that down, but what I don't have the cojones to admit, even to myself—*especially* to myself—is that if Doyle wants to forget, I only want to remember the version of us that I'm comfortable with. The version that's temporary and uncomplicated. So how is that any better?

He gets out of the car and slams the door hard, then stops short on the sidewalk, like he doesn't know what to do or where to go. The sound of that slamming door unleashes a hot, red fury in me, and I follow his lead, stalking onto the sidewalk in front of the restaurant in my ridiculously high heels, arms crossed, pissed as hell and not sure what to do about it. So I kick some gravel into the gorgeous little rock garden they have set up in front of the place. I pace back and forth, and one of my heels catches in the crack of the sidewalk.

Doyle rushes toward me as I'm righting myself.

"I've got it!" I yell, pushing him away. *"I don't need you!"*

He catches my wrists in his hands and holds them tight as we both breathe hard. He stares at me like he wants to eat me alive. I stare back like I want to lay myself on a platter and let him.

"You think I don't know that?" He relaxes his hold. His

hands slip down, and just when I think he's going to let me go, he yanks me into his arms. My face is crushed in the clean front of his shirt that smells like the old-fashioned starch my gram uses when she irons. There's no closer to get than how close we already are, but it's like I want to burrow into him. "You think that doesn't kill me?" he grinds out, one tortured word at a time.

"Why?" I wrap my arms around his body and ball my hands in the fabric at the back of his shirt, tugging him tighter, closer.

"Because if you need me, I actually got a chance. I got the slimmest chance you might not leave." He kisses me, just at my temple. "But you don't need me. You don't need anyone. The only chance I'd have to keep you is gettin' you to *want* me. And I got a feeling I'm gonna fail at that pretty bad."

"Stop," I beg in a whisper. "I do want you. And I *do* need you." I pull him tighter, twist harder at his shirt and blink like a maniac to beat the tears back. "Not to save me. To hold me. To tell me it'll be okay, that *we'll* be okay. Because I don't always know anymore."

He pulls back just enough so his eyes can meet mine. "We're gonna be okay, you and me. We're fighters."

I laugh around a wet hiccup. "Okay. I guess we might as well keep fighting then, since it's what we do best. But maybe we should stop fighting each other? It would make a lot more sense if we were on the same team."

"We're good at that." We both laugh, first quietly, then so hysterically, people walking past give us a wide berth as they head into the restaurant. We clutch each other and scream with laughter until our sides ache and we're gasping. "You still wanna go in?" he asks once we calm down. "We don't have to."

I stand up, press my hands on his now-wrinkled shirtfront,

adjust his collar, and smooth his hair back into place. "You look handsome."

"Thank ya." He blushes.

He's so beautiful. And warm and funny. He's also the only person I've ever been so afraid to love and so afraid to lose at the same time.

"You got all dressed up, and I promised you a date. Let's go." I push back all the crazy feelings running unleashed through me and tug his hand. We walk through the foyer and peer nervously into the dining area, which is romantically dim. The zen music adds to the mellow, adult ambiance I try to pretend I'm used to.

Doyle follows stiffly as a hostess leads us to a cozy corner table draped in heavy white linens. He opens the menu and says, "I don't think I've ever even noticed this place drivin' by here."

"It's kind of unexpected, right?" I glance around. "Mom told me she and her coworkers come here for dinner sometimes, but I didn't expect it to be so..." *Adult? Intimidating?* "Nice."

It's a little out of our league, I guess, but we're old pros at doing things that make us uncomfortable. The waitress is friendly, and Doyle looks super impressed when I ask for her recommendation. We wind up getting Kobe beef appetizers, pad thai, and sea scallops with basil sauce.

"This place is real nice." Doyle makes an extra effort to sit up very straight and keep his elbows off the table.

"Hey." He gives me a startled look. I smile and his face lights up. "Relax," I whisper. "It's just a restaurant."

"I guess I'm jest used to the kinda places where I can order through the window and eat in my truck."

"Doyle, Savannah has some of the country's most amazing restaurants. It's insane you haven't gone to more of them."

"You musta gone to some fancy places in New York. With your ex." He bats his lashes and tries pass it off as an innocent observation.

Right. Except I didn't just fall off the turnip cart, as my grandmother would say.

"Not exactly. We hung out all the time and did fun things when we were first dating, but the longer we were together, the more he wanted to party. And that's not exactly my scene." Before the night devolves into me reminiscing about everything that went wrong with my ex, I switch gears. "But Ollie and me? We had a column in our school paper called 'Besties' Best Bites in Brooklyn.' We'd pick some random food—cupcakes, spring rolls, hot dogs, *bizcocho dominicano*—and we'd spend the week hunting down the best places and rating them together. Then Ollie made our reviews into YouTube videos, and we became these minor celebrities." I wink at him. "I don't wanna brag, but if you're ever in Brooklyn, drop my name at a couple bagel shops or bakeries and you'll probably wind up with free food."

"She sounds real cool, your friend Ollie." Doyle starts to say something else, but stalls when the waitress drops off our appetizers—which are so mouthwatering, I wish Ollie was here to rate them with me. They'd earn five glitter-polish thumbs-up, no question.

"She *is* really cool," I say after we've each had a few bites. "It would be amazing if…if you two could meet."

The second I say my private wish out loud, I'm covered in goose bumps up and down my arms and over my neck.

"Meet?" Doyle stares at his plate. "Like me come to visit? New York?"

"Doesn't have to be New York." I poke his foot with mine

under the table, then wiggle out of my heel and draw my bare toes down his calf, shocked at how quickly a friendly poke is turning into full-blown footsie. His cool eyes burn with a fire that's as exciting as it is unnerving. I yank my foot back. "I think she's going to college in Ohio. If she does, I'll go see her on winter break from college. If I drive, company would be rad."

Ugh, it's shameless baiting but, as usual, I can't help myself.

"Winter break. From college." He rolls the words on his tongue, and I realize the whole thing—snow, cold, winter, college—is an alien world compared to the reality of our senior year in Georgia's blazing subtropical version of spring.

"Yeah." Our unspoken future yawns wide-open between us. I've been so focused on living in the moment—*surviving* in the moment actually—that I don't broach the future much. But, whether either one of us is ready or not, it's barreling at us full steam, and no amount of ignoring it can change that fact. "Both sets of our grandparents set up funds for my brother and me when we were babies that they put some money into every month, plus our parents are professors, so we have some ins." I cringe a little announcing this to Doyle. I have to imagine that, with raising four grandsons, his grandparents don't have a trust set up for him. "So. Have you given college any more thought?"

"Actually I got some letters from the schools on the list you gave me. Some calls. After the night those assholes lit the cross in your yard and the story kinda blew up, must've put me on their radars." He runs his hand through his hair. "A school in Connecticut. One in New Jersey. They wanted to talk about scholarships, mebbe. One asked about me joinin' their student equity club. They both have solid ag programs. I Googled 'em," he admits with this adorable sheepishness.

"Doyle, that's incredible. Congratulations! New Jersey? Connecticut?" I swallow hard. Neither one is New York, but they're both a short train ride. Or a drive.

Doyle Rahn on my home turf.

I wish we'd done a better job navigating all the tough stuff over these past months, so that I could be mildly confident about a future that involves me and Doyle—together. But, damn, we've messed everything up six ways till Sunday, and I'm not sure we'll be able to stop screwing up in the long run, if we stay together.

Who would Doyle be outside Georgia? Would he be as different a version of himself as the version of me is outside Brooklyn? We've both been so defined by where we grew up, our communities, the people who we love and don't want to leave.

The fact is, my geographical transplant changed me, but it also made me more eager than ever to get back to what I know, the place where I belong. At least for now.

So what's the use bothering to get excited about the possibility of having Doyle close to me, if there's a good chance he'd wind up as homesick as I've been?

"It's probably stupid." He runs his palms up and down the stiff denim of his jeans.

"No, it isn't." But I don't sound sure, even to myself. "You won't know unless you try. Plus it's not like this place will ever go away. No matter how much I may want it to," I joke.

His smile is stilted. "Has it been that bad?"

My throat goes tight. I shake my head hard. "No. That was a bad joke. It's been one of the best things I ever hated doing, actually."

I rub the back of his calf, and he reaches down, sets my foot in his lap and slides my shoe off again. Under the white linen, he runs his thumbs along my arch, and I sit up straight, shocked at how good it feels.

"Stop," I whisper.

"Are you sure?" he asks, his voice normal volume, like he's not touching me in a way that's perfectly innocent, but feels so freaking amazing.

"Don't stop yet," I decide, melting against his touch. "But you'll have to when dinner comes."

"We can pick up later." He keeps rubbing, and I clamp my bottom lip between my teeth to stop myself from moaning.

"Don't do that." He finally drops his voice.

"What?" I ask at normal volume.

"Bite that lip." His thumb slides over my arch with slow, sweet pressure. "You have no idea how beautiful you are, Nes."

It's not even the words so much as the *way* he says them, like he's in a little bit of pain.

There's a shift in the air, a spark that reignites flames I was sure were stomped dead. Whatever Doyle and I have been fanning bursts back to fiery life. And in the midst of this transformative relationship magic, life plods on like it always does. The food comes. He lets go of my foot, but keeps it in his lap. I press it up and down his thigh every now and then just to watch his face contort.

I'm sure everything tastes great, amazing, even, but my memory gets foggy. We talk. I have no clue about what. I try to grab the bill, but my mind is so wrapped up in his smile, he beats me to it. I argue with him, but not too much.

He's teaching me when to hold on and when to let go. Not always the easiest lesson for me.

After dinner, I drive him to a place my brother's friend, who lives in Savannah, recommended for great dancing. Which

I'm picky about because I've been dancing since before I could walk.

My parents used to dance in the living room on Friday and Saturday nights, putting on La Banda Gorda CDs and teaching Jasper and me to dance merengue, teaching us to focus on the feel of the music while we balanced with our little feet on their toes and followed the back and forth of their feet and the sway of their hips. My brother and I even competed locally until he got old enough to put his foot down about the gaudy sequined costumes and dancing to sexy Latin music *with his little sister.*

My friends and I went dancing all the time in the city, and Ollie and I used to make up our own intricate steps on the polished concrete floor of her living room. Lincoln said I never looked hotter than when I was dancing, especially if I sang along with the songs in loud, off-key Spanish.

I don't need to stoke the fire Doyle and I are building, but I don't want to play it safe again. And I want to be a little more me, a little more of that brave, crazy girl I feel like I left behind in Brooklyn.

The club is crushingly full and the music is ear-ringingly loud. I recognize the Oro Solido song filling the room. My grandmother has a soft spot for them because they're New York–based, local guys. The memories of all of us dancing at their concerts, my grandmother's feet flying along with the steps, her head tilted back as she laughed, make homesickness grip hard at my throat.

"I know you can dance," I yell over the beat that already has my hips rolling. "But do you think you can handle *this*?"

Doyle's watches with intense focus, taking in the frenetic foot movements and the slow turns, the joined hands and pressed bodies. After watching one song's worth of dancing, he grabs hold of my hand and drags me onto the floor.

He doesn't get every step just right. We have a few offbeat turns, a couple of false starts, but he picks it up fast. What he lacks in technique he makes up for in enthusiasm and a natural grace that's impressive.

Whatever disconnect has been tearing us apart the last few months, it's bridged right here on the dance floor. He pulls me close, my butt planted against his hips. I circle my arm back around his neck as our hips and legs move in perfect sync, and I pause to catch my breath when he draws the back of his fingers down my arm, taking my hand and twirling me again and again until I'm dizzy from laughter and out of breath.

We dance until we're covered in sweat, until my feet scream, and as we dance, he accepts less and less space between us. The rest of the dancers, the room, the music—everything—fades away and it's just the rhythm that's as natural as my heartbeat and the touch of his hands on my body.

When there's a break between songs, he tucks a stray piece of hair behind my ear, smiling that contagious smile again, and looking like he wants to ask me something. I lean close, not sure what I hope he'll ask—

"You want something to drink?" he blurts out.

The bubbles of excitement exploding through me fizz out.

I have a feeling it's not what he wanted to say, but I go with it. Plus I'm thirsty. "Sure. The water here is probably twelve dollars a bottle," I warn, reaching into the tiny pocket in my skirt where I stashed some cash.

"Dontcha dare." He puts his hand over mine and leans close. "Let me be a gentleman tonight—to make up for being such a jerk the last few weeks."

"You weren't," I object, but he moves in and brushes his lips, salty with sweat, over mine. It stops me from dissecting the last few weeks of our relationship in the middle of the dance floor, which was probably his goal.

The second he's out of sight, I feel someone sidle up next to me. A tall guy, muscled, handsome, and I'd guess in his early twenties.

His smile is so wide and bright, I can barely look straight at him. "I been watching you all night."

I have no idea how to answer this, so instead, I look over his shoulder and hope I'll see Doyle. The crush around the bar is several bodies deep, so that's pretty assuredly not happening.

"You're not from here, are you?" His eyes rake up and down my body. "The way you move? You've *got* to be Dominican."

"I am." The words fumble out. "How did you know? I mean, no one ever guesses right."

"Dominican women are the most beautiful women in the world, so you gotta be Dominican." He edges into my personal space with an ease that's disarming. The scent of his expensive cologne is so overpowering, it makes me nauseous. "Plus no female dances merengues the way you just did unless they have Dominican blood in their veins. *Dígame usted habla español.*"

"*Sí.*" I can't resist speaking Spanish to him, but I pull back. "*Estoy aquí con alguien.*" I point to Doyle, whose reddish-blond head is finally visible.

"*¿Quiere decir que el vaquero?*" He says it mockingly, dismissing Doyle out of hand, confident he's got me snared, I guess because we share some random cultural bond.

"He's not a cowboy." My voice instantly ices over. "He's my date. And I'm going to dance with him now. Nice meeting you."

"*Búscame cuando estés lista para un verdadero hombre,*" he taunts just as Doyle steps next to me.

Doyle looks from me to the guy, his expression hard and twisted.

"*Él es mucho mas hombre de lo que tú quisieras ser,*" I yell when the guy snorts and starts to walk away.

A few people turn around, nosy for the drama, and his handsome face goes dark. "*Puta.*" He spits the word out, and I feel the hot burn of shame roll over my face and neck.

"What did that asshole say to you?" Doyle demands. He drops the water bottles and starts stalking after the guy so quickly, I barely have time to yank him back.

"Stop. So not worth it. He's just an arrogant jerk who didn't like getting turned down." I clutch at his arm. "Seriously, no fighting."

"I can take him," Doyle insists.

I know size-wise Doyle would be sorely out of his depth, but it's not size that makes Doyle the fighter he is. That said, I'm not ready to see the guy I love getting violent again. I've seen enough hate, anger, pain, and suffering in the last few weeks to last me a lifetime.

"I never said you couldn't. But you don't need to. I'm actually pretty tired." I bend down to pick up the water bottles. "You know what I wanna do right now? I wanna drive to the beach and drink twenty-five dollars' worth of bottled water. You in?"

Doyle's pretty eyes are like sights zeroed in on this guy. His back is up, his shoulders stiff, but breath by breath, he relaxes and focuses on me like he's coming through some thick fog. "Yeah. Okay. That sounds good."

We leave the club, find our way to the car without further incident, and head for the beach. Doyle knows a stretch that's not crawling with tourists and navigates me to it. We eventually pull up at a huge house.

Make that a mansion. A massive, gated one.

"Uh, this is someone's private place." I glance around nervously, waiting for some hired-gun security guard to drive us off.

"My family does the landscapin' for all the Youngblood homes and businesses. I have insider knowledge that they're all in Europe right now. Croatia or Hungary or something." He raises his eyebrows and elbows his door open. "C'mon, scaredy-cat."

"I'm not a scaredy-cat." Despite my brushes with the school administration and law down here, I've managed to keep a squeaky-clean criminal record, and I'm not overly anxious to be caught trespassing.

Especially here, in this very ritzy, probably very *white* neighborhood.

Especially looking so very *Dominican* like I do tonight.

But Doyle is a natural-born leader, and I can't help but follow his lead. He leaves his boots and socks scattered on the cobblestoned driveway and cuffs his jeans high before he heads into the beachfront sand, waving his hand for me to follow. I kick off my heels and make a second set of prints just behind his.

"Gorgeous, ain't it?" He breathes the salty air in deep and wraps an arm around my shoulders.

The waves are calm tonight, their hiss and crash a purr that lulls us. The air hangs heavy, wet with cool water. My toes sink into the damp sand and maneuver through a million grains to find his.

I lean my head on his chest and hear his heart with one ear and the ocean with the other. I'm trapped between infinities.

"It's the same ocean you'd see in Connecticut. Or New Jersey." I nuzzle against him, waiting a few overlong seconds before I ask the question I don't know that I want to hear the answer to. "Does any part of you want to leave this?"

"Every part of me has thought about it every day since the first day I met you." His quiet words are almost lost in the crash of the waves. He switches gears fast, on purpose. To avoid. "You ever play I Never?"

"I think I have. Only we called it Never Have I Ever." I look at him curiously. "Why?"

"I think we should play it."

"I need to drive home. I'm not drinking."

"Not with alcohol." The up-tip of his lips manages to do so many things—dare me, tempt me, draw me in.

"So if you don't drink…?"

"You strip." He loosens two buttons on his shirt.

I whip my head left and right, scouring the beach for elderly strollers, families collecting shells, or optimistic surfers, but it's completely deserted.

"The same family owns the houses on either side. I promise, no one's gonna see."

"Are you sure?" Instead of answering directly, he starts a game I'm not sure either one of us is ready to play.

"I never got a naked pic of anyone I dated. Not for lack of trying," he adds with a twisted smile.

I blush, remembering the way I went light-headed when I got an unasked for—but much appreciated—texted picture from Lincoln, his toned body and dark skin so incredibly gorgeous my hand shook just from holding the phone. "Can I go put my shoes back on before we start stripping?"

One eyebrow elevates slowly. "Really?"

I'm not sure if he's shocked that I want to rewind and put on more clothing or that I'm agreeing to take something off at all.

I take off my bangles and lay them in the sand instead of

answering him or getting my shoes. "I never…" I pause and try to think about how to get Doyle Rahn out of his clothes. "I never…saw the Pacific."

"Cheater." He sheds his shirt without a second's hesitation. "You already knew I went to Hawaii."

"I forgot," I lie. Badly. I do make an effort not to stare at the lean, hard muscles of his body, the skin still faintly yellow around his ribs from the pummeling his father gave him.

"I never had a pet."

I don't make a move, and when he gives me a look that begs for an explanation, I oblige.

"Me neither. Apartment living. Also, my dad's allergic to dogs and my mom said keeping a litter box in a thousand square feet of apartment would kill her."

"My granddaddy's got coonhounds, but they ain't pets. They're huntin' dogs, and he keeps them outdoors in a barn on our far property. We're forbidden to interfere with their trainin'. They only listen to grandaddy anyway. When I'm on my own, I think I'll get myself a dog. A *pet* dog."

"A boy and his dog." I move my hand close to his and link our pinkies. "I like that plan."

"Your turn." He pulls my hand up to his lips and kisses the place where my palm meets my wrist.

I tell him I've never ridden a dirt bike.

The whine of his zipper pulling down makes the hairs on the back of my neck stand at attention.

He tells me he's never had braces, and I tug my top off, muttering, "Cheater." It was Doyle who unpacked the picture of Ollie and me at our eighth-grade dance, braced faces glowing with excitement.

I tell him I've never seen a *Godfather* movie, but he keeps his boxers on and tells me he's only seen *Scarface* and that we should have a gangster movie marathon.

When he tells me he's never been on the receiving end of oral sex, I shimmy out of my skirt with my face on fire.

I wonder if he's been on the giving end.

I wonder if he wants to try it. With me.

I wonder if it would be as good as it was with Lincoln.

Or even better.

I bet it would be better. Everything else has been.

I'm down to my lacy black underwear and leopard-print bra. Doyle's navy boxer briefs hang low on his hips. Our clothes lay crumpled in a heap next to us, just beyond where we sit. The moon is covered with clouds, the waves caress the soft sand. He reaches out and drags his fingers along my thigh, down to my knee and back again, then pulls away.

"That last one wasn't gentlemanly. There's havin' a good time, then there's pushing it, and I oughta know better than to cross that line." His words are heavy with an apology I don't need him to make.

"I can't play this game anymore, Doyle."

"I understand." He runs his hand through his hair and nods.

"No, you don't." I want to cover myself, but at the same time, I want him to see me exposed and vulnerable and to *like* what he sees. I want him to want me the way I want him. "If we go any further, I'm not going to say stop. And I don't want you to do anything you don't want to do."

"I've never wanted anything the way I want you." His words make my body shake. He reaches out to touch me, but pulls his hand back and fists it in the sand. "I'm a coward, Nes. You're the only person who's ever seen the real me. I'm sick of keepin' my head down and not being brave enough to say what I want or do what I want…with who I want."

440

Now he does touch me, but his hands tremble. I circle his wrists and hold his hands away from my skin.

"I don't want this to be another one of your regrets."

"I don't wanna be some temporary distraction till you head home."

"I feel like I *am* home… I feel like I'm home when I'm with you." I close my eyes and wait for his mouth on mine because I can feel what he wants to do next like my brain is in his body.

As he's kissing me and my head spins and my heart pounds like it's willing to work overtime for this, he whispers, "The only thing I'll ever regret is all that wasted time when I coulda been with you but was too scared."

We say each other's names like we're laying claim, like we're granting our own wishes and sealing a fate we refuse to be careful about anymore.

But I trounce the magic.

"Wait!" I fling a sandy hand through my disheveled hair, then push it between us. "Wait. Not here. Last time, we got caught up."

"I swear, I won't be a dick like I was last time—"

"It's not like that." I stand, and sand rains off my skin. I curse myself for choosing the tight clothes. Not good mixed with sand. Not good at all. "We can drive back. We'll drive, and I want you to think. When we get to my house, you can come in with me or…"

How will I survive this drive now? This is insane. And tortuous.

And *necessary*.

So necessary.

No regrets this time.

THIRTY-THREE

The drive is silent—no punk, no small talk. Just this thing we both want hanging uncertainly between us.

When we pull into my driveway, Doyle clears his throat before he says, "So."

"You don't have to come in," I assure him.

"I want...you. I want this." He stares at his hands.

Instead of answering, I get out of the car and head to the house, fumbling my key in the lock. I walk down the hall to the sound of his truck pulling away. My heart slip-and-slides into my stomach, but the way he looked at his hands instead of me? I should have known.

I remove my makeup and start to take off my jewelry, trying to be happy that Doyle and I had such an amazing date instead of sad that I'm spending tonight alone, when I hear a knock on the window and jump. I throw it up and pull him in under the arms.

"Why didn't you use the door?" I laugh.

"Didn't some dumb hick tell you he'd fix your doorbell? Guess he never got around to it." He presses my hair back and just looks at me.

"I thought you left," I breathe, reaching out to touch his face, tug on his collar so he's close enough to kiss, like I'm proving to myself he's really there in front of me, flesh and bone, complicated and mine.

"Jest moved my truck up the driveway."

"So, do you plan on hanging here with me tonight?"

"Oh, I got lots of plans. I'm not sure it's such a good idea to follow through on 'em though." His Adam's apple jumps when he swallows. Both my hands reach up and grab his collar again, and, this time, I drag him close and kiss him.

It moves from sweet and cautious to full-on, five-alarm steamy so fast, it steals my breath away. We don't break the kiss as we walk back and bump into the edge of my bed. He relaxes, falling back on my mattress, which is finally set up on the bed frame.

"You put your bed up," he says into my mouth. "The pyramid of boxes is gone."

I kiss down his jaw and bite his neck gently. "Someone told me to stop being such a coward and make a decision. I took his advice."

"Damn. Sounds like a smart fella."

"Oh, *he* sure thinks so."

Before the banter can go any further, we get ensnared in more heated kisses that lead to more frantic touches. My fingers fly over the buttons on his shirt. Once I push it off his shoulders, I can't stop running my hands over his skin, hard with muscle, warm with his freckled tan, scarred from fights I've witnessed and beatings I don't even want to imagine. I feel like I know him better than I've ever known anyone, and, at the same time, like he's a mystery I could spend the rest of my life unraveling.

His fingers play at the hem of my top and, as he closes his

hand around the fabric and tugs up an inch, then another, his eyes lock on mine. "Are you sure?"

"Does a bear shit in the woods?"

I love the way he chuckles as he pulls the cotton over my head. We have a near catastrophe when it catches on my earring, and then the straps somehow wind up bound around my elbows.

"Sorry," he mutters, tugging hard on the fabric and locking my arms behind my back tighter. "This is getting kinkier than I meant it to."

We're both laughing into each other's necks as we awkwardly unknot my shirt, and then his laugh cuts short. "I know I said this before, but you're so damn beautiful, Nes."

I feel beautiful with his eyes on me. And bold, like I'm not scared of messing this up anymore. We've already fallen for each other, broken the rules, been stupidly separated by misunderstanding and stubbornness, and now we're back together, maybe temporarily and maybe with regrets in our future. But this is us, me and Doyle, flawed and vulnerable, exposed and willing to fight for this thing we feel, whatever it is.

Though I know the name for it. It's *love*.

Damn, that's scary.

And wonderful.

My fingers brush down to his waistband, and I pause. "Are *you* sure?"

"Does Howdy Doody have wooden balls?"

He's so perfectly deadpan, I roll on the mattress laughing. "Who the hell is Howdy Doody?" I demand.

"Aw, you know, that little wooden puppet guy? My granddad used to watch him. You never heard of Howdy Doody?" he asks, one eyebrow raised like he doesn't believe me.

I shake my head and shrug. "I guess Brooklyn is just missing out when it comes to puppet exposure."

"It's a cryin' shame how you don't know about ole Howdy. Maybe Granddad will get out his tapes for ya."

"All this romantic talk! I can't take it." I bite my bottom lip solely to make his eyes go wide, then undo his pants. We both go still and silent. "Doyle?"

"Nes?"

"It'll be okay, right?" I brush my fingers over his face. "You and me? We'll be okay?"

Doyle Rahn prides himself on being honest, but I love the way he lies.

"Jest fine." He takes my hand and weaves his fingers through mine. "You and me are gonna be okay."

And then we don't talk for a long time. The few scraps of clothes that were keeping us from being completely naked get kicked off the mattress, and we touch like we're making up for all the weeks of avoiding touching we've just endured. Every single place his fingers brush is like another tripped lever pushing me closer to him until there's no space between us.

I bury my face in the pillows and shudder at the way he kisses places no one else has, taking his sweet time. And I make sure the next time he plays I Never, he'll take off his clothes and think about me and the way I made him bunch the sheets in his fists.

When I fumble for the condom and put it on him, he whispers, "I'm so sorry, Nes. I gotta feelin' this is gonna be the best three seconds of my life."

"Well, you'll just have to do better the second time."

Our laughs spiral into moans, and it keeps cycling like that—sex and sleep, sleep and laughs, laughs and kisses, kisses and moans—until the rosy light of dawn fills my room. Doyle

Rahn slides out of bed and pulls his jeans over his hips and his boots over his feet in the pastel light of early morning.

He kisses me like a promise before he slips out my window, even though he could've walked out the door, leaving me lying in the perfect, heavy contentment of the golden morning that follows a night full of risks taken and love finally seized, no regrets.

THIRTY-FOUR

In the midst of feeling all twitterpated and being in love and not caring who knows it, Doyle and I return to the bleach-and-fry-oil-scented halls of Ebenezer High and try to ignore the chaos. But it's like Romeo and Juliet trying to sneak back into Verona and just gaze into each other's eyes despite the civil unrest.

Bright and early Monday morning, we're all goose-stepped into the auditorium where Principal Armstrong and Officer Tomlin wait. Doyle squeezes my hand, and both our palms are sweaty. The cocoon of sweet, incredible love we've been wrapped in all weekend starts to unravel and let real life in.

"Ladies and gentlemen of Ebenezer High, I wish I didn't have to call you in this morning," Principal Armstrong begins grimly.

The speech doesn't improve from there.

Khalil is going to be okay, but his parents are pressing for an investigation, and we're all expected to be cooperative and come forward with any information we might have. There are flutters of nervous chatter at this announcement, but it quiets down at the next item.

"The race for Rose King and Queen was a *privilege* extended to students who could show goodwill for the community and strong character. A rash of harmful pranks culminated this weekend with a break-in at the school." He pauses as he scans the sea of our faces. "The office where we keep the ballots— as well as sensitive and private student information—was tampered with. It appears that only the ballot box was taken. I hate to punish everyone for what a few foolish students chose to do, but we are officially calling off the race. There will be no Rose Court at Ebenezer this year."

Saying the news is *not* well received is like saying the North's victory in the Civil War is all water under the bridge. But if the principal of your school tells you the punishment for your criminal behavior is that you can't enjoy your racist popularity contest, and you wanted to prove him wrong, you'd, I dunno, maybe *not erupt into a rioting mass of assholes.*

Alas, Ebenezer High hasn't established itself as a bastion of logic, and the screams, flying wads of balled-up paper, and nasty protest chants that follow this news don't exactly go far in convincing Armstrong he's made some awful judgment call.

In fact, no rational person would have blamed him if he announced his retirement, dropped the mic, and hightailed it out of this hellhole for good.

Officer Tomlin stalks the podium and announces that he will be happy to call for backup if we don't settle down. The crowd reduces itself to furious muttering and Armstrong continues.

"I expect you all to conduct yourself in a way that reflects well on your community, your family, your church, and this school. We are at absolute zero tolerance, folks. If you decide to involve yourself in *any* activity that harms another student or property, you will face suspension, expulsion, and possibly be denied the opportunity to walk in graduation. More serious than that, you will be turned over to the authorities, and your action may have legal consequences. I'm ashamed to say that I had to ask Officer Tomlin to be at the ready in case his police force is needed in the next few weeks."

Principal Armstrong leans on the podium, gray faced and sober. "I've been principal at this school for fifteen years, and I've never felt so let down by a body of students. But I'm a man who believes in redemption. We can start by getting to the bottom of what happened with Khalil Scott. I hope we can use these last few weeks of the school year to turn ourselves around and learn from our mistakes. I believe you can, I truly do. You are dismissed."

His shaky, uncertain words hang in the air as we gather our bags. There are still a few barbaric loudmouths in the crowd, but most of the students have the decency to look at least marginally ashamed.

"Heavy." Doyle uses his shoulder to wedge a path through the crowds as he holds my hand.

"It's gotten so out of—"

Before I can finish, Doyle is jostled hard from behind, sending him staggering to his knees and his books flying. I have to jump back to avoid falling on top of him. A group of big guys, football players, Confederate flag handkerchiefs dangling from their back pockets, snicker.

Ansley stands to the side, her smile unsure. It's clear we're in some murky moral territory if Ebenezer's Queen Mean Girl is uncomfortable with the level of bullying.

"Mudshark."

"Jungle fever."

"Coon lover."

There's a mixed reaction to the knife slice of those low,

hateful words—gasps, shocked silence, furious resignation. The rubbernecks file past like zombies as the goons start to move on.

"That's enough!" Ansley cries, tugging at one of the guys' jerseys. He throws his arms back and his chest out, laughing when Doyle scrambles to his feet.

"Coward," Doyle snarls.

"Clint, he's not even worth it." Ansley tries to say it with sass, but her voice snags when she catches Doyle staring at her, pure disgust on his face.

They shuffle away, Ansley with her bowed shoulders buckled under Clint's beefy arm.

I bend down to gather Doyle's books and he kneels to help me. "Mudshark?" I ask quietly, sticking his ag report back into its glossy binder.

"Douche bags can't even use a racial slur right," he snarls. When I raise my eyebrows, he grinds out, "*Mudshark* is slang for a white girl who dates black guys."

"Ah." I swallow back the lump in my throat. "Sorry."

"What are you sorry for? That they aren't even smart enough to rag on me with an accurate slur?" His smile is sad around the joking words. "Weird what you can ignore when it ain't directly affecting you."

We zip up his bag and lace our fingers together. "I hear you."

We ignore the hostile looks and nasty words in the halls. When we get to my classroom, Doyle's face is sharp with worry.

"People here are serious about the Rose Court, huh? It's gotten way uglier since Armstrong took it away."

"Ignore 'em," he commands, but I have a feeling he's saying it as much to himself as to me. "Couple weeks, we graduate and leave this all behind."

I pull a long breath in and hold it for a few hopeful seconds. "'Leave this all behind' like leave high school? Or..." I don't dare say it out loud.

His easy shrug is wide-open with possibility. "Or maybe I got a lot of thinkin' to do."

He bends down to kiss me, in the open, and that kiss leaves me too dazed to press him for clarification. I listen to him whistle as he walks away and feel brave enough to stare down the snide looks a few of Ansley's cohorts send me from their place at the main lockers.

He's thinking. If that means for Doyle what it usually means for me, he won't stop until he figures it out. I just hope his conclusion involves the two of us close enough for...

For whatever we want.

THIRTY-FIVE

As the lazy, numbered final weeks of school fly by, the graduating class comes to a shaky resolution. It isn't exactly like we join arms and sing "We Shall Overcome." More like the students of Ebenezer call an uneasy truce to keep ourselves from getting kicked out or arrested—and the administration figures out something important: control has to do with leverage. For years they'd been denying themselves a powerful tool capable of exerting massive amounts of control over horny, sentimental high school students.

Principal Armstrong realized that he who controls prom controls the actions of all students leading up to prom. It's obvious he regrets having to deal with prom chaos when he has no way to tighten the reins this year.

Tensions loosen a few days after the assembly, when a guy named Walter Jardin comes forward and claims sole credit for using a blowtorch stolen from his shop class to heat up the handle of Doyle's truck. He confesses it was a prank gone wrong, and he feels guilty for causing harm, especially to Khalil.

"Do you know Walter Jardin? Have you ever argued with

him or anything?" I grill Doyle all through lunch on the day Walter's taken out of the school in cuffs.

"Never said boo to the guy." Doyle sets his tray down.

"Never said boo to who?" asks Alonzo, chugging his third carton of milk. "Bulking up," he tells me as I watch, fascinated, expecting him to vomit from lactose overload at any second. "I need to build muscle mass. I got basketball camp for Loyola this summer."

"Congrats." I hold up my milk to toast and he says, "You drinking that?" I shake my head and pass it over so Alonzo can gain bulk or whatever.

"Walter Jardin got expelled and arrested for screwing with my truck and putting Khalil in the hospital," Doyle says as he wolfs down a ham sandwich. "He confessed and all that, but somethin' don't sit right."

"No doubt it had to do with your ex." When Alonzo mentions Ansley, Khabria and Bo scoot closer to us.

Khabria has been hot and cold to me since the day we watched Ansley freak out and accuse us of messing with her Jeep. I think she still assumes I had something to do with it, and since no one came forward, it's not likely she's going to change her mind.

On the other hand, I was there to help when Khalil got hurt, and I was the one who proposed opening alternaprom to sophomores the other day, just before she went to visit him in the hospital. She came to find me and let me know the news perked him up.

"Didn't that crackhead Walter Jardin fess up?" Khabria demands, tossing a dozen shiny braids behind one shoulder. "He and Ansley don't exactly run in the same circles."

"I don't think she's planning to take the dude to prom. I think it's weird Walter gave it up when there wasn't any evidence linking him. It's also pretty damn suspicious he got Ansley's granddaddy's law firm to represent him." Alonzo salutes Bo with his carton of milk, and I realize Bo has the same odd milk-chugging thing going on.

"How do you know all this?" Khabria demands.

"My cousin booked him." He holds up his phone. "He texted me, told me to keep my head down and stay out of trouble. We sure as hell can't afford to call Strickland Law Firm if something goes down. Plus my cousin is a dick about his reputation. He wants to be the youngest chief in the county or some crap."

"So that's it?" Khabria fumes, her fingers biting into the side of the table. "My baby brother is spending the end of his sophomore year bandaged and in pain, not able to play football, and they just take Walter's word for it and don't look into it any further?"

"He confessed, K. What do you expect them to do?" Alonzo chucks his milk cartons across the table and into the trash cans until a monitor calls for him to cut it out.

"I just expect… I guess I expect things to change. To really change. Is that too much to ask?" Her eyes fill up, and she lets Bo put an arm around her.

We're all silent in the face of her tears. It's strange to see someone as strong as Khabria lose it. Finally, Doyle breaks the silence.

"They might never change. But we did. And that's enough."

He takes my hand under the table, and I've never been prouder of him.

With Walter Jardin scapegoated for all the evils of Ebenezer, Principal Armstrong calls a second assembly, this one peppier than the first. He says he's proud of all of us, especially those "brave enough" to come forward with the information that allowed them to ensure justice was served.

I can hear Khabria's snort of disdain from across the auditorium.

When I crane my neck, I catch sight of Ansley's profile. She stares ahead, tight-lipped, eyes wide, no emotion on her face.

"Now that this has all settled, I'd like to discuss an issue the board members have been pondering for some years. We've decided that we have enough of an overflow of funds to offer a school-funded prom at Ebenezer High next school year. It will accommodate the entire junior and senior class. This will be the last year independently funded proms will be needed in our district." My jaw drops as Armstrong puffs out his chest like this was some wise idea he and "the board" came up with.

Like he didn't completely blow off Doyle and me when we proposed *exactly this idea*.

"Thank you all for giving me renewed faith in this fine school and its students. Y'all should be proud of yourselves."

I think that last part is a bit of a stretch, but this assembly ends in the Ebenezer Rebel chant instead of a near riot, so what do I know?

"What about the Rose Court? What about people who still want a segregated prom?" I ask, but Doyle takes the opportunity the happy chaos gives us and kisses me instead of answering.

When things calm down and people start to funnel out of the auditorium, he grins at me and says, "That's for them to figure out. We did it, Nes. We changed a tradition old as dirt at Ebenezer."

"They're only doing it so they have control of things in case it all goes to hell next year." I roll my eyes.

"Don't matter why." Doyle ignores my attempts at pessimism. "It's change. I never thought it'd be possible for this to happen. Now that it did, it's like there's a whole world of possibility. *Anything* can happen."

Doyle's always been pretty happy, but he's crossed into Pollyanna territory now.

"Right," I agree reluctantly.

A worry starts to gnaw away at my guts. I'm glad things are changing. Or I should be.

The truth is, selfishly, I'd wanted them to stay stagnant. Because now there's hope there will be bigger changes at Ebenezer, which may lead to opportunities for change across the community, and Doyle may want to stay here for good and be part of all that. Which would be a noble and awesome thing.

Or, at least an empathetic, big-hearted girlfriend would think so. A selfish, ornery wench like myself? No such warm fuzzies.

THIRTY-SIX

We make it to prom because we all stay happily distracted by the minor dramas of our own lives like the young narcissists we are. People debate the pros and cons of next year's school-funded prom and start to look to the alternaprom as a prototype for Ebenezer's future. We never asked about the dates they planned to hold the other proms, but it just so happens that alternaprom will fall on a totally separate weekend from both the black and the white prom. Sheer curiosity drives last-minute bid sales through the roof, and our little misfit prom starts to look like...well, pretty much like any normal, all-American high school prom.

That was always the point, but the rebel in me can't help but feel a tiny bit disappointed.

Though not everyone wants to party like it's the twenty-first century in the free and lawful United States of America. There is a vocal faction, led by a certain throne-crazed, plastic idiot, who would probably love it if we could roll back to the days of Scarlett O'Hara. Ansley and her tribe of clones vow to treasure the last year of their purist, segregated dance. I thought, after all the torture she put me through the last few months, that I'd want some kind of revenge, but I guess I really have experienced some personal growth despite my best efforts to stay a curmudgeon at heart.

She's in the hallway before school, handing out red-glittered, rose-shaped invitations, and, when she sees me, she whispers to some of her cronies.

"Ignore her." Doyle is back to his appear-out-of-nowhere hallway magic, and, this time around, I treat it like the incredible trick it is.

I slide my arm around his waist—filled out since he taught my mother his grandmother's biscuit recipe and we started perfecting batches after school—and kiss his neck, breaking my own PDA rule.

"Ansley doesn't bother me. Actually, I feel sorry for her."

His laugh borders on hysterical. "She'd pop a vessel if she heard that."

"Look at her bunch of backbiting friends." I nod to the table of girls who've started to give Ansley the side-eye as our tenure at Ebenezer winds to an end and they realize the very hard limits of her reach. "I mean, she works double time to keep them in line. She's gotta know they're all talking crap on each other and trying to win their own Rose Queen run or whatever."

"Yeah. It's like she really is Marie Antoinette—don't know who's on her side 'cause they wanna piece of what she's got and who genuinely likes her. Must suck, always watchin' your back."

"And she went from dating you to dating that Neanderthal, Clint. Talk about trading down."

Doyle laughs, but Clint is the main reason I can't hold a grudge against Ansley. Yes, she's awful. And shallow. But she got to date Doyle Rahn—gorgeous, funny, sexy, smart, romantic Doyle Rahn—and she lost him. And now she has brutish, arrogant, chauvinistic Clint, whose idea of a joke is knocking a person's books out of his hands.

"I think she's with a guy she deserves," Doyle says.

We both look at the table as Clint walks up, grabs one of the JV baseball players who was asking about voting, and crushes him in a headlock.

"Clint, cut it out!" Ansley cries, swatting at his arm and looking around for help. None of her cronies makes a move.

"I can't stand Ansley, but *no one* deserves to be with that dude."

I feel Doyle head over before I see him take his first step. By the time he's at the table, the kid in the headlock is turning a weird shade of purple.

"Hey! Knock it off." Doyle grabs Clint's arm and tugs. The surprise contact breaks Clint's hold on the kid, who squeaks out a hoarse thank-you and runs for his life.

"What the hell, Rahn? What I do ain't your business." Clint is taller than Doyle, broader shouldered with bigger muscles and a meanness that makes me nervous. There's no doubt in my mind he'd fight dirty if it came down to it. "Butt the hell out."

"It's my business if some jerkoff thinks he can pick on people who can't defend themselves. Why dontcha try to put *me* in a headlock."

"Step down, Rahn. I don't care if you are Ebenezer's hero. I'll take your ass down a peg." Clint lunges and Doyle steps forward.

"Stop," Ansley pleads, her eyes flat and dull, like she's seen some version of this before. From the tired way she begs, I deduce this isn't the first time Clint's macho act led to a brawl. "Please, just stop."

Doyle looks Ansley right in the eyes around Clint's beefy shoulder. "You pulled some crazy stunts this past year, Ansley Strickland. But dating this douche takes the cake. You deserve a hell of a lot better." He turns on his heel and comes back to me. Any leftover anger I was holding on to where Ansley was concerned officially melts away. I can tell from the look on her face when Doyle walks away that she knows exactly what she lost.

Even some otherwise rational people are opting to go to the independent proms "for old times' sake." The fact that this is the last year any independent proms will run gives them this added false sanctity on top of the all the usual, I'll-miss-these-people-I've-barely-been-able-to-stomach-for-the-last-four-years senior nostalgia.

I feel a little like I'm outside an aquarium looking at the exotic life floating around. I have intense feelings for my classmates—good and bad—but I've known them for only a few months. This has been a flash temporary journey to purgatory for me. I arrived in a foreign world like Alice or Dorothy, and I'm waking up from the experience changed in ways no one I love can truly understand. Soon, my Ebenezer friends and enemies will be part of a trippy blip in time—all except Doyle.

I hope.

Mom has been worried about everything lately, scouring the news for racist stories and investigating all the realities of race breakdown here—things she probably should have done when she was looking for a new place to move, except she was too brain addled from her affair gone sour. I've been doing my best to reassure, shield, or ignore her. Whichever is easiest.

When she gets particularly shrill over race-based graduation rates in our area, I try a desperate new tactic: distraction.

"I need a dress for prom!"

She was just comparing percentages across gender lines, but her eyes go wide and she gets this girly glow. "Prom dress shopping?" she squeals.

I try hard not to wince. "Yeah. I mean, I need a fancy dress. Do you…want to go?"

I take the squeals as a *yes*, and, even though I sigh a little, I'm happy to go with her. If she's keeping her current job, she'll be in Georgia when I move into my dorm this fall. After that, I'll be at college full-time, except around some holidays, so this is kind of…the end.

And now, like my dopey classmates, I'm looking back on everything and getting sentimental.

And a little regretful. Mom messed up, yes. But I refused to accept the fact that my mother is a human being who is going to make mistakes, and that is something *I* regret. I shouldn't have been so hard on her, especially when we were here with only each other to lean on. If shopping for a big, poofy dress helps erase some of the crappiness of the last few months, I'm game.

Mom is so into dress shopping, she decides we both need to play hooky.

"Can you afford to miss school on Friday?" she asks with slightly crazed, shiny eyes.

"Um, we're reviewing codes for our final assessment in computers—"

She waves her hand. "Great! You can miss that, right?"

You'd think a professor would value education over dress shopping, but professor is only one title my mother goes by. Obsessed Clothes Horse and *Vogue* Enthusiast is just as accurate.

Friday morning we're buzzing along in her Audi, listening to Lilith Fair mixes and sipping on Dunkin' Donuts cappuccinos.

"So, tell me, how serious are things with Doyle?"

I like that the last vestiges of Nervous Mom have evaporated.

"I like him, but he likes it here enough that he might stick around. I mean, this is his home, and he's helped make some amazing changes. His family and friends are here. And I definitely have no plans to stay." I take a long sip of my drink. "Place is important. Right?"

Mom lets out a long sigh. "You know, baby, I don't have a good answer for that one. Once upon a time, I would have said it all needed to be negotiated and worked out. Now?" She gives me a sidelong glance and winks. "Sorry. I was dwelling on my past. The answer is *yes*—for you, at this point in your life, you need to be where you can spread your wings. What's it down to? Did your father completely shoot down the idea of a year in Paris?"

"Jasper did, actually. He said he wasn't putting up with me being a Euro bum and messing up their nice neat life. And Dad is sticking to his 'no college, no free rent' rule... He said I'm welcome there as long as I'm attending university, but not for a gap year. You know how they like to micromanage everything...including my life, dreams, goals. The usual."

My mother laughs over the sound of some old-school Tori Amos. "Jasper really is his father's son. I love that boy with all my heart, but he and your father are two uptight, hyperfocused peas in a pod, and they both drive me up the damn wall. Has he made peace with your decision to go to NYU, or did Jasper want to show you the differential on all the other schools he wants you to transfer to? I bet he has a program on his computer for it."

"I cut him off before he tried. I'm happy with my choice, and I'm not being swayed by Jasper or anyone else."

Mom smiles at me. "I'm happy too. And ready to start planning! We need to find out about housing options, roommates, packing logistics. I can drive up with you early, after you get back from visiting Ollie's grandparents but before my fall semester prep. We need to channel a little bit of the men in this family and get our organizational checklists in order."

I know she's right, but my present is so all-encompassing, my future seems like a distant speck. I think about that as Mom pulls up at some swanky dress shop all decorated in that understated way that quietly lets you know any single item in the place is going to cost more than a car payment or twelve.

"Mom, this is too fancy. We could just go to Macy's."

She rolls her eyes and clucks her tongue. "Aggie, please. You've had a rough few months. This is something I want to do for you. Humor me."

She is air-kissed by a gorgeous woman she knows by name. "Navya, this is my daughter, Agnes. And she's about to go to prom with this Southern guy, all manners and big, broad shoulders."

"Mom, that's so pervy," I whine. "Stop."

But Navya is loving every second. "Really? I can't resist the accent here!" I'd classify Navya's accent as a combination of Bollywood and London. She's polished and beautiful, and I feel like a troll standing next to her in my cutoffs and vintage Luscious Jackson tank top, a pair of tattered Chucks on my feet.

"Look at that skin. Like silk," Navya gushes, taking me by the hand and turning me back and forward. "Oh, she got your cheekbones, for sure. And the same gorgeous eyes." She smiles, and Mom doesn't tell her that my cheekbones are from my abuela.

I look into the mirror as Navya fusses over the five million dresses I'm about to put on, and I stare at my mother and I, side by side. There's no question that we have dozens of very obvious differences, but there's also a basic facial bone structure, the way we both stand with our right foot tapping and our left hip jutted out, our eyes. You'd have to focus to see what we share, but it's there, and I'm glad.

Because my mother is still the most beautiful woman in the world as far as I'm concerned.

Before I have time to get too sappy, I'm pushed into a dressing room where I strip to my skivvies and start pulling things on. I come out of the dressing room over and over, and it's like I'm not even there.

"Hmm. A little too Scarlett O'Hara in the opening scene. If we're going to give a nod to that time, let's find something more like what Rhett gives her to wear to Ashley's birthday," Mom says.

White off, maroon on.

"I love this, but it's too formal for such a young person," Navya says, clicking her tongue. "And it's overly rich for summer. We need a jewel tone to pop against that perfect skin. Darling, what cream do you use on your face?"

"Um, sometimes I use sunscreen." I watch Navya's eyes widen in horror as I close the changing room door and slip out of the maroon dress and into a navy one.

I try every color, fit, and style and am about to die of exhaustion when I find one on the bottom of the pile. I slip it on. It's low cut, empire waisted, with a softly flared bottom.

And it's lavender. The exact shade of Doyle's eyes.

I come out in it and Mom and Navya stop talking about the benefits of salt scrub exfoliators.

"Oh, sweetie," Mom gasps coming to adjust zippers and tug on bunched fabric.

"Lavender," Navya says, her voice approving. "It would not have been my first guess, but it's extremely flattering. Have we decided?"

"I think her eyes say it all," Mom says. "She's glowing in this one!"

I'm super happy with my choice. And, in order to stay happy, I make a mental note not to flip the price tag over. Mom makes me pick new heels, even though I have a pair that would be fine, and we head out once she pays an amount I don't even want to imagine for all my stuff.

"Mom?"

"Mmm?" She's flipping through an app on her phone to find a good place to eat.

"Thank you. Seriously. Today was great, being with you. And I love my dress."

She leans over and pulls me into her arms, holding me tight. "Thank you, baby. Thank you for being the kind of daughter who never stops amazing me."

"Mom, you've been listening to too much Lilith Fair," I laugh, but my throat is scratchy.

"Okay. No tears today. Are you up for French, or do you want Southern family style?" She wipes under her eyes with her fingers and starts rattling off menu options.

I get this warm tingle through my body, like this is one of those days I'm going to look back on and appreciate when I'm older. But right now, fried chicken and fluffy home-cooked biscuits sound so good.

THIRTY-SEVEN

"So the place is set, Doyle is set, your dress is set. Are you ready for romance and memories and cheesiness galore?" Ollie is trying like mad to stay upbeat, but it's not quite working. I'm her best friend, and I can see through her fake smile.

"I want you here. You and Thao, dressed to the nines, here with me." I stomp my bare foot and glare at my phone screen. Ollie pops her bottom lip out like she's hurt. "I'm glaring at the unfairness of life, not at you. How is it possible I'm going to prom without you?"

"These last few months have been the weirdest," Ollie agrees. Her voice goes low and a little desperate. "Nes?"

"Yeah?" I rush over so I can be closer to the phone.

"We're still best friends, right?" She coils her silky dark hair around her index finger nervously.

"Why are you asking such *stupid* questions?" I demand. "No one could ever take your place in my heart. Or paint my nails the way you do. I'm so glad you can't see this botch job! I told her what I was wearing, then asked her to just go crazy with the design."

"Ugh, did she for real do French tips? That's *design*? Okay,

I'm a glutton for punishment. Let me see those bad boys." I hold up my hand and she tilts her head back and snorts.

We both laugh. "I'm glad you can't see them up close. No precision!"

Ollie clucks her tongue. "Does no one take pride in nail artistry anymore?" She taps the screen. "Hey, send me pictures, texts, updates, but get off the phone with me now. You need to get ready."

"Hey, I will. Also, PS—just wanted you to know, I've never missed another human being the way I miss you. I'll see you in a few weeks. Send me the new bassoon recording, the one that blew them away at the showcase."

"Will do. Kisses, Nes." She closes her eyes and puckers, and I fall in love with her all over again.

"Kisses, Olls."

Mom waltzes in a few minutes later to straighten my hair, help with my makeup, and chat. I know she knows I'm missing Ollie, and I think she is too.

"I miss that sweet Ollie chatting my ear off," she confirms like she's reading my mind. We both frown as she comes closer and slips the dress over my head.

"Me too." I sigh and wring my hands, pressing them down over the skirt of the dress. "I thought missing Paris was bad when I was in Brooklyn. Now I have more places and people to miss than I ever have before, and it's only going to get worse when I leave for college. Does it get easier to deal with?"

"I think your heart gets more elastic," Mom says as she pulls up the zipper. "And if you have kids, then you have your family living with you in the most elemental way. The people who matter never really lose touch, not completely. And when you get older you lose the luxury of wasting time on anyone who doesn't make the effort. So, yes, it gets easier, but only because life blunts all your young, passionate feelings."

"Geez, Mom. Are you running for mayor of Buzzkillville?" I mutter.

She squeezes me around the shoulders. "Just keeping it real, honey. You look *gorgeous*. I'm going to make sure the flash is on the good camera. Holler if you need me."

She leaves, and I glance at the picture she had printed and framed for me. It's from the night Doyle and I danced merengue before he snuck in my window.

Before that night, I thought we'd never get back to the place where we were before the first time we slept together, but we managed to look our insecurities in the face and find something better. The easy joking and fun flooded back as soon as we started letting go of the hurt, but there's a new dimension of respect underlying it all. We've both seen each other's darker sides, each other's weaknesses and fears, and we've stood up and fought through some scary times side by side. I run a finger over the picture, refusing to think too much about our future.

I have to live in the now as fully as I can, because now may be all I have left with Doyle.

I hear his knock as I slip into my shoes and give myself a last once-over.

When I walk out, he stops talking to my mother and grips the wall. He blinks and tries to say something. Tries again.

One more time.

But nothing comes out.

My heart dances a bachata at the look on his face, and I have to get my composure together when I walk his way. We've waited such a long time for this. Now that tonight's the night, it doesn't feel real.

"You wore a white suit." I make it over to him and adjust

his black tie, running my hands over his shirtfront. "You look amazing."

"Y-y-you look… That dress… *Damn*, Nes. I don't have a word for how beautiful you look." His eyes rake up and down my dress like he can't look enough.

"Don't you want to compare me to a speckled pup or something?" I ask, but he reaches out, dips me low, and kisses me, so long and hot and sweet, it takes my breath away. And he does it right in front of my mother.

Who snaps a picture.

"I'm sorry, ma'am. Your daughter makes me go crazy." He sets me on my feet and gives my mother this sheepish look he *knows* helps him get away with murder.

And, of course, my mother thinks his whole "aw, shucks, ma'am" routine is adorable.

Before the charm is even faded from his kiss and phony apology, he whips out the most gorgeous orchid I've ever seen. The petals are every shade of purple with soft hints of pale pink and cream stripes. He takes it from the box and ties it on my wrist with a silk ribbon.

"Doyle, this is gorgeous." He's a plant person; I'm not, but you'd have to be blind to not see this flower is a natural work of art.

"Hope so. I been growing it for four years."

"And you killed it for a corsage?" I gasp, feeling like I have the flower equivalent of the *Mona Lisa* just hanging out on my wrist.

"Hell yeah." He laughs softly and drops his voice so only I can hear. "I like flowers and all, but every time I see one that's 'specially beautiful, it reminds me of you. Trust me, that old orchid ain't nearly pretty enough to be sittin' on your wrist tonight."

This is why I can't keep my hands off this guy. I'm reduced to a whispered thanks and a watery smile. I guess my teenage hormones can't resist prom fever *and* Doyle Rahn.

I'm only human after all.

Mom takes her job as photographer seriously, snapping so many pictures, I can't believe she hasn't blown through all the memory on her card. When I tell her we need to go, she gives us long, slightly tipsy hugs. This time though, I'm glad she dug into the chardonnay. I know she wishes Dad was here so they could see me off together. I know she misses Ollie's always-happy chatter and our cozy apartment home and Grandmother coming over to try to pin my dress up so less cleavage shows.

We're both still deep in the throes of homesickness, and she doesn't have a Doyle in her life to take the edge off. I give her one last long hug and a kiss goodbye, then walk out the door Doyle holds open for me.

"I can't stop lookin' atcha." He leads me to his truck, which I insisted we take instead of wasting money on a limo.

"Thank you. You look pretty damn fine yourself." I let him twirl me before he helps me climb up into the cab.

"Are you excited?" He starts the engine, patting his pockets before he steps on the Gas. "Aha. Here it is."

I can't stop laughing the second I see what he has clamped between his teeth. "Is that a corncob pipe?"

"I hope this is doin' it for ya in a big way, 'cause you have no idea what a pain in the ass it was to find this thing." He holds his arms out and grins, the pipe rising up with his lips. "I hope I look like the Southern gentleman of your dreams."

"You look like something out of Scarlett O'Hara's dreams maybe. And every chicken's nightmares, Colonel Sanders." He makes me howl with laughter when he waggles his eyebrows.

"You got it all wrong. Colonel Sanders never smoked a pipe.

That was Popeye." He flexes his biceps, and I laugh so hard, I have to lean against the window. Doyle shakes his head as he pulls out of the driveway. "The things I do for you, woman."

He lets me fake-smoke his corncob pipe and we don't listen to music. We roll down the windows and listen instead to the never-ending hum and screech of the bugs and birds in the fields we pass because it's a sound he's loved since birth and one I've grown to love. I lean my head back, not caring that my carefully set hair is blowing all over my perfectly made-up face. I want to breathe deep the warm almost-summer air and feel the freedom that's so close, I swear I could close my fingers around it.

Doyle drives into the beautiful, throbbingly alive heart of historic Savannah, where everything is cobblestoned and columned, overhung with low-branched magnolias draped with Spanish moss and accented with two-sided marble staircases that lead to huge, glass-door-fronted foyers.

"The two sets of stairs was so that ladies could walk up one side and the guys the other, so they couldn't peek up under their big hoopskirt things," Doyle explains.

"I thought you guys were supposed to be gentlemen." I'm about to say something else about Peeping Toms and hoopskirts, but we pull up to a huge, Antebellum-style mansion, lit up and spilling over with music and dressed-up students. "Holy crap. Is this Tara?"

"No." He laughs and rolls his eyes. "Tara was near Atlanta. Also it was just a place in a book."

"You know a lot about *Gone with the Wind*," I say.

"My gram watches it every single year at Christmas, and we all gotta sit through the whole freaking three-hour deal." The thought of Doyle sitting through a three-hour epic romance with his gram is almost more than my overfull heart can deal with tonight.

Doyle parks, and I hang out the window, staring, mouth hanging open, and I don't care who sees me. This place is that impressive. Sure, Ollie sent us tons of pictures of the kind of decorating and setup they do for formal events like prom, but it's not the same as seeing it in real life. There are herds of people heading in, and I should recognize them, but everyone is too gorgeously decked out.

Doyle shoos me from the window and opens the door, then helps me down. He shuts the door behind me and wraps his arms around my waist. "Hey, beautiful, how 'bout you and me find somewhere to park for a while?"

It feels like a flock of rabid seagulls is beating its wings inside my stomach. "Oh, we're hard-core making out later, don't worry about that. All this romantic crap makes me crazy horny. But Ollie worked hard on this, and even though we cut back, this is like some raja's version of a prom, so I'd die of guilt if we didn't go enjoy."

"You're right." He offers me his arm. "Shall we?"

"Let's do this."

We smile at each other, then stand up straight and walk slowly up the stairs and into the massive black-and-white, marble-tiled foyer with enormous, sparkling crystal chandeliers. As I'm craning my neck back like an idiot to take it all in, a local reporter sticks a microphone in my face and asks for a comment.

For a second all the glitz and finery fades away, and I remember that if Doyle and I hadn't started this whole thing rolling, we wouldn't have been *allowed* to have this moment. The rules set in place by tradition would have dictated he and I go to separate proms. He never would have gone adorably stupid over my dress, I never would have laughed at his corncob pipe, there would have been no breathtaking moment walking up the stairs, arm in arm—and it would have been because the amount of pigment in our skin doesn't match.

I've been fairly tongue-tied around reporters since this all started, but something about being in the middle of what we worked so hard for opens me wide up.

I smile, I look at the camera, and I say, "Fifty years ago Dr. Martin Luther King Jr. gave his 'I Have a Dream' speech. Fifty years seems like a long time, until you consider this is Ebenezer High's *first ever* desegregated prom. I think Dr. King would have been proud that the students of Ebenezer finally made this happen."

The woman tells me she loves my quote and, when she takes my name, asks, "Aren't you one of the students behind all this?"

I stare at her blinding smile and glossy newscaster hair in a daze. Doyle nudges me gently. "This? Yes! I mean, I did. Help."

Her nod is pure approval. "Brava, Agnes. Well done."

Doyle gives her a quick wave as he pulls me away, and I feel floaty. And a little piece of me wonders if I should have given a few more interviews instead of avoiding it all. I should have let people know the crazy story of what we almost couldn't have for reasons so absurd we couldn't stand for it. But I have no time to think about any official regrets because I'm instantly hit in the face with so much pure, amazing, overwhelming *prom*!

There are so many brilliant, swishy dresses, it looks like a tank of tropical fish. The sweet smell of roses and lilies is wafting from the huge bouquets that are drooping with their lush, heavy blooms everywhere. There's bone china, gleaming silver, pristine white linens, a DJ playing something fast and danceable, and every single person we know is on the wooden dance floor, shaking what their mamas gave them.

"All right, let's show them how it's done," Doyle says with a whoop, pulling me onto the dance floor.

I love the way the boy moves, and I get drawn into moving with him. We dance hard, showing off in front of our cheering classmates and upping the ante with every new beat. When we're about to tear a hole in the dance floor, the DJ announces the theme song and the opening strains of "Stand by Me" float through the air. There's a roar of a cheer, and Doyle pulls me into his arms, grinning like the fool he is. My fool.

What I feel for him is so overwhelming, it closes my throat.

"I'm glad we didn't stay out in the truck and make out," he says. He's flushed, and his eyes are bright. He looks happy. Like he belongs.

I very much miss being somewhere I belong.

The thing is, I blend in here as long as I'm in Doyle's arms. But I don't want to have to rely on him—or anyone—like that. I want to be who I am on my own and still find my place.

"I'm really glad we came in too. After all the work and arguing over every tiny detail, this place is amazing, and everyone looks so fancy and happy." We glance around and see Critter tugging at his camouflage bow tie, Alonzo—dapper and cool in white—and Khabria in a shimmering red dress with handsome Bo staring like he knows better than to let her out of his sight.

I gaze around and see people I consider friends and people I only know by name or face, and they're all, thankfully, getting along.

"You did this, Nes. None of this would have happened without you." Doyle runs a thumb over my cheekbone.

"And you. And Khabria. And Ollie. I actually played a

pretty minor part in this whole thing." I wrap my arms tighter and sway to the music with him, inhaling his clean, green-leaves–and–just–Doyle smell.

"You got it all wrong. We were jest a pile of useless gunpowder. You were the match, Nes." He cups my face and tilts it up as Ben E. King croons that he won't be afraid. "You were the fire."

Who can resist kissing a guy who tells you you're the fire? I don't even try.

We'd probably have been attached at the mouth all night long if a peppy cheerleader type didn't snare the DJ's mic at the end of the song and yell, "Hey y'all!"

"Hey!" the crowd roars back.

"Is this the best prom *ever* or what?"

The screams and hollers are so enthusiastic and intense, I cup my hands over my ears.

"We've been collecting ballots since y'all came in, and we're just about down to the final count. Put your hands together for Ebenezer High's Rebel King and Queen!"

The thunderous applause give me goose bumps.

"All right, y'all, we got the official names. Our Rebel Queen by a landslide…"

At my core, I've got a gooey, girlish heart, and there is a second where everything in me is hoping and wishing and praying—

"Ms. Khabria Scott!"

—for the impossible.

But the feeling of wanting that crown for myself flies out the window when I see how ecstatic Khabria is. She fans her face and smiles so hard and wide, we all smile with her. Because, obviously, she's our queen.

"And to join Queen Khabria in the royal court…" The girl opens the ballot and blushes. "Mr. Doyle Rahn!"

He sighs and gives me a distressed look.

"Right. I'm sure it's so hard being the most loved guy in the entire school. Stop pouting and go get your crown." I shove him away, but it is a little shocking how completely I've started to consider Doyle mine. To the point where I forget lots of girls daydream about him and lots of guys wish they could be him.

Doyle jogs onto the stage, smiles while the girl crowns him with shaking hands, and hugs Khabria so hard, he lifts her off her feet. They hold their joined hands up high and scream along with the crowd.

The energy in the room buzzes like an open fuse, and I'm glad to be a part of it, but happier when Doyle comes down to take me back in his arms and Bo grabs Khabria and spins her around, laughing and congratulating her.

"I think you're supposed to dance one together," I say, but he pulls me closer.

"This whole prom exists because we wanted to be able to dance together in some fancy place, wearing dead-sexy clothes. Tonight I'm gonna dance with you every second I can, and screw anyone who don't like it."

My face burns with the kind of embarrassed-but-pleased blush I get when Doyle's take-charge attitude surfaces. I know it's all lame mascot symbolism, but he truly does make an awesome Rebel King.

When we've danced until our feet ache, eaten until our stomachs hurt, and talked to pretty much everyone at the prom, we finally walk back down the marble stairs and away from the party still raging inside. It's closer to dawn than it is to night, and Doyle drives to the beach without asking if that's where I want to go, because he doesn't need to ask.

We park, and he strips off his jacket, shoes, socks, and tie and unbuttons the top buttons on his shirt. Oh, and Doyle takes off his regal crown, of course. I slip my heels off and tuck my glitzy jewelry in the glove compartment. We head down the dunes and walk along the wet sand, watching the first rays of the orange sun creep up over the horizon.

"This night was amazing," I say, leaning hard on his arm. He kisses my temple and stares at the rising sun.

"Feels like so much happened to get to it. Fighting and planning and trouble. It was a whole lotta fun, but…"

I laugh. "But it was also, like, all this effort and craziness for the most normal, cliché high school dance?"

"Yeah." He runs his hand through his hair and shakes his head. "I mean, I can't bend my brain around how serious people have been about all this. Rules about who could come and who could bring who. All the squabbles and the pranks that got out of hand. Damn, someone went to the hospital. Someone went to jail. Over…what? A bunch of high school kids dancing to some cheesy music in their best duds, jest having a good time? God, it seems so stupid in the grand scheme of it all."

I let my toes sink into the damp sand and breathe the salty air into my lungs until it feels like they might pop. I don't want to bad-mouth the place he grew up in, the place he loves, but sometimes it's hard to see clearly what's too close.

I learned that lesson the hard way.

"I think that's the problem with not getting out of a town like this. You wind up with so little perspective, you'll fight like crazy over the strangest things."

"Ain't that the truth? Gotta say though, I'm glad I got to fight with you." He bumps his shoulder against mine. "I would always want to have you on my team, Nes."

"I think we make sense together." I stop and turn to him,

brushing his hair back off his forehead and tugging his mouth close. "I never would have imagined we'd make such a good team."

He brushes his lips against mine. "I knew. From that first day I saw you in that red bikini. I knew."

"What, that you wanted to get in my pants?" I joke, kissing his neck.

"Naw. That you weren't like anyone I ever met before. That I was gonna fall in love for the first time, and there wasn't a damn thing I could do about it. That you and me could change the world together." The waves crash at our feet, soak the hem of my dress and the bottom of his pants, but neither one of us moves back. We're wrapped completely in this moment together. "What I'm trying to say is I've never been so happy someone almost let an innocent tree die. What if I never jumped that fence to water that poor thing?" He swallows hard and licks his lips, looking at me with worried eyes when he says, "I don't like the idea of my life without you in it."

"I love you too," I answer back.

And then his mouth finds mine and we kiss until we can't keep our hands anywhere decent. We leave the beach and he drives me home, where I leave the window open.

Before I manage to get out of my dress and under the blankets, he's climbing over the sash. He crawls into bed next to me bringing in the cool, damp smell of earliest morning and the salty aftershocks of the beach. It's silent in the room except for the sound of our breathing and the urgent words we whisper now and then.

He reaches for me, and I roll into his waiting hands. We touch and move against each other until we have to muffle the noises we make and be satisfied pressing as close as we can. I arch my back when he buries his face in the side of my neck.

When our hearts finally slow from a race to a crawl, he spoons his body around mine. In the cool, silent gray of late dawn, we nestle in the middle of my bed, two perfectly flawed souls who found out our love strengthened and multiplied when we stood by each other's side.

"I love you, forever," I whisper when I'm sure he's sound asleep. "No matter where I go, no matter how far away I am, you can know that I love you, Doyle."

And somewhere in the murky dark of my dreams, I hear Doyle Rahn tell me he loves me more than anything. That he'll follow me to the ends of the earth. That our future together starts now, even if we have to be apart.

The problem with these drowsy, sleep-drunk confessions is that they need to hold up in the coldest reality of the light of day. I turn in my sleep, closer to him, and hope with all my heart we figure it out before we're out of time.

THIRTY-EIGHT

And then, even though I feel like I'm keeping an extra close eye on every second, we're out of time.

Principal Armstrong's drawl drones over the loudspeakers and echoes up through the moth-filled lights of the stadium. It's too hot for a daytime graduation here, so they wait for evening.

Kelwanda Smith is our valedictorian. She gives a beautiful speech about pride and community and things that would have made a lot more sense to this school a few months ago. But now's not the time for reflecting on just how screwed up everything got before graduation saved us from complete chaos. Instead, it's the last chance to cling to the selective memories of a time in our lives that's already rolling into the past.

Khabria Scott glides to the microphone like a goddess and makes a short speech about how the bulk of the money we raised for next year's prom is being put into a scholarship fund since prom will be a school-run event from now on. There is a polite smattering of applause, and I wonder who will come up on this stage next year to take a chunk of the money we raised by tearing down old traditions. It dawns on me that a small piece of what I did, what I helped with, will be a part of this high school for years. That feels strangely good.

Sometimes I feel like a donated organ spliced into a new body, trying so hard to do good, but always in danger of being rejected anyway. But, for this one fleeting moment at least, I belong. Doyle turns in his seat, his navy graduation cap making his eyes look darker, like indigo. He smiles and mouths, "Ready?"

I nod and smile back. He winks; we wait.

What comes next is my ticket out of here: my diploma.

The one Ma'am Lovett predicted I'd take and run, right back to Brooklyn and Ollie and my grandmother and everything I know and love.

The problem is, I have just as many things that I love right here, and running feels more like leaving so much behind than escaping.

When I returned Ma'am Lovett's books to her, she handed me a signed copy of the poetry of Maya Angelou.

"I got this a very long time ago, and I've treasured it. Her words helped me find my place when I felt very lost." Ma'am Lovett, teacher of steel, blinked her eyes like there were tears in them.

An impossibility.

"I can't accept this," I said, trying to hand it back. I love the dense weight of the book, the smooth paper of the cover, the old but perfectly preserved feel of it. I bet if I held it to my nose, it would smell like Ma'am Lovett's skin and old paper— two incredible smells. "I mean, if you have a copy she didn't sign to you, I'd take it, but this is yours, and it's precious. It obviously means a lot to you."

"Which is exactly why I want you to have it." She gave me a tight smile. "I had the pleasure of being your teacher for only a few months, Agnes, but you make me think of my favorite Maya Angelou quote." She let her eyes flutter shut and her voice roll out as she recited, "'My mission in life is not merely to survive, but to thrive; and to do so with some passion, some compassion, some humor, and some style.' You are the living embodiment of that quote, and I want you to have this. To remember me."

Her hand went up to her eyes and she swiped them, and I couldn't process this staggering emotion in a woman who'd always been a solid, unshakable rock.

But I had to process it.

Because I had only that moment. I would walk out of her room and never relive what was unfolding right now, right in front of me, again. If my time here had taught me anything, it was that life was lived in the tiny, fleeting moments, and you have to grab them while you can or risk losing them forever. So I clutched the book tight, then threw my arms around her, ignoring her shocked cry. I hugged her neck, holding on tight.

"Like I could ever forget you? C'mon, Ma'am Lovett, be real."

When they call my name, my dark, handsome father, wearing an immaculate seersucker suit and a Sammy Davis Jr. hat, rushes the stage and takes my picture, unaware that everyone else in the crowd—most of them in T-shirts, only the dressiest in polos and khakis—is giving him a judgmental once-over. Again, in another tiny way, I'm reminded of how much I don't belong.

Then I hear Doyle's voice yell, "I love that girl! I love you, Nes!"

Through a pretty intense blush, it occurs to me that I don't give a solitary damn who else likes having me here, as long as Doyle Rahn wants me around.

I watch the line of students move up, fist bump, crazy dance, curtsy, bow, wave, cheer, shake, and generally celebrate the fact that we made it—finally, despite nearly falling apart—and I realize how attached I got to all of this and all of them, despite myself.

I even get a tiny bit teary-eyed when Armstrong grips the podium, clears his throat, and tells us to move our tassels to the left.

Teary-eyed, because I never got to tell him where he could take his authoritarian policies and stick them—

"Congratulations, graduates!"

I toss my cap and let all the bad go. Breathe deep. Think Zen thoughts. *Moving on.*

"Agnes Penelope Murphy-Pujols, Ebenezer High graduate." Doyle stands in his navy dress pants, crisp white shirt, and those sexy cowboy boots.

"Doyle Ulysses Rahn, Ebenezer High graduate *and* recipient of the Future Farmers of America scholarship." I smooth my hands over his shoulders. "I'm proud of you."

He puts his arms around my waist. "C'mon, I never know what to do when you ain't pickin' on me."

"You could say, 'I owe it all to you,'" I tease, but his eyes aren't laughing back.

"Don't say it like it's a joke. I try to think what this year woulda been like without you. What I woulda been like. I can't do it, Nes. I don't want to imagine it." He leans close, his voice dropping low. "I know I was obsessed about you leavin' most of the time. Damn, this is gonna sound corny as hell, but oh well." He laughs softly and circles his finger on his chest, just to the left of center. "You ain't leavin'. You're here. Locked away tight, for good, like it or not."

So corny.

I blink hard and laugh around a sob.

"You're going to make my mascara run!" I croak, crushing him to me.

Our families are waiting, eyeing each other and us. I pull him down by his collar and kiss him hard.

"My dad and brother flew in from Paris. My grandmother flew in from Brooklyn, and she *hates* flying. They're going to kill me if I don't hang out with them." I take a deep breath. "And I want you to meet them."

"Me?" Doyle looks so surprised it's a little offensive.

"Yes, of course you. You and your family. Come here, right now, and let me prove that Southern people don't have the entire hospitality market cornered."

My family gathers in a loose horseshoe around me as Doyle waves his family over. We face each other like little kids about to play Red Rover, and I'm ready to call everyone over.

"Mom, Dad, Mama Patria, this is Doyle's grandma and grandpa," I begin. The invisible line between us is crossed. Mom hugs Doyle's grandmother as I keep going until cousins and brothers are also shaking hands. Soon our two families are in a knot of dark and light, dressed-up and casual. Different accents float through the air, every one of them congratulatory, welcoming, and happy for me and Doyle and all we've accomplished.

There are a few moments that have my heart racing:

"Now then, plantains are little bananas, am I correct? Do you think they'd suit for 'nana pudding with 'nilla wafters?" Doyle's grandma asks my abuela.

"So it's a college baseball team? *Dawgs*, with a *w*? No, I'd love to watch a baseball game at your place. Can I bring something? I was able to sneak some amazing foie gras and the most delicious claret in my luggage," Jasper is saying with a totally serious expression to Lee.

"I heard a rumor that in France you can't own your own firearm, no matter what," Doyle's grandfather says to my wide-eyed father.

"Let me know if you need help with your college essays. It's never too early to start writing them, Malachi," my mother lectures Doyle's introvert brother.

I don't pretend friendships between such different people would be completely smooth, but listening to them talk about food and sports and politics, and find common ground or civil tolerance reminds me that the point isn't to glide through life without causing a stir. It's to fight for what's right for yourself and the person you think you have nothing in common with—because chances are, under your accent and skin color and general worldview, you're just two people who want to...

"Celebrate!" Mom says. "That's what we're planning anyway. And what better way than with our friends? It's decided then. We'll see you for dinner. And I'm going to expect that banana pudding, Mrs. Rahn."

"Call me Lorraine." Doyle's grandmother smiles and Lee asks Jasper how big Mom's TV is and if we have the full ESPN package.

"Is this a good idea? Your brother is going to freak when he finds out my mom has the full BBC package, but no ESPN at all," I whisper to Doyle. I take his hand in mine as we watch our weird, amazing, frustrating families intermingle like old friends.

"He'll get over it." Doyle grins. "I heard my granddaddy say they ordered an entire roasted pig for tomorrow. You ever been to a pig roast?"

"I watched an episode of *Mind of a Chef* where they roasted a whole pig," my father is saying to Doyle's grandfather excitedly. "Do you need help digging the pit? I'll bring a shovel!"

"Looks like I'm going to one tomorrow." I can't keep the grin off my face. "One more Southern-tradition feather in my cap. I wonder what else our crazy families will plan for us in the next few days."

"No clue, but it'll be wild." He shifts closer and strokes my arms through the cheap fabric of my graduation gown. "So, what's happenin' after they all leave?"

The last few weeks have been so crazy good, we've avoided talking about the future. Living in the moment was the bravest thing I've ever done, and I don't regret it.

But here we are, the present quickly turning into the past and our future looming.

"I boxed my things. I'll hang out with you every second I can before I go," I admit, watching his face for signs of sadness about our limited time. "I leave in two weeks. I'll stay with my gram until Ollie graduates, and she and I are going to Vietnam to vacation at her grandparents' house for most of the summer. Then I'll be heading to our house in the Dominican Republic."

He nods, moving his hands down to hold mine. "Your mama staying here?"

"For now. I think my father might bring Celeste to our summer house, so she's opting out." I'm still not sure how I feel about the whole Celeste thing. Dad didn't bring her to graduation, which I appreciate, but if I've learned anything this year, it's that I have to have an open mind when it comes to the people I care about. "She got offered summer classes she's excited to teach. I'm not sure what happens after that." I clear my throat. "I hope...I hope it's not too weird for you, coming to water that stupid tree when I'm gone."

His shrug is aggravatingly casual. "Maybe a real cute girl will move in if your mama goes back up to New York."

I know we joke all the time and laugh things off constantly, but that one stings.

"Maybe you'll get to see her in her bikini," I say, and I'm unsuccessful at keeping the acid from my voice.

"Maybe Brookes will." He waits until I look up at him before he unfurls that slow smile. "He's the one who'll take over my runs. I'll be at some big ole college in New Jersey. Do you know there's a train that runs from a station at the edge of my campus right into New York City?" He reaches into his back pocket and pulls out a small folded map that already looks worn. "It's a subway map," he explains. "I been studying it. If I think of it as the roots of a tree, I think I'll be able to figure it all out."

"You'd come to the city?" My voice shakes with pure excitement.

"I'd come anywhere you were," he says in such an offhand way, he completely earns the kiss I lay on him.

I don't care who's watching, who's judging. I don't care that he's going to be the hot gentleman with the drawl and the cowboy boots that every girl at his college and mine will throw themselves at. I don't care that things between us will be unsettled and confusing, that we'll fight with each other as often as we fight for each other.

All I care about is the fact that we've become the kind of people ready to grow and change when times get tough, the kind of people who know how rare it is to find another person who tucks you into their heart and never lets you go. I've learned that the roots I put down are long and tangled. I never have to worry about losing what's been mine all along and always will be.

His lavender eyes crinkle at the sides, he's smiling so hard. "So we got two more weeks to drive each other crazy, then I'll see you at the Christopher Street–Sheridan Square Station this fall?"

My heart thumps out the answer: *yes, yes, yes!*

"It's a date."

"And while I'm gone…?"

A grin spreads slowly and surely over his face. "You'll be pretty busy. So will I. But I'd sure like to see a picture of Vietnam that's not black-and-white with soldiers in it."

I pretend to think while my heart squeals like a girl on the handlebars of her boyfriend's bike. "I guess. I mean, I don't want to force it, you know. Come to think of it though, I'll have to call you when Ollie's around. My imitation of your drawl isn't very convincing, so I think some firsthand evidence would be better. You guys are long past due a Face-Time session."

"You want me to FaceTime with Ollie? You imitate the way I talk?" he asks, his eyebrows high up in surprise.

"*Wa-a-ll* yes, sir. I ain't so good at it, but I only been 'round y'all for a bit now," I say, pretty sure I nailed it.

Doyle doubles over hooting with laughter. "Oh Jesus. Oh Lord, that is the worst damn accent I ever heard! Hell, you sound like Crocodile Dundee had a stroke! That's a damn mess."

I pull him close and revel in the happy gasps of his laughter. "I really will miss your voice this summer."

He looks back at me and winks, one slow drop of his eyelid. "We may be in the Deep South, but even we got these newfangled contraptions called phones."

"Doyle, I don't want this to… I don't want…don't want to bother you."

What am I trying to say? I don't want to be the lovelorn girl clinging on long-distance. I don't want to get my heart shattered again, even though a broken heart was the beginning of everything that went so right in my life.

Even though my broken heart healed stronger and loved harder after.

His face goes serious. "Only thing that bothers me is the itch I feel when I think 'bout all the time I gotta spend away from you. I ain't afraid to say how much I'll miss you. I'm not gonna be any good at letting you go. I know you're an independent woman. Hell, I respect that most about you. Doesn't stop the fact that being without you is gonna hurt."

"Doyle." I wipe my eyes off with the tips of my fingers, and I confess because I want things to be true between us. "I'll miss you so damn much."

"Not for long." His optimism bounces right back, and he says it like he means it. "Before you know it, you'll be seeing so much of me, you'll be sick of me."

Our families are drifting to their cars, calling their goodbyes and firming up plans for the big late-night celebration dinners and parties. A wave of happiness crashes over me when I realize the love Doyle and I have for each other just keeps rippling, keeps bringing people together and expanding the good.

That might be the most beautiful gift I've ever been lucky enough to give and receive.

I press my lips together and remind myself that there isn't anything left to prove. What we have, we worked hard for, and we liked the work enough to keep doing it. I'm not afraid to say goodbye to him anymore, no matter if it's just a few hours or a few months. I have faith in us.

"Aloha, Doyle." I wipe the tears away and smile.

"Aloha, Nes." He kisses me softly, then lets me go.

I watch him walk back to his family, and then I walk back to mine, saying a silent thanks to the little Southern town that taught me to fight for the things I love like the rebel I discovered I am.

★ ★ ★ ★ ★

ACKNOWLEDGMENTS

First, a short note to my husband:

Frank,
Your incredible love and loyalty inspire me to always push myself harder. Let's take one of those trips we keep planning, hot stuff! Writers are monsters, and your patience has earned you major points. First pick is all you! Thank you for being the coolest.

PS: I like you.
PPS: A lot.

I'd like to extend huge thank-yous to the following people.

My daughter, Amelia, whose passion for the things she loves is an inspiration. I'm eternally grateful that I get to hang with this fantastic, smart, funny kid who loves books as much as I do (yeah, genetics are *awesome!*).

My parents, Sonny and Suzanne Hansen, for their sometimes intimidatingly unshakable belief that I'll be successful at whatever I put my mind to. Their unwavering love laid the foundation for my success. Special smooches to my amazing sister Katie (move closer, kid… I miss you!), my sweet brothers, Zachary and Jack (who probably won't read this, but I'm a *good sister…*), and my fantastic sister-in-law, Brittany (the craziest, funniest

Southern belle)! Enthusiastic shout-out to the adorable gaggle of nieces and nephews I love with my whole heart! Love to my sisters, Jessica, Jillian, and Jamie, who are smart, well-traveled, beautiful young women.

My brilliant editor at Harlequin TEEN, Natashya Wilson. Her dedication and hard work has taken this book to levels I never imagined possible. Heartfelt thank-yous to Michael Strother for his warm, sensitive insight and enthusiasm. Sincere gratitude to Claribel Ortega and Perla Rodriguez for their thoughtful notes and awesome suggestions. I'm so grateful to you for allowing me to listen and learn from you. I'm well aware I have an editorial dream team!

Huge thanks to the Harlequin TEEN publicity and marketing teams—Siena Koncsol, Shara Alexander, Bryn Collier, Amy Jones, Evan Brown, Rebecca Snoddon, and Olivia Gissing—and the *Seventeen* magazine team for embracing the stories of girls and women everywhere and empowering them to speak up and be heard.

The cover-design team at Harlequin TEEN for bringing Nes and Doyle to life with their amazing artwork, and to Heather Martin for her attention to detail in copy edits and her supportive words throughout!

Kevan Lyon, my wonderful agent, who texted me one dreary night when I felt like my career might be a lost cause, and told me she loved the manuscript I sent her. I'm so appreciative of her hard work, professionalism and enthusiasm. Thank you to Patricia Nelson for her kind words and support for this book from day one!

Steph Campbell. You. Yes. You. (Always, bestie.)

The FP Ladies. It's been a long, crazy ride, but I love every one of your faces and can't wait to eat and laugh and celebrate with you all in person. Love you hard.

DATE DUE		

0 5005 00234033 3
Reinhardt, Liz.

Rebels like us

F
Rei

PARKWAY SOUTH HIGH SCHOOL
PARKWAY SCHOOL DISTRICT